Dreams to Dust

Also by Sheldon Russell

Empire
The Savage Trail
Requiem at Dawn

Dreams to Dust

A Tale of the
Oklahoma Land Rush

Sheldon Russell

UNIVERSITY OF OKLAHOMA PRESS : NORMAN

Publication of this book is made possible through the generosity of Edith Kinney Gaylord.

Library of Congress Cataloging-in-Publication Data

Russell, Sheldon.
    Dreams to dust : a tale of the Oklahoma Land Rush / Sheldon Russell.
        p.   cm.
    ISBN 0–8061–3721–5 (alk. paper)
    1. Oklahoma—History—Land Rush, 1889—Fiction. 2. Indians of North America—Fiction. 3. Racially mixed people—Fiction. 4. Newspaper publishing—Fiction. I. Title.

PS3568.U777D74 2006
813'.54—dc22

                                                                        2005052850

1   2   3   4   5   6   7   8   9   10

To my daughter, Shonda,
with love

Acknowledgments

I owe a debt of gratitude to my agents,
Michael Farris and Susan Morgan Farris,
for their guidance and patience
and to Karen Wieder at the University of Oklahoma Press
who never lost sight of the light at the end of the tunnel.
Further thanks is extended to Marian Stewart,
Associate Editor, University of Oklahoma Press,
for steering this project through the publication maze.
My thanks to Jay Fultz for the sensitive application
of his keen editorial skills.

Dreams to Dust

L ocking his legs against the inside of the rail car, Creed McReynolds pushed against the timbers. Even though it was April, the nights were cold, and when the train picked up speed, he would need shelter from the wind. The timbers refused to move. Once again he bore down, the muscles in his legs trembling against the weight of the lumber. As they gave way, first an inch and then a foot, the smell of resin rose into the night.

Leaning back, he adjusted his new hat and laid his rifle across his lap. He checked the medical bag at his side—his father's bag and all that was left of his memory. In it was everything that Creed now owned: a pair of socks, a shirt, gloves worn thin from loading timbers, the few remaining coins of Spanish silver brought out of the Territory so many years ago. The silver had educated him, made of him a civilized man or nearly so, bestowed upon him the credentials of Attorney at Law.

With what silver was left, he'd made payment on three freight cars of yellow pine, because this much he remembered from his childhood in the Territory: there was nothing so rare as lumber, unless it was water for drinking. After the stakes were driven and the claims were filed, there would be buildings to be built. For that there must be timber, strong and straight and true.

When that day arrived, he would be there with his pine, and they would come with their money and their smiles, because he would have what they needed most. It was not the way of his mother's tribe to profit from the needs of others, but in a world forever changed, that way seemed primitive and useless. With their money the settlers would come, this he knew, and when they did, they would no longer see the savage in his eyes, nor the black of his hair, nor the darkness of his skin.

In the distance, the light of the engine beam swept the horizon as the men filled the boiler with water and replenished the coal. Walking down the line, the railroad bull swung his lamp, stopping from time to time to check the cars for sooners. In his pocket was the hundred dollars Creed had handed him, along with the job application. Even though it had taken almost all Creed had, there was little option. No one got past the checkpoints into the Territory except soldiers and railroad employees. Without the badge Creed wore on his coat, his timbers would not make it to Guthrie station, where they would demand the price he needed.

From time to time the bull stopped, lifted on his toes, and peered between the boards into the blackness of the cars. A baton swung from his wrist, its end filled with lead to crush the skull of anyone foolish enough to hitch a free ride. As he approached, Creed drew down, not anxious to talk.

The bull stopped, listening against the chug of the steamer. Hooking his lamp over his arm, he swung onto the ladder with skill.

"Come up out of there," he said, laying the baton across his arm, "before you get a taste of my mate here."

Creed stood, moving into the light.

"It's me," he said, "the new car guard."

The bull held his lantern high.

"It's a smart man speaks up quick on the rails, boy. Been those left their brains hanging from the rods for less."

"You gave me my badge," Creed said, "to guard these cars. That's what I'm doing."

Setting down the lantern, the bull reached for his tobacco, rolling a paper between his fingers, tying off his Durham bag with his teeth. Leaning over the lantern, he drew on the cigarette until it glowed in the dark. The smell of tobacco drifted into the night. Leaning over, he pulled his lips back over the stumps of his teeth. Lines of coal dust glistened in the folds of his face, and his breath was raw and hot under the tobacco.

"So you are," he said, "but it's a way we have to go yet, isn't it. Last week we found a car guard choked dead with a packing wire. They'd dumped him over the side at the Cimarron bridge, but the wire snagged on the ladder. It was a surprise he had on his face when we found him, riding in on his wire. Being a guard can have its downside now and again."

"Where are we?" Creed asked.

"Winfield, Kansas," the bull said, "then Arkansas City, then on to Guthrie station, providing a hotbox don't hold us up."

"A hotbox?"

"Wheel bushing out of grease and running hot, white-hot sometimes, setting fires up and down the line. Likely burn this here lumber to ashes, wouldn't it? Be a real shame, wouldn't it, a man like you set on getting rich."

"That's what guards are for," Creed said, "to make certain nothing like that happens."

The bull spat a piece of tobacco from his tongue and hooked his baton under his belt.

"The Territory is crawling with sooners, down-and-outers from every dried-up town between here and London, England, come to get their free land, come for anything free and easy. Soon enough they could ride in on any of a dozen trains, but they want it first, don't they. Want it over your dead body, if it comes to that. They'll be getting theirs while those other poor bastards are sitting on the border with their mules and half-dozen kids waiting for the noon signal, waiting to claim what's left over so's they can starve in the promise land."

Steam shot from the sides of the engine, and the bell clanged its intent. The bull's eyes flickered under the light of his lamp.

"We break down or take a curve," he said, "sons of bitches hop out of the grass like fleas on a dog. Half-starved, most of them, eating grass-hoppers and living in holes under the ground so's the soldiers can't find them, thinking they can ride my train to glory. Well, let me tell you, there's more'n one wished he'd stayed in the city after he met up with my mate here."

"Maybe it's hope they're looking for. There's little enough of it."

"It's free land they're looking for. They want the best, and they want it first, smack in the middle of the Guthrie station town site so's they can make a fortune off their fellow man."

The bull fell silent, his eyes peering from under folds of skin, the flame of his lantern dancing on the breeze as he waited for Creed's reaction.

"That hundred dollars is in *your* pocket," Creed said, "and makes you no different than the rest of us."

Throwing his leg over the railing of the car, the bull flicked his cigarette into the darkness.

"Ain't nothing I hate worse than a sooner," he said, working his way down the ladder. When he reached the bottom, he looked up at Creed, "'less it's a red Indian."

Creed turned away, heat rising in his face. The one thing he'd learned in law school was to pick his battles with care. This bastard could wind up with his hundred dollars *and* the timber if he lost his head. Leaning back against the pine, he watched the bull's light bob as he worked his way to the front of the train.

A few minutes later the whistle blew—three blasts—and the train lurched, the report racing down its length. The smell of coal smoke rode in, the power and thrust of the engine pooling deep within him as the train gained speed.

Campfires stretched into the darkness, tents cropping from the earth like mushrooms. Thousands upon thousands were working their way to the border, sitting at their fires, their lights winking away as the train plunged into the night.

Pulling his collar up, Creed rested his head on a timber. When confident in the speed, he dozed against the clack of the wheels and the thrust of the engine. Once, he awoke, the night damp and cool about him. Overhead, stars stood sentry, indifferent to the train driving across the prairie below. Bones aching, he shifted positions against the jolt of the freight car.

Sometime in the morning hours they reached the border, the train pulling to a stop, brakes grinding, iron against iron, steam wheezing from the engine. A soldier rode the length of the train and then back again, the breath from his horse fogging into the cold. Moving to the top of the timbers, Creed laid his carbine across his arm.

When the soldier reined up, his horse squatted in reprieve, steam rising from the pool of piss gathering between its legs.

"Your badge?" the soldier asked, dusting his hat against his leg.

Creed held out the lapel of his coat.

"Much farther to Guthrie station, soldier?"

Putting his hat back on, the soldier shrugged.

"Depends whether you're sitting a ox or walking."

"How about riding a train?"

"Ain't that far riding a train."

Too long in law school, Creed had forgotten the simple logic of the Territory.

"I see," he said.

"From here on is the Territory, Mister. Might want to ride somewhere 'sides the top of that timber. Found a carcass dragged half-way to the switch point couple days back. Wasn't much left after scrubbing up three mile of track under a steam engine."

"Who was it?"

"Could've been a sooner riding the rods," he said, "or a Oklahoma colonist." Pausing, he slipped a glove from his hand. "Could've been President Harrison, though seems unlikely."

"Thanks," Creed said.

Tipping his hat, the soldier mounted and moved out, and within minutes they were underway. As the train banked to the left, a full moon rose and shadows rippled along the grade. From the horizon, scrub oaks lifted into the night.

As a little boy, he had stood in silence as they placed his Kiowa mother, Twobirds, on her burial scaffold. A detachment of the Seventh Cavalry had been lost and starving on the prairie. It had been she who saved them. Among the soldiers spared was an assistant surgeon, Dr. Joseph McReynolds, who sired him. It had been so long ago, like a dream. Now, he couldn't remember where she lay, but it was out there somewhere in the darkness of the Territory.

Clenching his fist against the knot in his stomach, Creed stared into the blackness. This was her place, her time snatched by circumstance and fate and a changing world. It was not a mistake he planned to repeat. The past was past, and the Indian way was as dead as the buffalo that once darkened the prairie. With little more than the ability to read, he had risen to the top of his law class, and before he was done, everyone would know that Creed McReynolds was not just a breed but a power to be reckoned with in any man's world.

At what point he fell asleep, or how long he slept, he couldn't be certain, lulled as he was by the clack of the wheels, the pull and rumble of the engine. But when he awoke, there was something foreign, something irregular and unsettling, like the skipped beat of a heart. Rubbing the sleep from his eyes, he adjusted the familiar weight of the rifle barrel across his lap. But when the moon slid from behind a cloud and the light spilled into the shadows, his heart stopped. The medical bag was gone, and the silver with it.

Standing, he gripped the side of the car, his jaw clenched. How could he have let it happen, the theft of his money while he slept? How could he have been so stupid? Without the silver, he could lose the timber, everything that he'd planned. Turning his face into the wind, he stared into the darkness, his eyes tearing with cold as the train drove into the heart of the Territory.

Leaping from one car to the next, Abaddon Damon stopped to pace the clack of the wheels, to gauge the slowing of the train as it pulled against the grade, steam erupting black and hot. As the train banked a curve, moonlight glinted from the rims of the drive wheels.

Up there was the enemy, those who would throw him into the darkness of the night and never look back. Crouching, he listened again, the medical bag he'd stolen from the sleeping guard held tight in his grip. If he could make it to the flatcar where he'd left his gear, there was safety in the stacks of telegraph poles destined for Guthrie station, sufficient room to hide, to move within them and away from the lantern of the railroad bull.

Balancing himself on the edge of the car roof, he drew a breath before blindly leaping the distance over the tracks below. Hitting hard, he shook his head and clawed at the wet slope of the roof. Feet dangling from over the side, he struggled to right himself onto the ridge at the top. Lying on the roof, he gasped for breath, the thump of the wheels drowning away the throb of his heart.

Scooting along its length, he clung on against the pull of the curve, against sliding over the edge into the wheels beneath. Pushing the bag ahead, he pulled himself to it, worming inch by inch to the ladder and to the safety of his poles.

Even now his hands trembled at the risk he'd taken in the darkness of the lumber car as he'd slid the medical bag from beneath the feet of the guard. It was an act contrary to his nature. He'd take persuasion over violence any day. It was more effective and far less dangerous. But it was a violent world in which he now found himself. When it came to his paper, he'd do what he must. As he opened the bag, his heart steadied. In the moonlight, he could see that it was silver, not a lot but enough to survive until his paper was under way.

Abaddon's skills as a newspaperman were limited. After an apprenticeship under trying conditions, he'd learned that, without exception, to control the word was to have power, a power to be reckoned with, even feared, if need be.

But he was not alone in this knowledge, and there would be others to come, others with backing and money. If he could be first, there before anyone else, selling his papers on that day, he would have an advantage.

Running his fingers through his hair, he opened the suitcase hidden between the stacks of poles, pulling out a copy of *The Capital City*. Predated, and in bold letters, it read, "Guthrie, 1889, Born in a Day, Destined for Glory." At the bottom it was signed, Abaddon Damon, Editor, *The Capital City*. Now but a single sheet, it would someday command all who fell under its spell. This was his vision. This was his plan, his promise, and no man would stand in his way.

At no small cost, he'd paid to smuggle a Washington Press into the Territory in a freight-car load of railroad ties. It was hidden near Cottonwood Creek under a tree split by lightning, at least so they'd told him, and covered with brush and rocks.

In his luggage was a small cache of salvaged type. By doubling up on the function of letters, he could manage for awhile, but it was newsprint that worried him most. Until a supply line was established, finding paper would be difficult indeed.

Leaning against the poles, he rested a moment before sifting through the articles of clothing, dropping the silver coins into his pocket, their weight cool against his leg. He'd paid the last of his own money to the brakeman for a slow signal at Guthrie station. Without it, jumping would be dangerous, with the risk of losing his gear, even his life. If there was one thing he'd learned, it was that everything could be had in the Territory, with proper payment.

From somewhere in the car, a thump resounded, and he held his breath to listen, his heart pounding in his ears. Perhaps it was the shifting of the load or the lurching against misaligned track.

The wheels clacked hollow as the train moved onto a bridge, moonlight shimmering on the water below, tributaries braiding through the sand, separating, and joining, and separating again. He guessed it to be the Cimarron, whose proclivity for salt and quicksand was well known among Texas cattlemen.

Guthrie station could not be far, and he fell to packing his gear. Three blasts of the engine's whistle, and the train would slow for one minute, enough time for him to throw off his things and jump. With luck, he'd locate a Guthrie town lot, remain hidden until the signal, and then make his claim.

The train slowed from the pull of the grade, and he steadied himself against the poles, listening for the blast of the whistle.

Holding the stolen medical bag to the light, he took a last look. It was old and worn from use, but of leather and sturdy in design. Embossed on the bottom was a signature, "Joseph McReynolds, M.D., Seventh Cavalry, U.S. Army."

Deciding to keep it, he dumped in the loose type and secured the leather straps before packing it away in the suitcase given to him by his mother.

Praying for his success, she'd pulled him onto his knees beside her in the kitchen, asking God to give him the courage to do what he must, to take the doubters and slackers of the world and shake them by their fat throats until they cried for mercy. "It's not knowing what you want that is the sin, Abaddon. The weak tremble under the power of conviction. It's God Hisself told Lot's wife to not look back. But in her own weakness she did. Now she's a pillar of salt for her trouble and none the better for it. God will drive the enemy from the righteous, so never move but straight ahead, you hear."

Holding her, smelling eucalyptus and sickness in the folds of her scarf, he'd promised what she asked.

Again the train slowed, brakes screeched, and Abaddon dragged the suitcase to the end of the car.

"Too fast to jump," a voice said.

Whirling about, Abaddon stared into the blackness.

"Who are you?"

A cigarette hung from his lip, and from his wrist dangled a baton, its handle shined with the heat of his hand.

"I'm the railroad bull, Mister. You got a ticket?"

"No. No ticket."

"Then let's be seeing your guard badge," he said, "to be riding this here railroad car."

"I don't have a badge, sir," he said, "not on me."

An ember from the bull's cigarette flared into the darkness, and the leather strap of the baton slipped into his hand. Squaring his legs against the movement of the car, he locked his eyes on Abaddon and shifted the cigarette to the corner of his mouth.

"U.S. Cavalry don't allow no sooners, and Uncle John don't allow no pikers on his train. My mate here sees to it."

Hooking his arm around a pole, Abaddon balanced against the slowing of the train.

"I've paid for a slow signal," he said.

"I don't know nothing about slow signals," the bull said. "But there's a badge fee for guarding these here cars."

"And what would that be?"

Dropping the stub of his cigarette to the floor, he squashed it away with his boot.

"Hundret," he said, "and the price of a ticket."

"And that is?"

"Another hundret."

"I see," Abaddon said.

"No charge for the mate," he said, tapping the baton into the palm of his hand. "Satisfaction guaranteed."

"There's a little silver," Abaddon said, "in the suitcase there."

Smiling, the bull stretched an arm across the aisle, his body swaying with the pitch of the car. In the distance the whistle blew, three blasts.

"Brakeman's slow signal," he said, "coming into Guthrie station. If a man was figuring on getting off, it would be now, wouldn't it. Seen 'em raw as skinned buffalo from jumping road speed. Scream for days, hided from bed gravel and begging to die, if they can beg at all." Pushing back his hat, he grinned, a red line stamped across his forehead from the band. "I'd be getting a move on, if I was thinking to jump."

Kneeling, Abaddon took out the medicine bag now filled with type, hearing the clack of the wheels and the beat of his heart, seeing the shine of the bull's oiled boots under the moonlight. Lifting the bag, he gauged the distance, the weight, the timing. "It's in here," he said.

Above him, the bull snorted his pleasure. Once, he started to speak, to warn against the folly of trickery, but there were few who'd dared in the past. Even as he hesitated, the weight of Abaddon's bag came down on his foot, and something wet and warm began to gather in the end of his boot. Against the din of the engine, his scream rose, and his baton rolled unnoticed at Abaddon's feet.

Sweeping it up, Abaddon brought it about and into the bull's shins.

"I'll kill you!" the bull screamed, clutching at his legs, but the baton, coming about once more, pitched him bubbling onto the floor of the car.

Wiping the sweat from his brow with his sleeve, Abaddon tossed the baton into the poles. The taste of blood was in his mouth, and it was sweeter than he could've imagined.

With a blast of the whistle, the engine bore down, venting heat and steam as it gathered speed against its load. After securing the suitcase, Abaddon dropped it over the edge. With collar flapping against the wind, he climbed out on the ladder, fear sweeping him, embracing the darkness, the speeds, the unknown terrain. Stories abounded of men impaled, decapitated, or dragged under the wheels, but there was no looking back now; there were no pillars of salt. Closing his eyes, he leapt unseeing into the night.

Lightning cut through the darkness, its rumble ebbing beyond the margins of Arkansas City. The smell of dust and rain swept under the edges of the tent, whose sides bellowed with the gusts like the lungs of an ancient beast. Sitting upright in the darkness, Alida Deventer waited for the thump of her heart to settle. Still exhausted from the train ride from Pittsburgh, she lay back down, bracing her knees against the slope of the floor, closing her eyes against the storm.

Even though they had arrived in Arkansas City a day later than planned, there was still time to make the run into the Unassigned Lands. Her father had insisted on leaving Pittsburgh early, for a cushion, he said, in the event something happened. As usual he was right, after a missed connection in Kansas City, another half-day sweltering on a siding north of Winfield, and then the crowds awaiting them in Arkansas City itself.

Stepping from the train, they were swept into the crowd, swollen with men, mothers and children, and all manner of horses and mules. Their supplies were unloaded, wheeled in on a baggage cart and tossed at their feet. Not knowing what else to do, they watched the train pull out, their courage fading with its whistle.

At the end of the depot, an old black man held up a cardboard sign. "Rig for Sale," it said. He smelled of peanuts and kerosene, and his bald head glistened with sweat as her father argued out the price.

It was a sad wagon with grain boards, sprawling wheels, and a broken seat. Trussed under the harness, a gray mare and bay gelding drooped against the heat, gnats swarming in the corners of their eyes, deer flies feasting at the tops of their hooves. They were a sad lot, but there was little else to be found. In the end her father paid the asking price, leaving them little enough to begin their new lives in the Territory.

Confused and tired, they were directed into Walnut Creek Encampment not far from the Arkansas River, a hollow blue with the smoke of campfires, smelling of pork fat and horse manure. Marshals marched them to the edge of the encampment. There, they staked their tent on the side of a hill, so steep that the ropes hung slack on the down-slope side, their coffee spilling from the cups when placed on the ground. It was here they were to spend the night, before moving at some point across the Cherokee Outlet to the starting line for the run.

From early in her life, Alida had known that, out there, someone special waited, a man whose love would know no bounds, whose devotion would stand between her and the coarseness of the world. Even though her parents had loved each other, loved her and Bram as well, their love had succumbed to duty, had eroded under the hardships of work and poverty and tragedy. For her, love would never yield, but triumph. It was written in the books she read. It was written in her heart.

Another flash ripped open the sky, lighting her father's back and broad shoulders, his thinning hair, his arm, now but a useless stump, the hand and forearm seared away under the crucible's heat. There'd been no need to sterilize, and he was sent home from the hospital within a week. In his shirt pocket was a month's extra paycheck from the steel mill, for his inconvenience, they said, and for assistance in finding a new job. No one knew what the mill had meant to him, to his pride, with his worth stamped out each month in dollars and cents for all to see. Without the job there was but a ruined man, his shame hidden each day under the sleeve of his shirt.

When her mother died, he'd toppled. Complaining of a toothache, she'd asked for camphor to ease the pain in her jaw, swollen with the abscess. But the pain did not abate, doubling and redoubling until she trembled under its pulse.

It was a squalid place where they took her, to the upstairs floor of a cigar store and the dentist with his blood-splattered coat, his hands stinking of saliva, his eyes clouded with age. Against her screams, he'd uprooted the molar, draining away the pus, sending her home with little for the pain.

Within a few days she was drinking liquids, then eating, her color returning, along with the light in her eyes, the smile, the laugh that bound them as a family. But the victory was short, the disease veiled and growing within her.

Her cries of anguish dropped them to their knees. Through the night she fought, her screams piercing the souls of all who heard, and as dawn broke, she calmed, not from truce but from surrender.

Sitting on a chair, Alida's brother, Bram, turned his face into the sun that streamed through the window. Standing in the doorway, their father, who had often waited for her opinion, braced his hand against facing confirmation of what he knew. Maybe it was a word, or no more than a sigh, but she was gone, and their lives were never the same.

In that single moment, Alida's dreams collapsed under the weight of a mother's duty, a role she neither wanted nor could fulfill. Often now, in the darkness of night, she cried for the loss of her youth and for the loss of her hope.

Now, Bram slept at his father's back, legs half-covered like strong, white saplings under the flash of lightning. A good boy with a tender heart, he was determined to prove himself among men, but like a young colt, he could bolt without notice, endangering all in his way.

"Go back to sleep, Alida," her father said from the darkness.

"The lightning," she whispered.

"It's a spring storm, Alida, and will pass as it came. There are many storms on the prairie, like squalls on the ocean. Maybe from now on you can sleep in the wagon, off the ground, until we build our house. It will be much better for you then."

"I don't mind the tent," she said.

"Soon we will have our farm, a place of our own. You sleep now. Tomorrow will be a hard day."

Turning over, she listened to the thunder, to the drum of the rain on the tent, and wished for her books, for the time and peace to read them. Heavy as they were, her father had brought them along, knowing their importance to her happiness. To read them was to escape for a bit from the hardness that life had become, from her father's grief, from Bram's, too. More often than not, her efforts fell short of what they needed most: her mother's touch, her voice, her reassurance. It was then that she turned to her books, into a world of her making.

The only other thing of value that Alida claimed was the ring she wore—a diamond on a golden mount. It was her mother's, passed down from her grandmother, a binding tie to the past. It was given to her as acknowledgment of her place in the family. Often she touched it, turned it on her finger to remember that she mattered and was more than a mother figure.

The smell of bacon steeped the valley. While Alida cooked cornbread in the skillet, Bram carried water from the creek for coffee and her father grazed the team at the edge of the camp.

"It's running full," Bram said, "and kids swinging out on a rope, dragging their feet in the current."

"A wonder they don't drown in this chill," Alida said, pouring herself a cup of coffee. "There's cornbread there, and it's hot. I'm saving the bacon for dinner tonight, maybe with some beans or something."

Taking a slice of cornbread from the skillet, Bram ate in silence.

"I'm too old to be swinging out on ropes," he said.

"I should think."

"Remember Mom's eggs, how she'd float them in a hot skillet, flipping grease over them until they bubbled up just ready to pop?"

"I don't have eggs, Bram, and not likely to until we get some chickens. You'll just have to eat the cornbread as it is. Besides, who says you can't fix your own breakfast once in awhile? I'm not your slave, you know, even though you seem to think I am. Maybe I've got a life of my own to lead. Maybe you should just take care of your own breakfast."

Taking a sip of coffee, he looked over the tents that filled the hollow.

"Jeez, I didn't mean nothing by it, Lidy," he said.

"Well, it's just hard, cooking on the go like this and with no food to be had. And don't call me Lidy. I don't like it."

Brushing the dirt from his knees, he looked up through his bangs.

"Where's Dad?" he asked.

"Taken the horses to graze. He says without grain they've got to have time to graze, early morning and late, or they won't make it to the starting line."

"I'm going to have a horse of my own when we get our place," he said. "Maybe a buckskin or pinto with glass eyes, one that loves to run on his own, you know, without me having to kick out his ribs just to get him going, and then I can work him, too, in the field with Dad. He'll earn his way, pay for himself."

Taking the cornbread out of the skillet, she placed it in a pie pan for her father to have later.

"Maybe," she said, "if we ever get a place of our own. Looks to me like half the country's living in this hollow, all wanting the same piece of land."

"Well, they got to beat us first," he said, "and that isn't going to be easy."

"You help Dad harness those horses in the mornings, Bram. It's a struggle with one arm. He liked to never have got a halter on that bay this morning."

"I'm good with horses," Bram said.

"You're good at bragging and eating cornbread," she said.

Wiping the crumbles from the front of his shirt, he shrugged his shoulders.

"Maybe I know as much as you."

"Maybe you don't," she said, flicking water onto his hair with her fingers.

The glint from the badge caught her eye first, a tall and slender figure working his way through the maze of tents. As he approached, he cocked his hat. A small feather tucked in the band fluttered in the wind.

Dropping his carbine to his side, he spoke, "Excuse me, ma'am, is your man about?"

"My father's grazing the team," Alida said. "Is there something I can do?"

Holding his hand against the sun, he looked out from behind the shadows of his hat.

"Word's come down to move into the Cherokee Outlet this morning, down to the starting line. It's a far trek with no stop. The Arkansas River's up, but there's a good bridge, if a bit narrow. Beyond that, there's the Salt Fork, with no bridge at all, 'cept a train trestle. Course, by that time, the water could be down, couldn't it." Switching his carbine to his other arm, he smiled down at her. It was not the first time men had smiled at her, or leveled their gaze from under their hats. It was her blue eyes, her father said, that caused them to gather like cats around a bowl. "Tell your pa we'll be crossing at nine," he said. "It's likely to be a considerable line."

"I'll tell him," she said, "and thank you."

Nodding his head, he smiled.

As he rode from tent to tent, she watched him, appraised the cut of his shoulders, the tilt of his hat, the way he sat a horse as an extension of his own lean body. Even after he'd disappeared into the valley, his smile lingered, and the sound of his voice, with its assurance and confidence to deliver her from the ugliness of the valley. For the briefest moment she thought that perhaps it was he who had filled her mind and dreams all those years.

By the time her father returned, the tent was down and the wagon packed. Bram helped harness the team, slapping the horses on the rear before stepping behind them, something he'd picked up from watching the others.

As the sun broke over the hill, they moved into the line. Hub-deep ruts jerked the wagon from side to side. The wagon seat with its broken spring gouged at Alida's kidneys. The stale smell of campfires hung over the morning.

Soon the line stalled, the bridge choked with wagons and horses. The sun rose hot above them, the day sultry with last night's rain. The team leaned into the harness, ears toppling under the swelter. Flies buzzed in swarms over the piles of manure dotting the encampment. Wagons spilled with children, and the cries of babies carried through the line.

By noon they still had not crossed the river, so Alida climbed into the back of the wagon to prepare slices of cornbread. Bram was right, they would have been better off with the bacon, but then there would have been no seasoning for supper beans. Why did it fall to her to make the decisions anyway, to take the responsibility? There wasn't that much difference between their ages. Why was it Bram got to be a boy, with his energy and will, and she but a mother worrying about bacon and cornbread? It was because she was a girl, someone to do the cleaning and cooking, that's all. What did they know of her dreams?

After eating their cornbread in silence, they fanned themselves with their hats against the heat as they inched along. Bram braided the gelding's tail and tossed pebbles into Bones's ears. The old bay's skeleton sagged beneath his skin, and his hips protruded like hatracks from under the harness.

"Stop it, Bram," she said.

Bram had dubbed him "Bones," deciding that the mare be called "Windy," for reasons obvious to anyone who rode behind her for any length of time. So fierce had been the bargaining that no one had thought to ask the old black man the horses' real names.

"There," her father said, pointing, "the Arkansas River."

Alida leaned into her father as they moved onto the narrow bridge, the floodwaters lapping and churning just inches below the roadbed. In single file they crept across the structure. With the creaking of the timbers, the horses' eyes grew wide with fear. When at last on solid ground, Alida slid off the wagon and clapped her hands.

By late afternoon, they were into the Cherokee Outlet, a gentle and rolling plain punctuated with clumps of trees that rose unannounced from the horizon. Most were blackjacks, scrub oaks, twisted and knurled from infancy by the winds that coursed from out of the desert. Others were locust, thin and straight, the sweet smell of their blooms drifting for miles across the prairie. There were hackberry with their bumps and warts, and cedar, and chinaberry with their clusters of gold, and bois d'arc with their milky apples and wood of iron. There were mesquite as well, survivors, these trees, banding together against the enemy, and with little to spare but for firewood, or a moment's shade.

Above them the sky opened, a blue canopy that teemed with life—birds orchestrated and swooping from out of the sun, vultures soaring in the heights, hawks circling low for game flushed by the wagons. Even Bones and Windy found new energy, ringing their tails and stealing nips of green here and there along the trail.

"Alida, take the team for awhile," her father said, rubbing at his shoulder. "It's easy going now. Just give 'em a pop from time to time so they know you mean business."

"Are you okay?" she asked, taking the reins.

"It's a load on the good arm, you know, and everything's more difficult to boot. Tires clean into my chest at times. Think I'll climb in the back and see if I can't get a little sleep. Bram, you get up here and help out. Wake me when we get to the Salt Fork if I'm not up."

Pulling in behind another wagon, Alida determined to keep pace, snapping the reins against the rumps of the team.

Taking out his pocketknife, Bram stropped it against his boot top.

"Want me to take the team for awhile?" he asked, testing the blade against his thumb.

"No, Bram, it's too hectic, and you don't have much experience."

"And you do, I suppose?"

"No, I don't, but then I'm older."

Folding his knife, he dropped it into his pocket.

"I'm going to have my own place soon enough," he said, "and my own team, too. Maybe I'll just file my own homestead."

"And maybe you won't. Besides, you'll be going to school."

"School," he shook his head, "talk, talk, talk, like hens scratching in the dirt. I'm going to make myself a real living, have money jangling in my pocket, go anywhere I want, when I want."

"Well, I can see where talking isn't going to help you much anyway."

As the afternoon wore away, she relaxed the reins, letting the team set its own pace. Whatever their shortcomings, the horses were well-trained, responding to her commands, to the touch of the rein. She suspected they could walk their way to the starting line by themselves given the opportunity.

When the wagons ahead ground to a halt, she pulled up.

"Bram, can you see?"

Standing on the seat, he held his hand over his eyes.

"It's the river, sure enough, and a railroad bridge, looks like."

"What is it?" her father asked, rubbing the sleep from his eyes.

"We're at the Salt Fork. Bram can see the train trestle."

"How long have I slept?"

"Several hours," she said, looking up at the sun.

"I best go take a look," he said, swinging his legs over the side.

"Can I go, too?" Bram asked.

"Alida?"

"Yes, go ahead," she said.

Jumping from the wagon, Bram flashed her a smile. Pushing her hair back from her eyes, she watched them walk away, Bram's swagger, her father's slower gait. He seemed so tired anymore, so silent and brooding and far away.

Wagons crowded in, the women talking of the river, of the crossing ahead, as they waited for the return of the men.

When Bram climbed into the wagon, he said, "Bank full and red as blood."

Wrapping her arms about herself, she asked, "Will they let us cross?"

"The army's built a temporary bridge," her father said.

"It's three feet under water," Bram said, "and breaking away. There were folks washed downstream, dead horses, too, scattered up and down the bank and smelling something awful."

"Hush, Bram," her father said. "There's no getting over, not till that water's down. An old ferry swamped under with a full load. Some of the people haven't been found."

"What do we do?"

"There's the trestle," he said, "four span and sturdy enough, but some of the railroad officials are demanding fare—five dollars a wagon to carry them across on flatcars. It's more than most can afford."

Coming forward, Bram hooked his elbows over the back of the seat, his chin in his hand.

"The men are threatening to tear up the track and take over the bridge," he said. "Shoot anyone who stands in their way."

"There's not going to be any shooting, Bram," his father said. "They've sent a telegram out of Arkansas City requesting permission to lay planks down over the ties and move wagons over by hand. It'll be morning before we know."

"Oh, dear," she said, "another night with all these people."

"We'll pull off a ways, Alida. There's no need to hurry now anyway, and you can sleep in the wagon tonight. It will be easier, more private for you."

Moving back through the wagons, they pulled under a cottonwood far from the encampment, pitching their tent on flat ground. Alida seasoned the beans with bacon and a handful of wild onions that Bram found growing in a buffalo wallow.

After supper, she made her bed in the back of the wagon and lay down, with her hands hooked behind her head. Her life was as distant as the stars, suspended in the blackness above her. How she longed to be that girl, pretty and smelling of sachet, secure in the arms of her dream. How she ached for his custody, and for deliverance from the smallness of her world.

Through the cracks of the sideboards, she could see her father huddled next to the fire. Turning back, she closed her eyes, helpless against his loneliness, and thought of the marshal, and of his gaze from beneath the hat.

Bram, who had gone into the encampment, returned with news that the railroad had agreed to let them cross the trestle, providing they lay aside for arriving trains.

"Overnight they brought in siding off a railroad shack," he said, "to put down over the ties. Wagons are crossing even now. They're charging twenty-five cents to pay the men who are doing the work, so we best get moving."

For hours they waited in line before the river came into view. From her vantage, Alida could see the waters, the color of blood, as Bram had said, rolling beneath the tracks. Limbs and debris gathered against the trestle piers, breaking away in a tumble as they succumbed to the water's force. There was no balustrade, no barrier, no rail between wagons and river, so the men stood shoulder to shoulder its length, forming a human wall between them and disaster.

Teams were uncoupled and led over by their owners, while the wagons were towed across by the men collecting fees. Everyone else walked between the tracks. The waters could be heard lapping at the ties of the trestle.

For Bones, the whole thing was an exercise in more human foolishness, and at the prospect of stepping onto the trestle, his legs stiffened, his front feet spiked, his ears drew back.

"Come on, Bones," her father yelled, leaning into the reins, "huh, huh. Come on now." Bones's eyes bulged, and his nostrils flared. "Come on, you old crow," he shouted, his arm trembling, "or I'll shoot you where you stand! Huh! Huh!" Sweat dripped from the end of his nose and onto the front of his shirt. Taking off his hat, he wiped at his forehead with his sleeve and yanked once more against the reins. "You ole son of a bitch! Huh! Huh!"

"Bram," Alida said, "you've got to help."

"Let me try to take Windy across first, Dad," Bram said. "Maybe Bones will follow."

"Try *something*," his father said, throwing down his hat. "We're holding up the line."

Gathering up Windy's reins, Bram stepped out onto the planking and gave her a tug. Lifting her head, she snorted and followed him onto the trestle, Bones dropping in behind as if on his way to the barn for corn.

Mopping the sweat from his face, Mr. Deventer shrugged. Midway, Bram turned to look back, his shoulders squared.

When Alida reached the end of the trestle, the rush of the waters still trembled in her legs, and she resisted the urge to drop to the ground onto her knees.

While Bram backed the team in, she pinned the wagon. As her father was positioning the hip straps, Windy lifted her tail.

"Damned ole plug," he said.

Behind them, the last of the wagons was towed across, and the men tore up the planking for the final time.

Resting against the wagon, her father pushed back his hat, his face pale.

"You okay?" Alida asked.

"Short of wind," he said, "unlike that ole nag there. Let's pull over in them trees a bit."

"Hadn't we ought to get on to the line, Dad?" Bram asked. "We're near the last wagon as it is."

"There's time, Bram. Both me and this wore-out team need a breathing spell."

The leaves of the mesquite had been stripped by grasshoppers and provided little relief against the heat of the sun. Pulling a blanket from the gear, Alida rolled it up for a pillow and placed it against the tree. Hanging his hat on a limb, her father lay down on the blanket.

"Would you like some water?" she asked.

There was a pallor about his face, his lips blue and thin against the chalkiness.

"It's a little rest I need, Alida. This wound has stole the vim right out of me."

"Get some water, Bram," she said.

"But he doesn't want any," he said, tucking his hands in his pockets.

"Get it anyway, Bram," she said, her eyes snapping.

"Now, Alida," her father said, turning on his side. "Let me rest for a spell. We'll catch up, Bram. Don't you worry."

From up the way, she could see the young marshal who had come to their tent the day before. He was checking the bridge, stepping from tie to tie over the trestle, making certain that all the planks had been removed. When finished, he mounted his horse and rode down the hill toward them.

"Miss," he said, bringing about his horse, a buckskin with black mane. It danced and pulled at its bit. "How's everything down here?"

"My father's resting," she said, pushing the hair back from her eyes. "We'll be along soon, I suspect."

"It's a good way to the line yet. Don't tarry too long, hear."

"Thanks for your concern," she said.

"Yes, ma'am," he said, turning about, riding back up the hill in a slow gallop.

When the last of the wagons pulled off down the trail, the marshal
fell in behind, turning in his saddle for a last look back.

Then all was silent, save for the whisper of the wind through the
branches of the mesquite.

"We better get some rest, too, Bram, while we can," she said. "You
get under the trees. I'll take the wagon."

"You always get the wagon," he said.

"Just do as I say for once, Bram."

Crawling under a mesquite, Bram dropped his hat over his eyes.

Unable to sleep herself, she waited an hour before awakening her
father.

"I think we better camp here tonight, Alida," he said. "There's a fire
between my shoulders, and things go awhirl when I move."

"But the others," she said.

"We'll get us an early start in the morning. Unhitch the team and
have Bram graze them up and down the right of way. They're not to
be ridden, hear. It's all they can do to manage the wagon. Now, I'm
going to rest a bit longer, Alida. I'll get up soon enough and help."

Awakening Bram, she reported their father's orders and sent him
south away from the river. In the meantime, she gathered wood for
camp, finding a cache of walnut drift close to the trestle, shuddering
at the thought that the water had been even higher than now.
Returning, she pitched the tent next to the mesquite and built a small
fire.

By the time Bram returned with the team, darkness had descended.
After warming beans in the skillet, she laid the remaining slices of
cornbread on top to heat, but her father refused to eat.

"Help me into the tent, Alida," he said, pulling himself up on an
overhanging limb. "All I need is a good night's sleep."

Standing in the doorway of the tent, she waited as he drew the
blanket about him.

"I'll cook up some more beans tonight," she said. "We won't have
to be stopping so much on the way then."

"I know how hard this is for you," he said. "A girl so young shouldn't
have to take on the duties of raising a family. A pretty girl like you should
be thinking of beaus and picnics and getting married some day. There
was time enough for all that, if only she had lived. I'm sorry, Alida. I
wouldn't have had it this way. I wouldn't have had it at all."

"I know, Father," she said, turning to leave.

Rolling onto his side, he lifted onto an elbow. "It's your mother's voice you have, Alida. Like she was standing right here."

"Good night, Father."

"Good night, Alida."

She and Bram ate in the wagon and watched the stars wink on in the blackness.

"Can I have more, Lidy?" he asked.

"One more helping, Bram, and no more. Father might want his for breakfast, and do stop calling me Lidy."

"Tuh, tuh," he said, "the queen herself out here on the prairie eating beans."

"My name's Alida, that's all."

Scooping beans onto his plate, he settled back against the sideboard.

"Uppity Alida," he said, chewing his beans, "walking around with her head in the clouds like she was too good for the rest of us. Well, you ain't no better than the rest of us, far as I can tell."

"What do you know about anything," she said, "strutting around like you was something other than a kid."

Bram fell silent, swabbing out his plate with the last of his cornbread.

"You figure the others got to the line today?" he asked.

"Father says we'll catch up tomorrow if we get an early start."

"It's his arm, I reckon," he said, wiping his mouth with his sleeve. "He can feel it, like it was still hooked on, till he remembers it's just a pile of ash on the mill floor."

"Hush, Bram," she said, "and go on to bed. We got to get an early start."

As she lay in the wagon, a loneliness swept through her, as if she'd stepped to the edge of her life, teetering there at the brink of eternity. Maybe Bram was right. Maybe she did act uppity, but it was not her fault that she felt so deeply about things.

The smell of mud rode in from the river, and Bones jingled his halter from somewhere in the darkness.

Sometime in the night she sat up, blood rushing in her ears as she struggled to remember where she was. Something had awakened her. When it came again, it was a rumbling, a trembling within the earth, and when the whistle blew, she leaned back against the wagon bed, her heart pounding. The light broke through the trestle spans as the train rushed over the river bridge, a dragon, angry and huffing into the night.

When she awoke again, it was daybreak. Shivering in the cool, she dressed and rekindled the fire, putting coffee water on to boil.

"Coffee's ready," she called. "Better get up if we're to catch the others. Bram, do as I say now. Get up and get the team ready." Putting the skillet on, she heated the beans, mixing cornmeal and water in a bowl. Fried in a little grease, it made a hearty breakfast.

"Bram," she called again. He could be difficult to roust, could fall into a trance anywhere. Once, back in Pittsburgh, he'd failed to come home and was discovered under the porch where he had gone to sleep with a green lizard clutched in his hand.

"Lidy," he said from behind.

When she turned, he was standing at the door of the tent, his hands clenched at his side.

"Bram, what is it?" she asked.

"It's Dad," he said.

With the broken spring from under the wagon seat, they scraped a shallow grave beneath the mesquite. Wrapping him in a blanket, they lowered him in as best they could, covering him with the iron-red earth. Alida wept, while Bram stood, arms folded across his chest.

After the team was harnessed and hitched to the wagon, they locked their arms at the grave. Alida hung her father's hat on the mesquite limb. It smelled of him, of sweat, of work, and of hard times, and her stomach burned with an emptiness.

"What do we do now?" she asked.

Looking back at the trestle, Bram shrugged.

"We could wait for the river to go down," he said. "We could sell the team in Arkansas City, make our way on back to Pittsburgh."

"Is that what you think, Bram?"

A morning breeze swept in from the southwest, and their father's hat turned on the limb.

"We've got to go on, Lidy," he said. "Bones and me crossed that river once."

After the cars of lumber were pushed onto the siding and the brakes set, Creed climbed atop the end car to wait for dawn. When the engine had disappeared down the track, the night fell silent and black about him. Thunder rumbled somewhere in the distance, and a coyote sounded its reply. A chill raced down Creed's spine. God's dogs, his mother had called them, seers on four legs.

She was a force in his life, even now, her courage and wisdom living in his memory. Many times she'd warned him against disturbing the dead. "Leave their names to the ages, Creed," she'd said, "and let them go in peace." But he thought of her often, more now than ever before, and always with pleasure and guilt.

Never would he violate her peace, but her memory rose strong from these hills. In this place where she'd lived and died, her spirit could not be denied. She was in the air that he breathed, in the bay of the coyote, in the hoot of the owl from down on the creek. He could hear her voice and its calm instruction, feel her touch, smell the smokiness of her hair, and when he was still, the sun-dance drums still beat in his heart.

Here in this land she'd carved out a world of her own, of both white and red, and of neither. Here, she'd built traps to feed her enemies, had forfeited her freedom for the love of a white man, had borne a halfbreed son despite the indignation of her people. It was for her that he now returned, and for himself, to take what had been taken.

He was uncertain how far the siding was from the depot, but it was farther than he'd hoped. Without a guard, the cars would be vulnerable, and there was little doubt but that he was in a nest of thieves.

Propping his rifle in the crook of his arm, he scanned the shadows for movement. But as the night wore on, his head bobbed with the weariness of his journey.

It was just an uneasiness at first, that feeling of someone's presence, and then the sound that caused the hair on his neck to crawl. When he spotted the figure on the ladder, he whirled about and leveled his rifle.

"You better have a damn good reason to be on this car, Mister," he said.

"Take it easy, friend," the man said, pulling himself up the last few steps. "I ain't armed, as you can see."

Staring into the darkness, Creed looked for others, hiding in the timbers, or behind him on the ladders.

"Maybe you're set on finishing me off, taking my clothes, leaving me barefoot and food for the coyotes."

"Boots won't fit," the man said, "and the hat's prissy. Someone's likely to knock it off, or stomp on it, or toss it in the air to see how high it'll go. What then? Kilt over a prissy hat."

"You're standing on everything I own, Mister, and I don't aim for it to be stolen. You best be moving on."

"Yes, sir," the figure said, "thought you might be riding in on your own goods. Most folks are hid out in these hills with no more'n fatback for eating and a wood stake for claiming a future, God help 'em."

"I'm a car guard for the railroad," Creed said, "and got the right to use this rifle."

"And who ain't, what with a hundret to spare."

"It's not land I'm after," he said. "These are my timbers, bought fair for business, that's all. It's timbers builds a town."

"We're all here for a reason, ain't we, legal or otherwise. Roop Walters is the name," he said, holding out his hand.

Since he was unarmed, Creed lowered his rifle.

"You know where I am from Guthrie station?" he asked.

"South," Roop said, "sitting in a patch of sooners, not to mention half the U.S. Cavalry. All of 'em looking for someone to shoot."

"I been robbed once, took all my money," Creed said. "I figure that's sufficient for one day."

Sitting down on the lumber, Roop pushed his hat back. His face seemed hewn from rock, with prominent nose, broken sometime in the past, and his brows swept upward from his eyes like fans. His hands were knurled and callused, and there was a ring of dust around the crown of his hat.

"Still have these here timbers," he said, "and that prissy hat."

"I figure to keep them both," Creed said.

"Watched 'em drag a railroad bull out of a car of telegraph poles," he said. "Looked like he couldn't walk too good."

"Some folks beg for it," Creed said, "but I didn't have the pleasure."

"Never knew a bull couldn't use his brains loosened," Roop said, pausing, listening. "Maybe we could go elsewhere's to chat, seeing as the railroad's touchy about their bulls, and seeing as how there's only one guard badge between us."

"What about my lumber?"

"Reckon it's safer than you, out here by yourself. It ain't that far, is it."

"And where would that be?"

"Just keep yourself low," he said. "Someone might mistake that hat for a government man or a preacher and get me kilt in my prime."

"You haven't said where yet, Mister."

"Home," Roop said, "for fresh-kilt squirrel. It ain't but a culvert, but it's a heap safer than walking these hills."

Too exhausted to protest, Creed followed him down the ladder. The last time he'd thought of food was in Kansas City after purchasing his timber, celebrating with several glasses of beer at the Town Saloon, finishing up with a beefsteak the size of a saddle blanket. But that was a thousand years ago now and in a different world.

Moving south, they cut into a grove of cottonwoods that cropped from a ridge and then looped back along the bank of a creek where they came on the culvert, not far from where they started. The smell of dampness rode down the bottom.

"Here," Roop said, whispering.

"It's full of water," Creed said, dabbing the sweat from his forehead.

"That's why I ain't been kilt," he said, "or robbed like other folk I know. Once inside, the water drops away. There's a ledge to sleep on and room for a small fire, if you don't turn over or breathe. You got to wade a little water, but I got wood for drying out and for cooking."

"Lead the way," Creed said. "It's your house."

As they slipped down the bank, the cold water rose to their knees, running shallow again as they approached the culvert. Ahead, Roop ducked into the opening, the water rippling behind him. No one in his right mind would hide in such a place, Creed thought, stooping into the dankness of the culvert, the smell of mud and crawdad thick in the air. Mud turtles scrambled from the bank and into the water as they worked their way in.

"What about cottonmouth?" Creed asked, his voice odd within the confines of the culvert.

The swishing of Roop's feet stopped. "It's fried squirrel or nothing, a little coffee maybe, if it ain't stole or eat up by crickets."

"And here I was all primed for cottonmouth," Creed said.

"Wait here," Roop said, laughing, "whilst I strike a light."

When the match struck, shadows leapt up the walls of the culvert. A dirt ledge stretched twenty feet its length, the width of a man's body, no more, deposited there by floodwaters that gathered and slowed within its bounds. Wood was sized and stacked, ready for a fire, and there was a bedroll spread out along the wall. A Mexican saddle lay on its side, a sterling band decorating the cantle, the horn leather sawed away from the scrub of a lariat.

"What about the smoke?" Creed asked, rubbing his hands together.

"Draft's east," Roop said, "with the water flow, 'less a train passes over. Then it sucks back west, taking out your lungs and eyeballs with it."

Pulling himself onto the ledge, Creed took off his boots and set them next to the fire. Slipping off his socks, he draped them over the tops of his boots to dry.

"Won't someone smell the smoke?" he asked.

"Sure," Roop said, tossing his hat on his bedroll, "but no way of knowing if it's ten mile off or smack under your nose. There's more fires burning on this prairie tonight than on the shores of hell."

"Sooners, I guess," Creed said.

"Most are scared," Roop said, "scared and hungry, and that makes 'em dangerous."

Creed held his toes in his hands to warm them.

"It's the hopeless most of all, I suppose."

"And those who live off others' hopes," Roop said. "It ain't just the poor waiting in these hills tonight, no sir, not by a long shot. There's bankers, builders, and scammers of every mettle, even a brew master hid in a coyote den where the creek turns, waiting to set up shop first chance. There's preachers and politicians enough to stall the progress of mankind for a hundret years. A whole colony of civil war widders is hid in a clump of locusts off the Cimarron, waiting to get a jump on their free claim of land. Don't even have to prove it up, just stake it out and it's theirs. East a mile, there's a half-starved family living out of a hollow tree stump, eating black walnuts and wild onions, drinking branch water swimming with skeeters. Them kids' eyes are big as wagon wheels, you know, but they're as apt to shoot you as the next.

Taking out his knife, he sharpened a small stick and picked at his teeth, parking it in the corner of his mouth.

"Every federal marshal between here and the Kansas line ain't but a shyster waiting to drop his badge in the dirt and race in for his town lot. Some say they are even working as railroad carpenters just so's they can get a Guthrie lot before anyone else." Tossing his toothpick into the water, Roop watched it drift away. "Hard to fathom, ain't it, even for stole' land."

"But then I'm a lawyer myself," Creed said, watching Roop's face.

Looking out from under his brows, Roop shrugged his shoulders.

"Guess I done things I ain't so proud of myself, although they don't come to me at the moment."

"We live off contention, Roop. There's likely to be plenty of it here when they start settling up claims."

Reaching under the bedroll, Roop pulled out the squirrel, still limp with body heat, its black eyes glinting in the light.

"Kilt him with a stick," he said, "while he was thinkin' things over. Here, take hold his feet."

Opening his knife, Roop gutted out the squirrel, tossing the entrails into the water, where turtles thrashed over the windfall. After threading the carcass onto a stick, he leaned back and propped it over the heel of his boot, lowering the squirrel against the heat of the coals.

When the aroma of roasting meat filled the culvert, Creed asked, "Who are you, Roop? Where do you come from?"

Turning the squirrel over, Roop checked it with the point of his knife, grease sizzling into the coals. Adjusting the stick, he turned onto his side, propping his hand under his head.

"It's a uncertainty," he said, "and a mystery."

"You don't know where you came from?"

"Left as a baby to be found, I reckon, or die, whichever came first. It was the William Barney Cattle Company out of Texas heard my wailing. William T. hisself took me home. Said I stank so bad he had to fight the buzzards off with his hat to keep 'em from picking out my eyes."

"An orphan?"

"Said all the Mexicans rode off without pay after two days of my mewling, and he'd wished a hundret times over he'd left me for the buzzards."

"It was Barney who raised you then?"

"A Mexican woman named Romona. She cooked and laundered for the Barney outfit, a widder with a new babe on the breast. Her man been knifed in the belly for bringing Manuel into a Juarez bar."

"Manuel?"

"His heel dog," he said, "with the disturbing habit of heeling everything he saw."

Crossing his feet, Roop turned the squirrel over before continuing.

"William T. rode in with me across his saddle, and said, 'Now Romona, it's your duty as a God-fearing Catholic to let this here boy milk. Anyone can see you got plenty just going to waste.'

"'A gringo,' she said, 'a Protestant smelling of death. No Catholic would leave her baby. Let it die as its mother intended.'

"'Now, Romona,' William T. said, 'you know we can't just throw this here baby away. I admit it ain't much of a baby, but it's against the law, ain't it?'

"'Then you suckle it, old man,' she said, 'because I will not.'"

"What did he do?" Creed asked, incredulous at the story that unfolded before him.

"Roped her right off his horse. Tied her to a wagon wheel and poked her tit through the spokes so's she couldn't get at me while I milked. Said she screamed so loud it took three days to get the cattle rounded back up. He had to rope her every day for a month before she'd stand without being tied. Even then, she'd stare off into the prairie and whistle the whole time like nothing was happening."

Pointing, Creed said, "Better turn that squirrel again 'fore you burn it to ash. That's the damndest story I ever heard."

"Yes, sir, but what can you expect from a feller thrown away by his mother and raised on the milk of rejection.

"Fact is, a man like me don't require much, Creed, a culvert for keeping off the rain, fried squirrel for eating, a pretty girl now and again to sweeten the soul. A man like me takes his days as they come, one at a time, squeezes them dry, and waits for the next to roll around. It's all I ever wanted. All I ever got, too, come to think on it."

"You never married one of those women, Roop?"

"Nope," he said. "Drank a whole quart of brandy one time, though. A man can get too much of a good thing. Here," he said, grinning, "let's eat this critter 'fore our fire goes out."

Ripping the squirrel apart, he handed half to Creed. Grease glistened on their fingers and chins as they ate.

"You grew up on the trail then?" Creed asked, wiping at his face with the sleeve of his shirt.

"Mostly, moving cattle north to market and then back, with just enough time and money to do it all over again. Then William T. took to leasing from the Indians, near twenty thousand acres at one point." Taking another bite of meat, he thought it over as he chewed. "Never learned to set a proper table, but I'm a fair hand on the trail. Guess that don't mean much anymore. It's a hard thing when a man's work is over. Like suckling a tit through a wagon spoke, ain't it. It's a unnatural state."

"Times change, Roop. You have to change with them."

Tossing the remains of his squirrel into the water, Roop wiped his hands on his pants.

"That's an odd stand to take, for a man like yourself," he said.

"A breed, you mean?"

"This land's going to be divvied up amongst strangers soon enough, Creed. That couldn't be something you've overlooked."

"I'm half Kiowa, Roop, and there's not a day goes by I don't feel it. My mother brought the first expedition out of Fort Gibson right up this valley. But she couldn't give up the past, nor see the future, couldn't see that things were never going to be the same. It cost her dear in the end."

"That's mighty hard against your own kind, Creed."

Turning his boots up, Creed shook out the last of the water.

"It's the way of things, no different than the end of the buffalo, or the cattle drives, I suppose. They're gone, that's all, replaced by the trains running over the top of this house of yours."

"Well, maybe so," Roop said. "Lord knows I got few enough answers."

Pulling his legs under him, Creed leaned in.

"Did you know the Kiowa developed a calendar, Roop, a kind of history of who they were?"

"Reckon I didn't."

"Well, they did, and they survived in these plains when no one else could, but those days are gone. A man can't live with one foot in the past and one in the present for the rest of his life. Things have to be set right so he can move on. This is one breed who's going to set it right, my friend. Everything I need's here in my head, and I'm going to wage my own kind of war. It all starts with those carloads of lumber out there. It's not about hunting buffalo and stealing horses anymore, Roop. It's about money and power."

Hooking his boot behind his knee, Roop pulled it off and set it by his saddle.

"So you're just another stray come home, like myself, I reckon?"

"I suppose that's so."

"I can understand a man making a new start," Roop said, taking off his other boot, "maybe even leaving his own kind behind in the doing, but why would he come home to do it?"

Creed studied the water as it eased by, the light of the fire flickering in its blackness.

"It's got to be here," he said.

"Lord help me," Roop said, "a Kiowa set on taking scalps."

Turning his socks over, Creed looked at Roop.

"The injustice was here and so must be the reckoning."

"It's the wound of the boy what drives the man to his glory and damnation, ain't it," Roop said.

Fatigue swept Creed, and he rolled over onto his side.

"Listen, I'm worn out. Would you mind if I rested here until morning?"

"It's the run you'll be making, then, when the time comes?"

"I'm going for a town lot, Roop. Guess it makes me no better than the rest of those sooners out there. But if I can claim a lot and hold it down for a few days, maybe I can sell it for enough cash to get by until the building of this new town starts."

"Maybe a angel will shit diamonds in your hand," Roop said, "though it's a rare event in these parts. In the meantime, you're welcome to hole up, I reckon."

It was the rush of the current against the wall and the cold water that swept at his legs that awakened Creed in the blackness of the culvert. Somewhere Roop called out, his voice lost in the torrent. Raising his arms above his head, Creed braced against the roof, against the water rising about him. Kneeling, he lifted his head as high as he could as the water rushed in, fear stripping away reason as he fought to breathe in the remaining inches of air. Maybe if he turned himself over to the current, rode it downstream, he could get out in the darkness. Once outside the culvert, there would at least be a chance. But the prospect of coming up short, of being trapped in the culvert was a thought he couldn't bear.

Reaching down inside, he searched for the courage to let go, to abandon the remaining moments of air for the uncertainty of the rushing water. It was but the length of a single breath any way it was cut. With a final gulp of air, he dropped away from the roof.

Counting, he steeled himself against the churn of the creek, against the trek along its bottom. From twenty, each second was a bonus as he tumbled weightless in the turbulence until his lungs ached, burst within his chest, and collapsed within him like useless bags.

Pushing off the bottom, he struggled upward, brush and limbs boiling about him, sucking him into the belly of the creek.

At first he didn't recognize it, the hand in his own, pulling him through the waters. Bursting through the surface, he filled his lungs, spewing and coughing and slapping. Hooking him about the neck, Roop hauled for shore, fighting against the tow.

When at last they reached the bank, they fell into the grass, rain sweeping about them, lightning crackling and thunder rumbling as the storm raced away.

Sitting up, Roop wiped the water from his eyes, slicking back his hair with his hand.

"I was awake anyways," he said, "though hadn't figured on getting up quite so sudden."

Rolling over, Creed lifted onto his elbows, the rain-washed breeze against his face. Unpinning the railroad guard badge, he tossed it to Roop.

"It's a hell of a way to make a man beholding, saving his life like that," he said.

Roop pinned the badge to his shirt and made his way to the bank of the creek where the stock of Creed's rifle protruded from the mud. Digging it free, he washed it off in the water before turning around.

"Saving a drowning sooner could ruin a man's reputation, if it got around," he said.

"I won't tell a soul," Creed said, "but thanks anyway, just between us."

"Least that prissy hat's downriver."

"Along with your Mexican saddle," Creed said.

Hooking the rifle over his arm, Roop shrugged.

"Where do we go from here?"

Standing, Creed steadied himself.

"You shoot the first son of a bitch that comes within range of our timber, Roop, because I'm going in for a claim. It's rich men I'm going to make of us, partner, whether you like it or not."

Shivering, Creed lowered himself into the grass along the grade for a look back. His three cars of timbers sat on the siding. From atop the lead car, Roop waved, his rifle cradled over his arm, the tracks gleaming behind him.

Turning, Creed headed back north to Guthrie station, swinging into the trees at the bend of the creek. Uncertain as to what might lie ahead, he pulled himself up into the fork of a cottonwood, working his way into the upper branches.

Below, the Cimarron valley stretched into the distance, red cliffs towering from the bends of the river, slabs of sandstone jutting from their banks, scarred by the fury of floodwaters, embattled but defiant. On the lee side, sand the color of straw swept into the blood-red earth. Between them, the Cimarron River crept to the sea, with boundaries of quicksand and brine-covered drift. As far as Creed could see, strokes of greens, reds, yellows, and blues emblazoned the prairie, shrubs, thickets of plum, colonies of sunflowers, and redbuds. Life flourished with the rain, but with a tentativeness, with eyes cast down in an intemperate land.

Striking a gait, he cut across an open field toward a grove of trees. He dropped to a knee to blow, sweat dripping from the end of his nose and onto his hand. The smell of rain hung in the branches and in the decaying leaves.

Moving into the shadows of a persimmon, he checked his watch. Timing was critical, early enough to beat the trains, dozens scheduled at fifteen-minute intervals from the starting line, but not so early as to raise suspicion with the authorities.

Vast numbers waited on horseback at the borders. There were reports of grain wagons stretching as far as the eye could see, farmers racing for homestead claims. But those wanting town lots would be riding the trains.

Creed understood the risk of going in too early, because sooner or later legal challenges would prevail or die on the basis of time.

Lifting onto his knees, he peered through the branches. To his surprise, he could see the depot across the creek, marshals gathering under its porch, leaning against its wall like blackbirds on a fence. From behind the depot, a hill rose into Guthrie station. To the south, soldiers' tents cropped in perfect rows up the hill, an American flag fluttering from a pole in the center of the encampment, steam boiling from pots suspended on a crossbar over a central fire. Aside from the two soldiers who tended the pots, the camp was deserted, the aroma of pintos and fatback wafting into the trees, smelling of home in a foreign land.

Settling down, he waited. The sounds of the grove were magnified in the quiet: the swish of feet through the leaves, the crack of twig or limb. From time to time he spotted others as they scurried into the shadows or dropped behind a tree.

Voices drifted from the depot, men gathering and laughing as they worked their way up the hill. The man at the lead was lank and spare, his coat black with a handkerchief tucked into the pocket. Fanning out on either side were a dozen marshals, picking their way through the brush, their hats pulled down over their eyes, their guns slung low on their hips. Behind them, a handful of railroad officials held onto their derbies against the breeze. Now and again they stopped to drive a stake into the ground as they lay claim to the choicest lots.

Dropping back, Creed waited. A cool head was the shortest route to justice, even revenge, one of the lessons of law that he'd learned, and so for now he waited.

As the sun arched overhead, the temperatures rose in the grove of trees. After checking his watch again, he took out his pocketknife and cut two persimmon sticks. From across the way, the marshals reconvened on the porch of the depot, joking and cursing as they awaited the arrival of the trains.

When it started, it was like a spring rain, a drop here, and then another, the first portent of the storm ahead: a man springing from his hiding place behind a brush, running across the prairie, his hat flying, another shooting from the grove of trees, his stakes flopping from his pockets like the wings of a bird. Both were cut short by the butts of the marshals' rifles. Like sides of beef, the transgressors were hauled to a railroad car, their heels dragging in the gravel bed behind them.

Others soon broke from the prairie, dashing from brush to brush, hurdling over the tracks and into the arms of the marshals. Some wormed through the grass or squatted in the open like rabbits. A few charged upright with war cries and raised arms. None was to make it past the marshals and into the site.

Creed pulled his knees into his arms. It was too soon. The timing must be right, or all would be lost. Determined to keep to his plan, he watched the sun ride its course across the sky, listened to the shouts from the prairie as the line was charged over and over.

Checking his watch again, he calculated the time. A man on a fast horse just might have made it from the line by now. Rising, he parted the branches of the persimmon. A line of soldiers now waited in reserve below the crest of the hill, their shoulders touching, their rifles leveled at their sides.

From the north a whistle sounded, smoke boiling into the sky as the engine broke over the horizon. Hundreds were leaning from the windows, hanging from the doorways, clinging atop the railcars. A woman with white hair straddled the cowcatcher, an avenging angel with her boots inches from the tracks, her skirt flapping in the breeze.

Panic seized Creed. The train, the marshals, the line of soldiers between him and the town! Then from the south, the northbound's whistle blew.

Sliding into the creek, he worked his way across and clawed up the bank. Dropping into the grass at the track's edge, he searched for a break in the line, but there was none, no quarter to be had. He could smell the creosote, feel the engine's rumble in his body, the heat of the rails against his face. Wind swept the grade, clogging his eyes with dirt, and he cursed.

When the engine slowed for the curve, bags, tents, and bedrolls filled the air, followed by people as they vaulted from the train. The soldiers and marshals pulled back, letting them through this time, and the morning came alive with the whoops and hollers of the charging crowd.

The only place open was the soldiers' camp itself, its eastern point coming within yards of the rim of the hill, within reach of the best real estate in the Territory. From that hill, the whole of the town spread out below, the heart of Guthrie station. If he could get to the tents, if he could work his way to that point, if he could do all that without detection, he might still beat the crowds.

Bounding over the tracks, he dove into a plum thicket at the bottom of the grade. From both directions, whistles screamed and brakes screeched as the engines pulled in to the depot.

Scratched and bleeding, he broke from the thicket, rolling under a tent flap, crouching in the shadows, smelling beans and canvas in the heat.

Dashing from tent to tent through the heart of the camp, he paused long enough to take a bearing, to clear his head before racing the final yards to the summit.

Below him, people boiled from the trains, running with abandon in every direction. With skirt flying, a woman dragged her startled child by his collar. Some drove stakes where they fell. Others fought their way to the front or turned to hold their ground against the crush of people from behind.

Taking off his boot to drive his stakes, Creed searched for some sign of survey or plat markings. Finding none, he drove in a persimmon stick, stepped off twenty-five feet, and drove in the second. Uncertain as to what to do next, he calculated the approximate center of the lot, sat down, and crossed his arms to wait.

Minutes passed before he noticed the figure hunkered under the sandstone outcrop. A wash undercut the stone, providing shade from the noon sun. An old man cradled a jug, the cork secured in the pocket of his overall bib. His socks drooped like rags about his ankles, and his whiskers faded to ash at the corners of his mouth. His smell was distinct and sour on the wind. Lifting the jug, he pulled and then dabbed at his mouth with the sleeve of his shirt.

"It's atop the goddamn world, ain't it," he said, his speech thick.

"Prime," Creed said.

"Have a drink," he said, holding out the jug. "Made from army taters and skeeter water, but it's a fine tune what plays."

"Thanks, anyway," Creed said.

Taking another pull, the old man dropped the jug into his lap. Moisture gathered at the corners of his mouth and raced into the thicket of whiskers. Leaning his head against the bank of the wash, he coughed.

"A celebration," he said, "for owning this goddamn mountain. It's real corn liquor I'll be having soon enough, whores, too, with bubbly tits and squeezy long legs, two at onct, maybe, or three to drown in, and pork ribs over a mesquite fire. Yes, sir," he said, "the capital right here, with marble steps and lions guarding the gates and a statue of me, covered with pigeon shit, taking this hill, looking heavenward into God's own eyes, like I knowed something no one else ever did." Pushing forward, he narrowed his focus on Creed. "Well, sir, it's theirs, ain't it, for a king's ransom and their own black souls."

"Just a piece of hill, Mister, and, not that, if they figure you for a sooner. It's a fast run you made, for a celebrating man."

Sounds rose from below them, encompassing the struggle up the hill, the ring of stakes in the hard pan, the whistle of another engine pulling the grade from the Cimarron valley.

Tipping the jug, he took another draw.

"Been driving a army slop wagon," he said, "three trips a day to the river, fightin' blowfly and stink in the heat whilst them soldiers live like goddamn kings with their white tents, eaten fatback and pintos, riding around in their pretty uniforms. Figured I'd just scout a way to prime land while I had the opportunity, figured a way to the top of the god-damn world right up through that soldiers' camp."

Standing, Creed walked the perimeter of his lot. The masses below were closing about him and the garrulous old man.

"It's against the law for government employees to stake a claim, slop wagon or otherwise."

"The law, is it," the old man said. "Who's to say I didn't quit a week ago and walk back to the border, come in on that train down there with them other dumb bastards? Who's to say I didn't?"

Before Creed could answer, his voice was lost in the din, in the clamor for lots, in the cries of joy and lost hopes.

A man broke from the crowd, his pate shining with sweat as he scrambled his way onto the lot next to Creed's. Under each arm was a bolt of cloth covered with tent canvas. A few feet behind, a large woman shoved her way through to join him, a scarf tied under her chin, a silver broach pinned over her breast. She, too, carried bolts of cloth, sweat glistening about her eyes and in her thin hair, the smell of stale bread about her clothes. With a piece of buggy axle, the man drove in stakes before joining her. Back to back they stood, buggy axle at the ready against any who dared jump their claim.

It was over as it began, in an instant, with the lots gone, even as thousands walked the hill, searching, waiting for the weak to falter, to fall from the heat, or step from their claim for want of water. Like coyotes, they ferreted out the helpless, taking from them what they could no longer protect.

From below, more trains rolled in, their whistles screaming as they disgorged yet more cargo into the bowels of the town site.

Throughout the afternoon, the heat forged disappointment into despair. From within the crowds, fights erupted, but never far away were the marshals, exacting swift and certain justice.

"Excuse me, sir," the man with the buggy axle said, holding out his hand to Creed, "my name is Samuel Lieberman. This is my wife, Lena. It seems we are to be neighbors if we survive this day."

"Creed McReynolds," he said, shaking his hand.

"We are from New York City," Samuel said, "my wife and I. It cost a hundred dollars to get the first train out of Arkansas City. The railroad employees are making more money than anyone, I think. Still, it was worth it, this fine lot."

"It's a beginning we all are looking for," Creed said, smiling.

"We will build our store here. Once we have a place to work, the cloth, under Lena's hand, will become the finest suits in all of the Territory, and at the best prices," he added. "It is enough for a start if we can make it through, enough for a beginning."

"A capital city will need its share of suits, I'd say."

Nodding confirmation, Lena pulled her scarf from about her face. Her eyes were dark and warm; her smiles, winning.

"And what of your neighbor there?" Samuel asked, pointing to the figure under the outcrop.

Chin resting against his chest, the old man snored, his hat cranked down over his eyes.

"Celebrating," Creed said, "as you can see. Says he's looking for a buyer with a king's ransom and a craving for the top of the hill. Says they're going to build a statue of him looking into God's own eyes. From the looks of it, he's been living in that wash for a considerable time."

"Not fit for God's eyes," Samuel said, shaking his head. "What is it that you do, Mr. McReynolds?"

"Call me Creed. I'm an attorney, like half the marshals in the Territory, I hear. I've got three cars of timber sitting on a siding, at least they were this morning. Hope to make a profit before I'm done. I figure to turn this lot into working cash."

"Timber," Samuel said. "Who won't need timber for building, and at what price?"

"It's a fair profit I'm after," Creed said.

Stepping back, Samuel examined Creed's clothes, lifting his brows.

"Maybe Lena can fix you with a nice suit," he said. "A businessman should have a nice suit."

"Clash with a plum thicket," Creed said, looking down at his torn shirt, "and a swim in the river. Must look a sight."

"You come to Lena, and she'll fix you with a nice suit like no other in the Territory. I guarantee it."

"I tell you what, Samuel, soon as my fortune's made, I'll order up the best suit you've got."

"It's a deal," he said.

With that, Samuel and Lena set about constructing a shelter by stacking the bolts of cloth into walls and placing another over the top for shade. From their home of cloth their legs protruded, and they laughed at this circumstance.

Pulling his knees under his chin, Creed locked his fingers behind his head against the afternoon heat and the eyes of the crowd. Sweat raced down his neck. Tearing off a piece of his shirt, he put it on his head, tying it off under his chin.

From behind their shelter, Samuel and Lena fell silent as they sipped water from the small canteen hidden in the folds of her skirt.

By afternoon, Creed's lips peeled from the dryness, and sweat stung his eyes. Dust boiled about him, rising from the trampling feet of the crowd.

When a boy passed by with a milk pail of water from the creek, Creed whistled him over.

"How much?" he asked.

A shock of yellow hair sprang from the boy's head, dirt gathering in its roots. The ends of his shoes were frayed, and he wore no socks. His clothes were soiled beyond repair, and his ankles were splotched with chigger bites. Pacing just beyond reach, he scanned the street, as if at any moment he might be snatched away. There was a ferocity in his eyes, but a flatness too, as if all feelings but one had been driven from him. He was a feral cat, half-starved and fierce, hunting at the margins of civilization.

"Fifty cents," he said, "and fifty more for use of the dipper."

"I'll pay you double come tomorrow," Creed said.

Setting his bucket down, the boy held his hand over his eyes for a closer look at Creed.

"It's a dollar, Mister, if you want a drink."

"Double, tomorrow," he said, "a fair promise."

"It's the promise of Jesus that's free," he said, "but cash for this here water."

"It's none too clean," Creed said, leaning over for a look, "and thieving high."

"Takes a man with no dollar for being particular, don't it," the boy said. "Anyway, it's the army horses upstream, and I ain't walking no two mile with a milk bucket full of water for nothing."

"Where you come from, boy?" Creed asked, growing impatient.

"A buzzard threw me up on a rock," he said, "if it's your concern." Stirring the concoction with his dipper, he looked up through his hair. "You want it or not?"

"I got this pocketknife," Creed said, holding it out, "deer-horn handle and worth more than a dipper of water."

Leaning in, the boy took the knife, holding it against the light.

"Handle's chipped," he said, "but worth a dipper, I reckon. Step out, and I'll draw you one."

"Two dippers," Creed said, "and you fetch it here."

Dropping the knife into his pocket, the boy shrugged, stepping in, handing him a dipper of the water. Unwilling of too close an inspection, Creed tossed it down, followed by a second. Throwing the dipper into the bucket with a splash, he seized the boy by the front of his shirt.

"Now get, 'fore I take that knife back and cut your balls off with it."

As the boy scrambled away, water sloshed from his bucket. When at a safe distance, he turned, dribbling a dipper of the water into the dust between his feet.

By late afternoon, the breeze died, and the crowd fell silent, resigned to the heat. As far as Creed could see, tents dotted the prairie. From across the way, the old man snored under his hat, his jug discarded at his feet, hands open at his sides. Beyond the tracks, a fiddle scratched out a song, and horses whinnied from the soldiers' corral.

Creed drifted into sleep. When he awoke, the valley shimmered with campfires, and the smells from cooking pots gathered in the cool. As night fell, beds were made in the tents, or in the backs of wagons, or in the grass where the last of the breeze might be caught. Here in this valley where his mother once walked, strangers from all over the world lay down within arm's reach of each other as the night descended. What would she have thought, he wondered, as they drove in their stakes, as they scrabbled over strips of land little bigger than a grave.

Creed watched as a band of men exited the depot, their lantern swinging in the dusk. At each lot they stopped, and then moved on.

Next door Samuel and Lena struck a fire, their voices hushed as they huddled about its light.

As the men made their way to the top of the hill, they approached Creed, their lantern high. The marshal's badge flashed under the light. His coat was tucked behind the handle of his revolver.

"This your claim?" he asked, checking his paper against the lantern.

"I'll be filing come daylight," Creed said, stepping back. "Is there a problem?"

"Oh, it's a fine lot, 'cept for being smack in the middle of the street."

"That can't be," Creed said, his heart ticking up. "There were no markers."

"Didn't get it done, did they, sitten on their asses, leaving it to the law to do. Ain't much comfort, but there's a good many folk in the same boat. I gave 'em till morning to get off. Will do the same for you. After that, you're trespassing on city property. You understand?"

"I have a choice?"

"Yes, sir," he said, folding up the paper, "but it's one apt to get you shot."

As the lantern moved on down the line, Creed kicked at the dirt. Without the lot, he'd lose everything, and after all he'd been through! Maybe they were wrong. Maybe there was some way he could file a protest come morning.

The old man from the wash stirred, searching for his jug in the darkness, tucking it away under his arm.

Moving to the back of his lot, Creed curled on the ground to await the coming of daylight. The light from Samuel's fire soon died away, and the night was desolate. Below, the town quieted except for the barking of a dog, the distant whinny of a horse.

Some time in the early hours he was awakened by the old man in the wash, who seemed to be hallucinating in his sleep. The thought popped into his head unannounced, as if it had been buried there all along, just beneath the surface.

Crawling toward the wash, Creed picked his way through the darkness, through the bullhead burrs that grew in abundance along the sandy bank, and before he realized, he was upon the old man, whose legs stuck from under the outcrop.

"Old man," he whispered.

When there was no answer, he shook his boot from side to side. Still there was no answer. The old man was passed out, just as he thought.

Hooking his legs under his arms, Creed pulled him from his den, the old man's hands trailing in the sand, his jug hooked over a finger. Creed's stomach lurched at the stink of liquor and slop wagon, but he was determined to see it through, inching the old man up the embankment, pulling him at last onto his own lot.

Winded, Creed mopped the sweat from his forehead while from the darkness the old man smacked his lips. Whores, Creed supposed, with bubbly tits and squeezy legs.

Only then did he realize that the jug had fallen off the old man's finger. Sliding back down the embankment, he worked his way back through the bullheads and kerosene weed, sweeping his hand in the darkness for the jug. On the verge of giving up, he found it, standing upright without a drop spilled.

As he scrambled up the bank for the second time, the first light of dawn broke on the horizon. Heart racing, he grabbed the old man's feet and hauled him a distance into the grass, propping him against a cottonwood stump, and squaring his hat on his head.

No sooner had he set the jug between the old man's legs than a hand seized his arm, pulling him forward.

"It's only a kiss, Lottie," the old man said.

Prying loose his fingers, Creed made his way back to the embankment and into the wash once more. From under the sandstone outcrop, he waited for his heart to steady and for dawn's light to awaken the citizens of Guthrie station.

It was midmorning when the marshals arrived, four of them, rigged with rifles and sidearms, and with the look of business in their eyes. Bringing up the rear was a black man, carrying leg irons over his arm for securing prisoners, his cheek bulging with tobacco.

Creed watched from the wash, his future hinging on the next few moments.

"Get up, Mister," the marshal said, kicking the bottom of the old man's foot.

"Huh," the old man said from under his hat.

Hooking him under the arms, they lifted him onto his feet.

"It's city property you're on," the head marshal said.

"Top of the goddamn world," he said. "You want marble lions, you gotta pay."

"Jesus," the deputy said, "smells like he died back in Kansas. Can we get on with it?"

"I told you last night, Mister, to be gone by morning. Looks like you had yourself a party instead." Turning, he nodded to the black man. "Give 'em an iron, Smitty. We'll take him before the buzzards carry us all off to Texas. Chain him under that tree so's he can air out a bit, boys."

Climbing out of the wash, Creed watched as they hauled him away.

"A shame," Samuel said, from the corner of his lot, "a man held in such high regard by God, and to be treated no more than a common criminal."

"It's a hard country," Creed said, "with little reprieve, even by God Himself."

Taking off his hat, Samuel rubbed at his bald head.

"Lena says that you are worth taking a chance on, that she can tell by the dark of your eyes. I have learned to trust what Lena says."

Picking burrs from the knees of his britches, Creed looked up at him.

"What is it you have in mind, Samuel?"

Reaching into his coat, he handed Creed a bill. "It is all we have, a hundred dollars, maybe enough for lumber to build our store, and we will guard your claim with this," he said, holding up the buggy axle, "until you've filed at the land office."

"You've got yourself a deal, neighbor," Creed said, tucking the bill into his pocket.

When finished at the land office, Creed walked to the Cottonwood. All about him life sprouted from the prairie, a city born in a day. The cries of children at play filled the streets, and the smells of civilization wafted from the tents. This primal valley stewed with humanity and the stink of the city. It was alone no more and would never be again.

At the bottom of the hill, he struck south toward the siding, Samuel's hundred-dollar bill crisp and cool in his pocket.

Twice now he'd placed his hopes and dreams in the hands of strangers, one with a broken buggy axle and six bolts of cloth, and the other, he hoped and prayed, still standing guard atop his cars of timber.

The lot was but a patch of cocklebur on the edge of the town site. From there Abaddon could see the Crosstimbers, a strip of hardwood trees cutting a diagonal swath across the Territory, most of them stunted from the heat and the scarcity of rain, or twisted by the winds, or split by lightning. Within its bounds, large areas of prairie flourished where the trees had burned, rivers of grass striking into its heart. Other parts were thick with vines, tangled with briar and brush so dense that it took man and axe to penetrate it.

Not long ago it had been a natural barrier between the Plains Indians and the tribes of the Southeast. It was still alive with black bear, cougar, honey bees, and opossum. Deer grazed at its borders in the morning dew, slept in its shade during the heat of the day, and when the wind was right the smell of honeysuckle and plum blossom filled the air.

Even though it was not the lot Abaddon wanted, he was lucky to have it, he supposed. After having removed most of his hide when he'd jumped from the rail car, and having spent the night in the rain searching for his bags, he was glad to be here at all. It had cost him twenty dollars to pay off the marshal who'd caught him. No more than a kid, he had thrown his marshal's badge into the bushes and disappeared into the dark.

More money was spent for the tent, a contraption made of branches and gutta-percha cloth, bought from an old man smelling of sheep. He'd stood mute, his hand out, his teeth black under his grin, until Abaddon paid him what he wanted. Even now the tent threatened collapse, weakened beyond repair with patches of mattress ticking.

There'd been little opportunity for Abaddon to retrieve his press from the cottonwoods or to do anything beyond surviving the day. Money was paid out to a line sitter at the land office, who'd abandoned the line when a fight broke out over a creek-bottom lot. Three hours later, his claim was filed.

In the heat the tent stank of smoke and bacon grease as Abaddon emptied his pockets onto the floor to count out the coins.

"Water, Mister?" a boy called from the edge of Abaddon's lot.

"It's a cool drink, is it?" he asked, sticking his head from the tent.

Holding up the milk pail, the boy nodded. "And pure as mountain snow."

"Well, I'll have a dipper," he said, "to wash the dust from my throat."

"Fifty cents, Mister, and fifty more for use of the dipper."

"It's a thief you are, then?"

Stepping out of reach, the boy dribbled the water into the pail.

"It's the love of Jesus that's free. This here water's fifty cents."

"It's a big mistake you're making, boy, selling what everybody's going to have free soon enough anyway. It's words will matter most when tomorrow comes. It's words going to make this town the capital city."

"'Fifty cents' is two words," the boy said, "and the price of this here water."

"Maybe we can strike a deal."

Dropping the dipper back into the pail, the boy looked over his shoulder.

"I got a can of lard," he said, "and a iron skillet, too, and a woman what opened her shirt for a dipper full. What I want is fifty cents."

"What did you say your name was?"

"Didn't."

"Well, what is it?"

"Jimmy."

"Don't you have a last name, Jimmy?"

"It's Jimmy, that's all, and when someone calls it out, I answer."

"Come on in to the shade, Jimmy."

"How do I know you ain't a murderer just waiting to cut off my head for a drink of this water?"

"Well, Jimmy, because my name is Abaddon Damon. I'm the owner and editor of *The Capital City*, the first newspaper in this Territory. Come on in. I want to talk to you. I'll leave the flap open, so you can call out if anyone sets out to cut off your head."

Jimmy looked over his shoulder before peeking into the tent.

"Maybe we ought talk out here," he said.

"It's a private matter, Jimmy, a business matter."

"Well, all right," he said, "but I'm a lot stronger than I look."

"Sit over there," Abaddon said.

Jimmy slid up on the stool, setting the bucket of water by his feet, folding his arms over his chest.

"What kind of business deal you got in mind, Mister?"

Pulling up a camp chair, Abaddon hooked his leg up on his knee, leaning into his hand. The boy reminded him of himself, the way he watched what was going on around him, the way he listened, the way he calculated every word.

"Where's your parents, Jimmy?" he asked.

"What's that got to do with a business deal?"

"Suppose I struck a deal, and they come along and change everything? That wouldn't do, would it?"

Leaning over, Jimmy looked out the flap of the tent.

"Dead," he said.

"Dead?"

"Kilt by Indians."

Abaddon pulled at his lip as he studied Jimmy.

"It's been a good long while since we had Indian depredations in these parts, Jimmy."

"I don't know nothing about that," he said, "but Indians scalped my ma and my pa."

"I see, and how is it they didn't scalp you, too, I wonder?"

Reaching into his pocket, Jimmy retrieved a knife.

"Cause I kilt them first with this here bone-handled knife," he said, opening the blade. "Ain't nobody scalping me long as I got this."

"Where do you stay then, without parents and all? How do you manage in such a place as Guthrie station?"

Folding up the knife, Jimmy slipped it back in his pocket and bobbed his legs as he considered the question.

"Well, I sleep in the tunnels mostly, back in the cracks where the drunks can't go, and sometimes, when the first sergeant is sleeping off a binge, the cook gives me food down at the army camp. On Saturday nights, the girls up to the Hotel-Springer give me tips for bringing men friends by, and once I found a whole keg of beer what rolled out from under the Sampson Beer Hall tent. Hunt Stovall gave me two dollars for it. And then there's this here spring water. It's a mighty good deal for fifty cents a dipper, given I got to haul it all the way up from the Cottonwood."

"You sound like an industrious lad to me, Jimmy."

"Hunt Stovall says I'm a natural-born businessman."

Standing, Abaddon walked the length of the tent, bending so as not to bump his head on the bed slat he'd tied in as cross bracing.

"Jimmy," he said, "I'm in need of someone to sell my papers."

"You pay money?"

"Fifty cents," he said, "if you sell 'em all, and the same every day after, providing you do me a good job."

"I can sell anything," Jimmy said, "even this dirty ole creek water."

"I expect a man's loyalty when he works for me, Jimmy. I expect him to give me all he's got. When he does, I take care of him. My success becomes his, do you see?"

"Yes."

"Well, then, you come back in an hour. I'll have them rolled and ready by then. There's more in it if you can find me some paint, and a wagon for hire, and one other thing before you go."

"What's that?" he asked.

"I want a dipper of that water, dirty or no."

By the time Jimmy returned, Abaddon had rolled the copies of *The Capital City*, making certain that the headline announcing the birth of Guthrie was the first thing seen when they were unrolled. Even with the rain, the copies had fared well, a bit wrinkled but readable enough.

Turning his milk pail upside down, Jimmy sat down on it.

"Use that bucket you're sittin' on," Abaddon said. "Come back for the rest as you need them. Did you find paint?"

Turning his milk pail over, Jimmy started filling it with papers. "Right there," he said, nodding to a can near the door of the tent. "Red barn paint. Cost me two dippers of water and a cussing 'cause it wasn't cold."

"Says ATS&F here on the label," Abaddon said, holding up the can. "Wouldn't that be railroad paint, I wonder? Well, never mind. Did you happen to steal a wagon from them while you were at it?"

"It's a slop wagon," Jimmy said, "with a team of mules. Stinks like the old drunk what owns it. He's chained under a tree yonder. Said the marshals took him off his lot so's they could build the capital on it."

Handing the last paper to him, Abaddon said, "I don't care what he smells like long as I get that wagon today. Here, take this paint with you."

"What for?" Jimmy asked, hefting the bucket of papers over his arm.

"I want you to sell subscriptions to *The Capital City*. After you collect the money, put a slash of paint on their tent pole so we'll know where to deliver come tomorrow. Tell them that every day they'll have the

latest news from back east, from their loved ones back home. Tell them
that's what they'll get from *The Capital City*, and more. Tell them it's
the first and the best paper in the Territory."

"See that sign on that tent yonder?" Jimmy said.

"What about it?" Abaddon replied, squinting into the sun.

"'*The Pathfinder*,' it says, 'Guthrie's First Newspaper.' I hear they're
looking for delivery boys."

His eyes narrowing, Abaddon took hold of Jimmy's arm.

"It's *The Capital City* that's first in this town, boy. I figure that's
something you might remember."

When the wagon pulled up, the reek of garbage reached under the flap
of Abaddon's tent. The old man atop the seat pulled down the brim of
his hat as dust boiled up from the wheels. Flies swarmed about the
army mules, lifting and landing between the swats of their tails.

"I'm looking for a Abaddon Damon," he said, spitting tobacco juice
into the dirt between the mules' legs.

"You've found him then," Abaddon said, stepping out of the tent.

"The boy said you was looking to hire a wagon?"

"Boy's right," he said. "I got a Washington Press I need hauled over
the creek. It's important I get it here today."

"Five dollars," he said, scratching at something in his beard, "and no
lifting. It's back trouble I got."

"Three dollars," Abaddon said, "and you help with the loading."
Walking over, he hooked his foot up on the wagon wheel. "Come
tonight, you can ease that bad back with corn liquor and know you've
set the world on the right course to boot."

Pushing back his hat, the old man looked at him.

"It's a risk I'm takin', what with my health and all, that's certain, but
don't want it said I denied my fellow man, nor beat my mules, either,
'less they had it coming." Picking up the reins, he looked down the
road. "Climb on," 'cause I'm wore out on drinkin' tater whiskey."

Tents were staked out on twenty-five-feet lots, hundreds of them
running from the creek to the top of the hill. Wares and services were
touted at every lot—haircuts, harness repair, cigars, and surgery. Everywhere, lawyer signs hung from the back of wagons. Leatherbound books
were stacked in the beds, testimonials to the credibility and knowledge
of their owners.

Flies buzzed in the back of the old man's wagon as they worked at the spoils in the crannies of the bed. People lifted their brows or pinched their noses as the wagon rumbled by. When they passed *The Pathfinder*, a man with derby and suspenders was working over an army press. A pot-bellied stove sat in the center of the tent, its pipe exiting a hole at the top. At the back of the lot, a woman pulled a roll of wallpaper from under a tarp and stretched it over a wagon bed.

"Looks like *The Pathfinder*'s found a little paper," Abaddon said.

The old man nodded, leaning into his reins, his feet propped on the footboard, his socks drooping about his ankles. From time to time he called to the mules.

As they eased down the bank of the Cottonwood Creek, one of the mules balked, his tail twisting, his ears laid back.

"Get on!" the old man said.

The smell of muck rode up from the wheels as they pulled into the creek, and turtles slipped from the bank, disappearing into the murky water. Cottonwoods towered above them, a canopy of leaves. Puffs of cotton drifted from their heights and settled on the surface of the water like sails on the sea. Crows scolded them from on high before flying off to more private accommodations.

As they climbed the bank, the old man leaned back against the seat.

"I been thinking," he said, "that a newspaper ought have a grand lot, up on a hill for all to see. Can't take a newspaper as important when it's sittin' in a weed patch at the edge of town."

"Best I could do," Abaddon said, "given half the lots were staked before noon signal came."

"Had a lot of my own," he said, sucking at a tooth, "atop the goddamn world it was, such a place for kings, for the capitol itself, with lions at the gate, and marble steps, and statues all about." Mopping at the sweat on his forehead with a soiled bandanna, he called out to the mules to pick up the pace. "Marshals dragged me off. Tied me to a tree like a dog. Said it was a street I staked out, that I was trespassing on city property, and that I was stinkin' up the town. Guess I was lucky they didn't burn up my wagon what with me in it."

"How is it a man comes to get a prime lot atop a hill," Abaddon said, "beating out the best with nothing but a slop wagon and mules?"

The old man shrugged his shoulders.

"Drove slop for the army all winter," he said, pointing to the tents, "soldiers living like goddamn kings, eatin' pintos and drinking corn liquor, sleeping in white tents whilst I froze in the cottonwoods. Said the wagon spoilt their breakfast, and I was not to come in, 'less they were on patrol, or dead, either one."

Taking out a twist, he chewed off a piece and rolled it into his jaw.

"Know what you're thinking," he continued, "but I ain't no goddamn sooner. Went back to the border and came in legal, just like everyone else, just like yourself. Knowed my way around a bit when I got here, that's all. Knowed where to go in the heat and rush of things."

"Didn't know enough not to squat on a city street," Abaddon said.

"Wasn't surveyed, was it," he said, working at his chew. "Course, I *did* have a touch of tater whiskey. Must've walked over a cliff," he said, rubbing at his shoulder, "or dragged off through a burr patch by one of these mules. When I woke, the hide was wore off my back, and my shoes were full of dirt, not to mention marshals offering to chain me to a tree."

"Head for those cottonwoods up there, and keep your eye out for lightning strike," Abaddon ordered.

As they approached the trees, the old man pulled up.

"Like that one yonder?" he said, pointing to a cottonwood that grew from the bank, its trunk split open from the force of a hit.

Abaddon looked for the rocks marking the spot. "That's it, I think."

Pulling back the stones and brush, Abaddon took a deep breath. The press was there. Yucca leaves had threaded through the gears, and a trade rat had covered it with paddle cactus, sticks, and cigar wrappings carried up from the depot. The plate was rusty but nothing a little time and oil couldn't fix.

The old man took off his hat, and arranged a wisp of hair over his bald head.

"Ain't it a sight," he said, "how a printing machine growed up under a rock out here in the middle of the Territory."

"Help heft," Abaddon said.

Together they wrestled the press into the back of the wagon, scooting it forward in the bed to center its weight. The mules balked at the first pull, threatening to quit altogether, until the old man unbuckled his belt.

Once out of the draw, they followed their own tracks back. When the going was easier, the old man leaned forward on his elbows.

"Hear tell they found a railroad bull in a carload of poles," he said.

"That a fact," Abaddon said.

"Yup," he answered, spitting a stream of tobacco juice over the side of the wagon. As they passed the depot, Abaddon watched the marshals watch him from under the shade of the platform

"It's a hard land," he said. "You'd think a railroad bull on this line would know that."

"Seems a shame, don't it," the old man said, "leavin' a bull alive, onct he was down."

"You can't defeat the enemy by killing him, 'cause there's another just 'round the bend," Abaddon said. "No, sir, it's the exercise of power that matters in the end."

The old man squinted against the sun.

"Well, I ain't educated, as you can tell, and you might be right, far as that goes. Still, it's hard seeing how a live railroad bull is better than a dead one."

Pulling up, the old man pointed to a rock outcrop. "Right there was my lot, right atop that goddamn hill."

Abaddon could see what the old man meant. From here, the whole of the town site could be seen. Better still, the whole of the town could see what would some day sit atop this hill. To their right, a man and a woman hunkered under a shade made from bolts of cloth. A broken axle lay across the woman's lap.

"Hold up a minute," Abaddon said. "I want to talk to these people." As he approached, the man climbed from under the shelter, and Abaddon held out his hand. "Excuse me," he said. "My name is Abaddon Damon, owner and editor of *The Capital City*."

"Samuel Lieberman," the man said, taking Abaddon's hand.

"Mr. Lieberman, there's little time for pleasantries, what with a city blooming up around us, so I'm going to get to the point. Fact is, I'm in need of a town lot on which to build my newspaper." Turning, he looked down on the tents stretched out below. "Appears to me, you have what I need, and I'm prepared to make you an offer, a profit for your industry and good luck."

Samuel shook his head. "Thank you, Mr. Damon, but this lot is not for sale. See those bolts of cloth? Those will be the finest suits in the Territory soon as our building is finished. No, I'm sorry, but this lot is not for sale. Lena and I are building our lives right here, right on top this hill."

"But you've not heard my offer," he said.

Stepping up beside Samuel, Lena crossed her arms over her breasts.

"The lot is not for sale, Mr. Damon."

"Mrs. Lieberman, if it's getting another lot you're worried about, I've filed on one just down the hill. I'm prepared to trade you out, with a nice profit to boot."

Her eyes darkening, Lena turned to Samuel.

"My husband and I will not be selling this lot, Mr. Damon. For years we've made suits for others to sell, for others to make the profits. Now, we will have our own place. So, if you will excuse us, please, we've much to do before the lumber arrives for our new store."

From behind, the mules rattled their harnesses.

"And that lot there?" Abaddon asked.

Reaching for Lena's hand, Samuel shook his head.

"That one is a city street, as your driver there knows well enough. The other belongs to a Mr. Creed McReynolds."

Abaddon's gaze fell on Samuel.

"And his whereabouts?"

"Mr. McReynolds has railroad cars of timbers on a siding south of here."

"Tell Mr. McReynolds that I'm anxious to talk with him when he returns, Mr. Lieberman, if you don't mind. My tent is marked *The Capital City*." As they started to pull off, Abaddon held up his hand for the old man to wait. "The railroad has yet to get newsprint in from Kansas City, Mr. Lieberman. Do you know where I might buy paper?"

"No, Mr. Damon, no paper."

The Washington Press was unloaded and carried into the tent. Sweat dripped from the end of the old man's nose as he held out his hand for his money.

"That'll be three dollars," he said, "for the hauling and loading."

"Yes," Abaddon said, circling the press, "but there *is* something I'd like for you to think about, Mr.—I don't believe you told me your name."

"Jess Clayborn," the old man said. "Don't think to say since most don't ask."

"Jess, you agree that it's a wise man who invests his money in the future. One day *The Capital City* is going to own the hearts of this town, of this state, when it comes to it. It's likely to rub off on a man."

"Yes, sir," Jess said, "I can see how it might go, but what does that have to do with my pay?"

Walking back over to the press, Abaddon rubbed his hand over the embossed portrait of George Washington on the frontal piece.

"I'll give you half for your services today. Soon as I collect on my first run, I'll pay you the other half and guarantee of all future hauling jobs."

Walking to the door, Jess looked out on his team.

"Well, I don't know, Mr. Damon," he said. "It wasn't just me, you know, but this team of mules and my wagon, too. 'Sides, this back of mine is killing me, what with being chained like a dog and then hefting that chunk of iron onto the wagon."

"Half will buy plenty of corn to ease that back tonight, Jess, and a lot more come tomorrow. By next week you ought to be making that much every day."

"Well, guess I could wait."

"Here, then," he said, "and a couple of other things, Jess."

"Yes, sir."

"Newsprint's what I need, but anything will do in a pinch. One way or the other I've got to get a paper out."

"I'll see what I can do, Mr. Damon," he said, "but where's a man to get newsprint in the middle of the Territory?"

"Then I want you to take that wagon down to the Cottonwood and wash it out. Wouldn't hurt for you to take a dip yourself, Jess. If you're going to work for *The Capital City*, you'll have to smell better than those mules out there."

No sooner had the wagon disappeared down the hill than Jimmy arrived, his bucket swinging on his arm.

"How'd we do, boy?" Abaddon asked, pitching his hat onto the press handle.

Emptying his pockets onto the top of the press, Jimmy grinned.

"Sold 'em all," he said. "Could've sold more if there had been any, and with a red slash on every tent pole for subscriptions."

Taking the money, Abaddon counted it out, stacking it in denominations on the platen plate.

"It's a fine job you did, Jimmy. We're going to do the same when tomorrow comes. It's a ride to the stars we're taking, boy."

"I was to get paid for the wagon, too, Mr. Damon."

"About that wagon," Abaddon said, laying his hands on Jimmy's shoulders. "It didn't work out too well. The old man was drunk on tater whiskey, near drowned me in the Cottonwood. On top of that, he had a bad back and refused to help me load that press. You can see yourself how heavy it is. Why, by the time I was finished, I figure he owed *me*. Still, a promise is a promise, so here's ten more cents. A man's word is his bond, and you'll find I keep my word."

"What about the subscriptions?" Jimmy asked.

"I'm going to take that money and invest it in the future of *The Capital City* for you, boy. It's going to be your stake in the stars."

"I'd as soon have it now if it's all the same to you," Jimmy said, looking at the small stack of coins.

"I know you would, 'cause the human will is weak, and sometimes it needs direction, someone with the courage to set the course. That's what I aim to do for you." Patting him on the shoulder, Abaddon smiled. "You've fine potential, Jimmy, and I aim to see it fulfilled. Now, be on your way."

Dropping the coins into his pocket, Jimmy picked up his pail.

"You want me here tomorrow, Mr. Damon?"

"Course I do. There's lots to be done."

Figuring there'd be little help from Jess tonight, Abaddon set out in search of printing paper. Goods of all nature abounded: kettles of beans; deer meat, cleaned and quartered; bread cooked over the open fire; fried rabbit; corn pone baked in a skillet. There was even a saloon at the base of the hill, a tent teeming with men and the smell of cigars. Near the soldiers' camp, there was much coming and going from a tent pitched at the edge of the Cottonwood, the laughter of women issuing from behind the flaps.

It was a city dropped from the sky, and in it, all a man could ask. There was in it everything, except the lot he wanted and the newsprint that *The Capital City* must have to survive. Those standing in his way would find that Abaddon Damon did not give up so easily.

Making his way back to his tent, he leaned against the press, closing his eyes. There in his head were the stories, the words written and ready, but without the printing paper, all would be lost. Lying down, he pulled his coat over him and tried to sleep.

Sometime in the night, a fog spilled into the valley and settled among the tents, muffling the voices, shrouding the flames that rose into the sky.

The smell of smoke hung in the dampness long after all had fallen dark and silent once more, save for the clack of a press and the flicker of a lantern from *The Capital City* tent.

When Jimmy arrived the next morning, the sun was just breaking, and Abaddon was waiting for him at the door. Bundles of newspapers were stacked in rows about the tent, counted, and secured with cotton string.

"You see Jess?" Abaddon asked.

"Sleeping it off in his wagon over by the land office," Jimmy said. "Left his mules hitched the whole night, I reckon."

Rubbing at his face, Abaddon said, "Get him up here, while I round up more delivery boys. There's two thousand papers got to be sold on this day. Take care, boy, 'cause wallpaper crumbles when its bent."

Jimmy watched as Abaddon walked away. When he was out of sight, he picked up one of the newspapers and held it into the light.

"*Pathfinder Burns*," it read.

The trail was clear as Alida and Bram moved into the Territory— tracks ploughed in the earth from the passage of wagons and marked by trees stripped of their limbs, discarded tins and coffee grounds, a rag doll half-buried in the sand. At night she and Bram slept in the wagon, the team tied close, the rifle lying between them. Each morning they grazed the team before harnessing them, to keep up their strength, as their father had advised.

Once, they passed a wagon in the distance, its wheel broken. A man and woman working at the hub looked up as they went by. Nearby, children played under the shade of a mesquite, their laughter ringing in the solitude of the prairie. The woman waved at Alida with the tips of her fingers before turning back to the wheel.

"Should we go over, Lidy?" Bram asked.

"No," she said, "And it's Alida, mind you. They've lost their race. There's nothing we can do."

Even in April, the heat was relentless, its fury causing their ears to sting. Lather gathered under the horses' harnesses, drying away to salt, corroding the leather and turning the buckles to green. Jackrabbits bound from the brush, zigzagging across the prairie, only to stop as if paralyzed as the wagon passed within inches of them.

That afternoon the earth turned red, clay so barren that it barely supported clumps of tamarisk and stunted cedar. Water gathered from the rain like puddles of blood, the clay cracking and peeling. Terrapins, with their legs flapping like oars on a stranded boat, struggled across the red flats.

"It's two days with nothing but sky," Bram said. "There wouldn't be no homestead land left between here and Texas by now." Tugging down his hat, he looked over at Alida. "We don't know where we're going or what we'll do when we get there."

"You're such a fuss, Bram. There's a little money left, and we have the team, too. With a team we could do a lot of things."

"Like start up a soap factory," he said.

"Just stop," she said. "Something will come along, you'll see."

Riding too late into the evening, they unharnessed the team in the dark. As the collars fell away, the horses shook the weariness from their necks and turned to pick at what green they could find. Taking a gunnysack from under the wagon seat, Alida rubbed down their backs, the smell of salt and sweat permeating the evening.

For supper they ate cornbread, drizzled with bacon grease, and a can of beans that Bram had found on a creek bottom. It was squashed but otherwise unharmed.

"Lidy, I've been thinking," he said. "All we got is this here rifle, you know, if trouble came up."

"What are you saying, Bram?"

"Well, it's a man's job, to protect the family, I mean."

"You're doing just fine, Bram."

"Truth is, Lidy, I'm not so good a shot. Dad was going to teach me but then . . ."

She could see in him their father's eyes. He had the cut of his chin.

"I think you're right, Bram. You and me need to learn how to shoot that rifle."

"Can't be far now, Lidy," Bram said, threading Windy's ear under the bridle. "Soon enough there's got to be people, don't you think?"

"Soon enough," she said. "Things will look brighter when there's other folks about. Maybe we can find work at Guthrie station. Everyone says it's going to be the capital."

"We going to shoot that rifle, like you said?"

Looking at the rifle leaning against the wagon seat, Alida shrugged her shoulders.

"How hard can it be?"

Between them it took half an hour to load it, and when the breech snapped and closed on Bram's finger, he spun in a circle, holding his hand between his legs.

"Jesus damn!" he said.

"Don't use that kind of language, Bram Deventer, or I'll not help you at all."

The bean can was safe under the barrage of gunfire, neither of them coming within range of the target. A mourning dove watched them from atop a mesquite, safely cooing its song. Windy and Bones snorted and stamped their hooves. When Windy sounded off, Bram and Alida broke into peals of laughter.

The terrain soon changed once again, now becoming a vast pile of rock. No trees grew from the desolation, no elm, no cedar, not even the mesquite. Rocks bulged onto the horizon, strewn there by demons unknown. Heat waves shimmered from their depths, and lizards watched on from their ledges.

Alida and Bram pulled over to eat under the shade of the wagon. Bram dropped his hat over his eyes to nap while Alida pinched sand into a lion ant's trap and listened to the zing of locusts rising and falling in the heat. Overhead, buzzards circled in the cobalt sky. Hipshot, Windy and Bones dozed, switching their tails against deer flies.

At first Alida thought she saw a mirage, but when the movement continued, she shook Bram's arm.

"Bram, I think someone is out there."

Rolling onto his stomach, Bram peered through the spokes of the wheel.

"A man and a woman by the looks of it. They're coming this way."

Climbing from under the wagon, he hung the rifle to his side, hooking the heel of his boot on the wagon spoke.

The man's gait was deliberate as he worked his way through the rocks toward them. As he approached, Alida could see the furrows that crisscrossed his face, and the fierce eyes that peered out from under folds of skin. Hair twisted from inside his ears like wire, and his hat was pulled low. The woman paced behind him, stopping from time to time to cock her hand on the curve of her hip. She wore a cotton dress, and a bandanna tied in her hair.

"Lo," the man said, dropping his hands into the pockets of his overalls. "We're the Ellisons. This here's Mavis. I'm Carl Ellison."

Lifting the rifle into the fold of his arm, Bram nodded his head. "We're the Deventers. I'm Bram, and this here's my sister, Alida."

"This property's been claimed," Carl said, "case you're thinking to stake it out."

"No, sir," Bram said. "We're just passing over. Sorry about trespassing. It ain't easy to know who owns what any more."

"No offense taken," he said, reaching into his bib for makings. "Ain't you folks a tad green to be out here on your own?"

"Didn't know there was an age limit on being in the Territory," Bram said.

Cupping a paper around the end of his finger, Carl opened a sack of Bull Durham and sprinkled in the tobacco, forming a cylinder.

"Reckon not," he said, sealing the edge with his tongue, "else they'd shot us old goats at the border, wouldn't they?"

Striking a match, he lit his cigarette. Smoke curled through a yellow path in his mustache, and he squinted up an eye.

"We lost our father a ways back," Alida said.

"Jesus takes his own," Carl said, blowing smoke out of the corner of his mouth, "when He's the notion."

"There was no reason for turning back," Alida said, glancing over at Bram, "so we figured to finish it out, come what may."

"Told Mavis someone gone to their Maker, didn't I, Mavis, what with that owl hootin' half the night. Said, 'Someone's died this very night.' Didn't I say that, Mavis?"

Mavis pulled her hair away from her youthful face and shook her head.

"Reckon we'll be on our way to Guthrie station, then," Bram said. "Sorry again about disturbing you and your daughter, Mr. Ellison."

"Mavis ain't no daughter," he said, drawing down on his cigarette, "though she might look so. Ordered her up through a catalogue, along with a cast-iron stove and a double-bit axe. Me and Mavis got a dugout started up there in them rocks. You folks welcome for a rest."

"We got people expecting us at Guthrie station," Bram said.

Putting her hands on her waist, Mavis pushed her breasts against her cotton dress.

"We got spring water," she said. "There's plenty to go 'round."

Shrugging his shoulders, Bram looked over at Alida.

"What do you think, Lidy?"

"We wouldn't be putting you out?" she asked.

"Wouldn't," Mavis said. "Ain't no one staked out this close to the starting line, 'cept us. Petered out before we even started, I reckon. Carl said he wasn't eating other men's dust for no quarter section of red dirt, so we just pulled up and set our stakes." Holding her hand over her eyes, she looked at Bram. "You're welcome, sure enough."

"Maybe we could rest for a bit," Alida said.

Slipping an arm around Mavis's waist, Carl rubbed at the small of her back.

"Take Alida on up, darlin'," he said, "while I help the boy with his team, and watch for them snakes sunning in the rocks."

As Alida and Mavis walked the path to the dugout, the rocks thickened, boulders the size of houses that had tumbled from the hill above. Where there were no boulders, there were rocks, or else pebbles that covered every inch of ground.

The dugout itself was not much bigger than a wagon bed, a hole carved into the bank. The steps were but footholds, scooped and worn by the tread of feet, and the smell of oil from the kerosene lantern rose from the dankness.

Lighting the lamp, Mavis dropped onto the bed, pulling her legs under her, motioning for Alida to sit down.

There was a stove in the center and, next to it, a table hewn from bois d'arc. A chair was pushed against the wall, and a trunk, secured with leather straps, doubled as a table. Behind the door, a man's hat hung on the wall, a feather tucked in the band. Against the wall was Carl's double-bit axe, just one of three items ordered from his catalogue.

"It ain't much," Mavis said, "'cept for keeping off the sun and the wind, but then the wind never stops out here, you know. It's a lonesome sound it makes in these rocks sometimes. Some folks say there's a ghost lives up there on the mountain. A monk, kilt by the Indians, they say. Sometimes I wonder if that's him just calling out my name."

"I'd forgotten the feel of walls altogether," Alida said.

"Ain't much room to sit, 'cept the bed," she said. "Spend my days *and* my nights on this here bed." She paused. "You ever been married?"

"I haven't even a steady boyfriend."

"Well, me either, not until Carl."

"I'm waiting for the right one," Alida said.

"Lot's of folks wonder 'bout Carl being so old," Mavis said, hooking her fingers behind her head. "Carl says it don't bother him none, and that he don't give a twit if men look at me that way. Carl says that a pretty woman ought to be enjoyed by everybody, like a statue in a park."

"You'll be planting a crop," Alida asked, looking out the door, "or raising cattle here on your homestead?"

"Lord, no," Mavis said, looking from under her elbow. "Carl's not up to farming in no real way. We're figuring on provin' it up and selling it later on. I kept telling Carl we needed to get on closer to Guthrie station, but he just sat down here. Carl can be like that." Standing, she hooked her fingers on the top of the doorway and looked out into the yard. "Guess your pa left you a little something to get by, enough for a start, I mean?"

"There's not much," Alida said, "but once we get to Guthrie station, we'll get work or something."

A grasshopper jumped onto the bed and scrubbed at its face. Mavis sat back down and thumped it away.

"I guess you haven't heard, then," she said.

"Heard what?"

"Guthrie station is brim full of folks already, a hundred men for every town lot, they say."

"No, I hadn't heard," Alida said.

"Homesteads are gone, too. People everywhere just wandering about, not knowing what to do next."

"We'll find something," Alida said. "We've got no choice."

Hooking her hands in the small of her back, Mavis twisted back and forth, the way little girls do.

"Why don't you stay a spell, Alida?" she asked. "There ain't no hurry now what with the run over. Wait a bit until things die down in Guthrie station. Carl says a run brings out the worst of the best of people and that most folks he saw wasn't the best to begin with. We got shade down on the meadow for your wagon, and you can graze out your team for a few days."

"Well, I don't know," she said. "We'd figured on getting in as soon as we could. Course, that team is right old, and we been driving them pretty hard."

Mavis clapped her hands. "Oh, do," she said. "I ain't had no one to talk to for ever so long."

"You sure your husband won't mind?"

"Carl? Lord, no. Carl likes folks about. Besides, there's sand plums coming on up on the mountain. You and me could go picking. It would be great fun, Alida. We could spend the day."

Alida watched Bram and Carl as they strolled their way up through the maze of rocks. It would be wonderful to take a few days. Bram and she were exhausted, and the team was near worn out, too.

"Fresh fruit," she said to herself.

"Then you'll stay?"

"Why not?" she said. "Bram and I could use some good company."

Alida, with towsack in hand, followed Mavis at arm's length up the rocky trail. Mavis's stride was strong, and her pace was steady. Alida struggled to keep up as the path grew steep ahead of them. On a ledge overlooking the dugout, Mavis stopped to rest, bending over to let her hair fall away from her neck.

"It's going to be a hot one today," she said. "We best take our time."

"Look," Alida said. "I can see Bram from here, with the team."

Running her fingers through her hair, Mavis nodded. "He's a good-looking man, your brother. I figure someone to take him up, soon enough."

Alida watched as Bram moved into the shadows of the mountain. She'd never thought of him as a man, nor as appealing to the opposite sex for that matter. Perhaps she'd been too caught up in her own life to notice.

"I suppose so," she said, "but he can be such a boy."

Pulling her knees into her arms, Mavis said, "Carl ain't no more than a boy hisself and never will be."

Alida tucked the towsack under her arm and walked to the edge of the precipice, her stomach knotting at the drop. Wind swept through the valley, tumbling and moaning through the rocks, trees bowing to its sway.

Mavis shuddered. "The wind never stops up here on the mountain," she said. "It blows on forever. We best get on to our picking. It ain't no place to be, come dark."

As they ascended into the rocks, a rift opened into the heart of the mountain, forcing them to cut around, and then up a precarious slide. Finding shade, Mavis sat down to wait for Alida, who had fallen a hundred yards behind.

When Alida dropped down beside her, Mavis pointed to the thickets that grew from the slide, now shimmering with noon heat.

"They're just right for picking," she said. "By the time we get down the mountain, juice will be running out our sack. They'll be wonderful on biscuits, won't they?"

The limbs of the thickets hung heavy with plums, and yellow jacket wasps lit and lifted in a frenzy above them. At every turn, inch-long thorns forbade entry. Skunk droppings littered the ground.

"I've never seen such plums," Alida said. "They're like rubies. How do they survive in such a place as this?"

Twisting one off, Mavis bit into it, scrunching up her face at its tartness.

"By living where nothing else wants to," she said, spitting out the pit, "like me and Carl sitting at the edge of things. There's not much to be had, but what there is, all belongs to us." Standing, she brushed off her hands, gathering up the folds of her skirt. "Come on," she said. "We've picking to do."

At times the thickets dropped away into crevices, void of a breeze, or rose into rocks too high to reach. Mavis and Alida talked as they picked, their fingers sticky with juice, arms bleeding from thorns, clothes wet with sweat. When at last their towsack brimmed with fruit, Mavis lifted it over her shoulder, bouncing it on her back. "There's enough for a hundred biscuits, and a plum pie to boot," she said. "Let's find some shade before we head back down."

Under the spread of a hackberry, they lay down their load. Mavis waited for Alida to drink from the canteen before tipping it herself, water dribbling onto the front of her dress.

Propping her head on her hand, Alida said, "I'm exhausted, but I can't remember when I've had so much fun."

"I'm sure glad you came along before the coons got them all," she said, taking another drink. "Carl won't do no picking, even if it means going without."

Taking a plum out of the sack, Alida bit into it and winked up her eye. "They're wonderful," she said, "and full of sunshine."

"What you figure you'll do when you get to Guthrie station, Alida?"

Flipping the seed into the rocks, she shrugged. "Maybe I'll get a job clerking at a store, or cooking at a hotel. I'm a fair cook since Mother died."

"Carl says I ain't good for cooking or keeping house. Carl says I ain't good for much of anything other than warming his feet. I guess if I cooked for a living, I'd starve out soon enough."

"I'll bet you could learn," Alida said.

Leaning against the tree, Mavis closed her eyes.

"I don't learn so fast, Alida, but sometimes when I'm up on the mountain, I close my eyes like this, and first thing you know, I can see myself with fancy clothes and a big hat, living in Kansas City, maybe, or Chicago, in one of them big hotels with people making my bed and fixing my breakfast, fussing over me from morning till night. Folks come along and talk to me like I was somebody. Sometimes, I think if I keep them closed long enough, it will all come true."

"Oh, " Alida said, "I dream all the time, too. Father always said I was a born dreamer."

Sitting up, Mavis pulled her legs under her. "What do you dream about, Alida?"

"You won't tell?"

"I won't," Mavis said, "if they gouge out my eyes."

"Well, I dream about the man I'm going to marry someday, about how he'll love me, and how he'll never think of anything but me. I dream about how I'll not have to worry about things because our love will be so strong that nothing could ever come between us. He'll be devoted to me, and I to him. That's what I dream about mostly, and sometimes about having a family, I suppose, about having kids."

"It's a dream and a danger most girls have," Mavis said.

"It's silly, I know, but I guess that's why they call them dreams." When Alida looked over, Mavis was dabbing at her eyes with the tail of her dress. "Mavis," she said, "what's the matter? Why are you crying?"

"Oh, it's nothing. I was just thinking."

"About what? You can tell me."

"Carl gets real mad when I talk about it."

"It's between you and me. I won't say a word," Alida said.

"I had a little boy of my own once. I had him right young. His father was no more than a boy hisself. He left town as soon as he found out. I never heard from him again. I thought he was going to be just like that dream of yours, Alida, but he wasn't. They ain't never."

"What did you do?"

"My pa said if I was to act like a stray, then by damn that's what I could be. He turned me out, and I ain't never seen any of my family since. After that, I got by best I could. Men do whatever I want," she said, slipping her hand down her thigh. "I learned to get by." Her eyes hardened. "I learned to do whatever it takes and the world be damned."

Alida fanned herself against the mounting heat.

"Where's your boy, Mavis?"

"When I heard they was wanting wives out west, I put my picture in that catalogue. That's when I met Carl. He was old, I know, and a hard man to boot, but I figured it was a way out for me and the boy." Picking up a stick, she drew circles in the sand between her feet. A fly worked at the plum juice that had spilled on her ankle. "I hadn't figured on him being so mean to the boy."

"Carl beat your boy?"

"No more than you'd figure," she said, slapping at the fly, "but he worked him right hard. A boy can't work like a man. He ain't got the spunk of a growed man, and he burns away from the inside out. The boy changed after that. I could see it in his eyes."

High in the branches of the hackberry, a crow scolded them. Hopping from branch to branch, wings drooped, it complained. A tingle raced between Alida's shoulders.

"Where is the boy, Mavis?"

"We were on a ferry, crossing the Salt Fork River. It was flooding high, terrible high. The ferry listed to the side the minute we shoved off the bank. I can feel it this minute, and the way the water rumbled against the side, and the way the froth gathered up. I remember the smell, too, like creek-bottom mud, and I remember how the light danced on the rolls of water.

"On the lower deck, the horses whinnied, the lot of them, like as if they knew, and steam rose up from the water in the morning cool. We were overloaded, everybody knew, sitting too low in the water, but nobody stopped it, like it didn't matter somehow, and when the horses shifted, crowding in on each other, the ferry swamped. I could hear the horses's cries from the lower deck as the water came over, and when it touched my feet, I screamed. I remember that, because the horses were quiet then, and I could hear myself screaming, and then we was swept into the current."

"How awful," Alida said, holding her hand over her mouth.

"I held onto the boy's hand," she said, gripping her knees. "I never stopped holding onto his hand, but when I washed up downriver, he was gone."

"Did they search for him?"

"Me and Carl walked the bank for awhile, but Carl said it wasn't no use and that it was time to move on."

The crow above them flapped away, and Alida took a drink from the canteen. She remembered the river, how it was, its rushing torrent.

"I'm sorry, Mavis, about the boy."

"I've come to figure it was just as well, for the boy, I mean. You won't say nothing to Carl?"

"No," Alida said.

"Maybe you and Bram can come tomorrow for plum butter and biscuits?"

"Yes," she said, standing. "I don't want to miss the plums."

"She's a mountain of dreams," Mavis said, looking back at the rocky summit, "what never comes true, and no place to be when dark comes."

By the time dinner was over, a breeze swept down from the north, wringing the moisture from the air and lifting their spirits. The rocks loomed about them like tombstones.

"Your biscuits and plum butter were excellent," Alida said.

"Thanks," Mavis said, picking up Carl's plate.

Rolling a cigarette, Carl struck a match, cupping his hands against the breeze.

"It's a fair place, ain't it, this ole mountain?" he said, pinching off the flame with the tips of his fingers.

"Must be a comfort having a place of your own," Alida said.

Taking another draw on his cigarette, Carl flipped off the ash.

"I was telling Mavis just this mornin' that, much as I love this land, I'm gettin' old, just too tired to see it out, I reckon. If the right folks came along, well, I might give it up, folks like yourself, young and strong and willin' to work, folks with a dream." Hooking the cigarette in the corner of his mouth, he looked over at Alida. "Ain't just anybody I'd sell this place to, 'cause land is a sacred trust. Ain't to be turned over to just anyone."

"That's generous of you, Mr. Ellison, but Bram and I don't have any money for buying land."

"Oh, I ain't saying it's great land, 'cause it ain't. Why, there's snakes of all kinds and more rocks than one might use. Just the other day I saw a hoop snake come rollin' down the hill. Rolled right past and into the bottom, and there's more joint snakes than necessary, too, although some say they keep down the rats. And there's even a few milk snakes up higher on the hill, though a rarity."

"I've never heard of those snakes," Bram said.

"No, sir, few have. It's right unusual to have them gathered all in one place like this. Must be the rocks for sunnin'. But when you think on it, makes this here land even more special, don't it."

"What is a hoop snake?" Bram asked.

"Grabs its own tail and rolls down the hill like a wagon wheel on the loose," Carl said. "Now I know it sounds peculiar, but it's so, on my mother's eyes. Sometimes they come by so fast you have to jump out of the way to keep from gettin' run over. And joint snakes can be a real nuisance, too, a hundret joints like links in a chain, and if you step on one, it breaks into pieces, and each piece turns into another snake. If you ever see a joint snake, don't step on it, 'cause its pure hell to get rid of 'em."

Bram looked at Alida and then at Mavis.

"I don't believe it," he said.

"God's truth," Carl declared, "and milk snakes are worst of all, especially for raisin' cows."

Bram lifted his brows. "Why's that?"

"They lay waitin' in the grass until a cow comes by. When it stops to graze, they latch on to a teat and suck out all the milk, leavin' your calves to starve or get et by coyotes. Sometimes a milk snake will be hangin' from every teat. It's a sight to behold."

"Don't you believe it, Bram," Mavis said. "It's Carl and his foolishness, that's all."

"Well, maybe I ain't seen a milk snake," Carl said, "they bein' so rare and all, but I've seen more than my share of them hoopers."

"Never mind the snakes," Mavis said, catching Bram's eye. "But maybe you folks *would* be interested in buying us out. We've a good start on the dugout. Soon enough you could have a place of your own, couldn't they, Carl?"

"There's a spring a quarter-mile east," Carl said, "where the rocks peter out, just beyond that hill. This land's bound to be worth a lot when things open up, but for you I'd sacrifice her for a hundret dollars this very day. Hell, I'll even throw in that ole cookstove. Mavis don't use it all that often anyways."

"I'm certain it's worth every penny, Mr. Ellison," Alida said, "but we don't have a hundred dollars."

"Maybe you'd be interested in tradin' out that wagon and that smoothed-mouthed team?"

"I'm afraid not, Mr. Ellison. We have to have a team, going or staying."

"It's a hard bargain you drive," Carl said. "What about that ring you're wearin'? It ain't much for a quarter of land, but then I ain't gettin' any younger."

"This was my mother's," Alida said, turning the ring on her finger. "It's all I have left."

"A fine ring for memories, though not much more," he said. "Still, I might consider a trade."

"I think not, Mr. Ellison. Bram and I don't know much about farming. We'd figured on getting work in Guthrie station."

Squashing out his cigarette with the heel of his shoe, Carl hooked his thumbs in his overalls.

"Mavis, darlin'," he said, "hand me that jug of corn. You folks like a shot for perkin' up the evening?"

"No, thank you, Mr. Ellison. Bram and I need to be getting back to the wagon."

"There's nothing ahead, Lidy," Bram said, mopping up his plate, "and it would be better than living out of a wagon."

"When it's a warm night like this, Carl and I sometimes sleep outside," Mavis said, handing Carl the jug. "It's so cool under the stars."

Looking up at Mavis, Bram said, "Maybe we could sleep up here tonight, Alida. That wagon ain't going nowhere."

"We must be getting back," Alida said. "I'd figured on an early start."

Tipping his jug, Carl said, "Well, you think about that trade some, Missy."

"I'll think on it, Mr. Ellison."

"This ole mountain's been here a long time. Reckon it will still be here come mornin'. You keep a hoe handy for them milk snakes, you hear," he said, laughing.

Neither Alida nor Bram spoke as they walked the path to the wagon. The warmth from the day's heat ebbed from the rocks as the sky filled with evening stars.

By the time Bram got back from checking on the team, Alida was in bed in the back of the wagon. Taking off his boots, he sat them on the wagon seat and reached for a blanket.

"The team's okay," he said. "Think I'll bunk under the wagon where I can catch a little breeze."

"What's the matter, Bram? You sound upset."

Some time passed before he spoke. "No," he said, crawling under the wagon, "I'm not upset. But I *could* turn this rock pile into a real ranch one day, Lidy, given a half a chance."

When Alida awoke, the moon was smokey behind the clouds. Lifting onto an elbow, she listened for Windy and Bones grazing in the darkness, or for Bram's snore beneath the wagon. It was then that she noticed Bram's boots missing from the wagon seat.

"Bram, are you there?" When there was no answer, she called again.

Neither Bram nor his blanket was under the wagon. Perhaps he'd moved higher into the rocks, or into the meadow for more breeze.

Slipping on her shoes, she started up the path. At the bend of the trail, she heard Bram's voice, low and thick, and then Mavis's laughter from somewhere in the darkness. Turning, she started back to the wagon, to flee from this place, when above her in the rocks, Carl's cigarette flared.

Lying awake in the wagon, she waited for Bram's return, hearing the rustle of his clothes as he undressed for bed. Once she thought to confront him, to call out his name, to demand to know what he'd been up to. Instead, she turned on her side, to think and to wait until no sound could be heard, save for Bram's snore and the first zing of locusts in the morning dawn.

Climbing from her bed, she dressed and slipped up the trail to the dugout. The smell of wood smoke drifted in, and a mockingbird sang from high up in the first light of the mountain.

Carl was sitting on a rock, smoking a cigarette, while Mavis slept in a bedroll on the ground. Her dress was tossed across a camp chair, her hair loose about her shoulders, her breasts bare beneath the thin blanket.

Carl looked up, and then at the end of his cigarette, flipping an ash onto the top of his boot.

"You come about tradin' for this here mountain, Missy?" he asked.

Taking off her ring, she held it out. "That's right," she said.

Carl took the ring, and rolled it in the palm of his hand.

"You've made yourself a deal, Missy."

"There's just one thing," she said.

Carl leaned back on his elbows and looked up at her through his brows.

"And what would that be?"

"I want you and her gone before Bram awakes."

Flipping his cigarette into the rocks, Carl looked over at Mavis, who was snoring quietly, a strand of hair caught in the corner of her open mouth.

"I reckon we could be gone 'fore mornin' breaks," he said.

Alida unloaded the bedding, the cooking utensils, and the boxes of books, setting them in the shade of the rocks, all before Bram awoke.

"Morning," Bram said, slipping his shirt over his head as he crawled from under the wagon.

"Morning's 'bout gone," she said, flipping back the canvas that covered the remaining store of clothes.

Running his fingers through his hair, Bram said, "What you doing, Lidy?"

"It's Alida, Bram, and I'm unloading this wagon. What does it look like?"

"But why? I thought we were going on to Guthrie station."

"Thing is, I traded for this pile of rocks this morning while you were sleeping."

"You did?" he asked, his face beaming. "You really did?"

"Now all we've got to do is figure how to keep from starving to death."

Slipping on his boots, Bram tucked in his shirt and slicked back his hair with his fingers.

"Think I'll see the Ellisons off, Lidy."

"Do as you like," she said, "but they left at sunrise."

"They left without saying a word?"

"They were in a hurry to get on their way, Bram. Now, fix yourself something to eat. All this stuff has to be carried up to the dugout, and then we have to find that spring. There's no water left for cooking or drinking either one."

The dugout was much smaller than Alida remembered, dank and dark and unwelcome. The smell of mildew hung in the air. Standing at the door, she held up the lantern.

"Lidy," Bram said from behind her, "these books are heavy. Where do you want me to put them?"

"They've taken the stove, Bram."

"Oh well, we can cook outside."

"They've taken everything from the looks of it."

"Don't worry, Lidy," he said, setting down the books. "We'll build us a house, with windows, and a porch, too. We can use this dugout for our potato cellar."

"I suppose you're right," she said. "We're lucky they didn't take the team."

By the time they'd finished unloading the wagon and storing things away, the afternoon was gone. Before making the last trip up, Bram moved the wagon out of sight and checked on the horses.

"We've got to have water, Bram," Alida said when he returned, "before we can do another thing."

"East, where the rocks peter out. That's what Carl said."

The path was worn and clear, twisting from out of the rift above. The lower they descended, the cooler the air became, with moss gathering on the rocks, ferns growing lush and green at the side of the path.

Alida spotted it first, a spring bubbling from the mountain, gathering in a basin worn in the rock. Watercress flourished in the icy water. Below the spillway, a bog gathered, smelling of moss and mud, and cattail reeds grew from its bank.

"It's beautiful here," Alida said, holding her hand under the water, "like a paradise."

"And cool," Bram said. "I thought I'd never be cool again."

Bram kneeled at the edge of the bog, his upturned face ashen.

"What's wrong, Bram?" she asked.

Standing, he pointed to an arm that reached from out of the mire. "It's a body, Lidy, buried in the mud."

"Oh, Bram," she said, turning away. "Who could it be? What are we going to do?"

Walking to the spring, Bram splashed water onto his face before he spoke.

"We've got to get it out, I reckon."

"But, Bram . . ."

"It's somebody died here, Lidy," he said. "We can't just leave them. We've got no choice."

Alida held onto Bram's belt as he pulled the body from the mud, the smell of marsh and decomposition thick in the cool air.

"He's been here awhile," Bram said, "and stripped naked clean. I reckon we'll never know who he was."

When Alida turned to look, her stomach lurched, and she waited for the nausea to pass.

"I know who it is, Bram," she said, wrapping her arms about herself.

"Who?"

"It's that young marshal from Walnut Creek," she said.

"You can't know that, Lidy."

"I remember him wearing a feather in his hatband."

"He doesn't have a hat, Lidy."

"I know," she said, "because it's hanging behind the door of the dugout."

Pulling down his derby, Jerome Bouchard walked out of the Arkansas City depot. Everything about him was foreign: the suit, the twist of his mustache, the shine of his shoes. The wind turned his eyes to water with its heat, and sweat trickled down his back.

Checking his coins, he dropped them into his pocket. The trip from France had all but depleted his resources. Arkansas City wasn't the Territory, but it was as far as he could get with the money he had. From here, he figured to walk in, if it came to that, but the heat was something he hadn't planned on.

It was in the Kansas City railroad station where he'd seen the circular advertising the settlement of Oklahoma Territory. With his money low and the land run over, the decision to come was ill-advised, but here he was.

Uncertain as to what to do next, he sat down on his bag. From under the shade of a cottonwood, an old black man watched him. Hitched to the tree was his horse and buggy, a "for sale" sign hanging from the back of the seat. The mare tugged twigs from the tree, working them under her bit. She watched Jerome with clouded eyes, ears drooping from the heat.

"You need a horse and buggy, Mister?"

Picking up his bag, Jerome moved into the shade of the cottonwood. "No," he said, turning up his hands. "I don't have money for a buggy."

Taking out a bandanna, the black man dabbed at the top of his head.

"It's a good rig," he said, "and Squirt here is as spirited as they come. Can't hold her back on a cool day, that's sure."

Perking her ears at the sound of her name, Squirt shook her head, flies lifting from the corners of her eyes and her nostrils.

Taking the coins from his pocket, Jerome held them out for the old man to see.

"That's all there is," he said. "I'm sorry."

Retrieving a plug of tobacco from his pocket, the old man cut off a piece, tucking it into his jaw.

"Everybody's going to the Territory, Mister," he said, "by train, wagon, or way of the angels. Which is it for you?"

"I was thinking to walk," Jerome said.

Giving his tobacco a turn, the old man gave aim at something scurrying across the ground.

"Where you from, Mister?"

"France," he said.

"France?"

"It's very far away," Jerome said.

"Near to the moon, I'd say," the old man said, "fer a man thinkin' to walk into the Territory. Fer ten dollars, ole Squirt and me ride you far south as the Salt Fork. A man just might make it afoot from there."

"River?" Jerome asked, waving his fingers through the air.

"That's right," the old man said, "Salt Fork River."

"And this is Squirt?"

"Yup, come spring grass or gyp water, either one," he said.

Jiggling the coins in his pocket, Jerome looked out onto the prairie's extent, heat quivering on the horizon.

"From there, I could walk to Guthrie station?"

"Might," he said.

"It's the Salt Fork, then," Jerome said, dropping the coins into his hand.

Without a word, the old man tossed Jerome's bag into the buggy. In it was everything he owned—a few clothes, the drawings, his buildings and dreams.

Climbing up on the seat, the old man looped the reins through his fingers.

"Climb aboard, Mister," he said.

"We're leaving in the heat?" Jerome asked.

"Don't get cooler in the Territory, Mister, just darker."

With a glance over his shoulder, Jerome bid farewell to Arkansas City and civilization as they disappeared from sight.

For miles they rode without speaking, mesmerized by the sway of the mare's rump, the clatter of the buggy along the path. Like ants, the men paled against the immensity and distances of the prairie.

When Madeline died, Jerome left France with little thought of the loneliness he might know in a strange country. It was a new start he needed, a land big enough and free enough for his dreams.

"Chew?" the old man asked, reaching into his pocket.

"Thanks, no," Jerome said.

"It's an old man's pleasure, when everything else fades," he said, smiling.

Nodding, Jerome watched as he sliced off his tobacco.

"How long will it take to get to Guthrie station from the Salt Fork?" he asked.

Settling in, the old man popped the reins against Squirt's rump and looked down the trail.

"Well, sir," he said, "depends on if you're ridin' a train, walkin', or an angel's spiritin' you acrost. Can't say much 'bout angels, myself." Hiking up his foot, he spit off the side of the buggy. "Did see my ma onct after she died. Come right up out of the grave, she did. 'John,' she said, 'you quit makin' liquor with that field corn. Slopped hogs eat their young.'" Looking over at Jerome, he squinted up an eye. "I ain't had a drop of corn liquor since."

"Good advice," Jerome said.

"Yes, sir, it was."

"What if I were to walk in?"

"Three days to a week," he said, "if you ain't snakebit or the river ain't up."

"How do I find my way?"

"Straight south," he said, pointing down the trail. "Keep the sun to your left in the mornin', to your right in the afternoon. If the sun ain't up, go to bed. If none of that works, then just follow the tracks, 'cause they lead smack into the heart of Guthrie station."

Pulling up the reins, the old man eased the carriage down a hill and over a dry streambed. Squirt stopped for a mouthful of grass.

"Giddup," the old man said.

"You ever think about going to the Territory yourself?" Jerome asked.

"No, sir," he said. "Some say they's startin' a colored settlement, not just on the edge of Guthrie station neither, but a real live town, and that it's goin' to have its own colored officials, too. Some say they's figurin' to have their own schools, and a college for colored folks to get educated right out here in the prairie. There's Negro colonists rode in here from all over the country lookin' to find the promise land, all fixin' to settle up their own towns across the Territory."

"I've seen the circulars asking for coloreds to come," Jerome said, "far away as Kansas City."

"Ain't to be no promise land," the old man said, tugging down his hat. "White folk won't have it, and all them people on the move. Most ain't got nothin', a broke-down wagon and a passel of kids. Don't even have shoes for walkin'.

"No, sir," he continued, shaking his head, "I'm stayin' right here where I can pick up a horse now and again for tradin', plant a patch of tomaters in the spring, butcher a hog come fall. Ain't much of a life, but ain't much for disappointment, neither."

For some time they rode in silence, the clop of Squirt's hooves on the trail.

"Wonder why a feller from France would come all the way out here so's he could cook his brains in this heat?" the old man asked.

Jerome shrugged. "A new land is like a new woman, I suppose, mysterious and unattainable. She stirs the blood."

"Hadn't thought of her like a woman," he said, looking up from under his hat. "Wouldn't neither, hadn't you come down from the moon. No, sir, just give me a tomater patch and butchering hog, and a good team under the rein, maybe a chew fer keepin' away the blues. I leave the women to you."

"I'm going to build buildings," Jerome said.

"Yes, sir," he said, turning over the information, "buildings are good. Most everyone's got one nowadays. Got one myself, a soddy, what with a dirt floor and a cedar table. Use it, too, when it rains, which ain't all that often. Skeeters come up river and eat a man alive when it rains."

"I'm going to build big ones, buildings like no man in this country has ever seen, buildings of stone with turrets and towers, buildings so beautiful you won't be able to get them from your mind. People die and take your heart with them into the grave, but buildings live on for generations. In France I've built palaces, and libraries, and homes. I can do it here, too, in this new land, in the way that I want."

"Yes, sir," he said, looking over at Jerome. "I can see you're set on it."

"It's a start," he said, "a place where anything is still possible."

"Not my aim to be givin' advice, Mister, but a man walkin' alone in this country ought to carry a weapon, 'specially one bent on buildin' palaces and such."

Reaching for his bag, Jerome dug through its contents, retrieving a revolver.

"I bought this in Kansas City," he said, "although I don't keep it loaded."

"Havin' it is what counts," the old man said. "Mostly."

When they crossed over the Arkansas River, Jerome leaned out of the buggy for a look. Below, the water ran green and deep as it twisted away into the prairie.

Once across the river, they pulled onto a plateau. The old man and Jerome dozed under the monotony of Squirt's clop. As evening fell, a flock of blackbirds banked against the orange sky. Pulling up, the old man took off his hat and dusted it against his knee.

"Well, there she is," he said, pointing down the path, "the Salt Fork, and a trestle for walkin' acrost, when there ain't no train coming. Follow them tracks south, and sooner or later you'll come to Guthrie station, or France, either one, I reckon."

Climbing down, Jerome lifted out his bag from the back of the buggy, watching as the old man wheeled about.

"Good-bye," Jerome called after him, but he neither turned nor answered, the dust from his wheels gathering in the dusk.

As he crossed the trestle, Jerome adjusted his stride to the spacing of the ties. Below, the sunset shimmered on the river. Beached on the shore was a ferry, mud covering its ramp, streaking from its windows. Farther downstream, dead horses had washed up on the bank. Crows perched on their swollen bellies, lifting and settling as they maneuvered for position. A heron watched on from the shore, a knight-errant with its head held high, with its plume and deportment intact in the midst of a grisly scene.

Once over, Jerome struck down the tracks, his bag slung over his shoulder, the crunch of rock under his feet. Off the right of way, he saw something move, a bird maybe, a hawk perched in a mesquite to await its night's catch. It was hard to tell, the odd way it moved in the darkness. The old man's warning about traveling alone and unarmed came rushing back.

Easing down the grade, he got a better look and laughed at his own foolishness. It was but a hat, turning in the wind, lost, or discarded, by someone passing by.

Night fell as he gathered twigs and leaves, striking a fire, blowing into the ember until a flame sputtered into life.

From his bag he took out a small pot, a wooden container of tea, and a piece of smoked meat. Filling the pot from his canteen, he set it on the fire to boil while he ate the meat. When the tea was finished, he sipped it from a tin cup, the aroma civil and reassuring. Tomorrow he would prepare hot food, but for tonight he was too weary, too uncertain of his course.

Pulling his blanket about his shoulders, he watched the stars ride through the sky above. He thought of Madeline, how often they'd taken their tea and talked of the day's events. He thought of how she'd died, how his heart had been torn from him. Unable to work, he'd walked the streets as a man lost, a man destroyed.

Pulling his bag under his head, he closed his eyes. What place more fitting, more distant from her memory than that in which he now found himself?

The train sat him upright, its whistle screaming as it steamed over the Salt Fork trestle in the morning light. Jerome watched the caboose disappear down the tracks, and his heart thumped in his chest.

After packing his bag, he swung it onto his shoulder, and with a last look back, struck down the tracks for Guthrie station.

The morning grew hot soon enough in spite of the wind. The shimmer of the rails and the smell of creosote overtook him. He drank from his canteen, and water dripped from his chin and onto his shirt, drying away under the wind. Twice he'd refilled the canteen, once from a creek green with moss, and again from a buffalo wallow. Neither source stood too close an inspection, so he now downed the water as one might medicine, pinching away the smell from his nostrils.

At noon, he chewed jerky under the shade of a trestle, a bony contraption that warded off neither the wind nor the sun. His lips cracked from the salt and smoke in the meat.

In the afternoon, the terrain changed with abruptness. His hand over his eyes, he turned in a circle. For as far as he could see, stones lay toppled like dominoes across the countryside. Rocks were scattered to the horizon, some stacked in layers, some cast in heaps, like piles of rubble, while others stood alone, like royal guards. In the distance a hill thrust from out of the earth's belly, jutting into the sky.

Below the hill was a wagon, its wheels turned against the slope of the ground. A pair of horses foraged from among the rocks below.

"You want something, Mister?" a voice said from behind him.

Hair rose on the back of Jerome's neck as he turned about, lifting his hands. A boy stood between him and the tracks, his rifle aimed at Jerome's chest.

"What seems to be the problem?" Jerome asked.

"This is Deventer land," the boy said. "We don't take to no claim jumper."

"I believe we are standing on railroad land," Jerome said.

"What's your name, Mister?"

"Jerome Bouchard. I'm on my way to Guthrie station."

Lowering his rifle, the boy looked him over.

"There's been a killing," he said, "a marshal shot down at our spring. Maybe it was you did it?"

"May I put my hands down?"

"See that you keep 'em in sight. I know how to use this rifle."

"What's your name, son?" he asked, lowering his hands.

"Bram," he said.

"Perhaps you could tell me how much farther to Guthrie station?"

"Never been to Guthrie station," Bram said.

"Maybe I could speak with your father."

"You wait up there by the wagon," Bram said. "I'll be back. And don't be stepping on no joint snake."

"Joint snake?"

"They're pure hell to get rid of."

Sitting in the back of the wagon, he watched the boy as he topped the hill. When he was out of sight, he located his revolver, dropping cartridges into the cylinder. Now, at least it was loaded, which was more than that boy could say for his rifle.

When Bram returned, a girl walked at his side, her blonde hair spilling over her shoulders.

"Hello, I'm Alida, Bram's sister."

"Jerome Bouchard," he said, taking her hand. "I'm just traveling through, on my way to Guthrie station. I'm an architect, you see, and I've heard that Guthrie station will be the new capital of the Territory."

"And state capital, too," Alida said.

"It's a funny talk you have, Mister," Bram said.

"I'm from France," he said, "as far away as the moon."

Alida pushed her hair from her eyes. "We'd invite you for supper, Mr. Bouchard, "but with all that's happened . . ."

"One must be careful of strangers," Jerome said, hefting his bag onto his shoulder. "In the future, Bram, you should make certain your rifle is loaded if you are going to aim it at a man. The breech is open."

Turning the rifle over, Bram looked into the empty chamber. "I'll be damned," he said.

"Wait, Mr. Bouchard," Alida said. "Bram and I would love to have you stay. We don't have much, but the company would be nice, wouldn't it, Bram?"

"Sure," he said. "I guess so. I've never known anyone from France before."

"It's done, then," Alida said. "Bram shot a rabbit this morning just outside our door. That's why his rifle is empty, I suppose. Anyway, we'd be happy to share."

"And I've some rice," Jerome said, "here in my bag. You wouldn't have any wine?"

"No, I'm afraid not, but we've the best spring water in the Territory."

It was with great interest that Jerome inspected their dugout, his hand following the natural arch of the rock.

"And this is where you live?" he asked, turning to Alida, who stood in the doorway.

"It isn't much, I know," she said, "but it's comfortable in the heat. Bram says we live like badgers but without the same good meals."

"It's dug from the mountain," Jerome observed, "like our ancestors who dwelled in caves."

Lighting the lantern, Alida placed it on the crate of unopened books. Soot drifted up from the chimney.

"I guess we do live like cavemen," she said.

"No, no," he said. "You misunderstand me. There is beauty here, in the change and surprise of the rock. Man destroys this in his penchant for symmetry. Do others live such as this?"

"Some live in soddies, I hear" she said, "cut from the prairie sod. Lots of folks live in their wagons, or under them, when the weather permits. There is little timber straight enough for building, nor even rocks like we have here. We have plenty of rocks, as you can see. There's people living in tents. Some dig holes into the ground, covering them with tarps or the slats from their wagon beds. Bram has found caves higher up with markings in them. I guess folks have always made do with what they have."

"Rabbit's cleaned," Bram called from outside, "and there's fresh water from the spring."

"I hope my stay will not run you short of food," Jerome said, following her out of the dugout.

"The meat doesn't keep for long anyway, Mr. Bouchard. Bram made a cedar box to store it in down by the spring, where it's cool, but even then it spoils. Sometimes the coons get to it no matter how many rocks we stack on top. It's best to eat it fresh."

After supper, they walked up the hill to sit on the ledge that over-looked the camp. The moon rose over them, poised and mute in the blackness.

"The evenings are exquisite here," Alida said, pulling her legs to her side, "but the days are torrid, and the wind never stops."

"What's France like, Mr. Bouchard?" Bram asked, hanging his legs over the ledge. "I figure someday I might go there."

"Well," Jerome said, "it's a beautiful place. Not like this, not in this way, but comfortable and predictable, a place where you know what to expect. Some of the world's most beautiful buildings are there, structures that took men their whole lives to build."

"There are only rocks here," Bram said, "and hoopers."

"But there is a beauty here, too, Bram, in the land itself. Like this place of yours, this mountain of stone is as grand as an Egyptian pyramid. Don't you agree, Alida?"

"It has its beauty," she said, "but it's a poor and hard land. What grass there is fails to nourish. Even though the horses graze for many hours a day, their bones rattle in their skins."

"Their stool is the color of chalk," Bram said, "from the rocks they eat, I guess, but the spring is pure and cold."

"That's where we found the young marshal," Alida said.

Standing, Jerome dusted off the seat of his pants.

"Do you have any idea who might have done it?"

"I traded my mother's ring for this land," she said, "to Carl and Mavis Ellison, an old man and his young wife. From the beginning, I felt something was wrong. There was a coldness in her eyes, but then . . . I guess I wanted the company, you know, someone to talk to, a girl my own age. She was so friendly, and we picked plums together."

Bram turned away, tossing a rock over the ledge, waiting for its thud below.

"After they'd gone," she continued, "after Bram and I found the body down at the spring, I remembered seeing the hat at Walnut Creek."

"What hat?" Jerome asked.

"The marshal's," she said. "I'd seen him wearing it. I remembered the feather in the band."

"The sort of thing a young girl might remember," Jerome said.

"The hat was behind the door of the dugout," Bram said, "the very same hat. It must have been Carl what killed him."

From down in the meadow, a horse whinnied, and a cloud drifted over the moon above them. Shadows grew from the rocks, sinking back into the mountain as the cloud passed away.

"I know this is not my business," Jerome said, "but you're so young to be living out here alone."

"Not so young," Bram said.

"I can see that you both are brave and strong, but to be out here alone like this could be very dangerous."

"We lost our father at the Salt Fork," Alida said. "It was too late to turn back."

"We buried him under a mesquite," Bram said, looking out into the darkness, "but this is our place now. We're doing just fine, ain't we, Lidy?"

From where Jerome stood, he could see the moonlight glinting on the distant railroad tracks.

"You left his hat on the tree?" he asked.

"You saw?" Alida asked.

"Yes, I suppose I did," he said.

"Sometimes it feels like it didn't happen at all, like it was a dream, and pretty soon I'll wake up, and everything will be like it used to be," she said.

"And your mother?"

Shrugging, Alida pushed her hair back from her face.

"She died of tetanus back in Pennsylvania, leaving us to fare on our own, and I've not been such a good mother, I'm afraid."

"Because in your heart you are still a girl," Jerome said, "with your own life ahead of you. These things will pass, Alida, and you will have what you want. I'm certain of it."

"But now I've bought this pile of rock," she said. "Sometimes I think we should have gone back home."

"Come on, Lidy," Bram said. "There was nothing back there. That's why we left in the first place."

"The future is here," Jerome said, "in this new land. We will make it ours, won't we?"

"Why don't you tell us about France?" Bram asked. "Are there lots of pretty girls in France?"

"None to compare, Bram, to what I've seen here."

Alida ducked her head and smiled.

"Bram doesn't think of me as a girl, but only as someone to cook his breakfast."

"Well, Bram," he said, smiling, "young men are often blind to the beauty about them. Now, if you two will forgive me, I'm going to take my rest down there in the bed of that wagon. I thank you both for the company and for supper. Tomorrow, I leave early. Is there anything I can do for you when I get to Guthrie station?"

"You might tell them about the marshal," Alida said. "Someone must be looking. Maybe they will come so that he can be buried proper with his own people."

"Yes," he said. "Well, good night, then, and thank you for your hospitality, and I wish you luck."

"Do keep an eye out for Carl and Mavis, Mr. Bouchard," Alida said. "They're out there somewhere, and if they killed once, they could do it again."

R olling out of his bunk, Buck Reed studied his toes and listened to the trumpeter's call to assemble. For twelve years his life had been dictated by the trumpet: when to rise, when to eat, when to sleep or water the horses. There were few decisions for the soldier to make in the U.S. Cavalry, even fewer for a colored soldier in a colored unit. But on this day the big decision was his, to reenlist or to muster out a free man.

In the past the decision had been easy. There was no other course for a colored man, nothing better than the army. But here in the Territory he'd heard rumor of the Negro colony for Oklahoma, and an all-black settlement being established near Guthrie station. Maybe there was something for everyone in this land.

His assignment at Camp Alice in Cimarron Horseshoe Bottom, north of Guthrie station, had been trying at best—six months of herding boomers from the Territory back into Kansas, only to have them return within weeks, better equipped, meaner, and more determined than before. For white soldiers it was difficult enough, for coloreds it was nigh impossible, their authority being challenged at every turn. On top of that, the equipment was worn and in disrepair, hand-me-downs from the Fifth Cavalry, clothing and bedding still smelling of men, tents weathered and torn by the prairie winds. The horses were jaded and diseased.

Squaring his hat, Buck dusted the front of his uniform. There were those who thought him odd, 'cause of the hex, 'cause of the voices he heard in the night, 'cause of the slant of his eyes passed through the womb whilst his ma watched the slaughter of a pig. But no man would deny that he was a power to reckon with, a man quick and certain, one commanding respect from even the white officers of the unit.

The cavalry had given him much, made of him more than he was without it. He could read words, fire a weapon with lethal accuracy, fight a man bare-fisted, ride broomtails until they stood quivering still. Soon enough even the most grudging forgave him the hex he bore.

Picking up his weapon, he stepped from his tent just as reveille sounded, as dust was gathering in the breaking light of Horseshoe Bottom. For a moment he watched the soldiers clamber from their tents, forming rank across the parade field. How often he'd stood at their sides awaiting muster. How often he'd awaited the bark of his name and the hardness of the hours to come. But today was to be different, because today his decision was made. Turning his back on the scramble below, he walked down the path to the captain's tent.

Slipping on a boot, the captain looked up at Buck. "What is it, Sergeant?"

"It's mustering day, sir."

"I see," he said, tugging on the second boot. "Reenlistment papers are signed with the clerk, Sergeant Reed."

"Yes, sir, but that's just it, Captain."

Standing, the captain strapped on his sidearm.

"You thinking on mustering out, Sergeant Reed?"

"Yes, sir," he said, his voice hollow and distant in his ears.

"I thought as much." Pulling the sleeves down on his jacket, he donned his hat, checking its tilt in a hand mirror. "Sergeant Reed, I've been in the army a good long while now, and I've seen this before, career men taking the notion to go it alone. Men like us need the army, Reed. Without it, we have no boundaries, no direction, drifting this way and that. Take my advice and forget it."

"It's a free man I'm going to be, Captain, just once 'fore I die."

"You're a good soldier, Sergeant, and I'd hate to lose you, but there's plenty more out there lookin' for a home. This army won't take a second breath when you ride out for the last time. The army doesn't need you. It's you needs the army." Picking up his gloves, he tucked them into his belt. "Guess you know this better than most, but there's damn small pickins out there for coloreds."

"There's a Negro colony organized east of Guthrie, Captain, and plans for a all-colored settlement."

"You been hearing them voices again, Sergeant? How you think a colored man is going to survive in this country without this here uniform on his back? Didn't those voices tell you them coloreds are living on forty-acre plots of the worst scrub in the Territory, eating opossum and cutting firewood for a living?"

"No, sir, I reckon they didn't."

"Well, that's the way it is, Sergeant Reed. This here army gives you a home, food, and stripes on your sleeve." Opening the tent flap, he looked down on the assembly below. "Take yourself a three-day pass. Think it over."

"My mind's set, sir. It's my pay I'll be needing."

The captain paused. "See the paymaster, Mr. Reed," he said, "and check in your gear. Take one of those Indian ponies we caught on the Bottom. They don't do nothing but eat anyway. Good luck to you, Reed. You're as good a soldier as I've ever had."

"Thank you, sir," he said, snapping a salute.

As the captain walked down the path, the beat of the cadence rose from the parade field, as measured and deliberate as Buck's own heart. He listened for the voice of the hex, for its authority, but it never came on decree, only unbidden in the night.

Within the hour, he rode from camp. Without a saddle, the Indian pony was stiff beneath him, and by the time he reached the trailhead, his trousers were soaked with sweat. Back at Horseshoe Bottom, mess call sounded for molasses and mush and pots of black coffee. Afterward, the men would gather under the cottonwood to smoke, to lie and tell jokes as they awaited the day's orders. It was a time of camaraderie, the laughter and kinship filling a man's emptiness. But for Buck Reed those days were over now, with naught but the backbone of this Indian pony removing his pride as he rode away.

By afternoon he could see the white tents of Guthrie station dotting the horizon, smoke curling from the steamers that idled at the depot. Voices rode small from across the prairie. Sliding off the pony, Buck brushed away the horsehair from the inside of his legs and leaned over the pony's back to watch the people as they scampered about.

Getting back on, he patted his pony's neck and reined him eastward. There would be time for Guthrie station later.

A leg of the Crosstimbers cut across the sandhills before him, a wall of scrub oak and vines. Bramble twisted like barbed wire and hung in curtains from the branches. Little light penetrated the canopy of leaves, and the sand under the trees was barren of grass. Clumps of sumac, with its fruit the color of tobacco, stretched for the patches of light. The smell of honeysuckle hung sweet in the air, the blossoms alive with the hum of bees.

Unable to ride in the thickets, Buck led his pony, picking his way through the undergrowth. But the going was slow, and dusk was setting when he came upon a wagon. An opening was chopped from the trees, leaving blackjack stumps like toadstools in the sand, cords of firewood around the perimeter. A black man leaned on the handle of his axe as he tended a pile of burning brush. A mule was tied in the shade, and a girl worked at a patchwork quilt draped over her lap. From behind the wagon, a woman watched him, her straw hat tied under her chin.

"Evening," Buck said to the man, tipping his hat to the woman who'd stepped out from behind the wagon. "Name's Buck Reed. Smelled the smoke from your fire."

The man leaned his axe against the wagon wheel. His beard was white against the frayed collar of his shirt. There was a pistol stuck in the belt of his pants.

"Lo," he said, touching the brim of his hat. "You ridin' that Indian pony alone or you got a war party hid in them trees?"

"Riding alone, sir," Buck said.

"This here's my wife, Bess, and over there's my girl, Rolondo."

Taking off his hat, Buck nodded. Rolondo smiled back, her dark eyes snapping. She wore overalls, cuffed to her knees, a faded shirt, one of her father's by the looks of it, and none of it managed to conceal the figure beneath.

"Nice meeting you," Buck said.

"Over there in the wagon is my boy, Junior. Oh, and I'm Roy, " he said. "We're from Pine Bluff way."

"It's a fair ride from Pine Bluff," Buck said.

"Uphill, too," Roy said.

"What's matter with his eyes, Ma?" Junior asked. "His lids droopin' down and lookin' like a pigs."

"Hush, boy," Bess said. "I'm sorry, Mr. Reed. It's from living like a mule day in and day out. He's lost his manners, I reckon."

"I'm right used to it," Buck said, putting his hat back on. "My ma watched a pig kilt whilst she carried me in the womb, and it came through the blood. Puts fear in a man when he looks into 'em, though I been told."

"Sam Bozen was hexed," Rolondo said, wiggling her toes into the sand, "but he just sat on the front porch rockin'." Linking her fingers, she pushed her hands out in front of her. "Is that what you do, Mr. Buck Reed, porch rockin'?"

"There's differences, I reckon," he said, tying his pony to the wagon, "some rockin', some talkin', some no one knows, 'cause they ain't said."

Kicking the sand from the tops of her feet, Rolondo looked up at him, "And what's yours?"

"Talkin'," he said, "comin' in the night, just mumblins mostly, but sometimes direct, callen my name in the dark."

"Sit down, Buck," Roy said. "Bess, get us some of that shine I been savin'. It's company we got calling."

"What that talk say?" Rolondo asked, the corners of her eyes crinkling. "'It's a good evening, ain't it, Mr. Reed,' or, 'I think it might be rainin' 'fore morning by the looks of it, Mr. Reed'?"

Pushing the needle through the quilt, Rolondo brought the thread up to her shoulder, holding it there as she waited for Buck's answer.

"Mostly it tell me what's in a man," he said, "down deep where he won't look. It's the truth what comes, the hard truth."

Rolondo studied him for a moment before feeding the needle back through the quilt.

"Seems a fearsome thing to me," she said.

"It's powerful and not to be made light of," he said, "a man seeing what others can't."

Taking the jug from Bess, Roy poured shine into the tin cups, handing one to Buck.

"Rolondo, go help your ma while Mr. Reed and I talk," he said. "You near wore him out."

Buck sipped on his shine as he watched Rolondo slip on her shoes.

"Right pretty girl, Roy, and smart, too, I figure."

"There's never any doubtin' what's on her mind," he said, taking a drink from his cup, "'cause she's done told you 'fore you can get it asked."

Taking another drink, Buck let the warmth work its way through him.

"It's a growin'," he said, "into a woman's strength."

"Lordee," Roy said, "I hope so."

"Yes, sir," Buck said, "I reckon it is."

Pouring them another drink, Roy rubbed at the numbness of his nose and pulled at his whiskers.

"It's a rare feller calls a man, sir, anymore, Buck, 'less he's been in the army, or got a rifle stuck in his ear."

"Mustered out this morning," Buck said, "out of Horseshoe Bottom. Handed in my sergeant stripes for that there razorback pony. Been chasing white folk back and forth over the border for six months now. Guess I couldn't take it no more."

"Seems a poor trade, don't it, sergeant stripes for a green Indian pony, what with no saddle?"

Setting down his cup, Buck leaned forward. "I heard tell that there was a Negro colony for Oklahoma started up, that they's building a colored settlement out here somewhere, a colored settlement run by coloreds and no one else."

"Yes, sir," Roy said, wiping at his mouth with his sleeve, "heard it far south as Pine Bluff. Sets over there where the Cimarron turns out, but there ain't much yet, a few soddies, a community garden. Most I know be choppin' firewood for sellin', or huntin' squirrels, or noodlin' catfish so's they won't starve. There's lots of us about, that's sure, up and down this here valley. Come from everywhere, didn't we, lookin' for the same thing, I reckon."

Pushing back his hat, Buck took a swig of the shine.

"I knowed there weren't no hope for the colored. I knowed that all along but just came anyway to be lookin'."

"Still," Roy said, studying the bottom of his cup. "It's a start, ain't it? It's our settlement, Buck, no more than it is."

"Oh, it will work, long as it's no more than a soddy or two, but what happens if it becomes a real town, a town run by coloreds? What happens when the whites get scart, Roy?"

Pouring more shine, Roy swirled it around and around as he thought.

"There's something different out here, Buck. Maybe it's 'cause of the heat, or 'cause it's starvin' poor, or 'cause it's the edge of the world, and we're all fixin' to fall over the side, but I got a notion that this time is different. Maybe out here white and colored got something to fight besides each other."

"Ain't the army I was in," Buck said.

"My neighbor's a white man yonder, livin' in a hole in the ground, with one mule, three kids, and a wife springin'. Me and him put our mules together to make up a team so's we could plant our sorghum. And I hear tell there's a colored doctor in Guthrie station, a doctor, you hear, and a politician, too, down from Kansas. Some say he's going to be governor some day."

Before Buck could answer, Bess appeared, a dishtowel draped over her shoulder.

"There's squirrel cooking, and lambs-quarter greens with fatback, if you ain't particular."

"No, ma'am, I ain't."

"Wash up in that bucket, and tie that pony somewhere's 'sides in my kitchen."

"Yes, ma'am," Buck said, finishing off his drink.

While Junior handed out tin lids for eating on, Buck watched Rolondo as she set the food on the back of the wagon. Bess served up the squirrel, leaving her own plate to the end. Heaping it with greens, she set aside the last piece of squirrel.

When Buck was finished, he mopped the drippings from his tin.

"There's plenty for seconds," Bess said, offering the last of the squirrel.

Over the years he'd done his share of complaining about army food, but it was rare there wasn't plenty to go around.

"I'm right full," he said, holding up his hand. "Give it to the boy, there. Look like he's growin' some."

From across the way, Rolondo flashed a smile.

"It's fillin' up a ditch with a teaspoon," Bess said, forking the last piece over to Junior, who took it with a broad grin.

Placing his tin lid into the bucket, Buck stretched his arms over his head.

"It's been a long day, folks. Think I'll be saying good night."

"You talkin' to the spirits tonight," Rolondo said. "I could use a pair of shoes 'fore winter sets in."

"I does the listening, little one," Buck said. "I just listens."

"You coming back this way, Buck Reed?" she asked.

"Best squirrel I had in a long time," he said. "Night everyone."

Buck lay on his blanket, his hands behind his head. Nearby, his pony nibbled at the weeds that grew tender and pale under the canopy of leaves. Laughter drifted from Roy's camp, the sounds of family, sounds foreign to army life.

He thought of Rolondo, the way she smiled, the dance of the light in her eyes, but it was her words that pleased him most, the way they tumbled from her like laughter.

He dozed, and when he awoke, the stars were fled, slipped away into the universe. Curling under his blanket, he waited for the voices that he knew would come, the call of his name.

The voices told of his anointment, of his charge and invincibility. They told of a purpose beyond the reach of his enemies and his own knowledge. In the end they sang, in requiem for him.

When Buck rose, he led his pony out of the Crosstimbers before mounting. Below him, brushfires smoldered, and the smell of smoke hung in the morning. Not far from the river, he could see the settlement, tucked in the valley, no more than a few huts built of blackjack and mud. Maybe someday he would come back and join them here at the river's bend.

As he topped the ridge, he saw a dugout below with white children playing at its door. A washtub was propped against a blackjack stump, and wet clothes hung from a rope strung between the trees. A mule stretched its neck through a pole corral and worked at the grass.

Buck watched the children play. Maybe Roy was right about this land. Maybe hunger and fear would drive them together, and something new and redeeming would be forged from it.

Snapping the reins, he turned his pony into the blackjacks and headed west toward Guthrie station.

The bare back of his pony scrubbed at Buck's legs, and when he could stand it no longer, he walked, trailing him behind. By evening, he could see the railroad tracks leading out of Guthrie station. Rail cars stacked with timbers sat on a siding. A small stream wound from out of a culvert and into a stand of cottonwoods. It was a good place for camping.

Pulling up, he patted his pony's neck. "You ready for a rest, boy?"

Leading him into the trees, Buck rubbed him down with a handful of leaves, before staking him up short in a patch of grass at the stream's edge. Taking off his boots, Buck eased his feet into the cool water.

"You're upstream of my coffee," someone said from behind him.

When Buck turned, two men were standing there. One sported a beard, and the arches of his boots were worn from the rub of stirrups. The other man was dark, the color of cinnamon, and his hair was straight and black. There was an uncompromising look in his eyes, a look Buck had seen often in the early days of the Territory.

"Sorry," Buck said. "Just coolin' my feet."

"Well, don't matter, I reckon. Might even be an improvement," the bearded one said.

"We got people set on stealing our lumber," the dark one said. "Carrying it off by the armload, right off our cars. It gets downright discouraging."

"I ain't stealin' no lumber," Buck said. "I'm Sergeant Buck Reed, or I was. I just mustered out of the cavalry over at Horseshoe Bottom."

"My name's Roop," the bearded one said, "and this here's Creed McReynolds."

Stepping to the side, Creed looked Buck over.

"We got a camp just on that rise," he said, "so we can keep watch on our cars. Why don't you join us?"

Slipping his boots on, Buck stood up and dusted the soil from his hands.

"Much obliged, Mr. McReynolds," he said, "but my horse is hobbled out, as you can see, so reckon I'll just stay put."

"Still," Creed said, "we'd like for you to join us. We insist on it, don't we, Roop?"

"That we do, Buck. We'd rather you be a guest in our camp, than a stranger in the dark, you understand. It's the nature of the times, ain't it, until you know about a man."

"You mean a colored man?" Buck asked.

"It ain't the colored been carrying off our lumber," Roop said, "but who's to say it won't come to that."

"In that case," Buck said, "lead the way, and I figure you'd like to carry my rifle for me, too?"

"I'd be proud," Roop said, "and you can bring along that Indian pony. What's his name?"

"Pony," Buck said, slipping the bridle over his head and loosening the hobble.

"That's a right proper name, ain't it," Roop said, looking over at Creed.

"Somethin' else you should know," Buck said.

"What's that?" Creed asked.

"I sometimes talk in my sleep."

"You *do*?"

"Yes, sir. I hear voices, too," Buck said.

"I won't hear them, will I?" Roop asked. "It's hard enough sleepin' with them bullfrogs honkin' half the night."

"Ain't likely," Buck said.

Once in camp, Creed put the coffee water on and pulled off his boots. Roop stood at the edge of the light with his hands stuck in his pockets. Buck sat down next to the fire, crossing his legs, the light playing in the blackness of his eyes.

"What you do in the army, Buck?" Roop asked.

"Most everything," he said, "'fore it was done."

"Why did you get out, I wonder?"

"A man can't stand with his knees locked for twenty year, without it eats up his soul," he said.

"Seems a steady job," Roop said, "what with grub and a mount, too."

"Oh, it's steady enough, all right. Ain't a day goes by with nothing to do. Chased boomers back to Kansas till our horses wore out. Boomers don't drive no better than turkeys, especially by no colored troops."

Roop held out two cups and waited as Creed filled them from the pot.

"I suppose a man could get killed in the army," he said. "Take some of the spin out of life, wouldn't it."

"There's a good many opportunities for that," Buck said, "and I've done my share of duckin'."

Rolling up his blanket, he lay down, tucking the roll under his elbow.

"Then I heard about the Negro colony of Oklahoma, coloreds comin' into the Territory by the hundreds, comin' from everywhere, all thinkin' of a new start. Said there was goin' to be a colored settlement, maybe even a colored state. I didn't believe it none, but figured it was somethin' a man ought see for himself."

Handing him a cup, Roop said, "If this coffee isn't good, wasn't my feet soaking in the creek."

"Seems like you boys would be staking out land somewheres," Buck said, "like other folk."

Sitting down at the fire, Creed balanced his cup on a piece of firewood.

"That's just it, Buck," he said. "Everyone's so busy thinking about land, they haven't considered what comes next."

Buck looked over at Roop, who shook his head. "Creed thinks on the backside of things a good deal," he said.

"What do come next?" Buck asked.

"Things have to be built—barns, businesses, everything that makes up a city. You've got to have lumber to do that."

"And that's what you got, ain't it." Buck said.

Taking a sip of his coffee, Creed shook his head. "Lumber is the lifeblood of a city. Already folks are buying it up, sometimes no more than a few sticks at a time, all they can afford, carrying it back in their arms. With luck I'll be sold out soon, and with that money, I'm going back for more lumber, because Guthrie station is going to be the capital, and lumber is going to be the king. Any man wants to build his place in the sun will have to come to my door."

"It's a big dream," Buck said. "The kind colored men can't have."

Standing, Creed walked to the edge of the camp, squaring his shoulders in the darkness.

"When they come for my lumber, they don't ask if I'm Kiowa, or black, or white. They don't care, Buck, because they need what I have."

The chug of a steamer pulling the grade out of Guthrie station rode in on the night. They could smell its smoke and see its light as it drove past the siding.

"What you figure on doin' when you get to Guthrie station?" Roop asked Buck.

"Anything what don't include Indian ponies," he said, rubbing the insides of his legs. "Fact is, I don't know much other than the army. I'm a good rider, and fair in a fist fight. Got a hard head, some say. It's a rare man I can't take when it comes to it." Taking off his hat, he stuck it on his knee and scratched at his head. "Don't mean to be braggin'," he said. "It's the hex doin' the fightin'."

"I'm going to bed," Creed said, taking up his bedroll. "First thing come morning, I'm headed to Guthrie station. There's lumber to sell. You want to ride along, Buck? I'll be leaving come sunrise."

"Yes, sir. I'd like that fine, providin' Pony don't saw off both my legs 'fore I get there."

As they slept, the moon rose from behind the cars of timbers. Roop snored quietly from beneath his blanket.

"Get up," Buck whispered, shaking Creed's shoulder.

"What is it?" Creed asked, reaching for his rifle.

"They're at your lumber," Buck said, "whilst you dreamin' of things unnatural."

Kicking the bottom of Roop's foot, Creed said, "They're stealing your half of the lumber, Roop."

Within moments, the three of them crouched in the shadows of the trees, rifles at the ready. Two figures labored under the moonlight as they passed timbers down from the car and loaded it into a wagon. Two others stood lookout at the end of the rail cars.

"What's that stink?" Roop whispered.

"Smells like garbage," Creed said.

"They're armed," Roop said. "What do we do now?"

"We go get them," Buck said, stepping into the moonlight, cranking a shell into the chamber of his rifle.

"Oh, hell," Creed said.

No sooner had he spoken than Buck opened up, fire spitting from the end of his rifle as he moved toward the cars. When the return fire came, shots smacked into the earth about them and ricocheted off the tracks, whining into the darkness.

From behind, Roop and Creed fired into the night, all strategy abandoned as Buck moved into the hail of bullets. But the fight was short-lived, the thieves dumbstruck under the fearless assault. Their wagon rattled off down the right of way as they shouted curses back at Buck.

"Lordee," Roop said, falling to his knees as he watched Buck amble back, his rifle at his side. "It's a wonder we ain't full of holes this very minute."

"I couldn't catch 'em up," Buck said, "what without my boots on. Wasn't keen on it anyway, by the smell of 'em."

"It's a wonder you aren't dead, and us along with you," Creed said. "What got into you, Buck?"

"It's the hex," he said, "can't be killed, can it, not till it flies out of my body, I reckon."

"Lordee," Roop said again, shaking his head. "I hope it flies straight into me 'fore this fool takes on the whole of the Territory."

After they'd loaded the timbers back on the car, they told their stories until dawn. Then Creed saddled his horse while Buck caught up Pony, hooking a leg over, pulling himself up.

"Like ridin' a picket fence," he said.

Mounting up, Creed turned to Roop.

"I'll be sending a wagon before nightfall for the Lieberman lumber. Then we'll be on our way, partner. You keep an eye out."

Rubbing at the stubble on his chin, Roop nodded.

"It was real excitin' to meet you, Buck."

Reining Pony about, Buck tipped his hat. "Same," he said. "Sorry about givin' you a start last night, Roop."

As they rode to the depot, a hot wind blew at their backs. The quiet of the prairie faded under the din of hammers and saws, the whinny of horses and the braying of mules, the laughter of children playing along the banks of the Cottonwood. The air was drenched with the smells of baking bread and smoking campfires. Tents covered the hills, their sides flapping in the wind like the sails of a thousand schooners.

Sweat ran down Creed's neck and onto his shirt collar. Ahead, Buck walked, leading Pony down the center of the tracks. A man stood under the shade of the depot and watched as they approached.

"A right strong interest he's takin'," Buck said over his shoulder.

Holding his hand against the sun, Creed said, "It's the marshal. We've met before, though I doubt he remembers."

When they came into range, the marshal walked out onto the baggage dock.

"Mornin'," he said, reaching for his handkerchief, dabbing at the perspiration on his forehead. "It's a hot one, ain't it?"

"Is there something we could do for you, Marshal?" Creed asked.

"Maybe," he said, "maybe not." Folding his handkerchief, he tucked it away into his back pocket. "Got three men complaining they was attacked last night. Run off the right of way, they said, without no cause."

"What's that got to do with us, Marshal?" Buck asked.

Looking at Buck, the marshal's face grew serious.

"What's your name?" he asked.

"Buck Reed, sir, just mustered out of the cavalry. Come lookin' for work at Guthrie station."

"Work, is it?" he asked, checking over Pony.

"Yes, sir."

"Well, Buck Reed, those boys said that a colored man just stepped out of the night and started shootin' 'em up. Said he just kept on comin'." Stroking his chin, he thought awhile. "Now, I ain't sayin' it was you, although it's a curiosity, you come strollin' down the tracks this very morning. Still, ain't for me to say, seeing as how coloreds is waltzin' up and down these tracks most every day now. Could have been anybody, couldn't it."

"Could have been the same boys who were trying to steal my lumber," Creed said.

"Yes, sir, could've."

"That would sort of make it even up, if that were the case?"

"If a man was stealin' lumber, like you say, and that's all there was to things."

Reaching into his pocket, he pulled out a badge, dropping it in a slow roll from one hand to the other.

"You see, my deputy was bringing up drag out of Walnut Creek Encampment, and now he's come up missing."

"We haven't been up Winfield way, Marshal," Creed said.

"No, sir, I reckon not, but it leaves me short-handed. Point is, I got an opening for a deputy marshal needs fillin'."

"I'm sorry, Marshal," Creed said, "but I've got a lumber business to run."

"Oh, I wasn't talking about you. No offense."

Buck kicked at the bedrock with the toe of his boot and looked out from under his hat.

"You asking a colored man to hire on as deputy, Marshal?"

"Appears so," the marshal said.

Catching Pony's reins up short, he asked, "Payin' work?"

"Some might argue that, Buck, but least you'd have a saddle for that Indian pony. You interested or no?"

"What would I be doin', Marshal?"

"Findin' my deputy, first thing. After that, just depends," he said. "If you're interested, come over to the office."

"Yes, sir," Buck said, "but there's one thing you ought to know."

"What would that be?"

"I got the hex."

Easing himself down from the dock, the marshal walked away.

"Hell, Buck," he said without turning, "I wouldn't hire no other kind."

C reed left Buck at the marshal's office before climbing the hill to find the Liebermans. The streets were crowded, the race for lots having given way to the building of a city. What lumber was available had been cut from the bottoms, most of it blackjack, elm, or cottonwood, all of it of poor quality and size. Bizarre dwellings grew on the hillsides, half-house, half-tent, some no more than wagon beds, or posts lashed together like teepee poles and wrapped with oilcloth.

Everywhere, lawyer signs touted claim settlement experience, but credentials were scarce. There was no way to distinguish between the blacksmith and lawyer or between the surgeon and horse doctor. A man was what his sign claimed, until proven otherwise.

As he turned south, Creed spotted a wagon and mule team hitched under the shade of an elm. An old man lay beneath the wagon, hat pulled over his eyes, ankles crossed. Curled next to him was a sleeping hound, brows twitching, legs kicking in chase. The smell of slop was strong in the heat, and flies buzzed about the wagon bed.

"Excuse me," Creed said. When there was no response, he touched the old man's shoulder. "Excuse me, sir."

The old man turned onto his side and smacked his lips. The hound lifted an ear, unwilling to open an eye yet. Maybe it was the whiskers, or the droop of his socks, or the smell of sour that caused Creed to recognize the old man. He was older than Creed remembered, but it had been dark the night he'd dragged him from the ravine. As Creed turned to leave, the old man lifted onto an elbow.

"Here," he said, "why you wakin' a man from his rest?"

"Sorry," Creed said. "I'll be on my way."

"Well, you got me woke now."

"Sorry," he said again. "Thought your wagon might be for hire."

Screwing down his hat, the old man looked him over.

"Ain't I seen you before?"

"You been to law school?" Creed asked.

"No, no, I ain't, but then I been tied up with my banking business, ain't I."

"I'll be on my way, Mister," Creed said.

"What you need a wagon for?"

"I've got timber to haul from the south siding, three cars in all."

Prying an eye open, the hound peeked over its bony shoulder at Creed.

"Well," the old man said, "I'm hired out full-time to *The Capital City*, and I've got a bad back, too."

"I'll find someone else," Creed said.

"And even if I did hire out, I couldn't do no loadin'. Ruined my back hauling slop for the army, didn't I, what with them livin' in their white tents like goddamn kings and me freezin' in the cottonwoods. 'Sides, I hear tell there's a crazy colored man down there, shootin' everyone what comes in sight."

Creed squatted on his haunches and picked a grass stem, sticking it in the corner of his mouth.

"My partner and I could do the loading." Pulling the bills from his pocket, he held it out. "I could make it worth your time, say, three dollars a load."

"I don't know," the old man said, looking down the road. "Strikes me that Mr. Damon ain't one for sharin' his wagon."

"What did you say your name was?"

"Didn't," he said, "but it's Jess Clayborn."

Folding the bills up, Creed put them back into his pocket.

"No need for anyone else to know, Jess. I'll be around this afternoon and ride out to the siding with you. You'll be here?"

"Providin' I ain't foreclosin' on widder women down at my bank."

"Nice dog," Creed said. "Real alert-like."

"Throwed rocks at him till my arm fell off, but there ain't no discouraging him onct he's made up his mind to come along."

Leaving Jess to his nap, Creed made his way to the Liebermans, where he found them clearing rocks, stacking them into a fence across the back of their lot. A smile spread across Samuel's face when he saw Creed.

"Lena said not to worry, that you would be back, and here you are."

"Glad to see you again, Samuel," he said. "I've made arrangements for your lumber to be delivered by this evening."

"Yes, yes," Samuel said, "I knew not to worry. We will have the first building in Guthrie station. Lena," he called, "Creed is here."

"Creed," she said, coming from the back of the lot. "You are safe. We heard there was trouble at the siding."

"A little," he said. "I've hired a wagon to bring your lumber. In fact, the driver was a neighbor of ours for a short spell."

"Ah," she said, hooking her arm through his, "and I hope he has taken a bath."

"That would be hoping for too much, I'm afraid."

Tucking her hair back under her scarf, Lena smiled.

"We have arranged for carpenters," she said, "or so they claim. Soon we will have our store. Come, I'll fix you something to eat."

"Thanks just the same, Lena, but I want to move the rest of the timbers as soon as possible."

"Before you go," Samuel said, "a man was here looking for you."

"A man?"

"A Mr. Abaddon Damon. He said he wants to buy your lot, maybe lumber, too. Mr. Damon is owner of *The Capital City* newspaper and is quick to let you know it."

"I'll go see him," Creed said. "Thanks, Samuel."

When he turned, he nearly stumbled over the old hound that was lying behind his feet. "Get," Creed said, but the hound moved just beyond reach, his tongue lolling from the side of his mouth as he panted against the heat.

"You've found yourself a dog," Lena said.

"An ole flea bag taken up with Jess. Get on now."

Taking a few steps back, the hound sat down again and wagged his tail.

"Are you sure you won't stay for some lunch?" Lena asked. "I've potatoes and onions from the grocer wagon down the street. More food comes in on the train each day now."

"It's tempting," Creed said, "after Roop's cooking, but I must be on my way."

"There's a sign on his tent," Samuel said, "but be careful, Creed. He is a man that gets what he wants, I think."

"Thanks," Creed said, "for everything, and, Lena, maybe I'll be needing that suit soon."

"You will be a big businessman, I think," she said, laughing, "to watch walking about the new capital city."

As he headed down the hill, Creed stopped at each tent, taking orders for lumber, insisting on wagon-load minimums, and there was no shortage of takers. The city teemed with new establishments, boot and tack shops, cigar stores, and banks. Every block boasted a saloon—Reeves Brothers, The Blue Belle, The Same Old Moses—all in need of lumber for completion.

A hot wind blew in from the prairie, as it did every morning, sweeping dust down the street, the smell of sage and gourd on its crest. Men held onto their hats, and the women wrapped their dresses about their knees to wait its passing. An engine idled down at the depot, steam hissing from its valves as from an impatient dragon. Creed picked his way through the streets that churned with wagons and horses and children.

The old hound trotted not far behind, and when Creed would stop, the dog would sit down, his tail sweeping like a pendulum.

"Get on," Creed hollered. "Get on out of here." Picking up a rock, he chucked it at the dog, who watched it roll past. Turning around twice, he lay down, chin between paws, peaking his brows this way and that. "Now, stay there," Creed shouted back at him.

The Capital City tent was located on an outlying lot, the prairie stretching away behind it. Like a beached ship, its hulk rose and fell with each gust of wind. Creed could hear the click of the hand press from under the flaps.

A man ducked out of the door. He was tall and thin, and his hair was slicked across his forehead. There was a delicacy in the turn of his mouth, but a hardness in his eyes. His high buttoned collar was ringed with sweat.

"Are you Mr. Abaddon Damon?" Creed asked.

"That's right," he said. "What is it you want?"

"Name's Creed McReynolds," he said. "Heard you were looking for me."

Taking his watch from his vest, Damon checked the time, winding the watch before dropping it back into his pocket.

"Come in," he said. "I've some business I'd like to discuss with you."

Even though the skirts of the tent were tied up, the inside was stifling. The press sat in the center of the tent, a pencil and pad on its top. Beneath it were several rolls of wallpaper. In one corner was a bedroll, a change of clothes hanging above it from a tent rope. A cedar water bucket, with a board on top to keep out the dust, sat in the other corner of the tent.

Reaching under the press, Abaddon pulled out a bottle of store-bought whiskey. "I understand you are in the lumber business, Mr. McReynolds?"

"In a fashion," Creed said. "Just getting started."

"As are we all here, but only the strongest will survive, as some have already discovered," he said. Pouring a couple of drinks into tin cups, he handed one to Creed. "You and I are going to do business together, Mr. McReynolds."

"You seem pretty certain of that, Mr. Damon," he said.

"That's store-bought whiskey. Soon enough it's going to be the best brandy a man can buy."

"Some would say it's illegal for you to give me a drink at all."

"Because of the color of your skin?"

"That's right."

"And what do you think?"

"I'm an attorney, a damn good one. It would be a mistake to think I'm not."

"I never take a man for granted."

Taking a drink from the cup, Creed said, "What is it you have on your mind?"

"As you can see, these are not the best quarters for running a paper. I'm going to need lumber for building *The Capital City*, Mr. McReynolds. It's my understanding you have such lumber."

"Why don't you call me Creed."

"How much lumber do you have, Creed?"

"Three cars," he said. "There's maybe one left. The demand for milled lumber in Guthrie station is pretty high these days."

"A smart move," Abaddon said. "Everyone but you forgot what they'd need once they got here."

The old hound stuck his head into the tent, twisting his nose at the smell of the whiskey.

"Get," Creed said. "How much lumber you figure to need, Mr. Damon?"

Setting his cup down on the press, Abaddon turned his full attention to Creed.

"All you got," he said. "And I want that lot of yours up there on top the hill." He held up his hand. "Before you say a word, I want you to hear me out, because this is going to be the most important decision of your life. What you see here in this tent is going to be the most powerful newspaper in the Territory some day. And out there in that scrabble is the makings of the new capital. It's going to be a grand and important place, and *The Capital City*'s going to be its paper."

"You're a confident man," Creed said.

"I guarantee it, and any man who signs on with me is in for the ride of his life. I'm going to the top, and I'm going there at full rein. *The Capital City* is the paper of record, my friend, the first and the best. My subscription rate is climbing so fast that I've hired on another man just to keep this press running. There's job work, too," he said, pouring himself another drink, "letterheads, envelopes, posters by the hundreds. Every man and jack between here and the Kansas border's starting a new business and is dead-set on advertising it. They want their ads with a winner, the biggest and the best, and that's what I've got.

"And here's something else," he continued, his eyes bearing down on Creed, "there's a government in the making here. This is going to be a state someday, and Guthrie station its capital. A government needs paperwork, legal notices, documents, school records, courthouse proceedings, forms of every sort, you name it. Who do you think's going to be in the position to provide them? The man with the press, that's who—Abaddon Damon, and *The Capital City*."

"I'm prepared to sell my lumber to anyone who needs it," Creed said. "Soon, I'll have more coming."

"And another thing," Abaddon said as he circled the press. "A paper needs a good attorney. You said you were a good attorney."

"That's right," Creed said, "but . . ."

"No other paper will take stronger positions than *The Capital City*. That means conflict, and lawsuits. I don't run from fights, Creed. What I'll need is a warrior, a man like yourself to help fight those battles. Do you see what I'm saying?"

Setting his cup down, Creed walked over to the tent flap and looked out on the street.

"I'm not a warrior, Mr. Damon, nor even half-warrior. My guess is that you don't have the money to buy my lumber. My guess is you want it on credit."

"A stake in the future," he said. "*The Capital City* paper needs to sit up there atop that hill where everyone can see it. The words will ring more certain and strong from up there."

"It's more than a salary that I'm looking for," Creed said.

Picking up his pencil, Abaddon walked around his press, his head brushing the roof of the tent. Clicking the pencil against his teeth, he studied Creed.

"Maybe it's revenge you're looking for," he said. "Maybe down deep you want to rub these bastards' noses in it." Smiling, he slipped the pencil behind his ear. "Well, it takes power to do that, my friend, and money. I'm offering both."

"I put the past behind me a long time ago," Creed said.

"There's too many folks and not enough to go around, Creed. Soon as things start getting hard, a good many aren't going to make it. Land won't get proved up, taxes won't get paid, bellies won't get filled."

"What's your point?"

"It's *The Capital City* will know it first," he said, pulling back his shoulders, "and those who work for her. This paper will have influence, plenty of it, and with you on the inside."

A breeze swept in, rippling the top of the tent.

"Here's how it is, Mr. Damon. I'm not interested in being your lawyer, but I am interested in your information. I would want it first. You tell me what's going on and when it's going to take place. I'll handle the rest. In turn, I'll sign over that hilltop lot up there and bring you what lumber's left for building *The Capital City*."

Abaddon sat down on top of the water bucket and pulled his long legs into his arms.

"You've made yourself a bargain," he said.

Reaching for the bottle, Creed poured himself a drink.

Taking a sip, he rolled it across his tongue. It tasted of fine brandy. "I want it in writing," he said.

"Such a thing could be used against me," Abaddon said.

"It cuts two ways."

Taking the pencil from behind his ear, Abaddon scratched out the agreement, tearing off the page and handing it to Creed.

After reading it over, Creed stuck the note into his pocket.

"The lumber will be delivered tomorrow, along with the claim for the lot," he said.

As he opened the tent flap, Abaddon said, "It's a rare man cheats me and profits in the end."

Pausing, Creed looked down the main street of Guthrie station.

"In that case you should know that I've hired your wagon for hauling timbers," he said, closing the tent flap.

As he left, he heard the press click up behind him. The old dog lay in the shade of the wagon. Rising, the creature shook off the dirt, and fell in at Creed's heel. Ears flopping, he trotted along behind, his tail sweeping from side to side.

"Damned ole flea bag," Creed said.

Jess had moved from under his wagon into the shade of a tree and was cutting a chew when Creed found him.

"Let's go," Creed said, "and stop at the depot on the way, so I can send a telegram. Seems I'm clean out of lumber and in need of ordering more."

While Creed sent the telegram to Kansas City for six more loads of lumber, Jess waited in the wagon.

When he came out, he climbed onto the seat next to Jess.

"Six more cars in a week," he said. "I'm in the lumber business now."

As they drove along the right of way, mourning doves gathered in the branches of the cottonwoods, and the sun eased onto the horizon, the clouds igniting above it, churning with oranges and golds. The wind faded to await the dawn, and the dust from their wheels hung in the air, obscuring the hound that trotted along behind the wagon.

"That flea bag's going to follow us the whole way," Creed said.

"Had a woman what did me the same way," Jess said, "with them sad eyes just hanging on every word."

"Why don't you feed him once in awhile, Jess? He looks half-starved."

"Ain't my dog. 'Sides, don't do no work, does he."

Lifting himself against the bounce of the seat, Creed settled back as they moved onto level ground.

"We been having our share of problems, keeping folks off our lumber," he said. "My partner's guarding the cars."

"Ain't colored, is he?" Jess asked, looking over his shoulder.

"No, sir. I don't believe he is."

It took a few moments for Creed to spot Roop sitting in the shadows of the freight cars. As they approached, Creed waved.

Stepping out, Roop lowered his rifle.

"It's a slop wagon you brought us," he said. "Ain't that fine."

Creed introduced Jess and said, "I've hired out his wagon to haul in our lumber."

"You sold more lumber, then?"

"And ordered six more cars."

Pushing back his hat, Roop grinned. "Sure beats looking up a cow's butt all day, don't it?"

"I could have sold a whole trainload, Roop. There isn't a man in Guthrie station doesn't need lumber."

Walking around the wagon, Roop wrinkled up his nose.

"No offense, Jess, but this wagon has a distinct smell."

"Jess here gets around, Roop," Creed said.

"That your hound, Jess?" Roop asked.

"No, it isn't," Creed said.

Laying down his rifle and slipping on work gloves, Roop said, "Guess Jess can't talk hisself, 'cause his vocal chords don't work."

"Ain't my dog," Jess said.

"Well, if it ain't your dog, and it ain't Creed's dog, then whose dog is it?"

Walking to the back of the wagon, Roop dropped the gate down. The dog moved off, circled once, and lay down.

"It's just a flea bag," Creed said.

"Looks like a egg sucker to me," Roop said.

By the time they'd finished loading the wagon, night had fallen, the smell of dust settling under the dew. Creed paid Jess his three dollars, giving him instructions on the delivery of the lumber.

"I'll need you again tomorrow," he said.

"Can't do it," Jess shook his head. "Mr. Damon would have my hide."

"That's taken care of, Jess. After Lieberman's lumber is unloaded, the remainder of this car goes to my lot. It's going to be the new site for *The Capital City* paper."

The old dog considered following Jess as he pulled off down the right of way, but then plopped down next to the track.

"He's as dumb as he is ugly," Roop said. "Come on, Flea Bag. Can't stay out here and get run over by a train."

Roop had fixed ham hock and beans and a skillet of cornbread for supper. The beans were good, as had been the day, and Creed scooped on his second helping. From the side, Flea Bag watched them as they ate.

"Mighty good, Roop," Creed said.

"Glad you like them, 'cause that's what you're getting for breakfast, too, since you didn't bring anything for tomorrow."

"Sorry," Creed said. "I was so busy selling lumber, I forgot to buy supplies."

Filling his plate, Roop set it on a stump, cutting himself a slab of cornbread.

"You going to tell me about this deal you've made, or are you just going to eat beans all night?"

Reaching into his pocket, Creed pulled out the paper Abaddon Damon had signed.

"I've agreed to turn over that hilltop lot," he said, "and the rest of this lumber to Abaddon Damon, owner of *The Capital City*. In turn, I get information, and I get it first."

"Seems a fair trade," Roop said, "land and lumber for nothing."

"He's a man knows where he's going, Roop. That paper's going to be the beating heart of this Territory. You and me are going to be there to take advantage of everything that falls our way." Unfolding the paper, Creed read it over. "This is an investment in our future, Roop, and puts us a leg up on every deal in the Territory."

"Here," Roop said, clapping his hands, "Flea Bag, get away from my beans, you son of a bitch. Look there," he said, "he's sneaked halfway to my beans whilst we were talking."

They watched as Flea Bag slid forward a paw, a movement so slow as to be nearly imperceptible.

"Get," Roop said again.

Taking yet another step, Flea Bag diverted his eyes.

Picking up a rock, Roop chunked it at the dog. "Look at him. He thinks if he can't see me, I can't see him. Get, now. Those are mine."

"Must be your dog, Roop," Creed said, "given his keen mind."

Flea Bag migrated yet closer.

"Here, god dang it!" Roop said, picking up a stick and whacking Flea Bag between the ears.

But even as he did, Flea Bag slurped the beans from Roop's plate, spinning it in a circle.

"It's a way you have with animals, Roop."

Throwing his hat on the ground, Roop said, "Well, I'll be god-danged if he didn't eat my beans."

"Shy on table manners, isn't he," Creed said, laughing.

Picking up his hat, Roop stuck it back on his head. A twig spun from a strand of web hanging from its brim.

"First you bring home a colored man damn near gets us shot full of holes," he said, "then that slop wagon, the same one stole our lumber just the night before, then this here flea bag what ate my supper. Now I just can't help but wonder what tomorrow will bring—Bill Doolin maybe, or a axe murderer lookin' to spend the night."

"Mighty good beans, Roop. I'm going to bed. See you in the morning."

The night was clear above as they bedded down. Across camp, Roop lay on his bedroll, hat dropped over his eyes, Flea Bag curled at his feet.

At the southern end of the mountain, Jerome Bouchard stopped to rest, studying the rift that opened into its center, cleaved there by the shifting of the earth. As he paused, he thought he saw something move, something high up on the rift, a lone figure in a robe perhaps, with outstretched arms. When he looked again, it was gone. In the distance the tracks cut through the horizon in a silver line. Turning east, he picked them up and headed toward Guthrie station.

The distances filled him with loneliness, and he thought of the young girl back on the mountain, and of her brother. There was no shortage of the likes of Carl and Mavis about, even in the isolation of these plains. But then Alida and Bram knew little of the ugliness of the world, of its indifference, or of its capacity for cruelty. Like birds fallen from the nest, they awaited their fate. Perhaps, if the gods were kind, they would be safe on their mountain.

As the day waned, weariness racked his body, and his feet ached from the unevenness of the bedrock. Cutting down a dry creek bed, he found willows growing from the bank of a small pool. Driftwood was plentiful for the building of a fire. There were tea leaves left for evening tea, and the rabbit Alida had insisted that he take.

When his fire was built, he made his tea. He thought of Madeline, the way she would call his name in the quiet of evenings like this, her voice singular like a bell, and how she would squeeze his arm sometimes, her nails biting into his flesh, and how she smelled of sachet and powder. Most of all, he thought of the way she believed in him, in his buildings, and how she would laugh with delight at his drawings. No matter his failures, her faith in him was undaunted, and he drew even now from her strength.

The first cool of evening swept in, and he shivered. When something moved in the dusk of his camp, he stood, spilling his tea.

"Who is it?" he asked.

An old man stepped from the darkness. "You traveling alone, Mister?"

"Yes," Jerome said, "I'm traveling alone. You're welcome to my camp if you mean no harm."

Squatting down, the old man set his rifle within reach, and pointed behind him.

"Harmless as a newborn," he said. "Back there's my wife, Mavis. She's a tad shy about strangers. Come on up here, darlin'."

Jerome's heart froze at her name.

Ducking her head and looking at Jerome from the corner of her eye, Mavis moved into the light. As she knelt into the sand of the creek bed, her skirt hiked above her knees. Putting her hands behind her, she leaned back, her cotton dress tight across her breasts.

"Hello," she said. "What's your name?"

"I'm Jerome Bouchard," he said, "on my way to Guthrie station. There's rabbit, though not much, I'm afraid."

"My name's Carl," the old man said, "Carl Ellison. Mighty nice of you to share your camp."

Jerome's stomach tightened as he looked about for his case.

"You say your words funny," Mavis said, sitting back on her heels.

"I'm from France," Jerome said. "My English is not so good. Would you care for some tea?"

"Oh, tea," she said, throwing her head back. "We don't never have tea. I'd like some just fine."

After pouring them tea, Jerome sat down, sliding his case within reach as he did.

"It's a bit dried-out from this eternal heat," he said, "but it still tastes of tea."

"I never knew anyone from France," Mavis said.

"I'm an architect."

Cocking her head, she looked at him. "What's an architect?"

"I build things," he said, "you know, design buildings."

"He's an architect, Carl," she said.

"All the way from France, too," Carl said, taking a piece of rabbit, "and he don't even have a sod plow. What you going to build 'em out of, Mister, buffalo chips?"

A breeze edged through the willows as Carl waited for Mavis's reaction. It came as a laugh, a liquid laugh, like water gurgling in a stream.

Jerome's face flushed. "I'll build from what the land provides," he said.

"Provides precious little," Carl said, wiping his hands on his overalls. "Take Mavis here, livin' in a dugout no bigger than a wagon bed, sleepin' with scorpions and black widders, wakin' in the mornings with webs dangling over her head. That's what the land provides in the Territory, Mister—a hole in the ground."

"It's my feeling that buildings should be an extension of the land," Jerome said, "of the place in which they are born, as if they sprouted from the soil in which they were planted." Slipping his hand under his case, he searched for the latch. "In other words, I don't know yet what I'll build them from. But you can rest assured that the beauty of the land will rise from them."

Carl squinted an eye, focusing it on Jerome, pulling at the corners of his mouth with his thumb and forefinger. Taking out his tobacco, he rolled a cigarette, lit it, the smoke lifting in curls. Mavis now sat still, her lips parted.

"You married, Mr. Bouchard?" she asked, digging her toes into the sand.

"I was married," Jerome said. "My wife is dead."

"You have kids?"

"No," he said. "We were both very busy with our careers. Madeline was an artist, a painter, you see."

"I'll bet she wanted children," Mavis said. "Most women do."

Carl looked over at Mavis. "You hush about all that. Mr. Bouchard been on a long dry spell and don't want to be talkin' about no kids."

"I miss my wife," he said, "a great deal."

"It's a hunger you got, ain't it," Carl said. "The kind what sets a fire in the guts? A man wants a woman, her heat and wet on a cold morning. Got my Mavis here from a catalogue, all tied up in one package, both glory and damnation arrivin' on the same day, all a man could hope for, but more than he could use."

"Come on, Carl," Mavis said, pulling her knees into her arms. "Mr. Bouchard don't want to hear 'bout that."

"Mavis is shy," Carl said, "till she gets a heat up, then there's no holding her back. Ain't that so, Mavis?"

Standing, Jerome said, "My wife and I loved each other. I'm certain we would have had children someday."

"Why, I'm right certain of that, Mr. Bouchard," he said, the coal glowing red on the end of his cigarette. "Just making conversation, that's all. Mavis, darlin', fetch that shine out of the wagon so's Mr. Bouchard and me can have a nip."

"I don't drink," Jerome said.

"Get the jug, girl," Carl said, leveling his gaze on Mavis.

Barefoot, Mavis picked her way through the darkness. She returned with a jug hooked over her finger. Spiking her hand on her hip, she handed it to Carl.

Jerome fumbled at the case at his side.

Lowering the jug, Carl sighed and wiped at his mouth with the sleeve of his shirt. "Here, darlin', give that to Mr. Bouchard."

Jerome started to protest, but Mavis shook her head, handing him the jug. The smell of tobacco was strong on its lip, and heat rose in his stomach when he drank. Clearing his throat, he handed the jug back to Mavis, who lifted it with both hands, a trickle racing down her chin and into the crevice of her breasts.

Fingers numbed, Jerome worked at the case. Carl drank again, his Adam's apple rising and falling.

"Whoa," he said. "It's a good goddamn batch, ain't it, if not a tad young." Handing the jug to Jerome, he leaned back on his elbows and laughed. "But we like 'em young, don't we? Here. Drink," he said. "Drink."

Lifting her hair off her neck, Mavis laughed.

"Do you like 'em young, Mr. Bouchard, or do you like 'em old? Carl says old is slow and easy like a summer day. What do you think, Mr. Bouchard?"

Taking a pull from the jug, Jerome handed it back to Mavis without answering, his head awhirl.

From across the way, Carl laughed, his chest rattling.

"Did you know that I was going to be a dancer?" Mavis asked, twirling about in the sand.

"No, no I didn't," Jerome said. "Why didn't you, I wonder?"

"It's 'cause of Carl," she said, leaning over, hands on her knees. "'Cause he said if I'd come out west, he'd make a rich woman out of me."

Moving his rifle to his lap, Carl picked up the jug and drank once more, shine gathering in the corners of his mouth.

"Said I'd make a *woman* outa you, and I done that," he said, laughing.

"I always been that," she said, lifting her breasts with the backs of her hands.

When the jug came again, Jerome drank with abandon, and the world tilted about him. He no longer cared about the danger, or the revolver, or the drawings in his case. He no longer cared about anything at all.

"Here," Carl said, kicking him on the bottom of the foot. "Don't you quit on us yet. Mavis is going to dance. Show us your dancin', darlin'."

"Without no music?" she said, twirling about, her feet twisting into the sand.

"Show us your pegs, Mavis," Carl said, lifting her skirt with the toe of his shoe. "Show us your dancin' pegs."

Mavis laughed her liquid laugh, and the moonlight caught the white of her throat.

"Whoeee!" Carl called, as he clapped out a beat.

Pointing her toe into the sand, Mavis bounced her knee to the beat. The tip of her tongue darted from between her teeth and traced the line of her mouth, her hips gyrating and thrusting to the old man's beat.

Jerome rose, his head whirling with shine, his hands about her waist, overcome by the smell of her, like the smell of wheat and earth, by her breath against his eyes, her probing tongue. Above, the moon and the stars warped through the blackness with silver tails, and behind, Carl laughed, his chest roaring as he beat the beat.

Legs folding, Jerome fell to his knees, the world spinning around him, swaying as her hips moved to the beat. With his head between her hands, she smothered him with open mouth. Jerome's heart tripped when the dress fell away to reveal the swell and ripeness of her body.

Stepping from her dress, she caught it on a toe, and pitched it onto Carl's lap, pushing Jerome to the ground.

When Jerome opened his eyes, the light shot through the willows and into his brain. His head throbbed, and his stomach twisted into a fist. His tongue was stuck to the roof of his mouth, reminiscent of an old shoe, and his heart pumped erratically in his chest. A wood tick dropped from the bark onto his ankle and paddled its way beneath his sock.

"Well there," Carl said, "if it ain't our Frenchman come back to the livin'."

Behind Carl, Mavis stood with a coffee can in her hands.

"What's going on?" Jerome asked.

Popping the lid off the can, Mavis sprinkled coffee into the boiling water and blew on the rising foam.

"Carl says strangers ain't to be trusted," Mavis said, looking up through the strands of hair that fell across her eyes. "Specially no Frenchman."

When Jerome pulled up, nausea swept through him. "Stranger?"

Stirring the coffee down, she took the pot from the fire with the tail of her dress. Carl rolled a cigarette while she poured the coffee.

"Carl says that what happened last night don't mean nothing," she said. "Carl says it's no more than havin' a fine horse to show around. What's the good of havin' a fine horse if no one don't ever see it? That's what he says," she said, holding the pot in front of her.

"I don't have anything worth stealing," Jerome said. "A little change, drawings for my buildings, nothing more."

"It ain't that we're thieves," Carl said, sucking at the hot coffee, "just folks lookin' out for themselves in a hard land. Hand me his case, Mavis."

Mavis did as she was told, keeping her eyes on Jerome the whole time.

"Leave it alone," Jerome said.

Carl smiled, dumping the contents onto the ground, rifling through the items, tossing them aside. Holding up the revolver, he turned it this way and that.

"Our Frenchman was armed, Mavis," he said, sticking it into his pocket, "just like I thought. Lucky he didn't shoot us both dead."

"My money is in the sock," Jerome said. "Take it and get out."

Opening the sock, Carl dropped the coins into his hand.

"Ain't much, is it?" he said, tucking them into his overall bib. "And what are these?"

"Just my drawings," Jerome said. "They are of no value to anyone."

"Then you won't mind if I burn 'em," he said, dropping them into the fire.

The drawings twisted in the coals and burst into flames, ashes rising into the branches of the willow tree.

"You murdering bastards!" Jerome screamed, spittle flying from his mouth.

The morning fell still. Mavis coughed, the sound like a gunshot in the quiet.

"What do you mean, *murdering*?" Carl asked.

"You think I don't know! You think I don't know what you've done to that marshal!"

When Carl flung the case at Jerome, it hit him in the chest, and he clutched it in his arms, gasping for breath. Reaching for Jerome's lip, Carl twisted it, his fingers smelling of tobacco. Water gathered in Jerome's eyes.

"What do you mean, *murdering*, you French Pox son of a bitch?"

When Carl released his hold, water dripped from Jerome's nose.

"It's you and her shot him to death and put him in the marsh," he said. "They'll be hanging you for it, and I hope to be there to watch."

"You get smart with me, Frenchy, and you won't live to breakfast, that's a promise. Now, who is *they* and how would *they* know anything one way or the other 'bout Mavis and me?"

"That girl and boy back there, the ones you sold your homestead to," Jerome said. "That's her ring right there on Mavis's finger. They found the body, recognized the marshal's hat hanging behind the door. They know it was you."

"I told you to get rid of that hat," he said, turning to Mavis, his voice flat.

"I just forgot, Carl," she said, "what with leaving so fast and all. I just forgot in the excitement."

"Now they know," he said.

The kick was fast for an old man, the toe of his boot catching her chin, rocking her with its savagery. Eyes rolling, she fell, dropping the coffee pot as blood trickled from the corner of her mouth.

Bending down, Carl cradled her head in his lap and waited as she gasped back into consciousness. Hanging her head over his knee, she spat blood into the sand.

"I'm sorry, Carl," she said. "I just forgot."

"It's the girl and the boy, then," he said to Jerome, "what know?"

"That's right," Jerome said.

"And you?"

"That's right, and they will hang the both of you for it."

"You hear that, Mavis?" Carl said, checking the cartridges in the revolver. "It's the three of 'em what knows?"

"I heard," Mavis said, tears running down her cheeks.

Jerome wondered if the tears were for him, for the suffering he bore, or for old Slow and Easy, who now stood with the pistol aimed at his chest. But it was a question unanswered as Carl pulled the trigger, and the morning exploded into blackness.

When Jerome opened an encrusted eye, he still clutched the case in his arms, a hole blown through its lid, its hinge dangling from the shot intended to take his life. Lifting onto an elbow, he touched the bruise that wrapped his chest and groaned with pain. Across the way, the campfire smoldered in the dampness of the evening, Mavis's coffee pot still lying where it had fallen. He drifted off again.

When he awoke the second time, the moon slid like a blood clot across the sky. A man in a robe knelt at Jerome's side, lifting his head to drink. There were scars about the man's arms, gouged into the flesh and sinew of his wrists.

"Who are you?" Jerome asked.

But no answer came as he moved away into the night.

C reed found Abaddon bent over his press. There was a smear of printer's ink across the end of his nose, and sweat glistened in the cup of his neck. At the back of the tent a boy rolled papers and packed them into buckets. Creed recognized him as the water peddler and new owner of his bone-handled knife.

"Morning," Creed said from the door.

When Abaddon turned, the blue of his eyes cut in the sunlight.

"That lumber delivered?" he asked, turning back to his paper.

"Most," Creed said, "except what I've promised the Liebermans."

"I need a full order," Abaddon said.

"I've telegraphed for another six cars from Kansas City."

"That's fine, and when it comes in, you can take care of the Liebermans. I need mine now, and double the order from Kansas City," he said, "and double the price, too. Do it soon, because the opportunity is now, and you're the man with the timber, aren't you?"

"I don't want to overextend," Creed said, stepping into the tent. "Lumber doesn't come cheap all the way from Kansas City."

"Double it," he said, stretching his arms over his head, rubbing the weariness from his face. "Look, there's only one way to get lumber into Guthrie station in any quantity and that's by rail."

Pulling up one of the buckets, Creed sat down. "I don't see the point."

Nodding for the boy to leave, Abaddon pulled up another of the buckets.

"It's in the interest of the railroad to have, let's say, a positive relationship with the leading paper in the Territory. That would be *The Capital City*. It's also in the interest of *The Capital City*, and of this Territory, to be supportive of such a railroad." Hooking his leg over his knee, he handed Creed a paper. "This editorial declares the gratitude of our citizenry, overcome with the generosity and service of this railroad, and promises support in every manner." A smile spread across his face. "In all their benevolence the railroad has agreed to provide the first year's seed wheat to any man willing to come pick it up, free of charge." Pausing, he turned over his ink-stained hands. "Did I mention they'll make a fortune hauling the harvest to market a year from now?"

"What does this have to do with my lumber?" Creed asked, glancing over the editorial.

Unfolding his legs, Abaddon lifted his brows. "It's the railroad keeps this town alive. A man ought know that."

"Still?" Creed said.

"The railroad can haul anyone's lumber it takes a notion to haul, wouldn't you agree?"

"Yes."

"Or not haul it, if it so desires?"

"I suppose so."

"And so whose lumber do they haul, and whose newsprint, too? Who gets it first and at the best price? That's right," he said, "*The Capital City*, that's who, me and you, Mr. McReynolds."

Creed moved to the door of the tent. He could feel Abaddon's blue eyes bearing down.

"I see," he said.

"One more thing."

"Yes?" Creed said, waiting.

"I received this notice this morning. There's a homestead up for sell. Seems the poor fellow died digging his well. Now his widow is set on going home. An enterprising man would be up there with an offer, I should think."

"Thanks," Creed said, tucking the paper into his pocket.

Turning back to his press, Abaddon said, "See to it that lumber's in place today. I've got to have more room, and I've got to have it soon."

Stepping from the tent, Creed took a deep breath. Talking to Abaddon was like teetering on the edge of a cliff.

Opening the notice, he read it over. "Homested for Sell," it said in an illegible hand, "to hiest offer, well mostly dug." At the bottom of the note was a map, section and quarter coordinates noted in the margins. As best he could make out, it was north, north even of Bear Creek, and farther out than he preferred. Still, if it was a bargain, it would be worth taking a look.

At the top of the hill, he found Roop and Jess waiting with a load of lumber. In the shade of the wagon, Flea Bag slept, legs jerking through yet another chase. Flies buzzed about the hound's ears and drank at the corners of its eyes.

Hooking a foot on the wagon wheel, Creed looked the lumber over.

"Abaddon wants his by day's end, Roop. Hire out some help if you need. Meanwhile, I'm telegraphing another order out of Kansas City."

Reaching down, Roop pulled Flea Bag's ear. "What about the Liebermans?" he asked.

"They can wait for the full order, Roop. It's doubtful they can build that fast anyway. I'll see they get first bid on the next load."

"Not up to me to tell you how to run your business," Roop said, "but it might be a fair jag between orders."

"We got to take our opportunities where we can get them. It's just the way things are out here."

"Yes, sir. Maybe you're right. Guess I've counted too many a calf to market, just to find 'em belly-up and ripen. Makes a man cautious."

Holding his back, Jess shook his head.

"I ought not be haulin' more timbers. Mr. Damon said he wanted this wagon for delivering papers."

"He wants his lumber," Creed said, "and he's a man you might not want to disappoint."

Scratching at his beard, Jess looked down the street where *The Capital City* sign hung near the entrance of Abaddon's tent.

"Well," he said, "maybe it won't take that long."

"I've got a tip on some land up north, Roop," Creed said, "and need to check it out. Think you might round up more orders while I'm gone?"

"Yes sir, I could do that, providin' there ain't no paperwork involved."

"Like tallying beef, Roop, how much and to whom."

"When will you be back?" he asked, slipping his gloves on.

"A few days. If we get a delivery, bring the first load to the Liebermans and then dole out the rest, first come, first served." As he turned to leave, he stopped. "By the way, next load's double the price, Roop, except for the Liebermans, of course."

"Double price?"

"That's right. Abaddon says the demand is there."

"Work a hardship on some folks, won't it?" he asked.

A dust devil formed in the street and wound its way down the hill like a brown rope.

"It's business," Creed said, "that's all."

At the bottom of the hill the dust devil spun off into the prairie, grass twisting into its vortex.

"Maybe so," Roop said, turning back to the lumber. "Maybe so."

Tonight, Creed determined to stay in town, leave with the dawn. A little luck and he could be home in a couple of days. For now, there was a horse to be bought, and supplies; besides, it had been awhile since he'd enjoyed real food.

The streets swarmed with people, children playing, women talking, men cursing and laughing around the blacksmith's forge. Not long ago it was the saw of the locust alone that broke the silence of this land.

The telegraph operator told him that there was a fair collection of horses "for sell" down at the stables near the marshal's tent, but that he might exercise care, seeing as how there was a crazy black man sleeping in the loft. Creed figured it was as good a place as any to get taken on a horse deal and maybe see Buck at the same time.

It was nearly dusk by the time he kicked his foot up on the railing to look over the horses. The stable boy circled them around the corral with a buggy whip.

"Scruffy lot, ain't they?" someone said from behind Creed. When he turned, Buck Reed was grinning at his shoulder.

"You sneak up on every one or just figure to scare the hell out of me?"

"It's from livin' too long in the woods, I reckon," Buck said.

"Look at you," Creed said, "badge, sidearm, and a new saddle, too."

"Yup," Buck said, hooking his thumb under his badge. "Silver. Course, it all comes out of my pay."

"I guess you're a full-fledged lawman now?"

Tying Pony to the fence rail, Buck looked the horses over.

"Sworn to uphold the law of this here Territory and shoot dead any son of a bitch, white or colored, set on breaking it. You ain't had more trouble with them timbers, have you?"

"No, sir," Creed said, turning back to the horses. "Seems you've established a fair reputation."

"That one there," Buck said, pointing to a roan mare standing with her head down in the corner. "Man needs a horse willing to think things through before she follows a crowd."

"I've seen better-looking animals, Buck."

"Yes, sir," he said.

"But if you say so."

"Yes, sir," he said.

When no further response was forthcoming, Creed motioned for the stable hand.

"How much?"

"Twenty dollars," the boy said. "Thirty, with the tack what came in on her."

"Fifteen," Buck said. "Twenty with the tack."

"You heard the man," Creed said, peeling off the bills and holding them out.

Shrugging, the boy tucked the bills in his pocket.

"You want her saddled?" he asked.

"I'll pick her up in the morning."

"What you need a horse for," Buck said, "if you don't mind me asking?"

"Checking on some land for sell up north."

Loosening the reins, Buck swung them around Pony's neck as he hooked his boot in the stirrup, arching his leg over the saddle.

"I'll be riding north come morning myself, to check on that young marshal. They ain't heard from him nor his horse since he was bringing up drag out of the Walnut Creek Encampment. Maybe we could ride out together, seeing as how I'm a deputy and all?"

"Sunrise?"

"Sunrise," he said, turning Pony's head about.

Creed checked in at the Lindel Hotel not far from the depot. Even though it was no longer a tent, it was not a building either, but a joining of the two, with porch of timbers and tarp. In the back, bunks made of cottonwood slabs and wagon-wheel spokes lined the walls. Crude as they were, they were off the ground and smelled clean.

For a quarter more, he had hot water drawn for a bath, soap, a mirror for combing his hair. The aroma of bread baking wafted from the kitchen next door. The canvas walls did little to stop the street noise, the sounds of a town newborn.

Soap bubbles popped in his ears as he eased into his bath. His eyes closed as memories swept over him: the smell of smoke and hides, the reds and yellows of a Kiowa camp, the roundness and softness of its teepees.

Surrounded here by thousands of people, he was as lonely as he'd ever been. Sometimes he felt as if he were drifting alone in a swelling sea of people. It was a feeling he'd not known as a boy. With all its affliction, there had been solace in the bosom of his mother's clan. Come what may, it came to all, a strength in the sum of the tribe.

He dreamed often of them, specters in the mist, their arms held out to him, their cries for help muted by the passage of time. But even as he reached for them, they faded and were gone.

After his bath, he dressed, balancing on first one foot and then the other against the coolness of the hard-pack floor. Holding the mirror in one hand, he combed his hair, studying his face in the light that seeped through the tent. The eyes were harder now, the lines more drawn, the jaw sharper.

Walking into the evening, he stopped at the door of the Blue Belle Saloon, filled with the laughter of women, the lantern light against the white of their skin, and the fiddler's song, sad and distant. From the Reeves Brothers, the stink of cigar wafted into the street, along with the clamor of men casting their dice. Inside, the lady in red danced alone, twirling about the floor.

But it was the smell of food from out of the double tent on the corner that caused him to enter. A cookstove squatted in the center with its smokestack rigged through a hole in the top of the tent. Wagon slats served as tables and spike kegs as chairs. A woman worked at her pan, her shoulders rounded, her arms winged and flopping as she stirred.

When she saw Creed come in, she dried her hands on a dishtowel slung over her shoulder.

"I'd ask you what you want, Mister, but we only got one thing, so do you want it or not?"

Creed pulled up a keg. "And what would that be?"

"Beef steak, white gravy, mashed taters, greens, fresh-picked, cooked in bacon grease and seasoned with vinegar, and something I ain't figured out yet, could be black pepper, could be flyspecks. There's sourdough bread, home brew, but no liquor, not up-front. It's agin Territorial law, and we abide by the law in this establishment."

"I'll have everything but the flyspecks," he said.

Wiping the sweat from under her eyes with the towel, she grinned.

"That's the best part, ain't it?"

When at last his meal arrived, Creed lifted the plate to savor the aromas. With his knife, he checked the steak, its crust and center. The mashed potatoes were puddled in butter, and the greens were bright emeralds, burnished with pepper and salt. The sourdough smelled of yeast and was still warm from the oven.

He ate like a man starved, wolfing his food, his chin shining with grease, washing the whole thing down with drafts of beer, still tepid and cheesy from the barrel. When finished, he pushed his chair back and studied his empty plate. The waitress poured him a cup of coffee and shook her head.

At the far end of the tent a man and his family came in. After placing his straw hat on the table, the man sat down, then his wife. The kids climbed onto their stools, their feet bare, their toes wiggling as they waited for the waitress. With hands folded, his wife listened as the menu was recited. Placing her fingers on her throat, she looked over at her husband.

With his coffee finished, Creed rose to leave just as the waitress arrived with their meals, greens and sourdough, and water all around. There was nothing said among them as they ate the greens, mopping their plates with the bread.

"How much?" Creed asked.

"One dollar," the waitress said.

Taking the roll of bills from his pocket, he peeled off six dollars.

"Fill out their meals," he said, "same as mine, except the beer, and the flyspecks of course. Tell them it's a house special. You keep the change."

When she took the money, her fingers lingered for a moment on his. Before she could say anything, he made his escape onto the streets of Guthrie station.

When the stableboy brought Creed's roan, she seemed a fair bargain, decked with California saddle and moss blanket. As they waited under the shade of a cottonwood for Buck, she nudged him with her nose and shook her head at his arm.

Buck arrived with a new hat, shaped and cocked against the wind.

"California," he said, pointing to Creed's saddle. "Good ride, green rawhide on the tree and a high pommel, like the Mexican."

"Yup," Creed said.

"What's her name?" Buck asked.

"Roan," Creed said.

"Good name."

"Yup," Creed said, smiling, as he mounted up.

Riding north out of Guthrie station, they were soon at the Cimarron, its bed an expanse of sand stretching a mile across. Rivulets of water no more than inches deep braided down its center. Tamarisk and sage grew from its banks, and clumps of river grass with blades like splintered glass. At the bends, or where rocks bore up from the earth, driftwood and brush gathered in stacks, deposited there by torrents of red water that rushed in during floods. Sand swept ahead of the winds, moving and circling in ever-changing patterns, rippling and waving. The smell of salt was in the air, as at the sea. A few inches below the surface of the sand, water gathered in pools, suspended there with neither top nor bottom.

"I'll walk out," Buck said, adjusting his new hat, already ringed with dust and sweat. "You bring up the horses in my tracks. Never know quicksand. First it's here and then it's there."

Making it over without incident, they led the horses up the bank, striking due north toward the border. When the blackjacks thickened, Buck and Creed walked, leading their horses through the maze of vine and thorn. By noon, the sun scorched its way overhead, and a hot wind drove at their backs. When Buck spotted shade in a canyon, they took refuge to eat.

"How much farther?" Creed asked, pulling his hat down over his face for a few moments of rest.

"Ain't that far, as the crow flies," Buck said.

"We get there today?"

Pulling his knees up, Buck located the sun's position and studied it for a moment.

"Dark," he said, "given we ain't crows."

Soon they exited the blackjacks onto a broad plain, grasses the color of salmon striking into the distance. Buck rode with his hat pulled low, his boots kicked out of the stirrups.

"Buck," Creed said, "you figuring on staying with this marshaling long? A man could get himself killed, you know, especially one who doesn't duck when the shooting starts."

Pushing his hat up, Buck said, "No, sir. If I'd wanted to chase people all over the prairie with a rifle the rest of my life, I could have stayed in the cavalry."

"What will you do, then?"

"Some folks from the Oklahoma Negro colony has started up a settlement east of Guthrie station. Oh, it ain't much right yet, a few soddies, a garden, but it ain't just a colored section what been pinched off a white town. No, sir. It's a place all its own, struck up by its own, where folks like me can make it rich or starve, any way they's see fit. It's a place of hope springing up right out there in that prairie. Maybe someday I can be part of that."

Kicking his leg over the saddle horn, Creed said, "My mother came through this country in thirty-four, with the Dragoons out of Fort Gibson. She had been captured, and they were taking her back to the Kiowa in hopes of appeasing them, of stopping the depredations."

"It's a far trip you've made from there, ain't it?" he said.

"I was but a child when she died. Her burial scaffold's out there somewhere."

"You remember her, then?"

"I remember her voice, and the black of her eyes, and the way she danced with her shoulders squared. I remember the bone whistle she made for me, and the smell of juniper in her hair. I remember all of those things, but I don't remember where she's buried."

"Memories ain't in a place," Buck said.

"It's just as well to forget," Creed said.

Pulling up, Buck looked out from under his hat. "No, sir," he said, "meaning no disrespect, but a man don't never forget who he is, no matter how much he wants. It's the one thing in life that don't never change."

Taking off his hat, Creed worked at its brim for a moment. "The world doesn't stand still for the way things were, Buck."

"Yes, sir, I can see what you got in mind. Just one thing," he said, turning Pony's head about.

"What's that?"

"Don't never sit in the quiet of your own thoughts, 'cause it's in there just like always, just waitin'."

The soddy was nestled at the bottom of a rise. A lantern flickered from the doorway, and the smell of smoke drifted on the wind.

"I've seen badger holes built better than that soddy," Buck said.

"Look at the sway of that chimney,'" Creed said.

"Now what?" Buck asked.

"Call out, I guess. She's got to be expecting someone sooner or later."

Cupping his hands about his mouth, Buck shouted, "Hellooo, anybody home?"

There was silence as they turned their ears into the wind.

"Maybe she's just scared," Creed said.

"Hellooo," Buck called again.

Even as he did, a bullet slammed into the sandstone just inches from where Creed stood, whining off into the distance.

Creed hit the ground rolling, coming up behind a fallen tree. When he dared look up, Buck was walking toward the cabin, Pony's reins over his shoulder. Bringing his rifle about, Creed took aim just as another round was fired off, its flame spitting from the darkness of the cabin.

Buck's new hat lifted from his head and dipped its way to the ground.

"Excuse me, ma'am," Buck said, hooking his thumb under his badge. "I'm a deputy marshal, and back there is my friend. He's here answering that sale bill you got out."

An old woman stepped from the soddy, her rifle leveled at Buck's chest.

"I ain't heard of no colored deputy before," she said.

"Yup," he said.

Pushing the hair from her eyes, she peered into the darkness.

"Tell your friend to come on out where I can see him."

Rising from behind the tree, Creed held his hands up for her to see.

"You colored, too?" she asked. "The whole guvment colored now? Wouldn't surprise me none, would it."

"I got your sale notice right here," Creed said, holding it up for her to see. "Might want to buy this place if you don't shoot us first."

"You come on up," she said, lowering her rifle.

Both Creed and Buck ducked low under the door as they followed her into the soddy. It was a dark room, dank with moisture from the earth, and the stink of bacon grease hung in the air. Without a foundation, the soddy had shifted, and the walls now leaned inward, the roof sagging so low that Buck had to slump his shoulders so as not to bump his head.

Turning up the lantern, the old woman placed it on a cottonwood stump that served as both table and kitchen work area. The lantern light struggled against the darkness, their shadows dancing up the walls. Hacking and wheezing into her apron, she made her way to the chair.

"Sit," she said, pointing to a bench next to the fireplace.

"Sorry to give you a start, ma'am," Creed said, "coming up on you in the dark like that."

"Thought it was one of them black bears," she said, pointing over at Buck. "Biggest one I ever saw, too. Last one come up from the creek bottom near tore my door off."

"That's Buck Reed, ma'am," Creed said. "New deputy marshal of Guthrie station."

"Ain't afraid of much, are you, Deputy?"

"No, ma'am," Buck said, hooking his new hat over his knee.

A breeze swept through the open door. The lantern flame lifted off its wick before settling back down.

"Got some cornbread," she said, "and some honey, too. Ran out of coffee and shine a week ago."

"Thanks anyway," Creed said, "but I'm here in response to this bill of sale you placed in *The Capital City* paper. It's my understanding that you are interested in selling your homestead."

"An old woman like me can't keep a place on her own, can't cut wood for heat, can't plant no crop, can't shoot neither, as you well know."

"How much are you asking?"

"It's a fair quarter," she said, looking over at Buck, "with forty acres broke out. There's a butchering hog free-ranging off acorns in them trees, a grasshopper plow for making up sod, and a well near dug. I need the team and wagon to get back home, Lord willing."

Standing, she walked to the door and looked out. From where Creed sat, he could see the bend of her legs and the beginnings of a dowager hump.

"I've a hundred dollars," Creed said, "for investing. I know it's worth more, but that's what I have."

"Henry died digging the well," she said. "Near to the bottom he was when he grabbed his chest and called out my name. 'Pauline,' he said, just like that, like he'd done a thousand times before, but I knew something bad was wrong.

"Well, I couldn't get to him. Arthritis," she added, rubbing at her knee.

"What did you do?" Creed asked.

"I just stood there at the top of that well and watched him die," she said. "Blue as my hat and his tongue swoll near out of his head. Onct I thought I heard him say something, but then I couldn't be sure. Don't matter, I suppose."

Taking up her chair again, she pushed the gray strands of hair from her eyes.

"Took me half a day to get a rope on him and pull him out with the horse, and another half to bury him yonder in them trees."

"I'm sorry you had to do that alone," Creed said.

"I was wore out, you see, and didn't get him covered good. That butchering hog rooted him right out of the ground. Found his hat blowed up against the door next morning. Wasn't nothing left to do but start over again."

Buck stood, sticking his hands in his pockets.

"I'll be making up camp back there in them trees," he said to Creed. "Give a whistle when you come in so's I'll know it's you."

"Sorry 'bout takin' that pot shot," the old lady said, looking up at Buck.

"Don't think nothing of it, ma'am," he said.

With Buck gone, Creed waited for her to speak. When she didn't, he said, "I know it's hard to talk business when you've just lost your husband, but if you still want to sell, I have the hundred dollars. It should be enough for you to start over."

"It's home where I want to be buried, Mister. I don't think I could stand it here no more, the wind howling night and day, crying out over my grave. No, sir, I'm going back to Carolina and stretch out under one of them pines. I told Henry from the start we had no business coming out here. We was too old, too tired to be taking it on, but he wouldn't hear otherwise."

"We can do this another time," he said.

"When you get old, it ain't property what matters, Mister, or a hundred dollars either. Things like that don't warm your feet at night or fill the emptiness inside you. When life goes wrong, and it most surely does, none of it matters a whit. It's those who shore you up and hold you close. It's the smell of pine trees early in the morning dew."

"I can see you're still grieving for your man," he said. "I'll come back another day."

"I can't bring my man back, can I, not tomorrow, or the next, or the next after that. There ain't no more left for me. Them papers are up there behind the chimney. Fetch them here for me to sign. I'll be out in a day or so."

After whistling at the edge of the trees, Creed followed the light of Buck's fire. There was the smell of bacon and coffee.

"There's a can of pears in that saddlebag," Creed said. "Thought the old lady might enjoy them, if you don't mind."

Taking the can of pears out, Buck tossed it to him and turned back to his bacon.

When Creed returned, supper was cooked, and they ate in silence. The light from the nearby soddy soon went out, and there was but the whisper of the trees in the evening.

Just as they were about to turn in, Buck held up his hand, motioning to Creed that something was out there. Reaching for his rifle, Creed stepped into the shadows. Buck waited at the fire, his rifle across his lap. Creed started a slow circle about the camp.

When the moon broke from behind a cloud, he spotted the figure hiding in the brush, his legs pulled into his arms, his head down.

"Step into the light," Creed ordered.

"Don't shoot," the man said. "I'm unarmed."

"We're coming out," Creed called to Buck.

Taking off the man's hat, Buck pitched it onto the ground.

"What you sneakin' about in the dark for?"

"My name's Jerome Bouchard," the man said. "I was on my way to Guthrie station when I was attacked. I thought I'd come up on them again."

Buck searched his pockets.

"He ain't armed. You don't sound like no farmer, Mister."

The man held his chest, and his mouth was split and swollen.

"Where are you from?" Creed asked.

"France," he said. "I'm on my way to Guthrie station. Hadn't planned on being killed just getting there."

"This is Deputy Buck Reed. I'm Creed McReynolds."

"Good way to get shot," Buck said, handing him a cup of coffee.

Rubbing at his chest, Jerome nodded, "Thanks. I should have called out, I know."

"Let's hear it," Buck said. "All of it."

And so Jerome told them of his encounter with Alida and Bram, of what they'd said about the young marshal buried at the spring. He told them of Carl and Mavis and of the hat behind the dugout door. After another sip of the coffee, he told them of the ambush, of Carl's sudden attack, and of the drawings now burned and gone forever. And finally, he told them how he'd been tied to the tree, and how in a moment of anger he'd spilled everything.

"Carl shot me pointblank and left me for dead. Hadn't been for my case stopping the bullet, I wouldn't be alive right now."

"No doubt they're headed back," Creed said, "to finish the job with that boy and girl."

Jerome nodded. "Yes. When I came to, someone was leaning over me, giving me water. He was wearing a robe, and there were scars about his wrist."

Untying his bedroll from his saddle, Buck tucked it under his arm, turning to Jerome.

"What business do you have in Guthrie station, Mr. Bouchard?" Creed asked.

"I'm an architect. I was going there to build my buildings, to grow with the city. But, they burned my drawings, all I had, and for no reason. Now, I don't know. Problem is," he said, taking another drink of his coffee, "there's less behind than there is ahead."

"It's a fair ride north I've got," Buck said, heading off into the darkness. "I'll see you men in the morning."

"Look," Creed said, "there's an old lady up there in that soddy with a wagon and team. She'll be heading to Guthrie station soon. Help her load out, and I'm certain she'll be happy to give you a ride."

"Thanks," Jerome said.

Picking up his bedding, Creed turned, "Is there anything else, Mr. Bouchard, anything else you need to tell us?"

"No," he said.

"Look, the Territory can be a hard land, and she's a stranger to beauty, and to those who make it. Maybe you need to reconsider. Good night, Mr. Bouchard, and best of luck."

The ground was hard beneath Jerome as he tried to sleep. For a moment he thought he heard Carl's laughter from out on the prairie. Turning over, he watched the embers flutter beneath the ash.

He'd told them everything, just as he said, except of Mavis, of her smell like wheat in the heat of the day, and of her dance under the blood-red moon.

When Creed awoke, Buck was saddling Pony, the stirrup tossed over the saddle seat, his hat hanging from the horn. Lifting with his legs, he tightened the cinch, and Pony snorted.

Bones aching, Creed tossed his blanket aside. "Morning," he said, running his hand through his hair, searching for his hat.

"Morning," Buck said, tying the cinch off. "Didn't mean to wake you. Pony here don't take to the cinch without complaint."

Donning his hat, Creed located his boots, knocking them against his hand to dislodge any stray scorpions.

"I'll get the coffee started."

"Need to be on my way," Buck said. "It's a fair ride out, and there could be some trouble."

"I'll saddle up," Creed said.

Pulling the stirrup down, Buck hooked the toe of his boot in and lifted into the saddle. Taking his hat from the horn, he checked the hole in the brim with his finger.

"Enjoyed the ride, Creed, but it's me getting paid for deputy work here."

Slipping the bit into Roan's mouth, Creed worked her ears under the bridle. Bringing her about, he tossed the moss blanket onto her back.

"I'm going along, either with you or behind you, Buck."

"That a fact?"

"Yup," he said, lifting the saddle onto her back.

Leaning on the saddle horn, Buck looked down at Creed.

"And who's going keep that Frenchman out of trouble?"

"Same one who shot that hole in your new hat," Creed said, mounting up. "What's it going to be, Buck?"

"Suit yourself," he said, bringing his heels into Pony's sides. "Don't want no breed trailin' me all day. Won't know if I'm goin' to get scalped by an Indian or hanged by a white man, will I?"

As they rode past the soddy, smoke twisted from the chimney and into the bright morning sun. A white hog grunted at the edge of the walnut trees, dirt stacked on the tip of his snout. It watched them pass before turning back to rooting.

By midmorning the smell of dust and sunflower was in the heat. Vultures ascended in the columns of heated air, spiraling into the heavens to circle and wait. A lizard scurried from out of nowhere, its tail whipping from side to side as it disappeared into the rocks.

Ahead, Pony set a slow but steady gait. Buck rode with his hat cocked, and his shoulders drawn against the heat of the day. Dust gathered in the wet of his shirt and in the crease of his neck. When at last they hit the open grade of the railroad right of way, they dismounted and drank from their canteens.

At noon they cut west to a stand of trees to garner shade while they ate their lunch. A stream twisted through the willows, minnows as clear as glass schooling and darting over the ripples of sand. After eating cold meat and bread, they took a moment for rest. Buck dozed under his hat. Pulling off his boots, Creed stuck his foot into the stream, his toes curling against the cold.

"A man comes all the way from France," he said, "to a land such as this, a man of refinement and culture, a man given to grand design and beauty. You have to wonder, don't you, Buck? What is it that brings them?"

"It's a fair land," he said, rolling onto his side. "A beginning, and an end, alpha and omega like the Bible says. It's a place where anything can happen, like a colored man wearing this here badge, for instance."

"It's a mix to behold," Creed said, slipping on his socks. "That's for sure."

"Course," Buck said, pulling himself up, "it could be the end of things, too, 'cause if it don't work here, it ain't never goin' to work nowhere."

"It's a last stand for many," Creed said, "and when a man's whole life is at stake, he can be dangerous and unpredictable."

Buck fell silent, peering into the trees where the sun sprinkled through the shadow of the leaves. Making his way over, he picked something up.

"What is it?" Creed asked.

"Looks like we found our Frenchman's camp," he said, holding up the damaged case. "There's wagon tracks, too, leading in here and then out again. They've doubled back, sure enough," he said, kicking at an empty whiskey jug that lay in the grass.

Pulling on his boots, Creed walked the perimeter of the camp.

"There's a set of tracks here," he said, "leading in from the trees and then back out that way."

Dropping to his knee, Buck examined the tracks.

"Weren't boots," he said, drawing a circle around the footprint with his finger. "No heel, flat like a moccasin or sandal. Must be the visitor that gave our Frenchman a drink."

Gathering up Roan, Creed led her to the creek to let her drink a last time. The water dribbled from around her bit.

"What do we do from here?" Creed asked.

"It ain't *we* no more," Buck said, mounting Pony, who pranced in a circle, tossing his head against the rein.

"What do you mean?"

"You ain't going on, Creed."

"I can't let you walk in there alone."

"This here is my business," he said, pointing to his badge. "It's my job. You get hurt or kilt goin' in there, then I ain't done my job, you see."

"I'm just supposed to wait here, then, while you make your arrest? That doesn't seem too smart to me, Buck."

"It ain't up to you," he said. "This here badge is mine. You follow me, and I'll put you under arrest, handcuff you to a tree if it comes to it. Now, you can go on back to Guthrie station or stay put here, don't matter none to me."

"You don't leave me much choice."

"No, sir."

"I'll wait here," he said. "When will you be back?"

"When it's done," Buck said, mounting up, spurring Pony away into a slow gallop.

Lying on his back under the willows, Creed tried to sleep, but the silence bore in. When the train whistle sounded in the distance, it was like a friend come visiting, and he stood on his toes to catch a glimpse as it thundered by. Behind him, Roan stamped a foot against heel flies and jangled her bit with a shake of her head.

From where he lay, the footprints were distinct in the sand. Whoever had visited Bouchard had given little thought to the scent they'd left behind.

Untying Roan, he followed the tracks along the creek bed, but at the bend they led off into the prairie. When the terrain turned rugged, he dismounted, leading Roan into a labyrinth of rock and canyons. Sweat soaked his shirt and raced from his brows into his eyes.

Stopping in the shade of a hackberry, he took off his boot and examined a blister that had formed on his heel. Impatient, Roan dropped her head and blew puffs of dust from the path, her ears swiveling about like a praying mantis. On foot, the ascent had been imperceptible, but now the prairie stretched out below. In the distance, a rock outcrop rose into the haze.

Taking up Roan's reins, he scratched her between the ears.

"We're going on, girl, until those tracks disappear or my heel falls off, whichever comes first."

Fluted columns of stone towered above him, and canyons yawned. Cedar trees shot from the crevices, green splashes of color in the dusk.

"The tracks stop here, girl," he said to Roan, tying her in the shade of a cedar. "I'll be back before dark."

A path, though faint, wound with purpose through the maze of stone. Heat bled from the rock into the cool of evening. High above, the rock face was fractured, a rift penetrating into the heart of the monolith. As evening fell, the last of the day's wind swept from the summit and howled through the canyons. Wrapping his arms about himself, he shivered, somehow certain that down there in the dark belly of the mountain were the footprints that he sought.

As he climbed higher, he checked each foothold against a fall. All about were slabs of stone, broken and jumbled by some momentous force. A draught rose from the depths of the rift, dank and stale, its smell pooling at the mouth of the cavern.

Perhaps it was the symmetry that caught his eye, the graceful dimensions of a cross carved in the face of the stone. The path was worn smooth beneath it, but without a torch, he dared not enter.

With darkness falling, he went back down the mountain, unsaddled Roan, and with a bread knife from his saddlebag cut the moss blanket into strips, knotting them onto cedar sticks. Tucking the knife into his belt, he made the climb back to the rift. If all else failed, he could cut kerosene weed for a bright, if brief, fire.

Within the hour he stood once more at the mouth of the rift, but the torch, saturated with salt and horse sweat, refused to light. After several tries, a flame sputtered into life, and the boundaries of the cavern pressed in about him.

As he worked his way down, the flame smoldered in the stillness. At first he thought it no more than his light refracted in the quartz of the sandstone. But then he saw them perched on the ledge—hundreds of rats, their red eyes, their twitching whiskers and bobbing heads. When he thrust forward his torch, the rodents scrambled into the protection of the deep.

Shuddering, Creed held the torch high, turning in a circle. In the center of the chamber was a mound of rat bones, and against the wall was a crucifix, carved of cedar and reaching to the ceiling. With face anguished and eyes cast down, the crucified Christ watched over this dark domain.

On the other side, ashes were banked up the cavern wall, from a hundred fires, from a thousand fires, built, no doubt, against the rats that waited from the ledge. Lye oozed from the ash and pooled at the base of the crucifix. A robe lay on the floor, as if dropped in haste. When Creed pulled aside the hood, empty eyes stared back.

A leg jutted from beneath the robe, the bone splintered, the sandal strap gnawed away. Creed's torch quivered from the draught below, carrying the dank and cold of the grave. Without a constant fire, there would have been naught but darkness, and the churn and squeak from the deep.

At the mouth of the cave, his torch sputtered in the rush of air. Holding it high, he chanced a look back, at the grotto and tomb, at the gathering red eyes below.

Roan stamped her foot when she heard Creed coming. In need of life, he pulled her against him for a moment, rubbing her nose and where her ears joined her skull.

Mounting up, he rode into the night. When the rift was distant, he drew up, overcome by a weariness like death itself, and he could not go on. After hobbling Roan, he fell to the earth, curling in the grass, his strength gone, bled away in the rift. He longed for the sweetness of sleep, and when it came, it was as a kiss riding in on the breeze.

When he awoke, Roan was munching a milkweed, watching him from behind a plum bush. Up there somewhere, the rift was but a shadow now, harmless in the dawn light.

As he saddled Roan, Creed debated his options: go back to Guthrie station, return to the camp, or find the dugout. The camp was out, since there was no way of knowing if Buck had already gone. But then Buck had made it clear that he wanted no interference. Any way he went, there was a good chance of doing the wrong thing.

Without the moss blanket, the saddle twisted sideways as he mounted. His boot caught in the cup of the stirrup, and that caused Roan to dance in a circle.

"Whoa! Whoa!" he shouted as Roan dragged him about, his weight spooking her yet more.

When at last his heel dislodged, he pitched backward into the dirt. Stretching out her neck, Roan sniffed at his sleeve. Cursing, Creed dusted off his britches, tightened the cinch, and swung into the saddle.

"Okay, girl," he said, patting her neck. "Let's find that dugout."

Uncertain which way to go, he turned down the path that wound into the tumble of rocks. The trail soon steepened, and he had to dismount. When a stirrup snagged on the wall of a narrow passage that led through a rock slide, Roan shied, then lunged ahead. "Whoa, whoa," he shouted, clinging to a single rein as she pitched her head, her front feet dancing. Talking her down, he rubbed her nose, and then tied the stirrups together over the top of the saddle. With that accomplished, they squeezed through the opening and down the path.

Even before he saw it, the smell of smoke caused him to rein up. Tying Roan in the shade of a cedar, he waited for her to discover the thistle sprouting from the crevices. Circling the smoke, he came upon a ledge that opened onto the valley below. Lying on his stomach, he worked his way to the edge. Below was the dugout, little more than a coyote den hacked from the rock. A fire still smoldered, but the camp was empty.

"Stand up," someone said from behind.

Lifting his hands, Creed stared into the rifle bore, big as a cannon and just inches from his face. Old eyes glared from under a sweep of brows at the other end of the rifle. A cigarette dangled from the old codger's lip, and a stub pencil with pinched eraser poked from his overall bib. There was the smell of stale and whiskey about him.

"Horse thief," he said.

"No, sir," Creed said.

"Breed, ain't you?"

"Yes, sir."

"Stealing horses to you is like breathing to a white man, ain't it?"

"I don't steal horses, Mister. I buy up homesteads from those who had enough of starving. By the looks of these rocks, that might be you."

"That a fact?" he said, leveling the rifle. "And you ain't come for that colored deputy, I reckon?"

"Never heard of a colored deputy before," Creed said.

"Get your horse up, and I'll show you one," he said, pointing his rifle down the trail.

When they got to the edge of the clearing, the old man put his hand on Creed's shoulder, moving him into the line of fire.

"Mavis?" he called out. When she didn't answer, he called again. "Mavis, goddang it, answer up."

"That you, Carl?" she called back from the dugout.

"No, it's the goddang king of England."

"Who you got caught up, Carl?"

"Horse thief," he said, "from up on the ridge."

Stepping from the dugout, she looked Creed over. Her hair was a tangle about her shoulders, and the top buttons of her cotton dress were undone.

"He a Indian deputy?" she asked.

"Says he's buying up starved-out homesteaders, and he ain't heard of no colored deputy before."

"He's kind of cute, ain't he," she said, pushing her hair back from her face.

"We ain't got time for dallying," Carl said, taking out his tobacco. "It's a clean sweep we got to make and get on our way."

"As cute as Bram," she said, moving in close to Creed, her breasts brushing his arm.

Striking his match, Carl let it burn before touching off his cigarette.

"Womanly, ain't she?" he said, blowing out the match, leaving sulfur in the air.

"Hadn't noticed," Creed said.

Looking up through his brows, Carl smiled and drew down on his cigarette, its end fluttering away.

"Never knowed a man not to notice Mavis," he said. "Even that colored deputy noticed Mavis."

Folding her hands over the mound of her stomach, Mavis looked over at the dugout.

"Never knowed a man wasn't afraid of getting kilt, like that deputy, neither," she said.

With a pull from his cigarette, Carl studied its end.

"Maybe breeds have the man took out of 'em, Mavis, like steers thinkin' on grass and eatin' all the time, what with their balls in a bucket."

"He's real cute, though, Carl."

"Mavis gets a heat up real fast," Carl said.

Leaning forward, Mavis laughed, a tinkling from somewhere deep within her. Sweat glistened between her breasts and in the sassy hair of her brown neck.

"What have you done with that deputy?" Creed asked.

"Bring 'em up, Mavis," Carl said, "the Deventers, too. We got business at the spring 'fore it gets hot."

Buck's hands were bound together with a saddle cinch. Behind him, a young man and girl followed, neither looking at nor acknowledging Creed. Not until they'd reached the top did Creed see the rope that bound them together and the dark bruise under the boy's eye.

"Buck?" Creed whispered, falling in beside him.

"Reckon you just had to follow," Buck said.

"Afraid so."

"Some kind of warrior you turned out," Buck said, his smile pulling crooked across his face.

"It's the white half lost me," Creed said, "and the Indian half's getting me killed."

Opening his hands, Buck showed him the cinch.

"Never thought I'd want to be back at Horseshoe Bottom," he said.

When the young girl's eyes lifted, Creed smiled at her. They were the color of sapphire and filled with dread.

"You first," Carl said to Creed, pointing his rifle toward the path, "and keep an eye out for them hoopers, thicker than grasshoppers, ain't they, Mavis."

The fragrance of cedar rose from the canyon as they followed the trail down the hill. Carl labored behind Creed, his lungs rattling, his rifled trained on Creed's back.

Buck walked behind the boy and the girl, Mavis behind him with Buck's own rifle slung across her arm. When Creed smelled the dampness from the spring below, he knew the time was short. If there was to be a chance, he must strike before they got to the spring, and he touched the stub knife still tucked beneath his shirt.

"Slow down, goddang it," Carl said from behind, just as the trail looped down and under a muscadine tangle.

Drawing the knife, Creed stepped aside, its handle cold as death in his hand. When Carl stooped in, his head was down, his rifle was lowered, and his eyes were on the path. Bringing the knife about, Creed drove it into Carl's chest. But the pencil in his overall's bib deflected the thrust, and Creed dropped the knife. Carl grunted, stumbling back from the blow, his rifle clattering into the rocks. Mavis was but moments behind, this Creed knew, and he prayed for strength and a few seconds more.

When the wide-eyed girl saw what happened, she muffled a scream with her hand.

"Get down, get down!" Creed shouted, knowing too well that the time had come, that Mavis was only a few steps behind. Buck stepped in, pushing himself against the rock wall, raising his hands above his head. Creed struggled to retrieve the knife, but it was too late, an explosion from Mavis's rifle blowing away the silence and what little hope remained. A white-hot pain shot through Creed's arm and pooled in his stomach.

Dropping at Mavis's feet, he braced himself for the finish, for the dispatching shot. Dust spun into his face and into the wet of his nose as he prepared to die. But just as Mavis aimed her weapon once more, Buck growled from behind, a sound both primeval and unnerving. With wrists still cinched, he grabbed her head in his huge hands, snapping her neck, the sound like a rifle shot in the canyon. Mavis crumpled across Creed's legs, her eyes open and unseeing. Spinning about, Buck then caught Carl under the chin with his boot, sending him sprawling into the rocks.

"Cut me loose, " Buck said, offering his hands to the boy. "Feel like Pony, all cinched up and ready to ride." Leaning over Creed, he asked, "How you doing?"

"Thought maybe you'd gone back to Horseshoe Bottom to reenlist," Creed said, gritting his teeth against the mounting pain.

"No, sir. Just waitin' to see if you was going to stop that old man or walk to your own funeral," he said, smiling.

Placing his hand over Creed's wound, Buck pushed down hard to stop the bleeding, and Creed's mouth went hot.

"What's your name?" Buck asked the young man who still hadn't moved.

"Bram Deventer," he said, his voice breaking. "This is my sister, Alida."

"Proud to meet you," Buck said. "I'm Deputy Marshal Buck Reed, come to fetch that deputy these two kilt. Guess you know where he's restin'?"

"Yes, sir, given as how we put him there. It's no more than a hundred yards into them trees."

"Alida, come here, sister," Buck said. "Think you could patch this breed up, tie off that bleed? Looks like the bone's busted up some, too."

"I think so," she said, looking down at Creed.

"Well, that's fine then. Can you walk, Creed?"

"Yes," he said, "but running's out of the question."

"Well, walkin' will do, won't it. Got a wagon and team I could borrow?"

"Carl and Mavis got the best wagon," Bram said, "team, too."

"Help me cinch ole Carl here up. You see him back to the dugout. We'll come back with a shovel for the deputy. I'll tote this Mavis girl back myself."

"Just a second," Alida said. "That ring on her finger is mine."

As soon as they'd disappeared around the bend, Alida set to work on Creed, slitting his sleeve with the knife, looking away to catch her breath.

"It's not so bad as it looks," Creed said.

Wrapping the sleeve tailing about his arm, she tightened it down against the flow of blood.

"There," she said, leaning back on her heels. "We're lucky. The bullet's passed through. That will do until we get you back to the dugout. I've sheets there for bandages and kerosene for soaking. Give me your arm, and I'll help you stand."

There was the smell of soap about her as he slipped his arm over her shoulder, and the world tilted under him.

"Whoa," he said, leaning into her.

"Take your time," she said, slipping her hand into his.

By the time they reached the dugout, sweat trickled down Creed's neck, and his legs trembled under him.

"Lost more blood than I thought," he said.

"Lie on the bed," she said, her voice hollow in the confines of the dugout.

Propping himself against the wall, Creed took a boot off, dropping it to the floor. "Have my boots on," he cautioned, mopping at his forehead, "and I'm covered in blood."

"It'll wash," she said.

Too weak to argue, he eased onto the bed as she guided him into the coolness of her pillow. Neither the blue of her eyes nor the throb of his wound could ward off the weariness that swept him.

Once, he awoke as she worked over him, her hair soft against his shoulder, her throat white in the lantern light. When he awoke a second time, the room was dark, save for a sliver of moonlight that spilled across the floor.

"Where's Buck?" he asked.

"They've gone with the wagon," she said from the darkness. "You sleep."

Closing his eyes, he did as she said, because at that moment the world out there was no place to be.

Without the burn of his heel blister, Creed might have tolerated the pain of his wound, but now it was more than he could bear. Sitting up, he rocked against its throb. Perhaps if the girl would awaken, or if daylight would come, there would be a reprieve.

"Miss?" he whispered into the blackness of the dugout. "Miss, are you still here?" His voice fell weak, and there was the smell of blood still about him. "Miss?" he called again.

"I'm here," she answered.

"Is it morning?"

"Soon," she said. "Try to sleep."

And so he did, moving into the ebb and flow of his pain.

When he awoke again, light filled the room, not with relief as he'd hoped, but with shards of glass.

How many hours or days he lay, he didn't know, stretched on the cycle of pain, disappointment of dawn, and yet more pain.

"Here," she said, cradling his head. "Drink this. It's tea and nearly the last for a while."

Opening his eyes, Creed waited for the pain, the nausea that he had come to expect, but felt weakness instead, the tremble of his muscles.

"How long?" he asked.

"Three days," she said. "There was a fever."

"Buck has come?"

"No," she said. "Bram is bringing Carl's wagon and team back from Guthrie station. Deputy Reed said it was ours, given the misery they put us through. Your horse is hobbled in the bottom when you're up to it."

Pulling himself up, Creed leaned against the coolness of the wall, taking in the room: a chair for sitting, a trunk pushed into the corner, a stack of books on its top, the deputy's hat still hanging behind the door.

"I must look for the worse," he said, running his fingers through his hair.

"Once I thought to put you in Bram's clothes," she said, lowering her eyes, "but each time you cried out."

Rubbing at the stubble on his chin, he worked at a smile. Having forgotten her features, he searched her face. A sadness registered in the turn of her mouth when she smiled at him.

"I can't remember your name," he said.

"Alida."

"Alida. Alida, I think I owe you my life."

Without answering; she rose to check the bandage as so often before, and again his hand turned in her own.

"We'd be at the spring by now, like that young deputy, if not for you," she said.

"I'm sure you didn't intend on a house guest for so long," he said, sampling her eyes. "My name's Creed."

"Yes, Buck told me."

"I've been in these clothes longer than I'd care to think. Suppose I go down to that spring for a bath?"

Standing, she cocked her hand on her waist, considering the particular ignorance of men.

"I should think not. It's a long walk to begin with and icy water when you get there. I'll not be responsible for pneumonia."

Edging his legs over the side of the bed, he sat for a moment, waiting for the spin in his head to subside.

"I don't mean to be unreasonable, but I've been in these clothes long as I can stand."

"We'll fix you a tub bath then," she said, whirling the tail of her skirt about, "but don't blame me if you drown on your own."

"The clothes, too, if you think Bram wouldn't mind," he said, picking at the shredded sleeve. "There's little enough left of these."

Setting the books aside with care, she opened the trunk. The cut of her waist was small, to fit in a man's arms with room to spare. Even though her clothes were simple and plain, she wore them with grace, the curve of her thighs like wind-whipped drifts.

"They're not much," she said, handing him the trousers and shirt, "but they're clean. I'll get the tub. The water will have to be heated outside. Carl and Mavis took the cookstove, Lord knows why, heavy as it was. It wasn't in their wagon when they came back—sold, I guess, or thrown overboard." Stepping to the door, she propped her hand on her knee and looked up into the day. "Could've used that stove. It was part of our bargain you know, least that's what they said."

The wind stirred the gold in her hair. She was no more than a girl, now that he could see.

"A dangerous pair," he said, "and with me such a bother."

Standing on her toes, she listened. "I can hear the train," she said, "like a bit of the city. It's a welcome answer to the wind out here on this mountain." Leaning against the doorway, she waited for it to pass into the distance. "I can't believe she's dead, you know. She didn't seem much older than me in a way."

"Buck had little choice," he said, "with her armed. She would've killed us all."

"Yes," she said. "I'll get that tub."

In short order the crackle of the fire filled the quiet, and the smell of wood smoke settled into the cool of the dugout. While he waited, he worked at his socks, removing each with the deliberation of a one-armed man. By the time he'd made it to his shirt, Alida came down the steps with the washtub in tow.

"It's not much of a tub," she said, setting it on the floor, "but it holds water, long enough for a bath, anyway."

"It will do fine," he said, steadying himself against the wall of the dugout.

"Let me help with the shirt," she said.

"I can manage."

"I've been taking care of your needs for several days now, Creed, so it's a little late for modesty; besides, my father lost an arm in the steel mills. Getting in and out of his shirt was one of the hardest things, he always said."

Dropping his arms, he shrugged, "Makes me feel a boy again."

"Men are forever boys," she said, smiling, her fingers turning the buttons through their holes. "Least that's what Mavis said. There, pull your good arm through first. That's it. Now the other. I'll get the water and a towel. You'll have to do the rest yourself."

Shivering in the cool of the dugout, he waited as she carried the hot water down, poured it into the tub, handed him a cake of soap. A strand of hair fell across her eye, and she brushed it aside with the back of her hand.

"It's lye soap for clothes, but it's all we have."

"It will do."

"You call when you're ready," she said, turning. "I'm fixing the last cup of tea at the fire."

Each time he bent to pull off his britches, his head went awhirl. Standing on the cuffs of his pants, he worked them off leg at a time. For a moment, the pain returned, swelling from his memory. Maybe Alida had been right about it being too soon.

Dragging the chair to the tub, he eased himself down. The lye soap clabbered in the hardness of the water and gathered white on the sides of the tub. An hour passed before he'd finished, causing Alida to call to him.

When finished, he lay down on the bed to gather his strength, to rest for a moment, but the moment passed into sleep, sweet sleep absent of pain.

He awoke to an itch tingling somewhere beneath his bandage and worked a finger under in a search of its source.

"Stop that," Alida said, sitting up from her pallet, straightening her dress. "You'll cause an infection."

"Itches," he said, "till I can't stand it."

"What do you expect?"

"Expect to scratch it," he said, swinging his legs over the side of the bed. "God made itches to be scratched, or they wouldn't itch in the first place."

Folding up her blanket, she tucked it away in the trunk.

"Scratching an itch shows lack of character, maybe even sinful."

"Nothing wrong with my character, but my stomach sure is empty."

"I'll gather wood," she said, straightening the blanket on his bed, "and fix something to eat."

"I'll gather the wood," he said. "No arguments."

"I don't have the wherewithal to get you back if you fall out or get bit by hoopers."

"Hoopers, is it," he said, laughing, reaching for his hat.

Filling his lungs with fresh air, he held his face to the sun. In the light, he could see the blue of his hand and the swelling under his arm. He worked his fingers back and forth and donned his hat.

A wind swept in from the southwest, dust lifting in its wake, as he walked down the path. Blackjack roots, washed from the soil, clung to the rocks like claws, and the smell of juniper drifted down from the rift.

Coon and opossum tracks led from the spring, and rabbit droppings were scattered among the rocks.

Small game was food of last resort for the Kiowa, for when the buffalo failed. Now the buffalo were gone, as certainly as the Kiowa ways. Maybe it was the breed in him, but right now fried rabbit sounded pretty good.

Below the locust grove, he found the horses grazing on the shoots of grass that sprang from the rocks, their tails whipping in unison against heel flies. Roan spotted him from a distance, but turned to graze with her friends.

When he got back, the fire was built, and Alida had finished in the dugout, joining him outside. There was a touch of rouge on her cheeks, and her hair was tied back with a bandanna, a splash of red against the white of her skin.

"I could do with some coffee," he said. "Seems a year since I had any."

"I don't have coffee," she snapped. "If this were Guthrie station, I'd go buy some, but this isn't Guthrie station."

"Are you okay?" he asked.

"Yes, I'm all right. It's just men I guess, like Bram, always wanting what I don't have or what he shouldn't have. Things are a little short, and it's not so easy to grow coffee in these rocks. And there's no tea, either, so don't ask."

Daubing bacon grease into the pan, she lay in slices of cornmeal mush, cut thin for browning, and blackened with pepper. Creed's stomach growled, and an itch set up under his bandage. Refusing to scratch, he turned his attention instead to a crow standing at the edge of camp, its head cocked as it watched him with eyes black as axle grease.

After eating, they walked to the meadow below.

"Is there something wrong, Alida?" he asked, taking her by the elbow. "Something you'd like to talk about?"

"I don't mean to be cranky, Creed, but it's a worry, you know. All we've got in the world is that worn-out team and this mountain of rock. Now, Bram's off to Guthrie station, and lord knows when he'll decide to come back. There's so much to be done."

"I think you're doing great, Alida. You've got your place here and the time to make it what you want."

"Bram's a good boy," she said, "but a boy nonetheless, and centers on himself. He's too young to be on his own and too old to raise. I don't know what we were thinking of when Father died. We should have turned back right then."

"I've wondered about your parents, why you were out here alone."

"And Mother, too, three years before. It was Father's idea to come here, 'to start anew,' he said. 'A man shouldn't have to work for other men,' he said, 'because it destroys him inch at a time.' He hadn't figured on dying, I guess."

Picking up a stick, Creed searched for his pocketknife. Remembering he no longer owned one, he tossed the stick back onto the ground.

"What about you, Alida?"

"Me?"

"It must be hard, a young girl like you, out here alone, and taking on the responsibility of a family."

"I'm getting by."

"But it's difficult?"

Biting her lip, she twisted the ring on her finger. "It's not the way I thought my life would be," she said. "Anyway, I'm sorry, about being short with you."

"Apology accepted," he said. "Things have a way of working out, Alida, sooner or later."

"At least you're here to listen to me complain. That's something, isn't it?"

"I've been listening to Roop Walters complain for some time now. Believe me, your complaining is a real pleasure."

"Who's Roop?"

"Oh, just a friend, a partner, a man keen on self-respect like your father."

"I think I'd like your friend, then, complaining or otherwise."

When they got to the wagon, they sat on the back to rest. Alida swung her legs, and watched a heron wing its way across the sky.

"I don't mean to pry, Alida, but how long since you've had meat in the camp?"

"I've not seen a deer since coming," she said, "the grass being so poor, I suppose. A deer couldn't find a safer place to be, though, with the way Bram and I shoot. There's lots of rabbits up in the rocks, but hardly seems worth the shells we burn up."

"You have an axe?"

"Yes," she said, looking up through her wind-blown hair.

"And corn?"

"A bit of cornmeal."

"That will do," he said, standing. "You're going to have to do most of the labor. With this gimpy arm of mine, I'm not much help, but I can supervise."

"Supervise what?"

"The building of rabbit traps," he said. "Now get that axe and let's get started."

First they cut cedar limbs for the traps. After that, they dragged them back to the dugout, split them, and ordered them by size and shape across the compound. While Alida fixed a drink of water, Creed checked over the wood. Its quality was good, straight and dry and easily worked.

By late afternoon, the temperature had mounted. Even in the shade, there was little relief against the heat that boiled from the sun-baked rock.

Determined to finish, Creed drove on, stopping only to mop the sweat from his eyes or drink from the water jug, which Alida replenished from the spring. Without complaint, she worked at his side, did for him whatever he could not, and at last six traps were built, baited with cornmeal, and ready for staking.

Too weary to cook, they ate bread slathered with bacon grease, washing it down with spring water. Alida lay her head on her knees, her eyes closed. Her legs were scratched from the brush, and her hair was tangled from the wind. She'd worn a blister on her hand from the ring she wore, but had refused to take it off, even with Creed's pleading.

"You should rest, Alida," he said.

Stretching, she crossed her legs, and studied him.

"So, are you going to tell me?"

"Tell you what?"

"Where you learned to make traps."

Falling silent, Creed struggled to remember his mother's face, each time more difficult now, more distant, like a deepening shadow.

"My mother taught me," he said. "She was Kiowa. Captured by the Dragoons, she was being returned to her tribe when the detachment fell on hard times. The bounty from her traps saved them from starvation. My white father was an assistant surgeon on that expedition. That makes me a breed, as they say."

"I see."

Standing, he walked to the edge of the camp.

"She died out here in the Territory. It was long ago now, somewhere out there. Anyway, I was reared by my father and stepmother, and sent off to law school when the time came. Now, I'm back, back where I started."

"I'm sorry, Creed."

"It's okay." he said. "The old ways are gone."

"If these traps work, I might disagree with you. Well, I'm exhausted," she said, rising.

"I think I'll sleep out here tonight, Alida."

Going into the dugout, Alida returned with blanket and pillow and handed them to Creed. As she turned to go back in, she hesitated.

"Carl said hoopers come thundering down the mountain like the wheels of a hundred wagons."

"Night, Alida."

"Night," she said, smiling.

The morning they checked traps, Creed led at a fast clip. With each passing day, his strength returned, as well as his concern about Roop and the business. If the traps were successful, Alida's and Bram's chances would be better, and his decision easier. But with so many years having passed since he'd built a trap, he could not be certain of his skills.

The first trap was empty, bait stolen, door ajar in its track, and his heart sank. But the second thumped with a cottontail.

"It worked," Alida said, clapping her hands.

"Was there ever a doubt?" he asked, smiling.

Catching the rabbit by the hind legs, he dashed its head against a rock, waiting for it to kick away.

"Oh, ick," Alida said, turning her head.

Afterward, he tied its feet together, looping its warm body over his arm.

In the second trap, a jackrabbit watched them with bulging eyes. It was lank as a Mexican mule and too tough to eat, so Creed turned it loose.

The remaining traps were untouched, their bait intact, with no tracks, neither in nor out. Tomorrow he would move them if he had no luck, closer to the spring perhaps.

By the time he'd skinned and dressed the rabbit, Alida had the fire ready, and soon the aroma filled the camp.

"It smells wonderful," she said.

Taking a piece from the pan, he handed it to her, blowing the heat from his fingers.

"Here," he said, "fried hooper."

"Stop," she said, taking a bite. "Oh, it's lovely."

After they'd eaten, they walked to the meadow to check on the horses, Alida at his side. He liked her next to him, the way her hair drifted in the wind, the way her hand brushed his, the way she took his arm when the pathway narrowed.

Stopping at the wagon, they counted the horses, and listened to the chug of the southbound headed for Guthrie station.

"Alida," he said. I think I'll take Roan out for a ride this morning, to stretch her legs, to get reacquainted, you know."

"Are you sure you're up to it?"

"Just a ride out," he said. "I'll be back before dark."

"You'll be careful?"

"Sure," he said. "I'll be fine."

"Okay. Maybe I'll do some reading. It's been awhile."

"I'll see you later then," he said, taking the bridle from under the wagon seat.

At the bend of the path, she turned back and waved.

Roan eyed him from the backside of the meadow, uncertain whether to stand or turn. Whistling, Creed held out his hand and clucked his tongue. Ducking her head, she ambled toward him.

With only one good arm, it took several tries to get her saddled. He looped the cinch over his shoulder, tightening it with the heft of his legs. Each time he tried to mount, Roan shied from under him, spooked by the unusual swing of his body. Leading her beside a rock, he checked to make certain Alida was not watching before he aimed a leg over and dropped into the saddle.

As he rode south along the base of the hill, he searched for the wagon trail. It was good to be out, and for the first time in a long while, he was able to think of his lumber company, of Abaddon, and of Guthrie station. Abaddon had been right—time was his advantage, and he was burning it up with each passing day.

In the heat of the afternoon, he rested under a tree, dozing while Roan pulled leaves from the branches, froth gathering green around her bit and in the corners of her mouth as she munched away.

From his vantage, he could see the base of the mountain as it gave way to the prairie, could see clusters of white daisies like drifts of snow and yuccas with blooms of wax, and could smell ragweed brewing in the heat. Grasses, the color of sand, waved their flags as the wind passed over them. A black beetle teetered by, flipping onto its back, its legs treading the air. With a stick, Creed turned it over, but each time it tumbled over onto its back again.

"So long," he said. "Can't help a fellow bent on suicide."

Cutting back west, he crossed the trail where it rose into the rocks. Carl's wagon tracks were still visible where the horses had struggled against the pull of the load. Where the grade fell away, he could see the cookstove, dirt-covered but undamaged at the bottom of the gulch. It would take horses and tackle to pull it up and more than a one-armed man to heft it into the wagon. He'd have to return.

Back at the meadow, he unsaddled Roan, hobbling her, turning her out to join her friends. Lifting their heads, they whinnied their welcome before turning back to their grass.

The smell of Alida's fire welcomed him as he approached.

Looking up from her work, she said, "I've been worried."

"I could smell your fire clear down at the meadow," he said.

"I checked all the traps, and we'd caught another near the bend, so it's fried rabbit again, and with greens, too, and wild garlic from the meadow."

Sitting down, he rubbed his hands together.

"I'm starved," he said, "and curious as to how you killed that rabbit."

"Shot him," she said. "I just couldn't bring myself to bash its poor brains out on a rock, Creed."

"Oh, I see."

"But now there's a hole in the back of your trap."

Chuckling, he took off his hat and ran his fingers through his hair. "I'll show you how to dispatch them with a stick. It saves on ammunition, not to mention traps."

"Fine," she said, pointing her chin at him, "in the meantime, I assume you'll eat the rabbit anyway?"

"Safe assumption, and I've some news of my own."

Dishing up his plate, she handed it to him.

"And what would that be?"

"I've located the cooking stove up in the hills. Looked like Carl and Mavis shoved it out the back of the wagon so they could make it up the grade. We'll get it tomorrow if you want."

"That's wonderful," she said, her eyes sparkling. "It will make things so much easier."

After dinner they washed dishes, talking as they worked, settling in about the fire as night fell. Alida showed him her collection of books, turning the pages, holding them to the firelight as she read favorite passages.

"My father brought these all the way from Pennsylvania," she said. Tears gathered in her eyes. "Bram and I buried him at the Salt Fork. I don't suppose he would have thought much of this rock farm I bought."

"You've done just fine, Alida," he said.

Laying the book down, she said, "You're thinking to go, aren't you, Creed?"

"I've started a lumber business in Guthrie station, Alida. With a city going up, the demand is high. There's orders to fill and deliveries to be made. I plan to invest in land when I can, but it requires my attention."

"I would be fine here alone," she said, "and Bram should be back any day. It's just that sometimes he forgets about things."

"I'll wait for Bram to come," Creed said. "There's time yet."

When the moon bobbed onto the horizon, full as a pumpkin, they both fell silent and watched it climb into the sky.

"Why did you come back to the Territory, Creed? You've a fine education. It seems an unlikely place for you to make a start."

"It's my home," he said, "where I was born, and it's where the future is. I've got carloads of lumber selling faster than the railroad can get them here, and there's land to be had, too. Many who came aren't going to make it and will be ready to sell for what they can get. I've struck a deal with Abaddon Damon, owner of *The Capital City* paper. He says that Guthrie station's going to be the capital, and his paper the instrument of power. All will be lifted in its tide, that's what he says. I figure to be a part of that."

There was something cold in his voice, causing Alida to pause.

"Is it so important?" she asked.

"I've seen what power and money can do to the powerless, Alida. One should never underestimate it."

Taking his hand, she held it for a moment. "I think you'll get what it is you want," she said.

He lay his finger across her mouth, and brought her into his arms, responding to the heat of her body, the trip of her heart, the sweetness of her kiss. When he drew her in again, she stopped him with her hand against his chest.

"Good night, Creed," she said, slipping away.

After locating the stove, they pulled it from the gorge with a rope half-hitched to the wagon axle. Windy and Bones hung their heads and lunged against their collars. Once the stove was freed, Alida and Creed loaded it by way of steps constructed from rock.

"It's going to be great," Alida said, "when it turns cold, and the wind races down that mountainside."

As they rattled over the rocky trail, the smell of gourd rose from under the wheels of the wagon. Neither spoke of what had happened between them.

When they passed the rift, Creed pulled up, helping Alida down from the wagon. Windy and Bones shook their harnesses and set to stripping a hackberry of its leaves.

"We better let the team rest," he said. "There's not a year left between them as it is."

Moving into the shade, Alida sat down, fanning herself with her hand. "A noble pair," she said, "no matter."

"Up there is a cave," Creed said, pointing to the rift, "a fracture that leads deep into the heart of the rock."

"You've been up there?"

"Someone came to that Frenchman, gave him a drink of water after Carl and Mavis had nearly done him in. He left his tracks behind, so I followed them. That's where they led."

Holding her hand over her eyes, Alida squinted up at the rift.

"Mavis and I were up there on the mountain to pick plums. It's so desolate, and the wind never stops," she said.

"I found a body in the cave, Alida."

"A body?"

"Or what was left of it. There was a cedar crucifix, carved big as life, and a pile of rat bones reaching to the ceiling." Moving from under the tree, he looked up at the rift. "There was a robe, and sandals, a monk or holy man of some sort, I don't know, and his leg was broken, a fall most likely. I think he'd lived on those rats, heaven knows how long. It's dangerous up there, and with him being all alone like that, I guess the rats did the rest."

Alida shuddered. "I'd heard rumors at the border that a monastery was started out here somewhere, that it had just disappeared, and no one was ever heard of again. Mavis told me she saw a man in a robe once, up in the rocks. Said when she looked up again, he was gone."

"Guess we'll never know for certain," he said. "It's a hell of a pile of rock though, isn't it, like it was shoved right up out of the heart of the earth and left to cool."

Untying the reins, he secured them around the handbrake and took Alida's hand to help her into the wagon. "We'd better go," he said, "while we have horses still breathing."

The meadow broke below them, and Windy and Bones kicked up their pace, causing the cookstove to rattle in the back.

"Look," Alida said. "It's Bram with the wagon."

Pulling up, Creed stood on the seat for a better look.

"Sure enough," he said. "He's back."

As they approached, Bram walked out to meet them, reaching for Creed's hand.

"Glad to see you're up," he said.

"The arm's much better," Creed said, helping Alida down. "Thanks to your sister. You got the wagon and team, just like Buck said?"

"That's about the only thing he said the whole blame time, except at night, talking and talking till wee hours, and me with no one about except Carl. It was downright spooky."

"I thought you'd left for good," Alida said.

"Buck handed over the reins and a five-dollar bill. Said it was for my deputy work, and that he'd get it back from the government one way or the other. Said I was as good a deputy as he ever had. Said I was to buy supplies and to tell Creed McReynolds half of Guthrie station is waiting on lumber, and that he best get back, if he wasn't kilt."

"You bought supplies?" Alida asked, her face lighting up.

"Flour, sugar, salted hog jowl, twenty pounds of beans, a sack of yellow onions, three cans of coffee, and a stick of licorice for my favorite sister. I didn't have enough money for fresh meat, nor figured it would last long in this heat."

"Well," she said, "we have all the rabbits we want, thanks to Creed and his trap-building skills."

"Rabbit traps," Bram said. "Why, I never even thought of it."

While Alida cooked, Bram and Creed dragged the cookstove up the trail, two feet at a time, and into the dugout. Soon the smell of beans cooking was unmistakable, beans flavored with salt-pork and onions, seasoned with cider vinegar and red pepper. Alida fried bread in the skillet and nestled a pot of coffee in the coals to brew.

"Sure could use a piece of apple pie," Bram said, rubbing at his stomach.

"If I had pie, he'd want cream," Alida said, "and if I had cream, he'd want it warmed and served with a silver spoon."

"A slice of yellow cheese on top would do me," Creed said, winking at Bram. "Course, I'm unspoiled and easy to please."

Pushing Creed's arm, Alida laughed.

As the evening cooled, they talked into the night. Bram's voice grew dark when he told of Mavis, of how alive she looked laid out in the wagon, without so much as a mark on her anywhere.

"When we rode into town, a crowd gathered up behind us," he said, "looking in at poor Mavis laying in that wagon bed. They followed us right up to the marshal's office. The whole time Carl was cussing and kicking the side of the wagon, yelling they was land jumpers, and sons of bitches, and that he'd see 'em all in hell soon enough. Some kid climbed up on the back of the wagon, calling Buck a killer, and threatening to cut him with his knife, right there in front of the whole crowd, until Buck conked him on the head with his buggy whip. All the time poor Mavis just lay there in the back of that wagon, looking up like she didn't have a care."

"Not for a young boy to be seeing," Alida said.

"Buck said I did good and that I had a natural way of it," Bram said, "though I did feel bad for Mavis."

"What are they going to do with Carl?" Creed asked.

"The marshal said they was going to give him a trial over to Fort Smith and then hang him. That's what he said. Then, we took Mavis out to the cemetery and buried her in a tarp. Hers was the first grave in the Guthrie station cemetery, setting out there on the hill all by itself."

Rising, Alida picked up the dishes, dropping them in the pan to soak.
"I'm going to bed," she said. "It's time for you to go to bed, too, Bram.
There's lots to done around here tomorrow."

That night Creed slept again by the fire. Bram was curled beneath his
blanket at camp's edge, his breathing slow and regular. Moon shadows
descended from the rock and eased into the stillness. Somewhere in
the distance, a train's whistle rose and fell, and rose again.

Turning on his side, Creed looked up at the mountain, the crags
spiraling into the sky, columns of stone, measureless stone that lifted
from out of the earth. The idea came to him, as the sleep itself came,
in the solitude of the night.

Awakening, he dressed in the dark, and followed the trail down to
the meadow where he whistled in Roan. Shaking her head, she waited
for her bridle and the touch of his hand. Dew gathered on her back and
clung to the hairs in her ears.

After saddling Roan, he led her to the trailhead, tying the reins high
on a limb to keep her from snapping them underfoot. Unlashing the
saddlebags, he threw them over his shoulder and headed back up the
trail.

Both Bram and Alida were awake, standing about the fire, sleep still
in their eyes.

"You're leaving, aren't you?" Alida asked.

"Yes," he said. "I need to talk to the both of you."

"Well, then," she said.

From the saddlebag, he took out money.

"There's a hundred dollars here, Alida, and more to come. I want to
lease your place."

"Lease? I don't understand."

"It's a good price," he said, "and you won't have to move. In fact, I
need you here, both of you."

"This place isn't worth it," Bram said. "Even I know that, unless you
have a call for rocks or hoopers."

"Bram's right," Alida said. "Maybe it's charity you have in mind."

"Not hoopers, nor charity either, for that matter," he said.

"Not rocks, surely," Alida said, looking over at Bram.

"The Frenchman said that a land must bear fruit from its own flesh,
Alida, and the more I thought about it, the more sense it made."

"I don't understand."

"Now, it's lumber that Guthrie station needs, but soon enough it's going to need more. It's going to be the state capital, everyone knows. Well a capital needs grand buildings, doesn't it, buildings of stone, don't you see. It will take a mountain of stone, like this mountain here, carved from the flesh of the land. The rail line is close. I can hear the whistle at night, and from there it's but a short haul to Guthrie station."

"But selling rock," Bram said, "seems an unlikely thing."

"I have money to raise and know little about the quarry business, but I can learn. There's arrangements to be made with the railroad, too, and then orders to fill."

"It'll take some doing to move this mountain," Alida said, looking up.

"Give me the rights to all I can haul," he said. "In turn, I'll give you ten percent of everything sold for as long as I sell it. I'll need a good man to help me, and I figure that's you, Bram. There will be a salary."

"A salary?"

"In addition to the lease and your share of the profits."

"Lidy?" Bram said.

"I don't know, Bram," she said. "This mountain's not much of a farm, I suppose, and we can't live on rabbit forever."

"It's a deal," Bram said, sticking out his hand.

"That's great," Creed said. "I'll draw up the papers."

"Now, have your breakfast," Alida said.

"I best be on my way. Roan's saddled, and there's much to be done."

Taking hold of his shirt sleeve, she stopped him. "Take what's left of the rabbit, Creed. It's a long ride to Guthrie station, and keep the bandage changed, you hear, until you've healed."

"I hear, and thank you for all you've done."

Letting go of his shirt, she looked up at him, her eyes glistening. "You'll be back soon, then?"

"Oh, I'll be back," he said. "There's unfinished business here."

Alida and Bram gleaned an average of two rabbits a week from the traps. With the supplies Bram had brought back from Guthrie station, their meals were hearty, if not a bit dreary. After a few weeks, Alida could dispatch a cottontail with a quick snap of a stick, skin it, and dress it out on the spot.

As the days passed, they soon fell into a routine. Sometimes, on a cloudy day, they would pick plums up on the rift or wild onion in the meadow. Each day, regardless of the weather, brought a trip to the spring for water, where they bathed and filled buckets to be carried back to the dugout. Bram took on the duties of caring for the horses and for keeping firewood stocked by the stove. She, in turn, did the cooking, washed clothes, and swept the hard-pack floor of the dugout.

In the sweltering heat of the afternoons, Bram took to the mountain, rarely returning before dusk, ranging high on the ridge where the cedars grew and the breeze never failed. Often he rode horseback. Other times he walked, poking his way through the labyrinth of rock, his hat squared against the boiling sun.

Alida read in the dugout, her bare feet propped up on the trunk, her hair lifted against the heat. Sometimes she would listen to the locusts, the rise and fall of their chant, their crescendo building in the afternoon, or take the deputy's hat from behind the door, with its feather and leather band, and remember the way he rode, the way he leaned into the gait of his horse as though it were a part of him. Then she would remember the way he died, his body left in the muck and slime of the bog. In her mind they were two different men, entirely separate in time and place.

But most of all she thought of Creed, of the way he kissed her, his mouth parted, and of the way his black hair fell over his eyes when he slipped on his boots. She thought of his skin, its smell of dust and smoke, and its color of saddle leather. She thought of the flame in his black eyes, of how it grew when he talked of the future. He was a man both Indian and white, and somehow neither, both strengthened and wounded by each.

In her heart it mattered little, though she knew it would to others, and that defying social rules had consequence. But what troubled her most, what crept into her thoughts in the quiet hours, was a question: Could a man driven by such needs of his own fulfill her dreams?

When Bram came home, his clothes were covered with sticktights, and his shirt was wet with perspiration.

Taking off his boots, he worked the sticktights from his socks, dropping them into his hand.

"It was hotter than billy hell up there today," he said. "On top of that, Windy refused to climb the last leg to the cedars. She ain't worth her salt, I tell you."

"She's old, that's all, Bram. It won't hurt you to walk a little."

Dumping the sticktights out the door, he poured himself a drink of water, emptying the glass.

"When do you figure Creed will be back, Lidy?"

"There's no way to know, is there?" she said, pausing from her reading. "Maybe he won't be back at all."

"He'll be back," he said.

"How can you be so sure?"

"He left money, didn't he?"

Leaning against the cool of the dugout wall, she looked at the hat hanging behind the door.

"I suppose he did," she said, "but it wasn't all that much, not for a man like Creed McReynolds."

"Besides," he said, pulling off his socks, stuffing them into his boots, "I saw the way he looked at you."

"Just stop, Bram."

"Hell, Lidy, a blind man could see he was taken with you."

Standing, she pushed her hair back and checked the ashes in the stove.

"Is it necessary to curse, Bram?"

"Maybe it's necessary if I want," he said, folding his arms across his chest.

"You're not as grown up as you think, Bram Deventer, and you've got no business saying things like that. I figure to take my time, that's all. It should be special. I want things special."

"Too good for anybody," he said, "with all the makin's of an old maid."

Spiking her hands on her waist, she glared at him. "You just shut up, Bram, just because you have no ideals."

"What does that mean?"

"I know about you and Mavis. That's what it means, and I think it's disgusting, being with her like that, and with that old man sitting in the night."

Bram stood, his neck splotched with anger. Picking up his boots, he walked to the door.

"You had no business spying on me one way or the other," he said, his jaw clenched. "I'm a growed man and don't need to come to you for such things. If you don't figure it that way, then maybe I should move on."

"Maybe you should," she snapped.

When she turned back, he was gone.

Alone, she passed the days as best she could, and at night she slept in the stillness of the mountain. Clouds raced through the night sky, shrouding her and the mountain in shadows. Somewhere out there, Bram, too, was alone, their argument lingering in his mind, as it did for her, words that she should never have spoken, words she'd give anything to retrieve. Things would never be the same between them, this she knew, their childhood having slipped away in that single exchange.

Unable to read, she checked the traps, and then checked them again. In between, she carried water from the spring and firewood from the draw. At the backside of the meadow, she found Windy gone, as well as the tack from the wagon. Bram had taken her, perhaps to Guthrie station, perhaps farther to some unknown place, but even so, she waited for his return. Together they had come here, the two of them against the world, and it was, for her, inconceivable that it should be otherwise.

Climbing to the ledge, she watched as the day cooled, the clouds rippling with the oranges and pinks. A breeze, tepid with heat, brushed the treetops, and the distant sound of a train lingered on the horizon. Perhaps Bram had been right. Perhaps there *was* room in Creed's life for more than his venture. Perhaps there was room there for her, if she'd only allow it.

Taking the hat from behind the dugout door, she headed down the rocky path toward the spring. The coolness of the spring rose up the trail to meet her, its gurgle throaty in the quiet. For a moment she stood quietly, turning the brim in her hand, before tossing the hat into the bog.

When she turned, Bram stood in the twilight at the foot of the trail, his hands tucked in his pockets.

"Lidy, I'm sorry, for what I said. It weren't true, none of it, about you being an old maid and all that. I was just striking out, just wanting to make my own way, you see."

Taking him by the hand, she leaned into him. "I'm glad you're back, Bram. It's been mighty lonesome on this mountain by myself."

"Oh, you was never alone, Lidy. I couldn't do that, so I been sleeping in the wagon down there every night."

Reaching up, she kissed him on the cheek. "I'll not be interfering in your life again, Bram. You're a grown man, just like you said, and that's the way it ought to be."

"Thanks, Lidy," he said, smiling, "but before you start not interfering, could you fry up one of them rabbits? I'm near starved clean to death."

Turning east at the Cimarron, Deputy Buck Reed kicked Pony into a fast walk, giving him lead along the path. Neither the promise of a hot day nor the hum of mosquitoes was sufficient to discourage him. It was only too good to be on the trail, away from the noise and clamor of Guthrie station. Where once tents stood, there were now buildings, ill-begotten constructions verging on collapse. Streets ran like tentacles throughout the town, and a ditch was dug to the Cottonwood for water, a wound rendering the town in half. The stink of grease and campfires was everywhere and shrouded the valley with its gloom.

Even though Buck had killed his share of men, mostly in the line of duty, the killing of Mavis Ellison weighed on his mind. In quiet moments, the sounds and feel of her squirming body, the smell of her heat and fear, swept him in waves of regret.

But, the marshal was pleased with his work, Buck's reward being three hours of paperwork and an assignment to bring in a thief running amuck at the colored settlement. He wasn't much of a thief, as thieves go, stealing turnips from a garden, chickens from a homesteader down on the Cimarron, overalls from a clothesline.

When a mule turned up half-eaten under a brush pile, concern had increased amongst the settlement, but still no one was willing to go to the law. Stirring up white marshals for turnips and mules was an uncertain trade. But then a young girl failed to come back from fishing one day. When her cane pole washed up on shore, there was little choice left but to go to the law.

After forming a committee, they'd gone to Guthrie station, taking comfort in their numbers. There, they were encouraged when the marshal promised to send out a deputy, soon as he got back from up north. Said they were to cooperate, to help bring in that thief, colored or white, and justice would be done. At first Buck resisted, being a colored deputy assigned to a colored community, but then he thought of Rolondo, of seeing her again.

When the day turned hot, as he knew it would, lather gathered about Pony's cinch and in the swell of his chest. At noon Buck led him to water, slipping the bridle over his ears, freeing the bit so that he could drink where the water pooled at the bend of the creek. Flipping back the scum with his nose, Pony slurped, water dribbling from the cup of his lip.

At the Crosstimbers, Buck cut north toward the Cimarron. The meander of the river would cost him in miles, but the going would be open and free of bramble. A hot wind blew in from the south, driving the last of the clouds from the sky. Heat quivered from the red earth, and Pony's ears drooped with boredom. A covey of quail lifted from the brush, wings whirring, pinfeathers floating to the ground.

"Easy, boy," Buck said, bringing Pony about.

When they came to a rise overlooking the Cimarron, Buck pulled up. The river twisted down the valley, shimmering in the sun, and the smell of salt and bog was strong on the wind. A sandstone cliff rose from the bend, swept and worn from the river's force. From its face, a pecan tree clung to life, its branches pregnant with nuts.

When they came upon a logjam caught at the river's edge, Buck dismounted. The sand beneath was cool and shaded. Tying Pony to a limb, Buck crawled under the drift to rest, lying on his back, his hands behind his head. Closing his eyes, he slept, free of demons and voices of the night.

It was the roar of a cannon in his head that caused him to crash his nose into the overhanging limb. "God dang!" he yelled. And then it came again, grinding, scraping, clawing with certainty into the core of his head. Scrambling from under the logjam, Buck screamed at the thing boring into his ear. Blood was dripping from his nose and onto his shirt.

Eyes stark white, Pony reared up, horrified by the monster crawling from beneath the woodpile. Reins snapping, the horse danced in a circle, nostrils flared, ears laid back, feet kicking as he raced down the shore of the river.

Frantic, Buck clawed at his ear, at the thing worming into his brain. Plunging in his little finger, cursing, he smashed away the intruder, holding it to the light. Smudged on the end of his finger was a pissant, its legs still struggling. "God dang it!" he said again, wiping it away in the sand.

Every time Buck reached for the reins Pony shied, prancing away just beyond reach. It took an hour and the whole of Buck's patience to catch up with him, and when he did, he whopped him across the nose with his hat, and had to chase him down all over again. It took another hour to retrieve the reins and splice them back with the rawhide string he kept in his saddlebag.

By the time they were on their way again, it was soon too dark to ride, so he made camp, having traveled far fewer miles than he'd planned. Still, it was a nice night and good to be on his own. Kicking back, he relaxed into the evening. There would always be thieves to be caught, he reckoned, and another day.

Opening a can of beans, he ate them with the curl of his fingers. After rolling out his blanket, he placed his saddle under his head, its smell of leather and salt. The air thickened, damp and moist from the river, and a fog soon gathered in the bottom. Tearing strips off his bandanna, he twisted them into his ears. Better to be kilt outright, he figured, than to have critters tromping through his head uninvited.

As he slept, the voices came, and they told of death, of time and outrage. They told of the unknowable, the unthinkable, and the unforgiven. An angel, with blonde hair flowing, came down upon him, her head slack and drooping, blood trickling from her nose and spreading across her front. Crowds gathered about, peering into his wagon, among them a boy shouting and cursing, waving his arms above his head.

When Buck awoke, his heart chugged in his chest, and a sadness lay heavy within him. Dew gathered on his blanket and in the thick of his beard. As dawn broke, he mounted Pony. Flanking him hard, he rode east toward the settlement.

The smell of the brush fires reached him first. When Junior spotted him on the rise, he ran back toward the wagon as fast as his bare feet would permit.

"It's him," he called out, pointing back at Buck, "the man with the eyes."

"Hush, boy," Roy said, taking off his hat for a better look.

"Lo," Buck said, dismounting. "Been smelling your brush fire. Like the whole valley's burnin', ain't it."

"Why, blow me down, if it ain't Buck Reed, wearin' a badge, too."

"Yes, sir," he said, looking down at his badge.

"A colored deputy marshal," Roy said, shaking his head. "I reckon I seen it all now."

"Here, Junior," Buck said. "Tie Pony to that wagon seat, and don't let him step on your toe, 'cause he's ignorant and can't be talked off."

Junior took Pony, holding him off to the side as he walked.

"Cutting hardwood for Guthrie station," Roy said, throwing a limb into his fire, "and burning brush for myself. Can't last, though, what with the railroad hauling in more coal everyday. Ain't nobody goin' to burn scrub oak if they can burn coal."

"It's a city changing," Buck said, "faster than a man can keep up."

"You forget to sidestep a gun butt," Roy asked, "huntin' outlaws and such?"

"Naw," Buck said, touching his nose, "just a pissant."

"Lordee," Roy said, "tore off your shirt, too, didn't he. Hope you shot him dead 'fore he tracks down my mules."

Wrinkling up an eye at Roy, Buck said, "Kilt with one shot, dressed out, too."

With his shovel, Roy pulled the twigs into a pile, and then scooped them into the fire, stepping back as they blazed up.

"Guess you come lookin' for that turnip thief?" he said.

"Guess so."

"Guess they didn't have no white deputy for such doin's?"

"I'm a bona fide deputy marshal, Roy," he said, "and will do what needs doin'."

Leaning on his shovel, Roy looked up at him. His white beard was filled with ash from the fire.

"No offense, Buck, but what we needs is our own deputy right here in the settlement."

"Just doing a job, Roy, makin' a little money. I don't want caught between folks, you understand."

"Between's a hard place," Roy said. "I been there plenty of times."

"Yes, sir," Buck said. "Sittin' on the fence scrunches up a man's balls."

"You kilt anybody?" Junior asked, sliding his hands under the bib of his overalls.

"Go find your ma," Roy said. "She's down on the bottom diggin' sweet taters."

"Oh, Pa."

"Tell her company's come. Go on now, get."

With pant legs dragging in the dirt, Junior sauntered off.

"Growed," Buck said.

"Eats more than my mules," Roy said, looking after him, "and ain't half as particular."

Rolling up a log, Buck sat down on it, hooking his hat on the toe of his boot.

"What you been hearing, Roy?"

"That girl's been found, Buck, least what was left of her, given the heat, and the mud turtles. Somebody kilt her, and worse, from what I hear."

"You figure it's whites come up from Guthrie station?" Buck asked.

Slipping his hands into his hip pockets, Roy walked to the edge of the clearing and looked down into the valley below.

"They found chicken bones and turnip tops scattered about a cold fire, and footprints, too, long as a man's forearm, they said."

"You got an idea who, Roy?"

Turning, Roy stuck his hands in his hip pockets and looked at him.

"It's Rolondo I worry 'bout, Buck. Wasn't for her, I wouldn't be tellin' the law spit, not even for you."

"Yes, sir."

Reaching into his bib pocket, Roy pulled out a twist, studying it for a moment, tearing off a chew and tucking it in his jaw.

"There's only one man I know could make tracks like that. I seen him noodlin' down on the river one day, big as a mule and with the look of mad in his eyes. He just stared at me for the longest time before sliding back under the water."

"What's his name?"

"They call him Shovelnose, 'cause he looks like the mudcat what he eats, smells like one, too, those what know. Strong as a draft horse, too, they say. Can pull a single bottom plow a hundred feet through buffalo sod with nothing but a shoulder rope. Say he kilt a man back in Georgia for a whippin' he took at the post. Say he walked the whole way to the Territory, following rivers, noodlin', stealin', Lord knows. Course, there's folks say lots of things, ain't they."

"Don't know where I could find him, do you, Roy?"

Taking aim, Roy spit onto the hub of the wagon wheel.

"No, sir, but he takes to water."

With bucket in hand, Bess crossed the clearing. Behind her, Rolondo followed, her skirt bulging with dirt-covered sweets.

"I'll be," Bess said, setting down her bucket, "if it ain't Buck Reed come back."

Rising, Buck shook her hand. "Hello, Bess."

Lowering her skirt, Rolondo rolled the sweet potatoes onto the ground, glancing up at him with her dark eyes.

"Lo, Mr. Reed, or should I call you Deputy Reed?"

"Call me Buck," he said.

"Oh, no, Deputy Reed," she said, smiling, "'cause I been brought up proper, ain't I." Lifting up on her toes, she looked at his nose and then at his shirt. "Guess you been killin' outlaws and fightin' red injuns?"

"Was a pissant," Roy said, "but a right mean one."

"Pissants are a hazard," Rolondo said. "Some say they're takin' cattle down at the river, dragging 'em right in, though I ain't seen it myself."

"Stop that foolishness," Bess said, "or Buck won't be coming back. You'll be staying for supper, won't you, Buck? Roy's been settin' trotline, and we got a mess of catfish, cornbread, too, and sweet tater pie, seein' as how we gotta wagonload fresh out of the garden."

"Why, yes, ma'am, if you think it's safe, what with pissants on the move."

"Pa's got a shotgun," Rolondo said, smiling, "and a dead eye, too."

"Well, I've been eatin' finger beans and drinkin' moss water for two days now. Maybe I'll just stay then."

That night Bess fried fish while cornbread baked in the Dutch oven. Roy and Buck sipped on shine and talked of the burgeoning Negro colony.

"They've plowed up a common garden," Roy said, taking a sip from his tin cup, "near eighty acres. A man puts in his work, gets equal shares. Keeps those with no plow or team from starvin'. Some say they've got papers for a township, filed legal, too, and soon enough there's goin' to be schools, and one day maybe there will even be a college where coloreds can get a education."

Taking a drink of shine, Buck let the fire in his stomach subside before answering.

"You and me been around some, Roy. It's but a dream."

"Well, maybe so, and maybe not. This is a new land, Buck. Look at you, wearin' that badge, takin' up the law like you was born to it. Maybe this time will be different."

Afterward, they ate supper, filling up on seconds, and a slice from a pie big as a man's hat. From across the way, Rolondo watched him as she ate catfish, her eyes sparkling.

Excusing himself, Buck stood. "I'll be bunking down in the scrub, Roy. That was a fine meal, Bess."

"We're going to need a deputy of our own someday, Buck," Bess said. "The settlement needs to be a place where a family can be raised without fear of no man."

"It's the last hope, this ole Territory," Buck said.

"You go huntin' down on the river," Roy said, "you take care."

Pulling her knees into her arms, Rolondo looked up at Buck, her thigh strong against the hem of her dress.

"Night, Deputy Reed," she said.

Buck picked his way through the blackjacks and onto a ridge overlooking the valley. Below, the river struck into the distance, and from the undergrowth crickets sawed with precision. Spreading his bedroll in the leaves, he lay down. Content with the evening and the meal, he dozed.

When he awoke, the moon rose with its creamy light, and a current of air eased through the scrub oak, the leaves whispering. She stood in the shadows of the trees, her smile flashing in the moonlight.

"It ain't the voices come callin' this time, Deputy Reed, " she said.

Taking her face between his hands, he pulled her to him, kissing her, melting into the rush of her embrace. When he touched her breasts, she groaned, and he rose into her.

Afterward, they lay trembling on his blanket, the night dew falling on their nakedness. Rolondo's breath was warm against his shoulder and her hand, callused from the garden hoe, lay on his stomach. With groin stirring, he wished for her to awaken, to do it again, and he ached, still, with the want of her.

Shivering, Buck pulled on his boots. During the night she'd slipped from his bed, leaving behind but her scent and memory. He recounted the night as he saddled up Pony.

After leading him to the ridge, Buck sat back on his haunches and studied the valley, the drifting river, the pink of dawn.

He wanted breakfast, but the smoke from a fire would give him away. If Shovelnose were waiting out there, he would know someone was hunting him, because his was a solitary life, a life clever in the ways of the wilderness.

Leading Pony through the blackjacks, he followed the trail into the valley. Even though the going was slow, he would be hard to detect in the undergrowth. Once he reached the river, he could walk the west bank, keeping out of sight in the brush. If it bore no fruit, he would cross over, double back along the east bank. With luck, he could make camp on the ridge tonight.

At the river, he dismounted and listened. Somewhere in the distance, a dog barked. The water was shallow here, but a few inches deep, too shallow for noodlin'. Catfish, the big ones, preferred the backwash, deep holes swirled beneath tree roots by floodwaters, caves populated by water snakes and the river mudcat, a creature that could grow to 120 pounds on its diet of carrion, a girth so large that a man's arms could not envelope it. Lifeless until touched, it would wait in the darkness, erupting in a fury of mud and slime as it sucked a man down.

Of this much Buck was certain, it took a desperate man to live off noodlin', a man both hungry and fearless, a man like Shovelnose. It wouldn't be in the shallows he'd find him, but in the river bends where the floodwaters churned against the banks.

By noon he'd seen not a thing, no tracks, no signs of camp nor trotlines. Squatting in the shade, he chewed on a piece of jerky and let Pony graze on the fescue that sprouted green in the damp of the river. After a rest, he took off his boots and led Pony across the shallows to the east bank. In the middle where the water was cool and deep, he stopped to listen once more.

Keeping the tree line between him and the river, he started down the east side. Disturbed by his presence, something splashed upstream. Buck turned his ear to the sound. Pony snorted, nudging his shoulder. There was no more than a ripple on the water as it slipped beneath the surface. A shirt hung from a willow limb that grew over the river, and on the shore, a pair of the biggest boots Buck had ever seen.

Tying Pony to a skunk brush, he slipped his rifle from the scabbard and eased his way through the undergrowth. The sun edged below the trees, its light reflecting on the surface of the river. Water bugs skimmed about like tiny sailboats, shuttled here and there by the breeze.

Buck listened again. There was another breaking of the water, like the rending of glass, and the rush of wet lungs, the blow of a whale as it prepares to sound.

When it slipped beneath the water, there was the smell of fish and mud. Buck moved to the bank, lifting his rifle to his shoulder. For ages

Buck waited for him to resurface—longer than a man could hold his breath, longer than a human could survive. Perhaps Shovelnose had met his end even now, had been dragged under a root, his arm swallowed in some murky hole. Buck strained to hear some sign of life, the sound of bubbles, or the stir of water, but there was naught but silence.

Shovelnose charged from out of nowhere, smelling of mud and marsh, eyes buried beneath his brows, head dwarfed atop his shoulders. The ensuing blow came with the weight and force of his body, with the intent to kill. Staggered, Buck fell to his knees, dropping his rifle.

Shovelnose roared, lifting Buck into the air as no more than a child, no more than the girl with the red-stringed pigtails, and flung him into the river.

Struggling to the surface, Buck gasped, his full boots towing him downward, sapping his strength. Shovelnose came from behind, his arm about Buck's throat, dragging him under. Locked in battle, they sank to the bottom, aliens in the river muck. Buck fought against Shovelnose's grip, against the endurance of his immense lungs, against his skill in the river. Overhead, shards of light pierced the darkness as the waters closed about them.

But the voices spoke, even then, of their power and invincibility. His arms dropping to his side, Buck waited in Shovelnose's grip as they sat on the bottom like fat, blinking frogs.

An eternity passed. Buck's body, now showing no signs of life, would float away soon enough, distended and corrupt, into the eddies of the river. But then he moved into that place of the gods, and of the voices, that place where no man but he might go.

When Shovelnose moved again, he did so with certainty and terror. He struggled to break free, for that breath of air, for the only thing on earth that any longer mattered.

Like a mudcat, Buck held on, his lungs ablaze as he clutched Shovelnose's leg, to hold him there until his great lungs filled with the river, to kill him. Even as Shovelnose thrashed above, Buck held on. Even as his own eyes darkened, and his heart flopped inside him, he held on. Even as the gods begged and the heavens wept, he held on, until there was no sound, no movement, no bubble left to rise.

When at last Shovelnose's arms floated upward, drifting in the current, Buck let go, pushing off the bottom. With the last of his will, he swam for the surface, to that single spot of light above him. Bursting through, he filled his lungs, spewing and sputtering and filling them again with life's sweet breath.

Afterward, he lay spent on the bank. When at last rested, he retrieved his rifle from the rocks and led Pony downstream. At the bend, he found Shovelnose snagged in the roots of a cottonwood. Climbing down, he tied a rope around Shovelnose's wrists and pulled him from the river. Pony snorted against the dead weight when Buck loaded the body across the saddle.

From the scrub, he could see Roy's trash fire up on the ridge, and the new-cut cord of blackjack in the clearing. At the edge, Roy worked brush into the fire, setting his shovel, as Buck approached.

Taking hold of Shovelnose's hair, Roy lifted up his enormous head. "It's him, sure enough. What you kill him with, a buffalo gun?"

"Kilt in the river," Buck said, "sittin' on the bottom like mud turtles, till one or the other of us drownt."

"Lordee," Roy said, taking out his chew. "I reckon we'll sleep better for it. Too late for that little girl, though." Scraping his shoe on the shoulder of his shovel, he looked up through his brows at Buck. "You're either the bravest man I ever knew, or the craziest, I ain't certain. We could sure use a man like you around here, Buck Reed."

Squatting down, Buck picked up a stick and drew circles in the sand. "It ain't me does the fightin', Roy, but something else living in my head. Ain't nothing brave 'bout that. Maybe someday, when I got a stake, something to buy a place of my own, maybe I will come back."

Clipping off a chew, Roy worked at it a bit before speaking.

"You'll be stayin' for supper then?"

Tossing his stick into the fire, Buck rose and gathered up Pony's reins.

"It's a temptin' offer, but I got a ways to walk yet, Roy."

"Sorry to hear it," Roy said, firing a shot of tobacco into the fire. "Rolondo's goin' to be right disappointed."

"**R**eckon I won't be going in to Guthrie station," the old lady said, pulling the wagon up at the depot. "Never was much for city folk, what with their talk and idle ways."

Climbing down, Jerome Bouchard dusted his hat against his leg.

"Thank you for the ride, ma'am. Are you certain you don't want to stay the night in a hotel, get some food and rest?"

Her gray hair stirred in the wind, and for a moment Jerome could see the beauty that had once been hers.

"I need to get on home," she said, gathering up the reins. "Comes a time when life loses its pleasures. Comes a time to wrap things up. Young folk don't understand. Nor should they."

"Well," he said, "I don't know what I would have done without the ride. Thank you."

"You ever get back to my place, check on my man's grave," she said. "There ain't no one left to care, and the prairie takes back what's hers soon enough."

"Yes, ma'am."

"And good luck on them buildings of yours, too. A man ought to have a dream, even if it's building buildings."

As he walked from the tracks and into Guthrie station, new buildings rose on both sides of the street. From behind him, a steamer pulled away from the depot, its chug deepening against the ascent out of the valley.

At the top of the hill, he turned and watched the smoke from the stack drift across the horizon. A bank of clouds was moving in over the prairie, and a cool wind blew in from the west. Lightning flashed, and thunder rumbled down the valley. There was the smell of rain in the air. From the Blue Belle Saloon, a fiddle sawed out a tune. Lamplights flickered like fireflies down the street, and horses whinnied from the soldiers' camp. The sky darkened, and rain spattered in the dust as children scrambled for home, their laughter pitched and shrill.

Ducking into the Blue Belle Saloon, Jerome took off his hat, drying his face on the sleeve of his shirt. Men sat at domino tables, chins in their hands. The fiddler played on as the rain drove against the window.

"What'll you have?" the bartender asked from behind the counter.

Touching his pocket, Jerome shook his head.

"I'm new in town and wonder if there is a place I might stay?"

Sliding his towel across the counter, the bartender looked Jerome over.

"Far away, by the sound of you," he said.

"France," Jerome said, laying his hat on the bar. "I'm an architect."

"You don't say. Well, I'm from Texas," he said, hanging the towel over his shoulder. "I ain't nothing as you can see."

"I've been on the trail a good long while. If you could direct me to a hotel."

"Guess you'd be wantin' a home-cooked meal, or female company to warm up the evening?"

"I thought perhaps there were stables, just a dry place for the night," he said.

"Say, you ain't that baby Jesus are you?"

"No, no," Jerome said. "I'm just a little short on money."

The men laughed and looked up from their game.

"Well, now," the bartender said, "guess you ain't the only broke man in Guthrie station, God help us. The law ain't forgivin' of sleepin' on the streets, but there's the tunnels. Course, they're full of packrats, and too dangerous for those goddamn marshals to go snoopin' around. Look," he said, pointing to a door, "through there is the hotel. Just inside is another door leading to the tunnels. A man can find a place to sleep, and 'bout everything else, too."

Picking up his hat, Jerome looked about the room. "Oh, I see."

"Why, they have whores in France, don't they?"

"Yes, but I don't. . ."

"We ain't got whores in the Territory. No one comin' and goin' to no whorehouses in Guthrie station, are there men?"

One of the men pushed his dominoes across the table and laughed. "No whores in Guthrie station," he said. "Oh, no, sir, just the righteous, that's all we got, righteous citizens enough to save every lost soul in the Territory, and that's saying something, ain't it, boys?"

The bartender drew a beer and slid it over to Jerome.

"Ain't enough do-gooders in the whole of America to save ole Henry's black soul," he said. "We see plenty of them whores when the town needs money, when it's time for collectin' fines. Yes, sir, we see plenty then— the mayor, the marshals, the city council, all come at collectin' time. So, we got tunnels, ain't we, like ants got tunnels, comin' and goin' in the dark."

"Oh," Jerome said.

"Go on now. Tunnels fill up fast when the weather's bad. Stop at the kitchen if you've a notion. It's cornbread and beans and poor fare for a Frenchman, I 'spect, but then what you goin' to do."

"I couldn't pay," Jerome said.

"Ain't chargin' baby Jesus for no beans, am I," he said, turning back to his work.

With the last of his cornbread, Jerome mopped his plate and watched the cook peel potatoes over a washtub. Whistling a tune through a missing tooth, he never looked up nor acknowledged Jerome's presence.

When he opened the door to the hotel, the smell of lavender hung in the hallway, and laughter came from one of the rooms. Somewhere a man cursed, and voices rose, muffled and angry from the darkness. Shivering, Jerome found the door to the tunnel where the bartender said it would be. It was secured with pulley and sadiron against the draft from below, and its hinges were rusted from the damp. When he opened it, the air smelled of earth and dank.

Following the steps down, he waited for his eyes to adjust to the darkness. Without the light from the street drains above, the darkness would have been complete. Water ran down the walls and collected in the stream that flowed at the path's edge.

Smaller tunnels intersected the passageway, freshly dug to accommodate the new establishments as they came on line. Shored with fieldstone, the walls were a haven for crickets and spiders. Grottoes were carved in the sides, retreats for the poor, for men like himself. They huddled with blankets or curled against the damp under threadbare coats.

"Either move or get off the goddamn path!" a voice said, moving away.

Finding an alcove, Jerome crawled in. Tomorrow he would look for work, anything until he could get on his feet. He was going to leave his mark on this city, whatever it took. Hunkering against the night and his loneliness, he was grateful for the weariness that at last brought him sleep.

Squinting, Jerome breathed in the morning air. With stomach empty, he walked the streets of Guthrie station at daybreak. All about, timber-framed construction was going up. At the top of the hill, a crew was busy assembling the walls of a building. From across the street, a man watched on. Next to him, a boy sat on a bucket rolling newspapers.

"Excuse me, sir," Jerome said to the man, "but I'm looking for work and wondered if you might direct me?"

The man was tall and lank, his eyes unwavering as he looked Jerome over.

"You smell of the tunnels," he said. "Why don't you sell papers like the boy here. It's enough to keep you above ground at least."

"Just don't sell 'em in my territory," the boy said, looking up at Jerome.

"Get on to your business, Jimmy," the man said. "Folks will be wanting their news with morning coffee."

Without looking back, the boy sauntered off, his bucket of papers hooked over his arm.

"I'm good with my hands," Jerome said, "and I've a head for building. I'm a trained architect, you see."

"You figure you could carpenter, then?"

"Yes, sir," he said.

"My name's Abaddon Damon, and that's going to be *The Capital City*, the first and the best newspaper in this Territory. When we become a state, and we will, this town's going to be the capital, and *The Capital City*'s going to be its voice."

"I don't have tools, Mr. Damon, but I'm a hard worker."

"Everybody loves a winner." Pushing back his hat, Abaddon looked at him as if for the first time. "What did you say your name was?"

"Jerome Bouchard."

"Where you from, Mr. Bouchard?"

"Paris, France. I'm an architect."

Scratching at his head, Abaddon mulled it over.

"You don't look like an architect to me."

"Nonetheless, I am, and what's more, that building won't stand the winter."

"What do you mean?"

"Those rafters are too far apart, and the headers should be doubled. The whole thing's going to sway soon as the roofing material is added."

"You don't say?" Abaddon said.

"Yes, sir."

"I could use a clean-up man. You go tell Bill up there that I've hired you on. Tell him to change those rafters and to pay you at day's end. I don't want my men sleeping in the tunnels. It's bad for *The Capital City*'s image."

"Yes, sir, and thank you," Jerome said.

That night Jerome collected his money and ate his dinner at the Blue Belle. It was cornbread and beans again, not in the kitchen this time but at a table. Afterward, he took a room in the hotel across the way.

When finished with his bath and shave, he soaked his blisters in kerosene from the lamp and then retired, happy for his escape from the tunnels. Neither the comings nor goings of the night, nor the fight that broke out in the hallway, could rouse him from his sleep.

For a week he worked the carpenter crew, cleaning up, carrying lumber, going for tools or drinks of water. A framework was started on the lot next door, but it soon fell behind for lack of lumber.

Each morning Abaddon watched from across the street, Jimmy sitting on his bucket at his side. Each night Jerome retired to his room, his body weary, and his spirit discontent.

It was on a Monday morning that Abaddon crossed over the street, motioning Jerome down from the scaffold.

Folding his arms across his chest, he said, "I've been watching you, Mr. Bouchard."

"Yes, sir."

"You seem to me to be a man who knows his business, a perfectionist, and you're driving my foreman mad. I like that in a man."

"Thank you, Mr. Damon. It's my work, you see."

"You said you were an architect, I believe?"

"Yes, sir. In France I was well known for my public buildings."

"Mr. Bouchard, I can't help but wonder why you are in Guthrie station."

Looking at his blistered hands, Jerome said, "I've wondered the same thing, Mr. Damon. I lost my wife and needed a challenge, I suppose, a new place."

"Well, Mr. Bouchard, I believe Guthrie station qualifies as a challenge."

"Yes, sir."

"Jimmy," Abaddon said, turning, "get on route. Tell those other boys I expect new subscriptions if they figure on working for *The Capital City*."

Hooking the bale over his arm, Jimmy trudged away. "I got more subscriptions than any of them," he said over his shoulder.

"Reminds me of myself at that age," Abaddon said, dabbing at the perspiration on his forehead. "Come by my tent tonight, Mr. Bouchard. We need to talk."

Jerome stacked lumber and gathered up tailings throughout the morning. At noon he ate an apple in the shade of the lumber wagon. While the other men rested, he worked on his drawings, sharpening his pencil on a sandstone. He wondered what Abaddon might want. Perhaps he was to be given more responsibility, or fired for annoying the foreman. Perhaps what happened between him and Mavis had been revealed. Reading Abaddon Damon was not an easy task. There was little to do but wait and see.

That afternoon the men shed their shirts in the heat. Thunderheads gathered, curdling and boiling into the blue, disappearing as they came, like ships at sea. The wind arrived on schedule from out of the west. The town swarmed with wagons and teams of horses, their heads drooping in the swelter. The stink of manure brought the buzz of flies. From all corners, the sounds of saws and hammers rang through the city.

When the day ended, Jerome walked to Abaddon's tent, where the publisher's shadow loomed through the canvas, his press clacking away.

"Mr. Damon?" Jerome called from the door.

"Come in," he said, shutting down his press.

"You wanted to see me?"

"Pull up a chair, Mr. Bouchard. Would you care for a whiskey?"

"Yes," Jerome said, hat in hand, "thank you."

Reaching under the press, Abaddon retrieved a bottle of whiskey and poured a shot for each of them.

"I like a man who'll have a drink. Shows character and flexibility."

Jerome sipped on the whiskey while Abaddon scrubbed at the ink on his hands.

"I like the suggestions you've made on the building, Mr. Bouchard," he said.

"Thank you, sir."

"You're wondering why you're here, I suppose?"

"Mr. Damon, I'm sorry about interfering with the foreman. It's just that he was going about it all wrong."

"That's not why I asked you to come," he said, pulling up a chair, rolling the whiskey in the glass. "Fact is, I've just signed a contract with the Territory of Oklahoma. *The Capital City* is hereafter more than just a newspaper office, Mr. Bouchard."

"I don't understand."

"It's a publishing house, too. *The Capital City* has the sole rights for printing every government document and book in the entire Territory. Whether it's a courthouse record, an arrest warrant, or a schoolchild's report card, *The Capital City* will print it and distribute it. Mr. Bouchard, this company's going to be running twenty-four hours a day, seven days a week to meet all the orders. There's going to be a steady income, a foundation from which to grow. In short, Mr. Bouchard, *The Capital City* is going to be the most powerful paper in all of the Territory. It will be the place to advertise, and that means money."

"Yes, sir, but I'm not certain what that has to do with me."

"Another whiskey?"

"Thank you, no," he said. "But what if we don't get the capital, Mr. Damon?"

"That's not possible, Bouchard," he said, his voice hardening.

"Yes, sir."

"That building up there is just a start. With this contract, I'm going to need room, lots of room, a basement for Mergenthaler linotypes, Babcock cylinder presses, and the Goss webb-fed. I'll need a place for job work, editorial offices, binderies, circulation, and sales rooms. Its got to be big, Bouchard, big and unforgettable. There will be thousands of legal notices, and orders from the railroad. There will be advertisements, and circulars, and accounting books. We are going to need a library, reception rooms, a telegraph office, space for a cartoonist. I want storage, lots of storage, and windows. I want people to see the working innards of this paper.

"I want a building that can be seen from ten mile out. I want them to feel it in their guts when they top the hill into Guthrie station. In short, build it worthy of the capital, Mr. Bouchard."

Sitting down his glass, Jerome stood. "You want *me* to design it?"

"That's right. I'm putting you on full carpenter's salary as of tomorrow. You get those drawings to me soon, you hear."

"Mr. Damon, I'm an architect, not a carpenter."

"It's just the beginning for you, Bouchard," he said, tossing back his whiskey. "You stick with me, and I'll see that you get every public building that comes along. Course, if you'd rather sleep in the tunnels, that's up to you."

"But your lot is too small for such a project."

"Turns out that the Liebermans are selling their lot," he said. "They couldn't come up with the lumber and decided to move on. I bought it this morning."

"Mr. Damon," Jerome said, sticking out his hand, "I'd be delighted to build your building."

Abaddon took a newspaper from the press and handed it to Jerome.

"Make it grand, Bouchard, one fitting of this newspaper. Bring me the drawings when you're ready. Don't take too long," he said, turning back to his press. "In the end, it's time that matters most."

Back in his room, Jerome turned up the lamp, opening *The Capital City*. The headline read:

Two Dead, One Wounded in Daring Capture

Deputy Buck Reed brought the bodies of Deputy Roland Treece and Mavis Ellison to Guthrie station on Monday. Treece disappeared while on his way from the Walnut Encampment to the Territory several weeks ago. The deputy's body was discovered by the Deventers, who had purchased a homestead from Carl and Mavis Ellison near the Kansas border. It was further reported that Mr. Jerome Bouchard, while on his way to Guthrie station, was attacked by the Ellison couple and relieved of his belongings.

The U.S. Marshal's Office stated that a gunfight ensued when the killers encountered Deputy Reed, who was conducting an investigation at the Deventers' homestead at the time. Mavis Ellison lost her life. Mr. Creed McReynolds, a local businessman and attorney, who had accompanied Deputy Reed to the Deventers, was wounded in the crossfire.

Deputy Reed suffered no injuries and was unavailable for comment, having ridden out to investigate thefts in the area. Mavis Ellison was buried in the Guthrie station cemetery. Carl Ellison has been transported to Fort Smith to stand trial.

Setting the newspaper aside, Jerome listened to the laughter of a woman in the next room. Taking out a tablet, he drew a line, his fingers awkward from the day's work. With broad sweeps, he sketched the foundation, the intersecting lines. He would make it of stone, of brick, and of glass. He would build a tower for all to see, with a capitol dome to reign supreme.

Through the night he labored, and as dawn broke he fell exhausted into his bed.

For a month he worked, rising, like the whores, at day's end. Each evening before starting, he would take his beans and cornbread at the Blue Belle. Afterward, he would work through the night under the lantern's light on Abaddon's publishing house.

"By god," Abaddon said, walking around his press with Jerome's drawings, "by god, just look at that."

"The first course is rough stone," Jerome said, "followed by brick, and at the top, as you can see, refined and elegant. It's born from the earth, its roots rugged and strong, its summit a bloom in the sunshine."

"By god, Bouchard, it's a fitting monument."

"Thank you, Mr. Damon. There's fifty thousand square feet, big enough to accommodate the growth of a state, big enough for a capital city, big enough for Abaddon Damon, I should think."

"But where do we get that kind of stone? It'll cost a king's ransom to freight it in."

"I know," Jerome said. "It's a problem I've yet to solve, but I will."

"She's a fine building," he said again. "Where the hell did you say you were from, Bouchard?"

"France."

Pulling out his whiskey bottle, Abaddon poured a drink for each of them.

"You're a hell of an architect, Bouchard. Here's to *The Capital City* building and its creator. May they both live long and prosperous lives."

"Thank you, sir," Jerome said.

Before turning back to his press, Abaddon said, "I'm a member of the City Council, Bouchard. There's a city hall to be built. I intend to recommend you for the job, but I expect *The Capital City* to be finished first. Get started on it as soon as possible."

"Yes, sir," Jerome said. "Tomorrow."

His head spinning with excitement, Jerome climbed the hill to the building site. From where he stood, he could see the Liebermans as they loaded the last of their things into the wagon. Hand in hand, they walked to the edge of their lot and looked down on the town. For the longest time they stood in silence, before climbing into the wagon and riding down the street.

From where Jerome stood, the town spread into the hills, the train tracks striking into the prairie. The aroma of beans and cornbread drifted from the Blue Belle, and he realized how hungry he was. But there was one more thing he must do. Before he ate, he visited the hilltop cemetery not far from the river, no more than a few graves scattered in the rawness of the earth. Standing at the foot of Mavis's grave, he held his hat in his hands.

"You danced your dance," he whispered, "and left your memory burned in my soul. Now, I will dance mine, and leave my mark upon this land."

The stiffness in Creed's arm had eased but was still uncomfortable. Once, he started to scratch at the itch beneath the bandage, but he didn't, Alida's warning still fresh in his memory. Along the dampness of the valley, sunflowers grew, their peppery smell on the wind. Snapping off a pigweed, Roan shook her head against the gnats and worked the stalk past her bit.

From a rise, he could see Bear Creek, no more than a silver string winding through the valley. Smoke twisted from a stand of trees that grew along the bank. A grain wagon was pulled into the shade, a tarp staking off its end and a small boy was playing in the sand beneath it. Creed figured to ride in. There were folks abandoning homesteads everywhere, and there was no sense in passing up an opportunity.

A woman worked over the fire, lifting her head as he reined up.

"Hello, ma'am. Name's Creed McReynolds. Saw your fire from up on the hill."

Standing, she dabbed at her forehead with the back of her sleeve.

"I'm Mary Sue Johnson," she said, "from Springfield, Missouri. This here's my boy, Johnny. Arnie's in Guthrie station on business. Expect him back any time soon. "

"Glad to meet you," he said.

"This here's our claim, up to that bend and then back south to the cottonwoods. We've got it staked off and filed."

"It's a fine piece of property," he said, "though prone to flooding in wet years, I suspect."

"They ain't no such thing as wet years in these parts, Mister," she said.

"I'm buying up land here and there," he said, "from folks who figure farming might not be what they expected. Don't know of anyone interested, do you?"

"Maybe you'd like to stay for squirrel?" she asked. "It's a young one. Shot it myself just this morning. Me and the boy was about to eat."

Putting his hat back on, Creed said, "I don't want to be of trouble, ma'am."

"No trouble. Almost forgot how to talk, though. It's a lonely place out here."

"I'd like it just fine," he said, dismounting.

The boy dug his toes in the sand and looked up at Creed through blond bangs.

After the squirrel and cornbread had been served, they found shade under the tarp, sitting on a drift log that had been pulled up from the creek. When they were finished eating, Johnny dug holes in the sand with a buffalo bone, burying and unburying his feet.

"What you figure to do with all that land you're buying?" she asked. "It won't grow but sage and skunkbrush, and precious little of that."

"It's an investment on the future, that's all. May come to something. May not," he replied. "Johnny, look in my saddlebag over there, and you'll find a stick of licorice. I been saving it just for you."

Digging through the bag, Johnny found the licorice, holding it up for his mother to see, a big smile on his face.

"You go on and play now Johnny," she said. "Me and Mr. McReynolds want to talk." After Johnny had disappeared into the trees, she said. "Thanks, Mister. He don't get much in the way of things a boy wants."

"Sure," he said. "He's a fine boy by the looks of him."

Standing, she leaned against the tarp rope, looking out on the prairie. "Fact is, Mr. McReynolds, Arnie's putting our place up in the paper, so I guess we might be one of those farmers you been looking for, and there's three more families up the valley here looking to do the same. This is a bitter land. It don't give nothing up. It never will.

"Our milk cow died of snakebite, died out there in the middle of the creek trying to cool off her swelling. We been living on squirrel and cornmeal ever since. I want to go back to Springfield where my people are and where apples grow on trees and every once in awhile the sky clouds up and it rains, one of those sweet, gentle rains that turns everything to life. I want Johnny to learn how to read and to have a real bed to sleep in, and I want other women to talk to. I seen what happens to them out here, how their skin turns to leather, and how their fingers knurl up from the work. I don't want it. I don't want it at all."

"How much did you have in mind for the place?" he asked.

"Arnie should be home soon," she said. "You could come back. He'd make you a right fair price of it. I'm sure."

"Maybe I'll ride up the valley and do some checking, come back by. I been paying a hundred dollars cash for good quarters. You and your husband talk it over. There's folks selling for less." Taking up Roan's reins, he mounted. "Thanks for the squirrel," he said, "and I'll see you in a few days."

It was closer to a week when Creed topped the hill once again. In his pocket were deeds for three quarter-sections of land, two of them at a hundred dollars each, the third, a rich quarter of bottom land, at a hundred and twenty-five.

He spotted the boy first, fishing in the creek with a willow stick, his overalls rolled high above his knees. Mary Sue stood at the back of the grain wagon folding a blanket. A man led a horse out of the trees, tugging his hat down, working his way toward the wagon. When Mary Sue saw Creed, she waved him over.

"Mr. McReynolds," she said, "I was beginning to wonder if you'd changed your mind." Taking his horse's reins, she waited for him to dismount. "I'd like for you to meet my husband, Arnie Johnson."

His stout handshake was testimony to hard work and honesty. "About my place, it's a fair quarter," he said, looking down the creek. "Good bottom land. I'd take a hundred and fifty for her and be on my way."

Pushing back his hat, Creed hooked his foot up on the wagon wheel. "I'm sure it's worth every penny, Mr. Johnson," he said, "but there's bottom land for sell all the way to Guthrie station. A hundred dollars is my top offer."

Arnie looked over at Mary Sue and then down to where Johnny was baiting his hook.

"Maybe a hundred and twenty-five, then. Our trip to Winfield was near that much. We're packed and ready to leave. Mary Sue wants to go home, and the boy, too. We'd be out of here by sunrise."

"I'd like to help you out, Mr. Johnson, but my offer stands."

Looking over at Mary Sue, Arnie shrugged. "It's a hundred then," he said, turning about. "Get him the deed, and good riddance to the whole of this Territory."

When she came back from the wagon with the deed, Creed peeled off a hundred-dollar bill. Tucking it into her dress pocket, she turned to leave.

"Here," he said, "a dollar for the boy, for when he gets to town. Buy him whatever he wants."

"Good bye, Mr. McReynolds," she said sharply, turning back to her blanket. "It's the boy's father what buys his needs."

As he rode out, Creed reined up, looking back on the valley. A trail of dust drifted up from the wheels of the Johnsons' wagon as it rumbled north to Kansas. In his pocket were deeds to a full section of prime bottom. In his stomach a spot burned sour and hot as he kicked Roan into a trot toward Guthrie station.

Forgoing a rest, he rode on through the heat of the day, and by evening Roan's head hung low. At dusk Creed dismounted and led her into a grove of trees. Camping alone was a dreary affair, one that he did not relish, but darkness prevailed over all on the prairie.

Water seeped from the rocks and gathered in a basin. After filling his canteen, he watered Roan, and hobbled her out to graze. Wood was plentiful, and he soon struck a fire against the night.

Wrapping his blanket about him, he listened to Roan pluck shoots of grass, to the munch of her jaws, and her snort of approval with each find. Soon he slept. He dreamed of Alida, of her voice, of her hands, and the gold of her hair.

When he awoke, the fire was dead, and the moon was stalled in the night. Something had awakened him.

The drumbeat came from the dark, from far away, but certain, like the beat of a heart. He fought the impulse to go. Something drew him, something ancient and compelling. Slipping on his boots, he followed its cadence. When he saw the light of their fire, he crawled to the canyon's edge. Below, the warriors danced to the beat, their heads bent, their shadows lifting and falling against the canyon wall. The women, too, danced, with arms locked and eyes ahead as they shuffled in a circle.

They were Kiowa, of this he was certain because of the colors, phallic symbols, and painted horses on their teepees. Their yips and cries called to him from out of the canyon, and he struggled against an impulse to join their dance once more.

Moving through the darkness, he found his way back to camp. Crawling beneath his blanket, he listened for the drums, but they were silent. Getting up, he stirred the coals of his fire, adding wood until the flames licked into the sky. He was not really of them—an accident of birth, that's all. No one, no people would drag him into the past, take from him what he'd earned, what he was to become. At this moment he was more successful than all who had gone before, and he owed no one for that. Unable to sleep, he stoked the fire again and waited for dawn.

Skipping breakfast, he caught up Roan and headed in to Guthrie station. Coming to the trailhead that descended into the Cimarron valley, he dismounted. The path coiled through the rocks and down to the river. In the distance, he could see dozens of new buildings sprawling across the hills. Dust rose from a wagon trekking along the bank of the river.

At the bottom of the trail, he turned south and into the sands of the Cimarron. When he made the bend, he thought he recognized the wagon and turned toward it. As he got closer, he could see Samuel's bald head, Lena with her scarf pulled about her ears. Dismounting, he waited for them to pull the last yards up the trail.

"Creed," Samuel said, leaning over to take his hand. "We heard that you had been wounded?"

"A close call," Creed said, holding up his arm, "but it's doing fine."

"And look at you," Lena said, adjusting her scarf, "half-starved if ever I've seen it."

"My appetite was a bit short for awhile," Creed said, tucking in his shirt, "but I'm making up for it now." Leaning against the wagon, he looked up at Lena. "Where are you headed?"

"Have some lunch with us," she said, "and we'll tell you all about it."

"There's a shade elm just back aways," he said, "with a sandy bottom for resting."

"We'll turn about," Samuel said, clucking his tongue at his team.

Samuel built a fire while Creed helped Lena with the food from the wagon. When she pulled back the tarp, he could see the bolts of cloth and the buggy axle they'd used to drive their stakes. He didn't say anything as she covered them up again.

The coffee pot boiled in the coals while Lena fried eggs, stacking them onto slices of sourdough. Topping each with a slice of onion, she seasoned them with salt and black pepper and placed them on a pie tin. With a smile she handed one to Creed.

After lunch, Samuel poured coffee all around and took up his place in the shade.

"That was great, Lena," Creed said, rubbing his stomach. "I didn't realize how hungry I was."

"Boys," she shrugged, "they never know what they need until they are told."

"I've been wondering," Creed said, "about the bolts of cloth in the wagon."

Lena sipped her coffee, looking down the river.

"It didn't work out for us, that's all. We're leaving Guthrie station, going back to New York."

"I don't understand," Creed said, glancing over at Samuel. "What about your plans? What about the store you dreamed of building? I thought things were coming along for you."

Tossing the end of her coffee into the sand, Lena watched it seep away.

"When you're young, you believe that your dream will set you apart. It's the dream that matters more than anything. It's the hope when all else fails.

Hooking the cup handle over her finger, she swung it back and forth like the pendulum of a clock.

"I was told once that your great-grandchildren will not be able to find your grave, that you will be forgotten forever from this earth within that short time." Setting the cup down, she looked at Creed. "This day I would not be able to find my own great-grandparents' graves. They're somewhere in New York, I think, but then I can't be certain."

"Oh, Lena," Samuel said, "you must stop talking that way."

"Samuel is right," she said. "These things are best reserved for the old to ponder."

"But what about your store?" Creed asked.

"We couldn't get the lumber," Samuel said. "No one gets the lumber without Abaddon Damon's approval."

"But that's ridiculous," Creed said. "It's my lumber company, and I make those decisions."

"It's your lumber company," Samuel said, "but Abaddon's railroad."

"What do you mean?"

"No lumber," Lena said, her dark eyes snapping, "nor anything else for that matter, comes into Guthrie station on the railroad without Abaddon's approval. In return he promotes the railroad each day in his *Capital City*. It's shameless, the power he wields. And the others, they are for him and for themselves, just as it was from the beginning."

"Even if we were to get our lumber, we could never depend on supplies for our store," Samuel added. "Sooner or later we'd lose, so we took his offer."

"What offer?"

"To sell our lot to *The Capital City*."

"You sold your lot?"

"It's enough to get us back home," Samuel said, "and Roop returned what was owed. It was not his fault, and we do not blame him, nor you. Abaddon's power grows each day, as does his wealth."

Taking a handful of sand, Lena shined the tin clean.

"Even now his editorials are blistering," she said. "Woe be to the man who crosses him."

"He has the printing contracts for all of the Territory," Samuel said, "and the ear of every politician."

"And all others are the peasants," Lena said, tossing the pan into the box.

Roan shook her head against the flies that had arrived with the smell of food, and that now gathered in her ears.

"It's home we're going, and not soon enough for me," Samuel said.

"The promise land," Lena scoffed, "the land of broken promises."

Brushing the sand from his pants, Samuel reached for Creed's hand. He was shorter than Creed remembered, older, and his face was drawn and tired.

"I am an old man," he said, "who has suffered too much disappointment, but I tell you, this is a city born of greed, a land stolen, and without regret. It will die from its own gluttony soon enough. They've gathered here like dregs at the drain. You beware, my boy, that you aren't next on Abaddon's hook."

"Shaw," Lena said, waving her hand, "you talk too much. Come, Samuel, let's be on our way, and leave our young friend here to his business."

Climbing onto the wagon seat, Samuel untied the reins and adjusted his hat.

"It's a long way home," he said, "and not without its shame. You forget an old man's complaints. They are of no consequence."

"I never thanked you," Creed said. "You know, about not saying anything when the marshal came to reclaim his street."

"It was but a small lie," he said, "unimportant among so many on that day."

With a snap of the reins they moved off down the river. Creed watched until the wagon disappeared.

By the time he reached the outskirts of Guthrie station, his arm ached from the wound, down deep where the healing was not yet complete.

The air was heavy and humid, and lather gathered beneath Roan's cinch.

There were now buildings and the bustle of people where open prairie once lay. Goods and services were advertised everywhere, claims as extravagant as the size and colors of their signs. Where raw excitement once reigned, there was but sober business at every turn. Stacks of lumber crowded the streets, and men swung from structures, hammering, sawing, climbing through the frameworks like chimpanzees in trees.

After taking Roan to the stable, Creed walked up the hill. Aside from a bath, he was uncertain of his next move. Samuel's warning was still nagging and fresh. But he was in need of some time to think things through, that was for certain, to make his plans. As Samuel said, why should he worry? An old man's complaint had little to do with Creed McReynolds in the end.

From the southwest, the clouds darkened, and the winds retreated into the belly of a storm. The smells of Guthrie mounted as they steeped in the heat.

At the entrance of the Blue Belle, he spotted Flea Bag curled against the wall, nostrils attracting flies, brows peaking at their intrusion. Flea Bag snorted a welcome and went back to sleep.

Roop was sitting at a table next to the window, having a drink, watching the storm clouds as they thickened on the horizon.

"What you drinking, partner?" Creed asked, pulling up a chair.

"Why, if ain't Creed McReynolds," he said, pushing back his hat. "Whiskey and water, mostly whiskey. Heard you been shot and left for dead."

"Well, you're half-right," Creed said, holding up his arm. "Had some pretty good care, or I'd *be* dead, that's for sure." Catching the bartender's eye, he pointed at Roop's glass. "Just rode in," he said. "It's like a different place around here."

"Yes, sir, it is," Roop said, sipping at his whiskey. "Every morning I have to ask my way around all over again. It's like the whole world's changed up while I slept. Onct even Flea Bag got lost. I found him sleeping down in the tunnels with the cats."

The bartender sat down Creed's whiskey and water.

"Start me a tab," Creed said.

When the bartender looked over at Roop, Roop shrugged, "This here man owns the McReynolds Lumber Company, Jake. I reckon he's good for his whiskey."

"Yes, sir, Mr. McReynolds," the bartender said. "You pay your tab anytime you've a notion."

"What's with all the attention?"

"Guess he knows more than you," Roop said, "which ain't all that surprising."

"Knows what?" Creed asked, taking back his whiskey.

"Knows the McReynolds Lumber Company is the richest company in Guthrie station, that's what."

"We're doing okay, then?"

Finishing off his whiskey, Roop slid his glass to the edge of the table. The bartender refilled it.

"Yesterday I deposited ten thousand in the bank, minus my own wages of course. The lumber can't get here fast enough, and every stick of it's coming through the McReynolds Lumber Company. You're going to need a warehouse soon. When that lumber gets wet, the customers fuss, although they take it in the end, since they got no choice."

A flash of lightning cut from the cloud, and thunder pealed in the distance.

"Guess you're not living in a culvert anymore, then?"

"Not 'less I'm too drunk to get home," he said. "I got a room in the hotel here. Keeps me from getting lost so much, and there's all the comforts of home."

Rain swept down the street, drops racing in rivulets down the dust-coated window.

"Blowing up a storm," Creed said.

"Make it a rule to never complain about the rain in this country," Roop said. "Man might not see it again for a hundret years."

The fiddler struck up a tune at the end of the bar, his head down, his fiddle worn and yellowed from the scrub of his whiskers. Flea Bag lifted his head and then lay back down. The men at the table laughed and cussed as they ended their game, stirring the dominoes for another set. The bartender brought Creed and Roop more drinks, wiping the table with his towel.

"Run into Samuel and Lena down on the river this morning, Roop," Creed said, sipping at his whiskey. "They told me they'd sold their lot to Abaddon Damon."

"That's how I hear it," Roop said.

"Lena said they couldn't get their lumber, that Abaddon squeezed them out because he had the railroad in his pocket."

Rubbing at his hands, Roop looked out the window.

"I gave them their money back, Creed. That was all I could do, given the circumstances."

"It's true then, about the railroad?"

"Oh, it's true enough. That order just never came in for one reason or the other. Once I thought to give them someone else's order, but I didn't. Fact is," he said, looking away, "I didn't have the grit. Orders for McReynolds Lumber could stop just as easy, I figured." Reaching for his drink, he downed it and dabbed at his mouth with the back of his hand. "Abaddon wanted that lot, and now it's his."

Creed ordered another round, and they drank as the storm deepened outside. Rain fell in torrents, and thunder rattled the windows of the Blue Belle. They drank a toast to McReynolds Lumber, and to their burgeoning bank account, ten thousand strong in the Territorial Bank. Taking out the deeds, Creed spread them across the table, and they drank to the land and more to follow.

"Roop," he said, "you ever wonder what would happen if Guthrie didn't get the capital?"

"It's like wondering about the end of the world," he said, "a desperate thought altogether, and precious little a man could do about it." Polishing off his drink, he drummed his fingers on the table. "But the way I figure it, the run out of Guthrie station would be filled with hate instead of hope, and she'd be a sight faster and more dangerous than the run in." Rising unsteady from the table, Roop let Flea Bag in out of the rain. Sitting back down, he waited for another round. "But it ain't going to happen, no more than the end of the world, 'cause there's just no reason for it to be. That's the way I see it."

"Of course, you're right," Creed said.

Watching Flea Bag curl up at their feet for a nap, he added, "Stinks like a wet dog, Roop."

Resting his boots on Flea Bag's back, Roop looked hurt.

"It's the way of a wet dog to smell such," he said, "though most object to being reminded. But this here's a special dog, as you can see, and slow to take offence, even at the coarseness of rich landowners."

"I apologize," Creed said, lifting his drink. "Here's to Flea Bag, and to any other dog, wet nor dry, who has been subjected to my insensitivity."

Afterward, as the liquor flowed, Creed told him of the encounter with Carl and Mavis, and of Alida, her hands so small and white, and of the books she kept on top of her trunk.

Roop listened until Creed had run his course.

"Sounds to me like you've taken a liking to this girl."

"It's just that she and her brother live out there alone, and both of them so young. It's a shame."

"Yes, a shame," Roop said, grinning.

"What, you ole goat?"

"What, yourself," he said.

"Something struck me while I was there, a plan," Creed said.

"Didn't have nothing to do with that girl's hands, did it?"

Creed finished his drink, and the room shifted a little under him. Outside, the storm raged, and the rain swept down the street.

"It's a mountain of stone they live on, Roop, stone so hard that neither grass nor tree will grow."

"How is it they make a living out there?" Roop asked.

"They don't," he said, "except for what they catch in a few traps, which isn't all that much."

"Say what's on your mind," Roop said, "'fore Flea Bag and me both die of old age." Reaching down, Roop pulled at Flea Bag's ear. "Think maybe Flea Bag's already gone."

"I made a deal for her place," Creed said, "leased it out for a quarry. I'm going to ship stone in on the railroad, right here into Guthrie station. These frame buildings are good enough for now, but what about when she becomes the capital, Roop? They're going to want grand buildings, buildings of stone, and McReynolds Lumber's going to have it ready to sell."

"Lordee," Roop said, looking at the bottom of his glass, "only Creed McReynolds would figure he could sell rocks and get by with it."

"Well, maybe so and maybe not," Creed said, hooking his elbows onto the table for support, "but you'll sing a different tune when the money rolls in."

"Come on, friend," Roop said, taking Creed under the arm. "I'll get you a room whilst one of us can still find it."

Moaning, Creed rubbed at the throb in his temples and scoured the fuzz from his tongue. After dressing, he made his way to the Blue Belle.

"How 'bout some breakfast?" the bartender asked.

"Thanks, no," Creed said, sipping at his coffee.

"Say, ain't you that McReynolds feller that was in here last night?"

"Maybe," Creed said. "What happened?"

"I liked to never got that danged hound out of here," he said, flipping the towel over his shoulder. "The more I pulled, the tighter he squeezed them eyes shut."

"That so," Creed said.

"I thought he'd died, or got into the rotgut. Why, I had to drag him out by his ears."

"That's Roop's dog," Creed said. "He's a tad backward."

"Roop or the dog?" he asked, checking the level in his coffee pot.

"Good point," Creed said. "Why don't you take it up with him when he comes in."

Grinning, the bartender turned about. "Yes, sir," he said, "I figure to do just that."

Creed's headache had downgraded to thumps by the time he found Abaddon Damon's tent. His operation had expanded to a maze of tents with tentacles stretching in all directions. Men were everywhere, working at presses, or hunched over their desks.

The wind whipped Abaddon's hair across his eyes, as he stepped to the door. "Well," he said, "if it isn't the Territorial crime fighter. You made headlines in *The Capital City* since we last met."

"Not by design," Creed said, shaking his hand.

"Come in out of the heat. You look a little pale."

Holding up his arm, Creed said, "It's the wound."

"Pull up a seat. I've got news. *The Capital City* has landed the printing contract for the whole of the Territory," he said, his eyes like the lit fuse of a firecracker. "On top of that, our subscriptions have quadrupled, not to mention our advertising. There's enough legals alone to keep us afloat, if worse comes to worse."

Hooking his foot up on a chair, Abaddon leaned into his knee. "Perhaps a whiskey," he said, "to ease the wound, I mean?"

"Thanks anyway," Creed said. "Fact is, I came to inquire about the lumber I'd set aside for the Liebermans."

"The Liebermans? Oh, yes," he said, pointing his chin in the direction of his lot, "the old couple with the bolts of cloth."

"They said you prevented them from getting lumber orders, orders that I had promised them."

Turning his chair around, Abaddon sat down, crossing his legs. Red crept from beneath the high-buttoned collar.

"I bought them out, and at a decent price, too. They weren't going to make it, you know. Everybody could see that. *The Capital City* needed that lot."

"I promised," Creed said.

"They were tired, as you know. How long could they have lasted, even with a store? This is a tough land; besides, they left with a good nest egg, and a grand adventure to tell back home."

Leaning forward, he locked his blue eyes onto Creed.

"We're growing fast, faster than I could've imagined. Nothing happens in this Territory that *The Capital City* doesn't know about. No one makes a move without its support. We could become a state any day now."

"Perhaps you're right," Creed said, "but it seems a shame."

"Now," he said, reaching into his table drawer and pulling out a stack of papers, "I guess you've come for these."

"The land notices?"

"Belly-up homesteaders, starved out and headed home. The price of a train ticket can buy every piece of land in there. Make some fine holdings for an ambitious lad like yourself."

"Thanks," Creed said, taking the notices.

Abaddon called over his shoulder, "Jimmy."

"Yes," Jimmy answered, stooping under the side flap of the tent.

"Go get Jerome Bouchard at the work site. Tell him I have someone I want him to meet."

"Yes, sir," he said.

"The architect?" Creed asked.

"You know him?"

"You might say."

"He's a man with a vision, Creed, and he's designing the new *Capital City* building."

"I see."

"And he's going to need lumber, lots of lumber. I guess you'd be the man he needs to talk to."

Walking to the door of the tent, Creed watched Jimmy sprint down the street. He'd changed since last he saw him, his arms grown too long, like the limbs of a spider. Across the street, Jess's wagon was parked under a shade tree, his team harnessed.

"Why is it you keep that boy around, Abaddon?"

"I like him," Abaddon said. "He's a tough kid, sleeping in the tunnels, living on his own. He's a feral cat and will scratch out your eyes for a scrap. Nobody takes what's his, and he figures it's all his. We understand each other, that's all."

"Where did he come from?"

"Says his folks was killed by Indians on the way into the Territory. Who knows where he came from, and he's not saying."

Sticking his hands in his pockets, Creed walked the length of the tent and back again.

"I have leased a place up near the Kansas border," he said. "It's stone as far as you can see, high-quality stone, quarry stone that could be used for buildings. I'm convinced there will be a demand for it in Guthrie station once this initial construction phase is over."

Moments passed as Abaddon processed the information.

"How do you propose to get it here?"

"It would take a railroad siding," he said. "Wagons wouldn't do, not for a quarry."

"The railroad has a mind of its own, Creed. Building a siding just for your business might not be high on their agenda."

"That's where I thought you might help out, Abaddon. People say you've some influence with the railroad."

Sitting down at his desk, Abaddon picked up a pencil, doodling on a pad of paper as he thought.

"I want twenty percent of the quarry," he said, "and of the lumber business, too."

"What?"

"I've kept my bargain with you," he said, "right there in that stack of papers, but things have changed. Without that railroad neither your quarry nor your lumber business comes out to much."

His eyes narrowed. "Look, we're closer than ever to getting the capital. There's nothing to stop us now. I hadn't planned to tell anyone this just yet, but I intend to run for a seat in the Territorial House of Representatives. When I win, and I will, there will be a capitol building to be built, and a city hall, and a hundred other buildings, all needing materials."

Tearing off the top sheet from his pad, he showed it to Creed. On it, he'd drawn a disk, a five-pointed star in its center. Smaller stars filled the background.

"You see this?"

"What is it?"

"This is going to be the Great Seal of Oklahoma. These stars represent the forty-five states. This large star is the forty-sixth, the state of Oklahoma. Each of those rays symbolizes one of the great Indian tribes of this fine land."

"What is your point, Abaddon?"

Tearing the sheet off the pad, he wadded it up, dropping it onto the floor.

"This seal is coming to Guthrie, my friend, to the capital, so rest assured you'll be getting your twenty percent's worth."

Creed moved to the door for air. Jimmy and Bouchard were walking up the hill. The smell of Jess's wagon drifted in ahead of them.

"Twenty percent," he said. "But I don't like it, Abaddon. I don't like it at all."

"Not necessary to like it. I'll make the arrangements with the railroad."

When Bouchard entered, he took off his hat, holding it in front of his lap.

"You wanted to see me?" he asked.

"This is Mr. Creed McReynolds," Abaddon said.

"We've met, I believe," Jerome said, shaking his hand, "under trying circumstances as I recall. How are you, Mr. McReynolds?"

"Mr. McReynolds owns the lumber company here in Guthrie station and has an idea for starting up a stone quarry," Abaddon said. "I thought you might take him down to the Blue Belle and work out the details for an order for *The Capital City* building. Oh, one other thing, Jerome. Creed and I have just gone into business together, so it's prime stone we'll need, isn't it, only the best for *The Capital City*."

At the Blue Belle, Jerome rolled out his drawings. His voice was pitched as he explained them in detail to Creed.

When he was finished, Creed sat back in his chair.

"It's beautiful, Jerome, overwhelming like Abaddon himself. And that dome on top of the tower, how could it be otherwise?"

"My soul is in this building," he said.

After they'd eaten, Creed told him of the monk he'd found dead in the cave of stone, and of the shooting that tore through his arm, and of his plans to build the quarry.

Jerome listened, his coffee growing cold.

"The monk," he said. "I wonder who he was?"

"We'll never know, I suppose."

"And the stone," Jerome said, his eyes lighting, "I remember the stone well. How could one forget its beauty or the beauty of the girl who lives there? From the best and the hardest stone, I will lay the first course of *The Capital City* building."

"It was you who gave me the idea," Creed said.

"Me?"

"With what you said, about buildings rising from the soil."

"Oh, yes, exactly," he said, "but it must be quarried with care, you must promise."

"I know little of quarrying," Creed said, "nor even how to find someone who does."

"There are those who do," Jerome said. "If not here, then back east."

"We'll start with Abaddon's order for *The Capital City* building," Creed said. "I'm sure he would have it no other way."

"Abaddon Damon is a man who gets what he wants," Jerome said, rolling up his plans. "But we both need him, I suppose."

"I'd like to leave soon before someone else gets the same idea on the quarry," Creed said, "and I have much to do. Do you think you could find a quarry man for me?"

"I never thanked you for the help you gave me," Jerome said. "I'll find someone."

"Thanks, Jerome," he said, standing.

That afternoon Creed bought three wagons, with mule teams for each, at the Hamsworth Barns. If there was to be a railroad siding, he'd have to have a good road built from the quarry.

At the Cottonwood bridge, he found a half-dozen men working rip-track for the railroad. With the promise of double pay and a week's advance, he had his first crew.

By five o'clock he'd purchased enough grub, tents, and hand tools to fill all three wagons, and then he set out to find Roop.

Flea Bag, asleep beneath the flatcar, lifted an ear, and lolled his tongue into the dirt. From atop the lumber, Roop called down as Creed approached.

"It's work we're doin' up here, Mister."

"Hello," Creed said. "Got a minute?"

Climbing down, Roop took off his gloves, and dusted his hat against his leg.

"Minute's about all I got. Busy making Creed McReynolds a rich man, ain't I."

Crawling under the car to escape the sun, Roop lit a cigarette.

"I've struck a deal on that quarry with Abaddon," Creed said, crawling under with him, "railroad siding and all. Fact is, I need you to handle the lumber orders for awhile longer, until I get things set up at the quarry. It's going to take a good while before I can get back. I've got supplies and men ready to go. Bouchard is tracking down a good quarry man for me."

Drawing on his cigarette, Roop looped his arms about his knees.

"I reckon I could do it awhile longer, although it ain't my cup of tea, you understand."

"Soon as I get things lined out, I'll take it off your hands, Roop." Reaching down, he pulled at Flea Bag's ear. "There's one more thing."

"Lordee," Roop, said, "who would of thought."

"I need a man to go around and offer bids on these homesteads. They're going for the price of a ticket home, even less some of the time. With the money we got coming in on lumber, we can buy plenty of land, Roop, and some day it's going to be worth a lot more."

Squashing out his cigarette on the car wheel, Roop shrugged.

"What you need is a bastard what don't mind taking a man's home."

"I need someone who knows how to drive a bargain."

"There's a whole town of bastards back there in Guthrie station. Odds of finding one ought be pretty high."

"I need a man I can trust, Roop."

Slipping his gloves under his belt, he pushed back his hat.

"I'll do it for awhile, as a favor to you."

"Thanks, Roop. You take what you need from the profits, including expenses. I'll talk to you soon as I get back."

On his way to the hotel, Creed stopped at Abaddon's building site. Bouchard was still there, as he'd hoped, and was going over the building plans.

"Have any luck finding a quarry man?" Creed asked.

"Maybe," Bouchard said, sticking his pencil behind his ear. "One of my carpenters says he rode in on the train with a quarry man. He told him he'd worked Missouri limestone most his life. He thinks he's staying down at the Ione. I should know by tomorrow."

"I'm leaving in the morning to get a road laid out, Jerome. I'd appreciate it if you'd send him on if you think he'll do. Tell him to contact Roop for the supplies and for the crew."

Taking his pencil from behind his ear, Jerome nodded. "Good luck, then. I'll be needing that stone soon myself."

"It'll be here," Creed said, "one way or the other."

On the way back, he thought to stop at the Blue Belle to eat. But a weariness swept him, and his appetite vanished.

Back at his room, he lay on his bed and watched as darkness fell across Guthrie station. He thought of his mother, of how they'd walked these hills with the silence about them. In the world of the Kiowa, no man owned the land. What would she think of him now? What would she think of this man who took this land and made it his own?

And then he thought of Alida back on Stone Mountain, the way she laughed, the way she faced hardships head-on, the way her heart beat against his chest when he kissed her. Her dreams were strong, but they were her dreams, not his. And he wondered if there was enough room for them in his world.

From the recesses of the hotel, laughter rose, shrill and false, as he turned to his sleep.

From where the trail dropped away into the rocks, Creed could see the rift and the opening of the monk's cave. It was a short ride to Alida's from here, and he kicked Roan into a trot. When Alida spotted him, she picked up the tail of her skirt and ran down the path.

"You're back," she said, breathless.

Dismounting, he slipped his hands into hers.

"You didn't doubt it, did you?"

"For just a moment," she said, holding her hand against her chest. "Will you forgive me?"

"You're forgiven," he said.

Falling in beside him, she hooked her arm through his.

"Bram's built a fence, so you won't have to hobble your horse."

"How's Bram doing?" Creed asked.

"Well, he's taken over the traps, and the team, too. Right now he's up on the ridge hunting rabbits. You'd think that no one else could do anything around here."

The smell of honeysuckle was sweet in the air, and from out of the rocks scrub oak and cedar clung to life. Alida walked ahead, lifting her hair to cool her neck. How beautiful she was, he thought, how she flourished even in this place. He remembered her kiss, the way it had touched him, the way it had changed him somewhere deep inside.

"Slow down," he said.

Cocking her hand on her waist, she said, "City boy."

When they reached the dugout, she poured them glasses of water, and they sat under the shade, their legs crossed.

"Oh, that's great," he said, finishing off his drink.

Watching him over the rim of her glass, she asked, "So, how's the arm?"

Turning it this way and that, he said, "Just like new. Must have been the nursing I had."

"Must of been."

"And what about you?"

"Oh," she said, "good. I've been reading a lot while Bram hunts. This mountain is quiet, and a bit lonely, too, I admit."

Setting his glass down, he pulled out a piece of paper, handing it to her.

"It's the quarry deal, Alida. It's all set."

"That's wonderful, Creed."

"And we have a partner."

"A partner?"

"Abaddon Damon."

"But you've got the lease and everything you need. Why a partner? Why Abaddon Damon?"

"*The Capital City* is the biggest paper in the Territory, Alida, and Abaddon owns it. He's a powerful man. No one gets anywhere in Guthrie station without his blessing. There's the railroad, the legals, and the sale notices on the land. Without Abaddon there would be no siding, no contract for hauling with the railroad."

Taking the paper back, he read it over. "I tell you, Alida, I think anyone connected to Abaddon Damon and *The Capital City* will reap the rewards someday."

"What's he to do with land sales?" she asked.

"His finger's on the pulse of every transaction in the Territory, every kind of business, every delinquent tax or claim gone sour. He knows what's going on politically, too. First there with the money gets the deal, Alida. It makes all the difference."

Pulling her knees into her arms, she studied him.

"Is it right, Creed, taking people's land when they're down on their luck?"

Standing, he looked down into the valley. Below, Roan leaned against Bram's gate, her neck stretched for the grass beyond reach.

"I don't make the rules. I just play by them. Look, Alida, there's a thousand things in my head, and they all have to come together. A quarry man's on his way for the start-up. A crew's been hired out, but they're green. Quality stone's got to be found. A road has to be built to the siding. Soon we'll need freight wagons for hauling stone. There's quarters for the crew to be built, and supplies have to be brought in from Guthrie station. There's a thousand things going on, that's all."

"We're a long way from anywhere out here, Creed, with nothing but stone and wind. Who's going to buy all this? What if no one wants it?"

"When Guthrie station gets the capital, there's no stopping us," he said. "Abaddon's running for the Territorial House right now. He's even got the state seal designed in his head, for the forty-sixth state. When the time comes, the capital will need buildings, fine buildings for the state's business, buildings of stone and brick. The first order's set even now for *The Capital City* paper, and there's plenty more to come.

"I'm going to buy land. I'm going to buy land until there's no more land to be bought. Some day you won't be able to cross this state without my permission."

Picking up the glasses, Alida went into the dugout. When she came back, she took his hand.

"You've told me *what* you're going to do, Creed. You haven't told me *why*. How much do you need to make you happy? Maybe there's more important things than owning land, than making money. What about friends, people you love?"

Pulling his hand away, he walked to where the trailhead led up to the rift. From there, he could see Bram coming.

"I've seen what money and power can do, Alida."

"I've never had power nor money," she said. "I've never wanted them, I guess, not when it comes down to it. I just want to be important in someone's life. I want someone to care about me as much as I care about them."

"I can't stand still. I can't go back."

"I try to understand," she said, laying her hand on his shoulder. "I know your mother's people lost a lot, but you can't spend your life settling scores."

"It isn't that," he said. "Those days are gone."

Just then, Bram rounded the corner, his rabbits held high for all to see.

"Welcome back to Stone Mountain, Creed," he said, laying the rabbits across a rock.

"Glad to be back. I see you're getting to be a pretty good shot."

"Thanks. Long as the shells hold out."

"What's this Stone Mountain business?" Creed asked.

"That's what we call it, ain't it, Lidy? Stone Mountain, 'cause that's what it is, no more and no less."

"Well, I like it," Creed said. "Stone Mountain Quarry. That's what we'll name it."

That evening Alida spread blankets on the ground and served biscuits and plum jam for dessert. Bram cleaned his rifle, laying each piece out on a rock as he finished with it.

Picking up the dishes, Alida dropped them into a bucket of water to soak, drying her hands.

"I wonder what it's like in Guthrie station?" she asked. "Are there lots of womenfolks about?"

"It's a wonder to see," Creed said, leaning onto an elbow. "There's womenfolks at every turn, walking arm and arm up the street, just talking and talking, about who belongs to the Shakespeare Club, or who has a new order of fabric coming in from Kansas City, or who is building a new home up on capitol hill."

"I reckon I prefer the quiet of Stone Mountain," Bram said, polishing the barrel of the rifle with his shirttail.

"And there's new businesses going up," Creed said, "cropping up everywhere. Everybody wants Jerome Bouchard to design his building. It's like owning a Paris original dress, owning something no one else has. I guess he's going to have his thumbprint on every building in Guthrie station before its done."

"Oh, it sounds so exciting," Alida said. "I can't wait to go see it."

Aiming the rifle at the firelight, Bram looked down the barrel. "Did you see Buck while you were in Guthrie station?"

"I didn't get a chance to look him up, Bram. Things were a bit hectic, but Buck's the talk of the town, made himself quite a reputation. Some say he's the best deputy Guthrie station has. Of course, there are those say he's daft and has no business with a gun at all, much less a badge. They don't like the way he killed Mavis, killing her with his own bare hands like that. Guess they didn't have Carl breathing down their neck, did they."

For a moment no one spoke, each reliving that moment down at the spring.

Breaking the silence, Bram said, "Rode Windy over to that place you bought. Right nice land."

"And how were things?"

"The roof fell in on the soddy, and the well's near washed full of silt. Guess it wasn't much for saving, anyway. There's a free-range sow rootin' up everything in sight, too. Found her litter in a plumb thicket, eight in all, not countin' the runt."

"You've got some salary coming, Bram," Creed said. "You get it figured up, and I'll pay you."

"I've been thinking," Bram said, "you know, about maybe fixing up a place of my own. There's a table rock down by the spring where a man could build. It would be cool in the summer and warm in the winter."

"What do you have on your mind, Bram?"

"I been thinking that I might build a house out of this here rock, but I'd need timbers for the roof. Maybe I could trade out my salary when the time comes."

"Bram," Alida said.

"Well, I'm growed up now, Lidy, and it's time I had a place of my own. It's not like you need me around every minute, not with the quarry coming, and with the lease and all." Picking up a rock, he threw it into the darkness, and tucked his hands into his back pockets. "Comes a time a man needs to be on his own."

"Let me think about it, Bram," Creed said, looking over at Alida.

"Just a small place," he said. "where I could be on my own."

"I'll let you know soon," Creed said.

"Well," Bram said, "I'm wore out chasing rabbits half the day. Guess I'll turn in. Night Creed. Night, Lidy."

Alida turned her back, wrapping her arms about her.

"Make sure you turn out the lantern, Bram," she said.

After Bram had gone, Creed put his arm around her.

"How about a walk, Alida?"

"In the dark?"

"You afraid of the dark?"

"Who wouldn't be," she said, "with those hoopers rolling around like they do."

As they walked the path leading to the ledge, the moon rose, bathing Stone Mountain in its light.

At the ledge, where he'd first seen Carl, they sat down and hung their legs over the side. Cool air rose from the valley, and the heat from Alida's arm was warm against his own.

"I feel like a mother who's losing her son sometimes," she said.

Putting his arm about her shoulder, he pulled her against him.

"It's not about you, Alida. He's needing to be a man, that's all."

Leaning onto his shoulder, she sighed. "I know. I don't want to be his mother, Creed. I want a life of my own, too."

"Well, then you understand how he feels?"

"Yes," she said, "I suppose I do, but it feels like I'm losing him in a way, too. He's all I have left."

"It would be fine with me if Bram wants a place of his own, Alida, but I thought we should talk about it first."

"Sometimes Bram is ungrateful, you know, after all I've done."

"I know it must seem that way, Alida, but a boy steps into a man's world on his own. It's in his nature, and only he knows when that time has come."

Looking up at him, her eyes glistened. "I guess he wouldn't be that far away."

"I'm sure Bram is grateful you were here for him, Alida. You gave him the time that he needed."

"What about you?" she asked. "Did you have the time you needed?"

"There were folks to care about me, like you care for Bram."

"I'm sorry to be so selfish sometimes," she said, touching his cheek.

Opening his arms, he folded her into him, experiencing her warmth, the smell of her hair, like lilacs, and the ivory of her throat.

"I've missed you, Alida. It was like being on the other side of the world."

"Me too," she said, snuggling against him.

Slipping his arms about her waist, he held her tight. Crickets tuned up for the night, instruments a thousand strong, playing but a single note.

"I'm not always a good person," she said. "Sometimes I'm weak and selfish."

"It's in our nature to be both," he said.

"And you could do better than me, Creed, much better."

Taking her face into his hands, he looked into those eyes.

"But it's you I want, Alida."

When she kissed him, it was with abandon, boundless, a falling away into the universe.

"I love you," she said, burying her face into the warmth of his neck. "I didn't know it possible to love another person this way, but it makes me afraid."

With the tips of his fingers, he pushed back the strand of hair that had fallen across her face, brushing his lips across hers.

"We should go back," he said.

"I want to stay here," she said. "I want to be with you."

"But Alida, there is so much to be done. There is so much to be finished."

Taking his hand she held it to her breasts. "Make love with me," she whispered. "Here, tonight."

When her dress fell away, Creed hesitated at her beauty, the lilt of her breasts, the curve of her waist, the eyes, turquoise under the ivory light.

"Are you certain, Alida?"

Lying back, she lifted her arms to him.

When he lay down beside her, their bodies touched, warm in the coolness of the evening. But he waited, laying his hand on her stomach for her to know his presence. He waited for the rise and fall of her breasts, and for her abdication. As the sky brightened above them, he kissed her breasts, her nipples already erect under the warmth of his breath, and savored the salt of her skin, the smell of her, like earth and lilacs and sun. "Alida," he said, moving into her.

"I love you," she moaned, locking her fingers behind his neck, rising to him, taking him for who he was, as he was, here on Stone Mountain.

Afterward, they held each other, Alida tucked in the hollow of his shoulder. The stars spun through the sky, and a train whistle rose from out of the valley.

"Alida," he said, "I don't want it to be this way."

"What do you mean?" she asked, lifting onto an elbow.

"I love you. I want to ask you to be my wife."

Laying her arm over his chest, she pulled him close to her. "Then why don't you?"

"I've followed a straight path for a long time now, giving no thought but to my own ways."

"You must know now how I feel?" she said.

"Yes," he said. "I think I do."

"Well?"

Turning her face to him, he kissed her. "Will you marry me, then?"

The wedding took place in Guthrie station at the Ione Hotel. Bram and Roop served as witnesses, while Flea Bag slept at the door, one ear trained for any prospect of food. With so much to be done, Creed and Alida returned to Stone Mountain after a short stay at the Ione. While waiting for the crew to arrive, Creed worked on the plans for the quarry. Alida set up household, and turned a garden in the meadow.

Bram spent his days hauling and sorting stones for his house down at the spring, and as the weeks passed, they saw less and less of him. On occasion, he would come for a cup of coffee at breakfast, or for biscuits from the larder at day's end. Sometimes, early mornings, Creed would see him hitching up the team down on the meadow.

"I feel like we've run him off," Alida said, laying aside her book.

"He'll be fine," Creed said, putting his arm about her shoulders. "Soon as the quarry's up, we'll be seeing a lot more of him. Right now, he's staking out his future." Reaching over, he kissed her. "Meanwhile, we've all this time to ourselves, haven't we?"

"I've a garden to plant," she said, "and you've a road to build. Of course, that doesn't mean we have to work all the time."

"No," he said, smiling, "not all of the time."

When the plans were finished, Creed saddled up Roan and rode east toward the tracks. At the end of the meadow he planted a flag. Before losing sight of that flag, he planted another, repeating the process until the tracks were in sight. Without surveying equipment, it wasn't perfect, but it was as straight as he could make it.

In the evenings, after the winds died away, he and Alida walked, or explored Stone Mountain. Often they would lie on the ledge above the dugout to make love in the balmy open air, or sometimes they would listen to the coyote packs gathering for the night hunt. The solitude of Stone Mountain quieted all with its peace. Creed slept and ate and made love under its spell. He grew brown from the sun, and strong from the work, and came to understand why the monk had chosen such a place. He flourished under Alida's mindfulness, the sweetness of her soul, and there were times that Guthrie station was far away and small in his life.

But Alida's disapproval of his quest for land often overrode her gentleness. Even so, each day he loved her more than the last.

Once, Bram came to replenish his supplies and to see if the quarry man had yet arrived.

"It's a bit lonely, I admit," he said, finishing his second helping of food, "and I miss Alida's cooking something awful."

"You're skinny as a jackrabbit," Alida said. "Why don't you come back home, Bram?"

"I've nearly got the walls up," he said, "and when the timbers come, I can finish the roof. You let me know when the crew gets here, Creed, or if there's anything else I can do."

"I've got the road laid out. There's little left but to wait now, Bram."

The day the quarry man arrived, Alida and Creed were washing dishes in the bucket that doubled as a footstool.

"Look," Alida said, pointing, "they're coming. See, there, just beyond the meadow."

Dust rose from the horizon as the horses and wagons wound down the trail, and Creed's heart leapt. Hugging Alida, he watched as they moved onto the meadow.

"They're here," he said. "Let's go."

Clutching his hand, Alida held him for a moment.

"Now I'll have to share you," she said.

"You'll never have to share me, Alida. Now, let's hurry before they tear out the whole of Bram's fence."

The man who climbed down from the wagon was all chest and arms, his legs mere stumps beneath him. Mounted on his shoulders was an enormous head, planted there without the accommodation of a neck. His felt hat was ringed with the grime of the trail. Dust gathered on eyebrows that sprouted like wire from his forehead, and his eyes were the color of speckled bird eggs.

"You Creed McReynolds?" he asked.

"That's me," Creed said, "and this is Alida, my wife."

"Max Bode," he said, pumping Creed's hand. "I'm the quarry man, and this back here's the crew you hired. Mexicans mostly, workin' track for the railroad. Good hands, I 'spect, if not a tad superstitious."

"Welcome to Stone Mountain," Creed said. "We've been waiting. The men can make camp over there in that locust stand. There's wood cut for their fire, and a spring is just down that trail over there. The meadow's fenced, so you can turn out the teams for grazing."

"Obliged," Max said, tipping his hat. "I took the liberty of hiring out a few more hands, what with a road to be built. Them wagons back there are loaded with all the equipment a man needs for quarrying: explosives, ratchet hoists, stone and mason hammers, pitching tools, wedges, and some McReynolds kiln-dried lumber for scaffolding. Bought good mules, too, big as elephants for hauling rock. They're smarter than most and know more English than the crew. The tack's used, but good, and there's three new tumblebugs for moving road dirt."

"Seems you've done a thorough job, Max."

"Yes, sir, and that fancy Frenchman said to charge it all to the McReynolds Lumber Company, so that's what I did. Without quality stone, they're sure to hang you and me both right here atop this mountain."

"It's a tiring journey, Max," Creed said. "You and the men make camp and get some rest. We'll talk in the morning."

"Why don't you come for breakfast?" Alida said, shading her eyes with her hand. "We'd be happy for the company."

"Why, I'd like that fine, Miss."

"Sunrise?" Creed asked.

"Figure that's why God made the sun," Max said, squinting up an eye, "so's I'd know when to stand up."

When Creed awoke, Alida had breakfast on, the aroma of bacon and coffee filling the dugout. Pulling on his boots, he walked to where he could see the meadow. Smoke rose from the campfires in the locust grove below. Stretching his arms above his head, he yawned and rubbed at his face. There was a lot riding on this day, and he'd slept little last night.

"Morning," Max said as he sauntered up the path. "It's a beautiful day atop Stone Mountain."

"Morning," Creed said. "Come on in. Breakfast is nearly ready."

Stooping into the dugout, he handed Alida a paper sack. "Here, Miss. This is for you."

"Oh, Creed," she said, peeking in, "it's fresh eggs. How many would you like, Max?"

"Three or four will get me by till noon, Miss," he said, smiling. "You and your husband enjoy the rest of 'em."

Pouring a cup of coffee, Creed handed it to Max.

"Alida and I are business partners, too," he said, "besides being husband and wife, and Alida's brother is half owner in the land."

"Three foremen," he said, smiling. "Ought be an interesting project."

After breakfast, they drank coffee outside and watched the new day fill the valley. Retrieving his pipe, Max loaded it with tobacco, hooking it in the corner of his mouth.

"Have you had a chance to take a look at the stone yet?" Creed asked.

"Can't say as I have," Max said, tamping his pipe with his forefinger. "We'll have to go up aways to find out what you got here. Most of this stuff at the bottom is top stone, come rolling down the mountain a hundret years ago. Too much rain and wind weakens it, changes its nature, you might say. We need to go up to find stone with a little sap left in her."

"Sap?" Alida asked.

"Yes 'em, stone fresh out of the ground with the moisture still in her. That's when you can tell for sure what you've got."

"It's beautiful stone," Creed said, leaning forward, "red, with streaks of purple and white."

Striking a match on a button, Max lit his pipe, sending puffs of smoke into the air.

"Oh, it's handsome stone, but it's got to be strong, too. It's got to have shear strength to make fine buildings. We'll have to have fresh stone for that."

"We best be on our way, then," Creed said. "Alida, you're welcome to come, but it's likely to be a hard climb. We've got to know what this mountain has to offer, top to bottom."

"You go on. I've things to be done, anyway."

Creed struggled to keep up with Max, his energy boundless as they ascended into the rift. Horned toads perched on the rocks to warm themselves, cocking their heads as they passed, and snakes slithered into the crevices at every turn of the path. Not far from the ledge, they found the remains of a coyote kill, nothing left but hair caught in the thorns of a cactus. Coyote droppings, filled with plum seeds and undigested fur, were scattered about the site.

Short legs and all, Max leapt from rock to rock, digging stone loose with his bar, probing the strata for quantity and accessibility. Striking the stone with his hammer, he would listen for the telling ring. When satisfied, he'd climb higher, doing it all over again.

Sweat dripped from Creed's nose as he watched Max pry yet another slab from the ground.

"What do you think?" Creed asked, seeking out the shade of a rock.

"It's good enough stone, but the quality's up there," he said, pointing to the rift. "Up there's the stuff of eternity."

"But it's so high, Max."

"See where the stone's shifted like that? Well, there's apt to be beds, good beds with clean layers."

"How would we ever get it down?"

"Don't take much to go downhill, does it. We'll use stone boats. If that's quality, and I 'spect it is, it will be worth it."

"Stone boats?"

"Sleds," he said, lighting his pipe. "Course, takes a heap of running to stay out of their way once they get moving."

Taking advantage of the break, Creed fanned himself with his hat.

"Fact is, Max, there's a grave up there I'd as soon not disturb."

"A grave?"

"An ole monk, a hermit, I guess, and he died up there. It's like a sacred place."

Dusting off his hands, Max shrugged.

"Suit yourself, but there's no quarry material down here, not for the kinds of buildings that Frenchman was talking about. Oh, it's good enough for bridge work, foundations and such. But for buildings, you've got to have quality, and size, big enough for keystones, cappings, things like that. You ain't got it down here, Creed, not like that."

Creed studied the rift. "I don't know," he said. "Doesn't seem right."

"Well, that's up to you, ain't it, but for me, bones is bones and soon enough dust. What difference does it make?"

"Maybe we could take a look. I don't see any harm in looking."

When they reached the rift, the last of the moisture had been wrung from the wind. Leaning against the entry of the rift, Max peered into the darkness.

"Can't see a goddamn thing," he said. "Hand me that pry bar. I'll check one here just inside to see what we got."

"Watch the overhead," Creed said. "Looks like it could come down without much persuasion."

With his shoulder, Max leaned into the bar, and the slab loosened. Once again he heaved, this time the slab giving way. Crawling into the opening, Creed positioned himself at the other end. Air rose, damp and cool, from out of the rift. Down there somewhere lay the monk, the cross, the rats on the ledge.

On the count of three, they hefted the slab into the pathway. Moisture wept from its face, its color rich and sumptuous in the light. Taking his hammer from his back pocket, Max gave it a blow, its ring clear and uniform.

"Looks like they ain't going to hang us, after all," he said, sweat dripping from his brows. "It's quality, and look at those layers working back into that rift, unbroken as far as you can see. And that color . . . Well, by god, it just speaks for itself, don't it."

"It's good, then?" Creed asked.

"It's handsome, and it goes deep into the heart of this mountain. We might just be able to supply that Frenchman with all he can use and then some."

On the way down the mountain, Creed suggested they stop off at the spring for a cool-down.

"Couldn't hurt," Max said, wiping at his brow.

"This way," Creed said, turning onto the path that wound its way into the canopy of trees.

Above the spring, they found Bram at work stacking rocks. Taking off his gloves, he waited for Creed's introduction.

"Hello, Bram," Max said, shaking his hand. "We found some fine stone up there on your mountain."

"That's great," Bram said, putting his gloves in his back pocket. "When do we get started?"

"First, I could use a drink of that spring water, if you got no objection."

"Of course not. Help yourself."

Max took off his hat, holding his head under the icy water. After drinking out of the cup of his hand, he shook his head. "Whoeee," he said, "ain't that grand."

Afterward, they sat in the shade and rested.

"You think it will produce good stone, then?" Bram asked.

"Yes, sir, it's good stone, about the best I ever did see, if you want to know." Picking up a stick, he poked it into the mud. Taking the mud off the stick, he rubbed it between his thumb and forefinger. "All it takes now is a sure buyer, and looks to me like that's on its way."

"I just dry-stacked these stones," Bram said. "I figure it's good enough down here below the hill."

"Hell, son, I hear tell they got dry-stacked fences in England been there two-hundret years. I reckon you done just fine. But up there on that rift there's high-quality stone, the kind men need to build monuments to themselves. Man wants to live for eternity, don't he, even if it's just stacking stones one upon the other to say that he was here. It's been going on since he lived in caves, and there ain't no stopping it now."

"We start then," Creed said, "as soon as possible."

"Yes, sir," he said, "tomorrow. By the way, you know if this spring ever goes dry?"

"Same water, day and night and forever, as far as I can tell," Bram said.

Taking out his pipe, Max knocked it against his foot.

"I ain't getting any younger, boys," he said, "and quarrying stone is a young man's work."

Taking off his hat, Creed splashed cold water onto his face, drying it off with a bandanna from his pocket.

"What you trying to say, Max?"

"Fact is, I got an idea that could make a good deal of money for all of us." Holding his hand under the water, he gauged its volume. "Fact is, I'd like to share that idea, you might say. Take a cut of the profits for my old age."

"We've already made a deal on the quarry, Max."

"I ain't talking just the quarry, here, Creed. Now, there ain't nothing to lose, 'cept the time it takes to listen. I been around some, and could bring the know-how to bear. If you like my idea, I want ten percent of all she earns. If you don't, we'll get on about the quarry business and let her go at that."

"Okay, Max," he said. "I'm listening."

Reaching for his tobacco, Max pulled the string with his teeth. "There will be lots of folks needing to show off their fine homes so's others can see how important they are." Loading his pipe, he clicked it against his teeth as he thought. "It's brick they'll want, you see, and there will be streets to pave and sidewalks to lay, and factories to build, too. There will be a thousand things what needs bricks."

"Bricks?" Bram asked.

"And where would a man get bricks, I wonder?" Max said, touching off his pipe. "Kansas I reckon, or the other side of the world." Blowing out his match, he tossed it into the water, watching it drift away into the rocks. "Now, if a man had brick right here in the Territory, that would be a different story altogether."

"Go on," Creed said.

"All of Stone Mountain ain't up there no more, like I said. The wind and the rain wore her away, washed her right down here under your feet." Picking up a handful of mud, he smelled it. "Now it's clay, slick as axle grease and perfect for brick-making. And there's power here, too, in this spring, you see, a flume and overshot wheel for running a pugmill. We could pump out brick day and night just like this water, never stopping until Stone Mountain's covered with money. And there's plenty of sun for drying, god knows, and wood yonder for firing salt-glazed. There will be a road already built to the tracks, and wagons for hauling, crews for working, and a railroad for taking brick out and bringing money in. Hell, you even got a foreman's shack near finished right here at the spring, ain't ya', Bram?

Lighting his pipe again, he looked up through his brows at Creed.

"Anyway," he said, "that's my idea, and I figure she's worth a ten percent cut."

"You have brick-making experience, Max?" Creed asked.

"Experienced everything," he said, "'cept bedding of the queen, but then I ain't dead yet."

Walking over to the clearing, Creed looked up at Stone Mountain. When he came back, he scooped up a handful of the mud and lifted it to his nose. It smelled ancient and clean.

Taking Max's hand, he shook it, the mud squeezing from between their fingers.

"Max," he said, "welcome to Stone Mountain Brick Works."

Creed and Alida walked the path to the ledge above the dugout. Taking up their usual spots, they listened to the sounds of the evening. The smell of food rose from the locust grove down on the meadow, and a guitar strummed out a tune. One of the mules brayed as if wounded, and the men laughed.

With nothing on, but a cotton dress, Alida shivered against the cool breeze.

"I'm exhausted," Creed said, "from following Max over this mountain all day."

"Tell me what he said, about the quarry. What does he think?" she asked, pulling up her knees.

"It's good stone, the best he's ever seen, and he's not a man who's easily impressed. It's high-quality, and there's lots of it. With a good market, we're going to do just fine."

"I see."

"And there's more, too," he said, his voice lifting. "Max says the clay down at the spring is perfect for brick and that we can harness power from the spring to run a pugmill. The infrastructure for the quarry will double for making brick. It's perfect. Who knows but someday we'll be making brick for the whole of the Territory."

"But that's even more to take your time, Creed. You're involved in so much already."

"But this is perfect, Alida—Stone Mountain Brick Works. Max is going to build the waterwheel, the pugmill, and the road. I'm going to clear a slide for the quarry, and then there's quarters to be built. In the meantime, we'll be sending Gomez for equipment and for more men for the mill. Max says Gomez is a good hand, knowledgeable, and his English is excellent. I figure to put Bram in charge of the brickyard soon as he learns it."

"Stone Mountain Quarry, and now Stone Mountain Brick Works," she said, standing. "And then there's Roop buying more land by the day. Why can't we just have our life here? We could be so happy, you and I."

"It's an opportunity that can't be passed up, Alida."

Turning her back to him, she locked her arms.

"I thought we could start a family, a child, you know."

The music from the locust grove faded on the breeze, the smell of sage from the prairie easing through the valley.

"There will be time for that, Alida," he said, "when we're established."

"Sometimes I think you don't want a family. Sometimes I think you don't want to be with me at all."

"It's not true, Alida. You knew when we got married that my life was full, that there were things I wanted to accomplish."

"Maybe a family connects you to your past," she said, pushing her hair back with her fingers. "Maybe that's why you fill your life with everything else."

"Any child of mine is going to start at the head of the pack, not at the back. With enough money and time, no one will remember, or care to remember where I came from." Taking her by the arm, he turned her around. "Look, there's plenty of time for a family. We'll have one I promise, but not now."

"Maybe you're right," she said. "Maybe now is not the time."

"There is one problem," he said, "but it's one that can be solved."

"A problem?"

"The quality stone is high up the mountain. Up there," he said, pointing to the rift.

For some time Alida did not answer.

Darkness gathered on the horizon, and the wind fell away.

"That's where the monk is buried," she said.

Lightning lit in the distant bank, a flash somewhere deep within the clouds. Thunder rumbled away, and there was the smell of rain, of dust laden with moisture.

"It's not going to be easy, getting the stone down. We'll have to clear a run for it, build stone boats and sled it to the bottom. Eventually we'll cut switchbacks up the mountain."

Walking to the edge of the overlook, Alida fell silent. Below, in the locust grove, the crew had quieted.

"It's the monk's place," she said.

"I know, Alida, but it can't be helped. That's where the stone is; besides, bones are bones and soon enough dust."

"You shouldn't talk that way," she said.

"I don't mean to be disrespectful, but the fact that some stranger died up there is not my problem. We all live on the bones of the past."

"I think nothing could stop you from what you want, Creed, not even me."

"We have to be realistic, Alida, that's all. Look," he said, turning her about, "I promise you that if there's any way possible, we'll leave the monk's cave intact. And the first thing to be built is a stone house for you. It's high time you had a place of your own."

"Sometimes I think it's the *taking* that's important to you, Creed. In any case, it's your lease," she said, her voice lost in the thunder that pealed through the valley.

In silence they made their way back down the mountain, the rain splattering about them, fading inevitably into the plains.

Not until three of his white marshals were summoned to Federal Court in Wichita did Marshal J. A. Jones assign Deputy Buck Reed to patrol in Guthrie station proper. Up until then, Buck's assignments consisted of forays into the countryside, settling claim disputes, soothing family quarrels, and ferreting out petty thieves. Short-handed and up against it, the marshal called Buck into his office.

"It ain't that you're not a fine hand," Jones said, leaning back in his chair, "but folks in these parts ain't used to a colored deputy. And then there was that thing with the girl—you know what I mean, Buck."

Pushing back his hat, Buck looked out the window and down the street. Guthrie station was a town alive with activity, a city dropped from the sky.

"Yes, sir," he said. "Guess I know better than most."

Putting his feet up on the desk, the marshal locked his fingers over his belly.

"Anyway, I figure it's high time they get used to things around here. There ain't a man in Guthrie station don't know who brought in Carl, ole Shovelnose, too, for that matter. The word's out about you, Buck, about you having some kind of spell, not that they believe it, but then it might be true, and that's just as good, I figure."

Sitting back down, Buck took off his hat to let the breeze from the window blow over him.

"Some things is out of a man's hands, Marshal."

Looking more like a businessman than a lawman, Marshal Jones stood up and paced the short distance behind his desk. It was a reputation he enjoyed, that of a scrapper in spite of his size, a man prone to dropping the hat without provocation.

"There's more whores down at the White Elephant Dance Hall than's necessary, Deputy. There's an ordinance against them, you know, fines to be paid." Arranging his belt into a more comfortable spot beneath his stomach, he looked over at Buck. "Them girls ain't paying up their fines like they ought, Buck, and it's putting the whole of Guthrie station in jeopardy."

"What do you want me to do?" Buck asked, sticking his hat back on.

"I'm short-handed," the marshal said, hooking his thumbs in his belt, "and them fines need collecting. It's a delicate process, Deputy. You understand what I'm saying?"

"Yes, sir. I figure I do."

Sitting down, the marshal turned to his papers.

"Take a turn through those tunnels now and again. It's got to where a man can't go about his business down there without risking his life."

"Yes, sir," he said.

After leaving the marshal's office, Buck checked on Pony down at the stables. With a whinny, Pony trotted to the fence, burying his nose in the palm of Buck's hand.

"How you doin', boy?" Buck asked, scratching him behind his ear.

Dropping his head, Pony ambled back to the other horses.

It was the shade of the barn, and the prospect of standing on his feet all night, that drew Buck to the hay for a nap. When he awoke, his stomach growled with hunger. For a dime he could eat a meal of fried rabbit and greens at the Red Horse, a cafe on the edge of town that catered to coloreds.

Before entering, he took off his badge and slipped it into his pocket. The windows were adorned with flour-sack curtains, and the salt-shakers were no more than tin cans with holes punched in their tops. The chairs were made of nail kegs, horse blankets having been draped over them against the sharpness of the rims. But the food was good, and the establishment clean, in spite of the flies that buzzed against the screen door.

The cook watched Buck eat, slapping her leg as he finished up the last of his plate.

"Lordee," she said, as he paid out his dime, "I ain't seen a man eat like that since I left Arkansas."

"It was mighty good, ma'am," he said, donning his hat, "'bout the best rabbit I ever did eat."

"If there's more you're needing," she smiled, fixing her hair, "it's another dime well-spent."

"Thanks all the same," he said. "Maybe some other time."

Once in the street, he pinned on his badge, and checked to make certain that his sidearm was loaded. It was quiet for now, but Guthrie station had its share of misfits. It was as if a depression had opened up in the earth, and everyone without a good hold on life had come sliding in.

Dealing with whores required the cover of darkness, so Buck walked the streets awaiting night. The citizenry passed him by, dropping their eyes or turning away. Even though they'd seen their share of colored soldiers, the colored deputy, the one who had no fear, the one who had killed with his bare hands, was another matter altogether.

As he turned south off Harrison, the evening darkened, and lamplights glowed from down the street. The smell of liquor gathered like day-old perfume, and the peal of laughter rose from out of the establishments. As always, the night would bring many, men coming and going. For every drunk stumbling through the front door of a whorehouse, there were ten citizens skulking through the shadows of the tunnels.

At the corner a boy stepped from the doorway, his arms full of *The Capital City* paper. Stepping on Buck's toe, he spun away. A cigarette hung from the corner of his mouth, and his hat was cocked to one side.

"Hey," Buck said, "you take off a man's toe, you ought apologize."

"Watch where you put your big foot," he said.

Snapping him up by his overalls' strap, Buck asked, "What's your name, boy?"

"You keep off me," the boy said, sticking out his chest, "or you'll wish you had."

"I asked what's your name," Buck said, twisting up the strap until the boy's face reddened.

"Jimmy," he said, his lip curling above the white of his teeth, "and I'm delivering *The Capital City* paper for Mr. Damon. He'll see you hung off the Cottonwood bridge."

"Ain't I seen you before?"

"Maybe, and maybe you ain't."

"Well, Jimmy, I'm the law here in Guthrie station, and I figure you owe me an apology for takin' off my toe."

"Ain't no colored man the real law," he said.

"Won't take off a boy what I wouldn't take off a growed man, Jimmy," Buck said, lifting him up onto his toes. "Now, what do you say?"

"I ain't apologizing to no crazy colored man," Jimmy said.

With a shove, Buck spilled him backward and into the street, his papers lifting in the wind.

"It's a small feller can't say he's sorry, Jimmy."

Brushing the dirt off his knees, Jimmy grabbed at the papers swirling about his feet.

"I'll get you!" he yelled, poking the papers under his arms. "You just wait!"

Buck's first stop was the White Elephant, a house renowned for its collection of beauties. Buck knocked on the doors along the darkened hallway. At each, he showed his badge, repeated the ordinance against prostitution within the city limits of Guthrie station, and collected the required fine. Digging coins from their pockets, most of the girls paid. A few sweet-talked him, or offered trade, or begged to postpone payment until better times, but in the end all divvied up.

Afterward, he walked the street to the marshal's office, where he counted out the fines before placing them in the safe. Hungry again, he strolled back down to the Red Horse.

"If you're here to spend that other dime, I wore out from cookin'," she said, wiping at her brow.

"Ham and eggs will do for tonight, Missy," he said.

"Lordee," she said, cracking eggs onto the griddle, "that a marshal badge you wearing?"

Touching the badge, he said, "Reckon it is."

"It's a dangerous thing," she said, setting down his plate, "a colored man wearing a badge."

"You see these eyes I got, Missy?" he asked, dipping his bread into the egg.

"Reckon I do," she said, "meaning no harm."

Lifting half an egg onto his fork, he slid it into his mouth, washing it down with coffee. "And something else I got, too," he said.

"Like all men," she said, grinning, "looking to poke it somewhere."

"I got the hex."

"Do?"

"There ain't no harm can come with that, you know."

"Like Jesus Hisself," she said, "walkin' the water and bringin' down walls."

Pushing back his plate, he wiped at the corners of his mouth.

"Makes this here marshal job easy, when you think on it, 'cause there ain't no man to fear one way or the other."

"Lord Jesus," she said, holding the ladle over her head, "it's a fine thing, ain't it?"

"Here's a extra nickel," he said, standing.

"Oh, that too much, Deputy."

"Them whores drop nickels all the time figuring to keep from paying out their fines. Why, I didn't even know I had it till I just now looked."

The night quieted as it moved into the morning hours. Checking his sidearm again, Buck walked down to the Ione, a hotel known for its quiet and promise of a good night's sleep. Built of clapboard and timbers, it was clean and inviting. A woman sat behind a desk, a pencil in her hand.

"There's the Red Horse Cafe on the edge of town," she said, "if you're lookin' for food."

"I'm Deputy Reed," he said. "Just keepin' an eye out."

"No trouble here, 'less you count them two drunks."

Buck leaned against the wall. There were two hours still left till dawn, and his toes cramped in the ends of his boots.

"What two drunks would that be, Missy?"

"One riding on the other's back," she said, clicking her teeth with her pencil, "whooping and hollering like they hadn't a lick of sense. Leave it to boys to be the fool, I'd say."

"Ain't many thinks ahead. It's what leads 'em at the moment, ain't it. You want me to round them up?"

"I never heard of no colored deputy before," she said.

"It's a sight most get over, Missy."

"You the one broke that girl's neck with his bare hands?"

"It's all I had on me at the time," he said. "You want them boys rounded up or not?"

"They weren't hurting nothing, just fooling around, givin' me a time, if you know what I mean."

"Night, then," he said, tipping his hat.

"Night, Deputy."

Stepping out onto the walk, he rubbed at his face and yawned. It was then that he saw them in the alley across the street, arms hooked over each other's necks, bottles in their hands.

"Hey, Deputy," one of them called, "you in the wrong part of town?"

The other laughed, slapping his leg with his hat, pointing at Buck.

Without speaking, Buck approached them. The exchange of words to follow would be fruitless, this he knew, and as predictable as the coming of the day.

"You come to arrest us, darkey," the tall one said, "you best bring a posse."

Buck's huge hands came about, cupping the tall one's ears with a pop. Too shocked to scream, he fell to his knees, his eyes wide with the pain worming into his head.

"Hey," the other one said, but even as he said it, Buck drove his fist under his rib cage, emptying him of air and of hope as he fell to the ground. There was a time he would've waited for the exchange, the insults, the humiliation that was his by birthright, but not any more. Maybe it was the times. Maybe it was the place. Whatever it was, change was in the air. He could smell it, stand on his toes and see it just there in the future.

After locking them up, Buck finished his report just as the first light of morning eased onto the horizon. Dew gathered on the grass and glistened in the morning dawn. As he stepped into an alley to relieve himself, he heard an owl hoot somewhere above. Leaning against the wall, he waited, to hear it again, to make certain of what it said. When it came, it was as a child calling out to him. "Buck Reed," it said, "Buck Reed," and chills raced down his spine.

Remembering his promise to check the tunnels, he walked down the hill to where there was an opening that led from the Cottonwood. Having been in them once with the marshal, he knew their smell, the stink of sewer, the stillness of the air.

He held his lantern high, soot drifting from the chimney and into the gloom as he eased himself into the tunnel. Bending low so as not to hit his head on the roof, he made his way down. A hundred feet in, he heard something, like a rat scurrying from beneath a rock.

"Who goes?" he asked, moving into the shadows of his lamp. "Who goes, I say?"

"It's me," someone said.

"Who's that?" Buck asked again, peering into the darkness, his voice echoing in his ears. "Step on out here where's I can see you."

"It's me, Jimmy."

Lowering his lantern, Buck took a deep breath.

"What you doing down here anyway, boy?"

"This is for you," Jimmy said, bringing his knife across Buck's arm with a slash.

Sliding down the wall, Buck clutched at the wound, blood oozing from between his fingers, the pain settling in his stomach like a red-hot ball. Jimmy stood in the shadows, his knife at the ready.

Reaching for his revolver, Buck brought it about. "Throw down that knife 'fore I decide to use this, boy."

The lantern light flickered in Jimmy's eyes as he brandished the knife.

"Do it," Buck said again.

Throwing down the knife, Jimmy backed into the shadows.

"I told you I'd get you," he said. "I told you so."

"I heard the owl callin' out my name," Buck said. "It was a child callin' out. Who are you, boy?"

"Jimmy Ellison," he said. "You kilt my ma, laying her out in the wagon for all to see."

"Mavis Ellison was your ma?"

"I got away at the river," he said, "and weren't never going back, but she was my ma. You shouldn't have kilt her like that, laying her out for all to see."

The lantern flame danced above the wick, fluttering against Buck's breath as he gasped against the pain that crawled up his arm.

"It's a pity about your ma, boy, but sometimes a man's faced to do mighty hard things. Now you get on outta here and leave that knife where it be."

Turning, Jimmy ran into the tunnel, into its blackness. "You ain't got the spell no more," he yelled back. "I seen to that."

Tearing the tail off his shirt, Buck wrapped it about his arm, tightening the knot with his teeth. The pain that flashed through him bore out the truth of Jimmy's words.

When he stepped from the tunnel, he breathed in the fresh air and waited for the throb to subside. At the stables, he saddled up Pony, leading him up the hill to the marshal's office. There, he uncinched the saddle and tossed it over the fence rail. Taking off his badge, he pitched it onto the porch.

Mounting Pony, he rode from Guthrie station. At the river he reined eastward, to the settlement, to Rolondo, to freedom at last.

Within the week, Bram moved in with the men at the locust grove.

"It's not necessary that you stay with the men, Bram," Creed said. "Stone Mountain is your home, after all."

Tossing his hat into the corner of the tent, Bram sat down on the bunk.

"I want to do my share, do what the others do, that's all. I hope to have weekends for working on the Spring House, if it works out."

"Independence must run in the family," Creed said, unrolling the quarry plans. "As you can see, we've got to go high. We'll have to clear a sled run from this point here down to here where the wagons can back in for loading. It's a matter of moving surface stone and lots of it."

Holding the plans to the light, Bram studied them for a moment.

"It goes to the rift, Creed. Isn't that where that monk is?"

"Yes, but with a little luck, we won't have to disturb our monk."

Rolling the plans back up and handing them to Creed, he asked, "How do we go about it?"

"You and I will take a crew up to clear stone. We'll build stone boats and start at the bottom, work our way up, straight as possible. Gravity is going to work for us, so we want it steep but not so steep that we get run over by our boats. Max and I have marked the route and picked the crew."

"What's Max going to be doing?"

"Dragging the road, bringing in fill for low spots, that sort of thing. There's a low-water bridge and an over-shot wheel to be built. Word is that a section gang unloaded ties for the siding yesterday. Soon as Gomez gets back with the pugmill, we'll be ready for production. When the time comes, I'll be wanting you to take that part of the business. It's important that you learn as much as possible from Max. Stone Mountain is coming together, Bram. It's coming together fast."

"Let's do it," Bram said, tugging his hat down onto his head.

"One other thing," Creed said. "Max says surface stone is good rubble wall and would suit this mountain just fine. I think we should use it to build a house for Alida. Lord knows we have enough masons to do the job."

Walking to the tent flap, Bram looked up at the twist of smoke rising from the dugout.

"I worry about Alida," he said. "She spends so much time alone, without friends to talk to."

"It's difficult for her, I know," Creed said, "but as soon as I get the quarry underway, things will be different. There will be more time for us all. In the meantime, there is the new house. It will be a grand house, Bram. What woman would not like that?"

From where he stood, Bram could see the old wagon he and Alida came in on, Windy and Bones grazing along the fence line, their tails switching in unison.

"She lives in her books," he said, "and in her heart. This is not a place for either. It's been harder on her than the rest of us. My father knew this, I think. She misses him a great deal."

Placing his hand on Bram's shoulder, Creed said, "This won't go on forever, but if we don't strike now, someone else will. It's time that matters, you see. Alida understands this."

"Well, then," Bram said. "Let's build our quarry."

As they cleared the path up the mountain, they lifted stone upon stone onto the walnut boats, dragging them to the bottom like mules at the doubletree. At times a boat would beach, requiring a half-dozen men to dislodge it. Other times it would slide at breakneck speeds, forcing the men to jump aside so as not to be crushed beneath. At the bottom, the stones were stacked and sized for the masons, and the boats were hauled once again up the slide.

While the crews worked at the slide, the masons lay stone for Alida's house, walls of rubble rock that rose higher each day at the base of Stone Mountain. But it was the rare day that found Alida out of the dugout, a place now dwarfed by the immensity of the quarry operation.

The slide crew found the going tough, and there was no end to their grumbling. Each day there was a new complaint, a new reason to delay, or another repair to make. It was Bram who worked without complaint, keeping up with the best and strongest of them. His shirt soaked with sweat, he heaved the stones onto the boat, his eyes snapping with satisfaction.

Dropping into the shade for a break, the men drank from dippers, water dripping from their chins as they slapped at mosquitoes or dug gnats from their ears. Joseph Cervantes, the crew foreman, approached Creed, hat in hand.

"Mr. McReynolds," he said, "the men have asked me to talk to you."

"What is it now?" Creed asked.

"The men feel that it is no longer safe to work. Some fear for their lives."

Creed looked at the men gathered under the shade. They shook their heads in agreement.

"There's nothing to fear, Joseph, except hard work and heat."

Looking over his shoulder at the men, Joseph shrugged.

"It's the snakes," he said. "The men are afraid."

"Snakes?" Creed asked, looking over at Bram, who was busy beneath his hat.

"The men have heard of the hoopers and of the rattlers. They say it is too dangerous to work, and for such a small sum."

"Joseph, what if I told you there was no such thing as hoopers? They're folk tales."

Looking at his feet, Joseph gave it careful thought before answering.

"I would never call you a liar, Mr. McReynolds, but the men say they should be paid more, that the rocks are alive with snakes. This is what they believe."

"I see," Creed said, "and who told the men of these snakes, I wonder?"

Looking over at Bram, Joseph shrugged. "It is a well-known fact."

Hooking his foot on the stone boat, Creed scraped at the dirt that had hardened where the sole met the heel.

"What is it the men want, Joseph?" he asked.

"The men are willing to risk their lives for a bonus of twenty dollars each month."

"I'm paying more than the railroad as it is."

"But now the men think of their safety, and of their families."

"Well, Joseph, I have a bargain for the men. For every snake killed, I'll pay two hundred dollars. For every hooper, a month's salary. Seems a fair price, wouldn't you agree, Bram?"

Nodding, Bram stuck his hands into his back pockets and kicked at the dirt with the toe of his boot.

Joseph looked at the men, who agreed with a nod of their heads.

"The men will do this, Mr. McReynolds, even at the risk of their lives."

So each morning they rose again, like ants from the den, to move the stone and curse the heat, and to watch for snakes from the corners of their eyes. And at the end of each day, Max would appear atop the point to appraise their progress.

At night Creed fell exhausted into bed, his muscles aching. Sensing Alida's unhappiness, he found the fatigue convenient, sleep welcome. At times, late in the day, he would spot her standing at a distance, or walking along the path to the spring. But no longer did they talk of family, nor walk hand in hand to the ledge, nor hold each other under the evening stars.

It was on a Friday, at the end of the day, when Joseph approached from the clearing.

"Mr. McReynolds," he shouted, excitement in his voice.

"What is it, Joseph?" Creed asked, wondering what new scam was now in the making.

"We have killed one. You must come and see."

"Killed what, Joseph?"

"A hooper," he said, holding out his arms, "as big as this, and by the grace of God no one was hurt."

"You don't say, a real hooper?"

"Yes," he said, "from up there. Manuel has killed him and is deserving of his money, I think."

Pulling off his gloves, Creed looked over at Bram.

"Well let's go see. I can't remember a hooper ever being sighted, can you, Bram?"

Picking up his shovel, Bram worked at the stone.

"I think I'll finish out here, if it's all the same."

"I insist," he said, "you being a hooper expert and all."

Laid out was the biggest snake Creed had ever seen. Its tail had been threaded into its mouth to complete the circle.

"See," Joseph said, "just as I said."

Kneeling down, Creed examined the snake, glancing up at Bram.

"Looks like a hooper to me," he said. "Rolled right down this mountain." Peeling off the bills, he stuck them in Joseph's shirt pocket. "I always keep my word, Joseph. Now, tell your men that if they reach that rift within the next ten days, every last man of them will receive the same."

"I'll tell them, Mr. McReynolds," Joseph said, smiling. "Soon we make the rift, I think."

As they walked away, Bram shook his head.

"Now why would you do a thing like that, Creed? You know as well as I do that was no hooper."

"Because soon we make the rift, I think," he said, tossing the snake into the bushes below.

Just as Creed was having the last of his morning coffee, word came that Gomez was at the siding with pugmill and crew. Creed found Max harnessing mules in the meadow, his pipe hooked in the corner of his mouth.

"It's here," Creed said, "and they are in need of wagon and ropes."

"About time, ain't it," Max said, grinning. "I was beginning to think ole Gomez jumped the traces."

Max followed the new road through the meadow. The mules balked at the low-water bridge, forcing him to lead them across. Frogs bound from the banks, disappearing into swirls of mud, and crawdads darted backward into their adobes.

Climbing back in the wagon, Max popped the reins. "Goddang mules ain't happy unless they get your feet wet," he said.

But as they rode on, both knew that this was the moment they'd been waiting for. With the slide all but cleared and the pugmill in place, they would be in business soon enough.

The crew hopped down from the flatcar to greet them. On one end of the car was the pugmill. On the other end were the timbers that Creed had ordered for Bram's Spring House.

"Morning," Gomez said, touching the brim of his hat. "There's a little coffee left from breakfast, if you'd like some."

"Don't mind if I do," Max said, handing him the reins. "How about you, Creed?"

"Sounds good."

"Why don't you have the boys load up that pugmill while we talk," Max said to Gomez.

Gomez gave the order in Spanish, pointing to the tie-downs that secured the pugmill to the flatbed.

"Coffee's over here," he said. "It tastes of axle grease but guaranteed to keep you awake."

"That mill's a beauty," Max said, taking a sip of the coffee. "Where did you get her?"

"Telegraphed an order right out of Guthrie station to Kansas City. They telegraphed me back that the siding was complete and that the order could be put off here. Didn't even have time to sober up," he said, smiling. "The crew and me hopped the next passenger going north, and here she was, just like they said."

"Don't look like there's a Mexican left working on the railroad either," Max said, taking out his pipe.

"I told them that Stone Mountain Quarry paid the best wages in the Territory and that once a year they could go home to Mexico to visit their families. I assume you approve, Mr. McReynolds?"

Sitting down on a tie, Creed propped his elbows on his knees and sipped at the coffee.

"We need men," he said, "providing we have customers to buy all this stuff."

Hooking his thumbs into his belt, Gomez watched as the men worked at the chains. Even though he'd abandoned most of his Mexican attire, his boots jingled with spurs, and a turquoise bracelet hung loose about his wrist.

"Oh, you'll have customers, Mr. McReynolds," he said, "because the capital is coming, they say. There's no doubt about that. There's a constitutional convention gathering in Guthrie station, and a new capitol building is to be built soon. Abaddon Damon has been elected to the Territorial House of Representatives. Looks like you'll provide the stone and brick for the new capital city."

"We'll be ready, " Creed said, looking over at Max.

Gomez barked out an order to one of the men, and then showed him how to release the tie-down.

"They are good men," he said, when he came back, "but not accustomed to working with machinery."

"How is *The Capital City* building coming along?" Creed asked.

"The Frenchman says he will soon need stone. I think Abaddon Damon does not like to wait. Even the politicians come to Guthrie station to find out what they believe. If they don't, they are killed with his pen."

"And what of the town?"

"Each day the wagons gather at the railroad siding. There's freight cars of McReynolds lumber stretching as far as the eye can see. You are to be a rich man."

"And brick?" Max asked, dipping his pipe into his tobacco pouch. "We going to have any use for that pugmill now that we have her?"

"All the streets are to be paved with brick," Gomez said, "and side-walks, too, they say. Even now people are asking for brick to build their homes, but it must come from far away and is too expensive. Stone Mountain brick will be in much demand."

Lighting his pipe, Max puffed clouds of smoke about his head and grinned.

"Yes," he said. "So I thought."

"Any other news?" Creed asked.

"While Deputy Buck Reed was working the tunnels, that newspaper boy came at him with a knife. Turns out the deputy kilt the boy's mom, right here on Stone Mountain. Course the boy, being in the employee of Abaddon Damon, got off without so much as a whuppin'."

"Mavis Ellison was Jimmy's mom?"

"Yes, sir. So Deputy Reed quit that very day. They say he built a soddy at the colored settlement and took a woman. They say he cuts scrub and no longer even carries a gun."

Swirling the dregs of his cup, Creed studied them for a moment before tossing them into the grass.

"Guess Buck's joined the mortals," he said. "Come on men, let's get this pugmill on the road."

Soon an expanse of mud spread across an opening above the spring, to be weathered and to wait its turn at the pugmill. Once the main drive was engaged with the over-shot wheel, the pugmill groaned like an angry mantis waking from its sleep. As the mud fed in, the mill chewed and churned and birthed brick from its orifice. Smoke from kiln fires settled in the meadow, and within a few days rows of brick awaited their ride to the siding. Bram worked hand in hand with Max the whole of the time and proved to be a quick learner.

On a Saturday, all of the hands helped Bram raise the roof of the Spring House, and by day's end, he was moved in.

Creed was hopeful that things might improve between Alida and him, but they didn't. More and more, she spent her days with her books, or on walks alone up on the mountain. Even though they talked—of the brick works, of the quarry slide, of the hands and their chicanery—the distance between them widened. In the quiet hours, there was a loneliness that crept into Creed, doubts that had not been there before, and he struggled to keep them at bay.

On a hot morning, Joseph stood at Creed's doorway, his shoulders squared, a smile spread across his face.

"What is it, Joseph? Not more hoopers, I hope."

"The slide is open, Mr. McReynolds. We are at the rift."

"Let's go get Max and Bram," he said, reaching for his hat.

At the rift, a hot wind blew down the valley, the smell of cedar steeping in the heat. Locusts zinged and lizards scampered over the blistering rocks.

Looking down the slide, Max wiped at his brow with his handkerchief.

"It's a damn good job, men," he said. "All we have to do now is blast that rock out of there, load it on them stone boats and get the hell out of the way. Joseph, go tell the men to bring up some rope and a charge. We'll soon enough see what we got."

"Wait a minute, Max," Creed said, catching his breath from the climb. "There's a grave down there, as you know, and I promised Alida not to disturb it unless there was no other way."

Walking to the edge, Max looked down into the rift. Taking out his pipe, he knocked it out on a rock and then packed it with tobacco.

"You and me both know that's where the stone is, Creed," he said, striking a match, drawing on the pipe, "and that's where we got to go. We knowed it all along, didn't we?"

"Couldn't we take the body out," Bram said, "bury it on the overlook? A man's got a right to a proper grave."

Stepping to the entrance of the cave, Creed peered into the darkness. Dankness rose from the depths, the smell of death on its current.

"It might not be stable, now with all this activity about," he said.

"Someone's got to place the charge, anyway," Bram said. "We'll tie the rope around my waist. I'll send up the remains and plant the charge while I'm at it. Max will show me how, won't you, Max?"

"That's up to Creed here," Max said. "Plantin' a charge ain't all that hard to learn, I reckon, but she will have to be set as far down into that stratum as she can go; otherwise, she's going to blow out this hole like a cannon and take off your hat, along with your head in it."

Above him, Creed could see the cross in the dome of the entrance, carved there by the monk's own hand.

"I'll go," Creed said. "I've been down before and know the way."

"The way is down, like it's always been, Creed," Bram said, taking hold of his shoulder, "and my turn to go."

Seeing that he was determined, Creed nodded.

"If that's what you want, then."

Max finished his instructions, and stood at the entrance. Creed fed the rope out as Bram crawled down into the rift. Soon the light of his lantern disappeared in the darkness, its smell oily on the current from below.

Repositioning himself, Creed moved down until he could once more see the lantern. From time to time, Bram called back, each time his voice smaller and more uncertain.

When the tug on the rope came, Creed knew what it was. Hand over hand he lifted up the monk's body, little more than a bundle of bones. After untying it, he lowered the rope back down.

"I'm going to set the charge," Bram called up.

"Be careful," Creed said.

Soon the ring of Bram's chisel reverberated in the confines of the rift as he worked at the rock face. And then it stopped as suddenly as it had begun.

"Bram?" Creed called into the darkness.

But there was no answer, so Creed worked his way down yet farther until once more he could see the lantern, just a point of light now, like a star in a distant universe.

"Bram?" he called again, but it was the mountain that answered back, a shuddering from within its depths.

"She's shifting," Max yelled from above. "Get the hell out of there!"

"I've got to get Bram," he said.

"Creed!" Bram called from below.

"Follow the rope, Bram."

But even as he spoke, the mountain groaned, and Bram's lantern winked away. Rock showered from overhead, filling the passage. Creed prayed, prayed for mercy and deliverance.

When he opened his eyes, there was but blackness, no glimmer of light to center him in the darkness. Nose and mouth clogged with earth, he gasped for breath and clawed at his face.

"Bram?" he called out, but no answer came.

He dug at the rocks about his legs. How long he dug, he didn't know. Without light, there was no time, no gauge nor measure of life, save the roar of his lungs and the thud of his heart.

When the floor gave way, Creed fell, hitting hard, his lungs collapsing.

"Bram?" he called when he could get his breath. "Bram, where are you?"

"Creed," Bram whispered from somewhere in the darkness. "Creed, I'm bad hurt."

Searching the floor with the sweep of his arms, Creed found the lantern, its globe broken.

"Oh, god," he said. "I've no matches."

"In my pocket," Bram said.

Shaking, Creed searched the darkness until he felt the warmth of Bram's shoulder. Finding the box in his pocket, he struck a match, and the cavern flooded with light. Bram lay against the wall, his leg jutting to the side. When Creed tried to move him, he cried out in pain.

"Your leg is broken," Creed said. "Don't worry. They will get us out."

For hours they waited, and when the lantern sputtered with the last of the fuel, the rats came from out of the darkness, their eyes shining. They moved as one, these monsters of the rift, to await the dying of the light, to feed on the flesh of their victims. Bram moaned, pulling close. Neither said, but both understood, what awaited. Both knew the horror of the monk.

When the light broke above, washing the cavern, they shouted with joy.

"We're here," Joseph said, kneeling at Creed's side, his breath smelling of tobacco and onion.

"Joseph, you have no idea how good you look," Creed said.

"Oh, yes," he said, "I am a pretty man. Many women have told me this."

"Thanks, Joseph," Bram said.

"It's best to leave the gringo to his own makings," he said, smiling, "but then there would be no one to pay money for killing hoopers?"

That day, Creed watched on as Alida held Bram's hand as he was carried into the dugout on a stone sled. Standing at the door, he remembered how she had nursed his own wounds, how she'd bathed him and cared for him in the confines of the tiny dugout. But this time, as she looked back at him, there was anger and hurt in her eyes.

On the second trip to the rift, Max set the charge and brought out the monk's cross. Joseph raised it on the overlook to be seen from the meadow below. Beneath it, they buried the remains of the monk.

The next day the charge brought down the rift. Columns of stone rose from its depths, and dust darkened the sun. All within its sound knew that Stone Mountain Quarry was born.

Alida stood at the overlook, her hands clasped, her hair blowing in the wind. Here on this place, they had made love, had been in love. Now there was but the silence of the grave behind her, and the emptiness of her heart within her.

For Alida, Mavis's death was even more sad in light of the news about her son being alive, and about what he'd done to poor Buck Reed. But with Bram's injury, she had little time to dwell on it. Creed moved in with the crews down at the locust grove to make room for Bram in the dugout while his wound healed. About the only time Alida saw Creed was at day's end, when he'd make his way down from the quarry, dust-covered and weary, to check on the progress of the new house.

Creed's requests for her to come with him to see the house were to no avail. It was, she said, something that could wait until Bram was better, and even though the walls rose up, and the new tiled roof cut away the sun, and the grounds buzzed with the comings and goings of workers, Alida did not budge from that course.

The break in Bram's leg was clean and healed quickly under Alida's constant attention. With the demands placed on her, Alida brightened, rising to the occasion with energy and enthusiasm. She took to reading her books once more. Sometimes, in the heat of the day, she would read aloud, Bram feigning disinterest as he worked at his plans for the Spring House, or dozed in his chair, his leg propped on Alida's trunk.

One day Bram limped from the dugout, his broken leg almost healed. Outside, Creed waited by the dugout door.

"You look ready to go back to work to me," he said, slapping Bram on the shoulder.

Smiling, Bram pointed his crutch at the mountain. "Long as I don't have to go back up there."

"Max is waiting with the wagon," Creed said. "We need you at the pugmill. There's more orders than we can get filled and new ones coming in every day."

Kissing Alida on the forehead, Bram said, "Thanks, Lidy. I couldn't have made it without you."

"I'll come by the Spring House and check on you."

Tapping his leg with the crutch, he said, "As you can see, I'm in no need of nursing. You take care of Creed. I'll take care of me."

Alida and Creed watched as Bram climbed into the wagon, waving as he pulled away.

Somewhere high on the rift, a charge blew, rumbling beneath their feet, dust boiling into the sky, drifting downwind into the valley.

"Now," Creed said, taking her by the arm, "I want you to come see what I've done. They've finished the house, and the last load of furniture arrived from Kansas City yesterday."

"Furniture?"

"I've taken the liberty to furnish the house, Alida. Of course, I'll leave the final touches to you. Come on, you must see it."

When they stepped into the house, Alida gasped at its extravagance; the rooms were plush with hutches, secretaries, and tables. A large cherry desk filled Creed's office. "It took four men to load it on the wagon," he said, running his fingers across its top. The bedrooms were decorated with cannonball beds, mahogany armoires, and marble-topped commodes. There were great chairs of leather, and footstools of oak. There were velvet couches, woven tapestries, and oriental vases in every room. The library took her breath with its carved mahogany panels, leaded glass doors, volumes of vellum and morocco. Taking her hand, he led her into the kitchen with its tiled floors, steel cutlery, and stately cast-iron stove.

"Enough for a king," she said, "but how can we afford all this, Creed?"

"It's only the beginning, Alida. The quarry's making more than I could ever have dreamed. I'm expanding each day, and Abaddon's landed the contract for the Capital Convention Hall. It's just the beginning for us. We can afford this, and more, much more. You're going to be the richest woman in the Territory, Alida. You're going to have the finest of everything."

"It's beautiful, Creed," she said, sitting down, "but it's only you that I ever wanted."

"And you have me, Alida, and everything I own. I know I've been pretty busy, but that's not going to go on forever. Soon, when the quarry's up and running, then we'll have more time together."

Folding her hands in her lap, she looked about. "Time is the one thing you can't get back, Creed."

Leaning over, he kissed her. "You deserve all this, Alida. Now, I need to run. The railroad is building a spur from the siding right here to Stone Mountain. What with all the business we're bringing them, they've sent an official out. I shouldn't be long."

"I see," she said. "Perhaps we can talk later?"

"You arrange all this any way you want it. It's yours, you know. I mean, that's why it's here."

When he got to the door, Alida called after him.

"Yes?" he said.

"Could you have my trunk and books moved from the dugout?"

"I'll send someone," he said, closing the door behind him.

The demands on Creed's time increased as the days passed. If it wasn't a breakdown at the quarry, it was trouble at the pugmill, or discontent among the crew. Often, he would not return until dark, and then only to eat and leave again. Exhausted at day's end, he seldom came to her bed anymore. Rarely did they talk, and when they did, it was of orders, or land, or the problems of the quarry. When she would bring up family, or the loneliness of the Big House, he would stiffen, or fall silent, or excuse himself to attend to the quarry.

She found the new library cold and imposing, the bound books stiff and unfamiliar in her hands. Swallowed in the immensity of the house, she wandered from room to room in search of solace, of warmth, of some necessity in coming or going.

Sometimes, while waiting on Creed's return, she would walk to the dugout, to its welcome smells of dank and kerosene, because it was here with Creed that her days had been most happy, her life most complete. Other times she would climb to the ledge to watch the wagons as they rumbled down the road, their beds loaded with quarried stone or salt-glazed brick. Day and night, dynamite blasts rocked the mountain until the valley reeked of dust and smoke

Late one evening upon returning from the quarry, Creed pulled his boots off at the door.

"Would you like something to eat?" she asked.

"I ate with the night crew," he said. "Shouldn't you be asleep?"

"I thought I would wait up for you. We so seldom talk anymore."

Setting his boots by the side of the door, he eased into a chair.

"I'm awfully tired, Alida. Maybe it could wait until morning?"

"How about a cup of tea?"

"All right, then," he said, "a cup of tea."

When the tea was brewed, she set the cup next to his chair, easing down beside him.

"It's sweetened with honey," she said, "and will help you sleep."

"Cervantes let a bushing go dry on the pugmill," he said, sipping on the tea, "and burned the damn thing up. Anyway, we've patched it together until another can be ordered out of Chicago. I hope it holds because we have an order for a hundred-thousand brick for paving Oklahoma Avenue in Guthrie station. We don't have time for this kind of problem. For a little, I'd send Cervantes packing."

"I'm sure he didn't mean to," she said.

"It was his job to keep those greased, and he damn well should have done it. On top of that, Roop's sent word that he's in need of cash. These homesteaders are going bust faster than we can buy them out."

"I don't understand the hurry with all this, Creed. We've got everything we need."

"Land will never be this cheap again, Alida. The opportunity is now, and it can't be missed."

Leaning onto his knee, she said. "I've been thinking that maybe you and I could take a few days, you know, take a wagon to Winfield. On the way we could stop by where my father's buried. Then, maybe we could catch the train out of Winfield to Kansas City or Chicago, just you and me for a few days. Wouldn't it be lovely, Creed? It's been so long since we've been really alone."

"It's not a good time, Alida. We've got the order for pavers, and then there's the convention hall. Abaddon says they will be starting construction on a new city hall soon enough and that we should be gearing up for it now. And then there's Roop waiting for cash. I just don't see how I could get away."

Gathering up the teacups, she took them to the kitchen. When she came back, Creed was bent over his desk.

"Perhaps Bram could take me?" she said. "After all, we have the same father."

"Bram?" he said, looking up from his papers.

"You know, my brother, the one who operates your pugmill."

"Yes, I know who Bram is, Alida. I suppose we could spare him. I'll talk to him tomorrow."

"Jeez, Lidy," Bram said, putting her things in the wagon, "you've enough here for a trip around the world."

"Well, I know how you eat for one thing," she said, climbing up in the seat, adjusting her hat. "Anyway, there's no reason we can't be comfortable."

A rumble rolled down the mountain, and a dust cloud boiled up from high on the rift.

"They've gone to twelve-hour shifts," Bram said, taking his place next to Alida. "Creed's paying time and a half, plus a bonus if they make their quota." Popping the reins against the rumps of the team, he pulled off down the road. "Guess I won't be collecting mine, seeing as how my sister needs a driver."

Catching her hat against the wind, Alida held it on with her hand, looking at Bram from under the brim.

"I'll see you get your bonus, Bram," she said, "if that's all that's worrying you."

Smiling, he hooked the reins between his fingers, leaning forward with elbows on his knees. "Reckon it is," he said, "unless you're going to talk me to death before we get back."

As they moved north toward Winfield, the dynamite blasts rolled like distant thunder behind them, soon giving way to the solitude of the prairie. This time the team was strong and young and prone to trot without Bram's constant attention. The miles passed with ease, and the sky opened before them.

Now expert with a team, Bram coaxed them over Bear Creek, clucking his tongue as the horses struggled up the bank. His arms were browned, and strong, and his hair was bleached. He rode with his thoughts, as a man rode, and drank sparingly from the canteen under the seat.

For Alida, the peace was a balm for the wounds that had opened in her, her feelings settling from out of the noise and dust of the quarry. It was good to be quiet with her thoughts.

When they stopped to eat, under the shade of a cedar, or the spread of an elm, or the lee of a creek bank, they would talk of the way things had been, and sometimes they would laugh, their laughter evoking childhood, when things had been simple and bright and clean.

The day they stopped on the rise overlooking the Salt Fork, both climbed down from the wagon, and stood arm and arm. It had been a long time since they had ridden over its swollen waters.

"Do you know where the grave is?" Bram asked.

"There," she said, pointing, "not far from the trestle."

"We'll camp there tonight," Bram said, "if that's what you want."

Somehow Alida had expected her father's hat to still be there, stirring in the wind, but it wasn't, and even the grave was uncertain, the winds having swept the area clean. They stood for awhile, remembering his voice, the way he cursed the team with such fondness, the way he forgave them with his gruffness.

Afterward, they walked to the river and stood on the trestle, smelling the creosote and mud. The Salt Fork was small and inconsequential now, no more than a stream twisting through the sands. On the opposite shore, the old ferry cropped from the bank, its bow deserted and rusting in the river drift.

That night they ate in the firelight, and watched the stars roll overhead, some seeming so close as to be touched.

"I wonder what Dad would think of us now?" Bram asked, finishing off his plate. "He was set on getting a farm, and here we are selling rock."

"I guess he'd be proud we made it, Bram, one way or the other. That's what he would've done."

"I ain't sure we would have made it, Lidy, not without Creed come along. A man can eat only so many rabbits before he goes stark mad."

"I suppose you're right, Bram. He's a man who turns the world to cash, and it's spilled over the both of us."

Cleaning off his plate, Bram stored it in the box Alida had prepared for their trip. Snapping a twig off the mesquite, he sharpened the end with his knife before sticking it in the corner of his mouth.

"I don't mean to pry, Alida, but a man would have to be blind not to see that things ain't what they should be between you and Creed."

Walking to the wagon, Alida leaned against it.

"It's funny," she said, "how a girl gets ideas about what she wants, how she thinks things are going to be. I had this picture in my mind, you know, of how I would someday be a wife, the heartbeat of a man's life, the thing he lived for. I know it sounds silly, but that's how I felt— like Father and Mother, Bram, like the way they used to look at each other when they did the dishes or when they were sitting on the front porch. You remember, don't you? I thought it was going to be that way with Creed and me. I thought he was that man. I thought I could love him enough to make him that man."

Opening the box, she pulled out a pan, taking off the cover. "I brought a plum pie."

"I love plum pie," he said.

After serving him a piece, she cut one for herself, and sat at the fire, balancing the plate on her knee.

"Fact is," she said, "I'm no longer certain if I made the right choice. What happens to a man like Creed if someday it all goes away? What's left for him then? I'd give everything away tomorrow, Bram, and take that dugout back, if Creed were in it. Now, all I've got is a big house, a house as empty and lonesome as me."

Finishing off his pie, Bram laid his fork in the plate. "I don't know, Lidy. It's a powerful future he's building, you know. You've things that most women can only dream about."

"But that's just it, Bram. I'm mighty far down the list of things that Creed McReynolds lives for."

Taking up the plates, Bram cleaned them and put them away. "That was mighty good plum pie."

"Thanks," she said. "Creed doesn't favor it."

"Listen, Lidy, Creed McReynolds is a man with a hole cut out of him, somewhere deep inside, and he's filling it up, that's all. He's filling it up with land and lumber and stone."

"Maybe he's missing what matters most, with his lumber and stone," she said.

After giving Bram his bedroll, she made her own bed in the back of the wagon and lay down. Bram prepared his bed beneath the wagon, and the smell of camp smoke hung in the dampness from the river. Soon he slept, his soft snore familiar in the night.

It was here where her father lay, where her own life both ended and began. She'd thought to start anew by returning, she supposed, to begin again at the river's edge. But it was hard truth she'd found instead, and when the train rumbled over the trestle, its light sweeping the night like an angry eye, she pulled the blanket about her.

The horses picked up pace as Stone Mountain came into view. The earth trembled from a quarry blast, and a plume of dust gathered on the horizon. As Bram and Alida crossed the meadow, they could see the old wagon that they'd come in on from Winfield. It was pulled under the shade of an elm, long since retired, now filled with barbed wire and fence posts and worn-out tack. One wheel was cocked, broken away at the axle, and the seat was weathered beyond repair. Windy and Bones sauntered toward them, but enticed by a patch of clover near the fence, stopped to graze, forgetting for the moment their welcome home.

After taking Alida's things out of the wagon, Bram stood in the door-way of the new house.

"I'll be going on to the Spring House," he said, "if that's all you'll be needing."

Hooking her hat on the chair, Alida sat down at the table. "Thanks for taking me, Bram. I'll see to it that you get your bonus."

"Aw," he said, "I was just going on about that, Lidy. I'm glad we went. It was a circle needed finishing, I guess."

"Yes," she said.

As he started to leave, he turned, "Lidy, if there's anything I can do, you know I will."

"I know," she said. "You always have."

She waited for the sound of Bram's wagon to disappear down the road before pouring her bath in the footed tub Creed had shipped in from New York. Afterward, she packed clean clothes, putting them in the trunk, along with the books her father had brought from Pennsylvania. After combing out her hair, she polished her nails and cleaned her mother's ring. The trunk was heavy, but she managed to slide it next to the front door. Standing in front of the mirror, she studied her face. She had changed here on Stone Mountain. It was there behind her eyes, something spent and false.

When Creed returned from the quarry, he unlaced his boots at the front door. "Hello," he called. "Anyone home?"

Stepping from the bedroom, she set her purse and hat on the chair. "Yes," she said.

"We've had a hell of a day," he said, slipping off a boot. "That bushing didn't hold, and the pugmill was shut down for nearly twelve hours. It's going to be a horse race to meet that order now."

"I want you to pay Bram his bonus, Creed. It was my fault that he was not able to meet his quota."

Slipping off the other boot, he looked up at her, and then at the trunk next to the door. His black hair fell across his face. "Okay," he said.

"I'm leaving, Creed."

"Yes," he said, "so I see."

"I want you to arrange for someone to take me to Guthrie station, and I would appreciate it if you would ask Roop to set up an account for me. I'll leave word at the Post Office as to my location."

"When will you be back?"

"I won't be back."

"I've given you everything," he said. "Everything."

"It's not enough, Creed," she said. "It never was."

"So it's my pride you must have?"

"You gave that up a long time ago."

Slipping on his boots, he stood, his black eyes crackling.

"I'll get Max to drive you," he said.

T he buildings of Guthrie station rose up before Alida like ancient shrines.

"It's unbelievable," she said to Max, who rode silent at her side. "Where did it all come from?"

Urging the horses across the Cottonwood bridge, he said, "Up from Hades, I reckon, or down from the sky. Either way, here she was in a wink."

As they turned onto Oklahoma Avenue, men were laying brick, row upon row of McReynolds's salt-glazed, their shirts wet with the heat of the day. A stream of mule-drawn wagons made their way from the track siding with their cargoes of brick. The men worked in unison, each move practiced and efficient, stopping only long enough to gaze at the woman who rode by.

To Alida's left was the Starr Building, with its limestone stars and leaded windows, and farther down, the New York Hardware store, with its façade of brick and budded crosses. To her right, the Swan Hotel lifted three stories high, bristling with railroaders and train passengers.

Each street was the same, a city born from the world: the Germania Beer Hall, the Reeves Brothers' Saloon, the Bank of Indian Territory, the McKennon Opera House, the Oklahoma Building. But overlooking all was the Capital City Publishing Company. It sat on a foundation of Stone Mountain rock, and its dome was perched atop towering pilasters. All around its girth, great windows opened onto the street, and the clack of the presses hummed in the valley. A boy sat on the stoop, folding papers, his eyes following them as they rode by.

"Where do you think I should stay, Max?" she asked.

"There's the Ione," he said, "right new and fine."

"Anywhere but the Ione," she said.

"Capitol Hotel is a good as any, ma'am," he said, pointing to a white-framed building. "It's clean, you know, in more ways than one, and the rates are fair."

"Take me there," she said.

Pulling up, Max unloaded her bags, carrying them to the front desk.

"This here's Mrs. Creed McReynolds," he said, "of McReynolds Lumber. She'll be staying at your establishment for a spell. Mr. McReynolds says she's to be taken care of—you understand, whatever she needs."

The man nodded, entering her name, turning the ledger about for her to sign.

"It's our honor to have you here, Mrs. McReynolds," he said. "We have a double room on the second floor, if that would do?"

"That will do fine," she said.

"And meals are served in the dinning room. Breakfast is at eight."

"Thank you," she said.

"Will that be all, ma'am?" Max asked, squaring his hat.

"Yes, thank you for bringing me. Oh, perhaps you could leave my address at the Post Office?"

"On my way out," he said, pausing. "I hope things settle out for you, ma'am."

"Thank you, Max. You take care of things on Stone Mountain."

Smiling, he touched his hat on his way out the door.

At loose ends, Alida stayed in her room, leaving only to eat, searching out tables near the window where she could sit without engaging others. At night, the sounds of Guthrie station seeped into her room and into her dreams. Sometimes, she would awaken, sitting upright in her bed, certain that she'd heard a knock, or that someone had called her name.

In the darkest hours she thought about what had gone wrong. Why had things turned out the way they had? It was Creed she'd loved, Creed she'd wanted, Creed she'd married, but somehow it was not Creed she'd gotten. He'd moved beyond her reach, obsessed with his land and lumber, and there was nothing she could do to get him back.

The days passed, and in her isolation her melancholy deepened, settling over her as thick and suffocating as river mud.

When the knock came, her heart leapt, and she waited for it to settle before opening the door. Roop stood foursquare before her, hat in hand.

"It's Roop Walters," he said. "They gave me your address over to the Post Office."

"Oh, Roop," she said.

"I seen that look of disappointment on many a woman's face in my day, though I can't say I've gotten used to it."

Stepping aside, she said, "I'm sorry. Won't you come in?"

"Thanks the same. I just came to tell you that an account has been opened up for you over to the Bank of Indian Territory."

"Oh, yes. Thank you, Roop."

"And that ain't all," he said, shifting to the other foot.

"Yes?"

"Well, it's going about that you ain't been seen on the streets of Guthrie since your arrival."

Looking away, she said, "I've been busy getting things settled, Roop. You know how it is."

"Oh, yes, indeed," he said, "but I'm wore out eating with ole Flea Bag and thought maybe you'd keep me company for dinner?"

"I'm pretty busy, Roop, I mean, with the bills to pay now that an account is opened."

"Yes 'em, I can see where it's important chores you have, but then, I *was* part of your wedding."

Straightening her dress, she looked out the window and then back at Roop.

"It's a sad picture," she said, "a man eating alone with his dog."

"Flea Bag don't like it none too much hisself," he said, sticking his hat back on. "I'll meet you in the lobby."

After changing her dress, Alida went downstairs. Roop was standing at the door, his boot kicked up on the jam. When they exited onto the street, Flea Bag sauntered across to meet them, stopping in the center of the road to scratch at his ear.

"Would the Lindel do?" Roop asked. "There's less explaining Flea Bag's manners there."

"It will do fine," she said.

At the Lindel, they took a table near the door, and Roop ordered them dinner without looking at the menu. Building himself a cigarette, he lit it in the cup of his hands, blowing out his match. Flea Bag watched on from the doorway, sighing heavily as he settled into a doze.

"You're looking a little pale, Alida. A young lady like you oughta be getting out once in awhile. There's lots going on in Guthrie station these days, a good many of them legal, too."

"I plan to, Roop. I just need a little time."

"I guess you ain't been keeping up on things," he said. "I guess you ain't heard."

"Heard what?"

"We're a state now, a bona fide state. Hodson's been elected governor. Course, he's a Democrat and none too fond of Abaddon Damon, but we got the capital, didn't we, and the Great Seal of Oklahoma to prove it."

"Yes, I know. Abaddon Damon was right all along."

Roop waited as the waitress served their food. When she left, he squashed out his cigarette.

"Abaddon Damon's always right, even when he's wrong. He's not happy about having a Jack Democrat in office, and he's been firing off editorials too hot to touch. Sometimes a man like Abaddon don't know when to quit. It can be a dangerous thing to corner a man like Governor Hodson. Things could turn ugly in a hurry. This here town ain't got but a single taproot. If it gets chopped off, she's in mighty big trouble."

Picking at her food, Alida said, "Looks like Creed stands to do well. With Guthrie having the capital, things are bound to prosper."

Looking up, Roop nodded. "Yes, ma'am, if things pan out as planned. That boy can track a deal where no one else can. It's the lawyer in him, or the Indian maybe. Creed McReynolds is likely to be a powerful man some day. The rest of us just have to figure how to fit in."

Flea Bag watched as Alida tore off a piece of bread, his ears perking. "Have you seen him, Roop?" she asked.

"Not for a good long while," he said. "He sent a bundle of money for buying up more land and word that I was to set up an account for you. I figure he's mighty busy. All you have to do is look around to see that the Stone Mountain Quarry's in high gear."

"They're building a spur from the main line to the quarry," she said. "Creed says it will double production."

Pushing back from the table, Roop said, "It's none of my business, Alida, and I won't bring it up again, but I'm right sorry about your trouble."

Tears gathered in her eyes, and she looked away. "Things didn't turn out the way I thought, Roop. It's like I'm on the outside of his life, like I'm not part of it somehow."

"You ever watch a trade rat build his nest, Alida?"

"No, I don't think so."

"Well he spends his days making his nest pretty, collecting bits of glass and paper, anything what glitters. Sometimes he drags stuff for miles, things so big that you wouldn't think he could move them. Then, if he sees something prettier, he throws it down and starts all over again. It's rare he ever gets back with what he intended."

"What are you saying, Roop?"

"Well, that stack gets bigger and bigger, and pretty soon he's got the biggest pile of junk on the desert. But that trade rat ain't never happy, going back for more, for something shinier, prettier. Soon, he's got a great stack of glittering trash." Pausing, he took out his makings. "But it ain't a nest, you see, no matter how big or how pretty it gets. There's only one thing makes it a nest."

"Thank you, Roop, for the encouragement, and for the dinner."

A train whistle blew from down at the tracks, its engine chugging and throbbing on the way out of town. Flea Bag lifted his head and then dismissed the sound as unimportant. Roop lit his cigarette, squinting against the smoke.

"There's lots for a young lady like you to do in a town like Guthrie station, Alida. Maybe Creed will figure out what's important in his life and maybe he won't. Either way, other folks got to keep on living and doing what they have to do."

"I feel so empty, Roop, like my life's been spilled out of me."

"We got a marble bathhouse for taking away the blues, and a Shakespeare Club, and a new Carnegie Library for reading folks. I hear they're looking for help over there, someone what can spell and smells pretty, like yourself. Now, given your bank account, I see no reason why you couldn't just go ahead and do whatever you want to do."

As they walked back to the hotel, Flea Bag trotted along behind them. At the door, Roop took off his hat. Alida dropped her hand in his for a moment.

"You're a good friend, Roop."

"I'll be around to check on you now and again. You think about what I said, about getting on with things."

Standing at the window of her room, Alida watched Roop and Flea Bag as they disappeared down the street. Opening her closet, she went through her things, laying them out. Afterward, she sat down on the bed. Roop was right, but the thought of getting on alone left her cold inside.

Picking up her purse, she headed for the door. A new life began somewhere, she supposed. Perhaps it began with a new set of clothes.

T he smell of fall was in the air, the first signs of gold touching the trees. Sometimes, in the early mornings, fog moved through the valley, drifting like a deep and silent current.

Creed stood in the doorway and watched Max come up from the meadow. The last section of track had been laid yesterday, and the final inspection completed. Today was an important day for Stone Mountain Quarry.

To meet the orders from Guthrie station, the quarry face was expanded, and switchbacks were built to replace the stone-boat slides. With the completion of the spur, stone could be loaded directly from the quarry onto freight cars for their trek to Guthrie. New quarters were built in the locust grove to accommodate the ever-increasing crews, and a blacksmith shop down at the Spring House was nearly finished. A steam jenny now replaced the over-shot wheel as a power source for the pugmill. It ran day and night off the coke that was freighted in from Pittsburgh.

Often Creed worked into the night, only to rise in the darkness to begin again. The crews complained of the pace, of the long hours, but the money was good, and nobody worked harder or longer than Creed himself. It was the work that sustained him; it was salve for his soul, retribution for his heart. Even Bram, who had proven his mettle at the pugmill, sometimes complained of the pressure, the hours, the heat of the kilns, once stomping off to the Spring House and not returning for an entire day.

But when Creed was alone in the Big House, when all others were gone and the problems of the day had passed away, he would wander from room to room, or stand at the window, or sit at his desk with a glass of whiskey. He'd not heard from Alida since her departure, except from Max, whose reports were spare indeed. But at times like these, when his thoughts pressed in, he could feel her presence. Steeling himself, he would force her from his mind and turn his thoughts back to the mountain.

Max took off his gloves, sticking them in his back pocket, shaking his head as he came across the yard.

"What is it?" Creed asked, sensing something was wrong.

"The pugmill's down," he said. "We've got crews sitting around, and a backlog that stretches from here to Kansas City."

Reaching for his hat, Creed said, "What's happened to it now?"

"Same thing. Bushing was dry."

"Again?" Creed asked, closing the door behind him.

"Burned to a goddang crisp, and there's no fixing it this time. She'll have to be replaced."

"A bushing doesn't burn up if it's greased, Max. Who the hell let that bushing go dry?"

"Bram's in charge of the pugmill. If it wasn't greased, he's the man you'll have to talk to."

Creed said nothing as they walked to the Spring House, where they found Bram bent over the pugmill, a grease smear across his face.

"What the hell is this about, Bram?" Creed asked.

"The bushing's burned up," he said, pitching his wrench into the dirt, "and it looks to me like she's finished."

"Why wasn't that bushing greased? Do you have any idea what this is going to cost Stone Mountain Quarry?"

"It was Cervantes' job," Bram said, rolling up his sleeves. "I told him it had to be greased every two hours. I told him it had to be done."

Kicking at the dirt, Creed walked to where the spring used to flow, having now been covered with planking to accommodate the jenny. Water from the spring was pumped into the boiler, where great clouds of steam churned into the sky. When he turned, his jaw was set.

"Tell Cervantes he's fired. I don't want to see him on Stone Mountain again. Is that understood?"

"Yes," Bram said, looking over at Max.

"But you were in charge, Bram. It was your job to see that bushing was greased. The responsibility was yours."

Picking up his wrench, Bram stuck it in his back pocket, wiping his hands on his britches. His face was flushed, and beads of sweat gathered on his forehead.

"I'll go tell Cervantes," he said.

It was late in the night before Creed got back to the house. All efforts to repair the pugmill had failed. In the end, there was little to do but wait for the parts to be shipped in, just as Max had predicted.

He was on his third glass of whiskey when someone knocked at the door. Bram was standing there.

"I fired Cervantes," he said. "Gave him what pay he had coming."

"Come in, Bram."

"Thanks, no. I've come to tell you that I'm quitting Stone Mountain Quarry."

"That's not necessary. Come in and have a drink."

Stuffing his hands in his pockets, Bram rocked up on his heels. "It's necessary for me, Creed. You were right. Greasing that bushing was my responsibility, and I didn't do my job. I figure it's time I go, just like Cervantes."

"I was angry, that's all. There's no reason for you to quit."

"I hear that Southwest Ironworks in Guthrie station is needing men for coking their blast furnace. I figure to do that for awhile."

Taking down his whiskey, Creed shrugged. "You'll find it mighty hard work, Bram. Maybe you ought to rethink things."

"I've made up my mind. Shoveling coke might be hard and it might be simple, but it's work I can do. I figure that's better all around."

"If that's what you want," Creed said, "there's a team and wagon in the stable. Leave it with Roop when you get to town."

"Thanks the same, but I fixed the wheel on that ole wagon Lidy and I came in on. Windy and Bones ought to have enough life left to make it to Guthrie station."

"Suit yourself, then. I'll deposit what you got coming from the quarry in the Bank of Indian Territory."

"That will do," he said, looking at his feet. "I hope things work out for you, Creed. I'm sorry about shutting down the operation."

Studying the bottom of his glass for a moment, Creed said, "Stubbornness must run in the family."

"Yes, sir, I figure that's the case," Bram said.

The snowstorm arrived early and without warning, snowflakes the size of silver dollars. When the winds blew in from the north, drifts clotted the roads, and a bitter cold settled into the valley. Steam from the jenny gathered like a giant thunderhead, and the horses stood with their rumps to the wind, steam rising from their backs in the plummeting temperatures.

By noon the water lines that ran from the spring to the jenny froze up, and the pugmill was shut down. Within the hour, the switch engines could no longer breach the snowdrifts that clogged the spur. Exasperated, Creed closed down the quarry, sending the crews to their quarters until further notice.

As he walked the path to the Big House, his breath rose in the cold. The house was dark and lonely, and at the last moment, he cut north up the path. Snow swirled from the mountain, stinging his face, the wind tearing his eyes. Without the thunder of dynamite from the rift and the chug of engines climbing the switchbacks, Stone Mountain was silent under the quieting snow.

When he spotted the trap, he kneeled down, dusting the snow from its top. The cedar had turned the color of ash, its trip-string having long since rotted away. Holes from Alida's gun were still visible in the end of the trap, and he smiled to himself.

He'd heard from neither Alida nor Bram since their departures from Stone Mountain Quarry. Both lease payments and royalties were deposited as agreed, but neither Alida nor Bram had ever acknowledged their receipt. Neither understood what it took, the sacrifices he'd made. Neither understood the ramifications of money and power nor the consequences of its absence. Neither had suffered the helplessness of defeat at the hands of an enemy. Anyone who had would never forget.

At the ledge, he paused for a moment at the monk's grave, snow gathering on the cross that had been raised there. It was here that Alida had first turned away from him, that day they'd brought the monk's body from out of the rift. Creed had felt her withdrawal then. After that, things were never the same between them.

Just as he turned to leave, he spotted a figure riding with experienced ease across the meadow, his horse lunging through the drifts. Behind him, a dog leaped from drift to drift, sometimes disappearing from sight altogether. A bandanna was tied under the rider's chin to hold his hat against the wind, and a scarf was wrapped about his neck. As the rider approached the camp, Creed recognized Roop Walters and hurried off to greet him.

Climbing down from his horse, Roop held out his hand.

"Hell," he said, "I near froze from the Cimarron on north. Nobody told me it was going to blizzard. For awhile there, I thought I would have to tie poor ole Flea Bag behind the saddle."

"Hello, Roop," Creed said, shaking his hand. "I figured you'd show up on the one day when no work's going on. Put your horse in the stable over there. I'll get him some oats."

"Get me some, too," he said. "I'm damn-near starved."

"We'll go up to the house," Creed said, taking the reins. "I got a pan of enchiladas the cook put together."

Creed fed the horse, while Roop brushed him down with a burlap bag and hung his saddle over the gate to dry. Afterward, they walked up to the Big House, drifts high as their knees in places where the wind cut through the draws. Flea Bag followed behind, crystals of ice gathering between his toes and dangling off his tail.

Brushing off his pants, Roop said, "A man's either cooking his brains or freezing off his balls in this dang country, and I ain't got that much of either to spare."

"Kick off your boots inside the door there," Creed said. "I got a pair of dry socks you can wear."

Leaning back, Roop took in the house as snow gathered in his beard and brows.

"Will you look at that," he said, "a mansion right out here in the middle of all these rocks. That's the biggest house I ever did see. You should've let me brought my horse along, so's I could ride him from room to room."

Taking Roop's coat, Creed hung it behind the door. "It's a bit bigger than I need," he said, "as it turns out."

"I remember the day you called a culvert home," Roop said. "Least till that little shower came up."

Throwing a rug down by the door, Creed said, "Flea Bag can sleep here. That wind's getting more bitter by the hour."

"Lay down," Roop said, pointing to the rug. Flea Bag looked up and wagged his tail. "How'd you like to spend the night in a snowdrift?" Roop added, opening a crack in the door. Flea Bag peeked outside at the swirling snow, circled a couple of times and lay down on the rug.

"I believe that dog's smarter than he used to be, Roop."

"Yes, sir. There's an advantage to being dead ignorant, 'cause there's only one way to go and that's up. A lot of it comes from hanging out at the saloon and watching them boys play checkers. It's improved his judgment considerable."

"You pour us a couple of whiskies while I build a fire," Creed said. "It's a night in the making for both."

After putting kindling in the kitchen stove, Creed dribbled in a little kerosene from the lantern and lit it. Soon the room warmed, and the smell of wood smoke filled the kitchen. Roop slipped on dry socks and poured Creed and himself a drink. The wind rattled the windows of the Big House, and snow gathered on the sills.

Pulling up to the table, Creed sipped his drink. "So tell me what's going on in Guthrie station, Roop? It's been awhile since I've had any news."

Taking a drink, Roop turned his glass against the lantern light. "It's mighty good whiskey you're drinking."

"I have it shipped in," he said.

"Well," he said, pouring another drink, "they hung Carl Ellison, I hear, over to Fort Smith. Said he cussed them with all he had right up to the time they cracked his neck.

"And they say ole Buck Reed's raising mules over to the settlement, and got himself a little Buck Reed on the way. They say he ain't one for coming to town, not even for a sack of flour or sugar. They say he makes that young bride of his, or her pa, ride in for all their needs."

"Maybe he figures a man who's taken the chances he has better not press his luck," Creed said.

Taking out his makings, Roop rolled a cigarette, lighting it over the lantern chimney.

"Abaddon's picked a fight with that Democrat Governor Hodson. Says Hodson's out to take the capital. Says he's a scoundrel, and he'll see the end of him soon enough. We got the capital," he says, "and the Great Seal of Oklahoma to prove it. Swears there ain't no man nor party big enough to take it." Drawing on his cigarette, he studied the lantern flame. "Abaddon don't know when to back off, which is a dangerous thing. Get a man cornered, he's nothing left to do but fight or die. Them editorials of Abaddon's is fighting words, I tell you. Man talk to me that way, I'd have to kill him, that's all."

"Guthrie's the capital, Roop. It always has been, always will be. Everyone's known it from the beginning, and Abaddon's done a hell of a lot for Guthrie station. Without him, it would be nothing, a collection of misfits and ne're-do-wells who couldn't make it anywhere else. He's done a hell of a lot for us, too, Roop. That spur wouldn't be out there right now without Abaddon's influence."

"The governor's told Abaddon to back off," Roop said. "Told him more'n onct, but Abaddon don't listen. He's like a badger. Grab him by the throat, and he rolls over in his skin and digs out your belly with his claws. There's citizens in town who are scared that he's going too far this time."

"Why did you ride out, Roop? What's going on?"

Putting out his cigarette, Roop crossed his legs, rubbing the cold from his toes.

"Abaddon's sent me. He says it's time for you to come back to Guthrie station, 'cause the fight's on, and he's going to drive the heathens from the gates."

Creed poured them another round, and then slipped the enchiladas into the oven to heat. Taking up his chair, he rolled the whiskey in the bottom of the glass as he thought over what Roop had said.

"It's not a good time for me, Roop. There's the quarry and the brick works, and the new spur opening up. We've got a breakdown at the pugmill on top of it all."

"Abaddon says Guthrie's a town fixing to blow, that there's a thousand kinds of people with a thousand wants, and a man better look out for what's his. He says you are to come, that he has a plan. I don't know what it is. Don't know that I want to know for that matter, but I figured I owed you a ride out."

The smell of enchiladas alerted Creed, and he took them from the oven, dishing them up. Roop fell to, hooking his elbows on the table. When finished, he pushed back his plate.

"More?" Creed asked.

"Not unless you want to roll me down this mountain come morning," he said.

Setting his plate on the floor, Roop called Flea Bag, who trotted in to slick the plate, his tail wagging in gratitude.

"When you going to ask what you really want to know?" Roop said.

"I don't know what you mean."

Roop picked up the plate, and sent Flea Bag back to his rug.

"She's staying at the Capitol Hotel," he said. "Last I heard she'd taken a job over to the Carnegie Library. Always was one for the books, wasn't she. I heard she'd joined the Cambridge Club, and the Sorosis Club, too. Folks seek her out, serving on this committee, or taking up one cause or another, her being the wife of a rich man like yourself, and she ain't no slouch when it comes to thinking or holding her own, neither. I see Bram here and there, too. He's working out to Southwest Ironworks, and living over at the Lindel. He's growing into man on his own."

"She's doing okay, then?"

"Managing, I'd say, and making herself useful to the community. Course, there are those who lost their land to the McReynolds Company, or failed to get their lumber, or brick, or stone, or are just plain unhappy with the success of any man. It's the way of things. She's dealing with them best she can."

Standing, Creed walked to the window, looking out into the snow. A light blinked from the crew quarters down in the locust grove, and the wind swept against the house.

"If I go to Guthrie station, would you take over here for me, Roop?"

"What do I know about stone or brick?"

"But you know how to handle men, and I need someone I can trust."

Leaning back in his chair, Roop pulled at his beard. "Fact is, I came here on a matter of my own as well. You see, I've bought up eighty sections of land since we began. That's near fifty thousand acres you ain't even rode over, and it's nowhere's near done. In my way of thinking, it's enough for any man. Anyway, it's enough for me. Every one of those deeds is sittin' in Abaddon Damon's vault in case you've been wondering."

"Can't see that buying up land is a crime, Roop."

"No, sir," he said, "but then I ain't no trade rat, picking up sparklies for an empty nest. I'm wore out taking land from starved-out families and widder women what can't prove up their places. Sometimes I wake up nights in a sweat. Fact is, I'm here to tell you I'm quitting. Guess I just don't want to do it no more."

Turning, Creed said, "I came here with no more than a few cars of lumber, Roop, and turned it into an empire. Do you know how that happens? It happens when a man knows what he wants and never wavers from that goal. If you feel it's time for you to move on, then so be it. You're not the first to feel that way, but I have to follow my course."

Rising from his chair, Roop extended his hand. "No hard feelings."

"No," Creed said. "As I see it every man follows his own trail, Roop. Max can run the quarry, and I'll take the land deals until I can arrange for someone to take them over."

"I'll get some rest, then," Roop said, "if you can put me somewhere besides a snowbank."

"Take the front bedroom. It's closer to the stove and a warmer sleep."

"Oh, the back room will do just fine for me. I got Flea Bag for company and for keeping my feet warm." When he got to the door, he paused. "I hope you find what you want, my friend. I hope it's everything you thought it would be, 'cause life is precious short for hunting cold trails."

Long after Roop's light went out behind the door, Creed sat at the table while the stove crackled against the bitter cold. He drank the last of the whiskey and opened another as the winds howled down the mountain. Sometime in the morning hours, he lay his head on the table and slept.

After bundling up, Alida left the hotel and headed for the Carnegie Library. It was no more than a few blocks away, but the wind was bitter, sweeping from between the buildings and sending her into a shiver. Leaves spun down the street ahead of her like frenzied birds, and the dawn rose gray and cold in the east. Pulling up her collar, she pushed on, her head down, her hands shoved into her pockets.

Each day was the same: rising at six, eating breakfast alone in the dining room, going to work at the library. Most often she shelved books there, or organized the index file. On occasion she ordered new titles, her favorite job, or checked books from behind the oak counter near the door. It was not that she needed the money. Her account at the Bank of Indian Territory was fat indeed, with a stream of royalty checks pouring in from Stone Mountain Quarry.

Her acceptance into the social life of Guthrie had been swift and certain. There were few who didn't recognize the wealth and influence of the McReynolds name. She'd joined the Excelsior Literary Club, and then the Sorosis Club, but they'd left her wanting and unsatisfied in the end. The part-time job at the Carnegie gave her purpose, filled her days, and kept her informed and involved in things.

Hanging her coat behind the door, she rubbed her hands to warm them. The aroma of coffee wafted from the head librarian's office. Mrs. Hollis was a quiet sort, efficient and patient, and with a keen intelligence unsuspected by most everyone who knew her.

"Good morning," Alida said, helping herself to a cup of coffee.

"Good morning," she said. "We've a new shipment in this morning. Perhaps you'd care to catalog them?"

"I'd be happy to," Alida said, blowing into her cup.

"They're upstairs in the rotunda. I'll be up later to help if I have time."

As Alida climbed the stairs, she paused on the landing to warm herself at the radiator. From the window, the whole of Oklahoma Avenue stretched out before her, the grand buildings of brick and stone, their boisterous turrets, their kaleidoscopic colors and patterns and schemes. None of these buildings could have risen without Stone Mountain Quarry, without the will and tenacity of Creed McReynolds. This Alida knew better than most. But in that certainty was both pain and pleasure, because it had torn her life in two.

Her favorite room in the library, the rotunda had a high-domed ceiling of plaster and oak wall panels. Stacks of books awaited the day's readers. When the midmorning sun shone through the windows, the smell of wood and books and wax permeated the room. In its assemblage was peace, solace, a serenity that she'd known only once before, in a dugout on Stone Mountain.

She'd not heard from Creed since leaving, except through Bram, and then mostly just details about the pugmill, and about how Creed was driving everyone mad with his ever-increasing demands. Later, she'd heard that Roop Walters was now working with the section gang for the railroad, and that he, too, had quit Stone Mountain Quarry. In her heart she knew that Roop's departure had been a blow for Creed, and it pained her to think of him alone now on Stone Mountain. Once, she thought she'd seen him on Harrison Street, had briefly glimpsed his black hair as he rounded the corner, but then he was gone. She could not be certain.

By noon she'd finished cataloging the new books. Rather than go back to her room, she walked the block, returning to the library to read for awhile. No sooner had she settled into one of the leather chairs than a man approached. Though he looked familiar, she couldn't place him as he sat next to her.

"Mrs. McReynolds," he said, "please forgive me for disturbing you, but I wonder if I might have a word?"

Laying her book aside, she said, "Do I know you?"

"My name is Jerome Bouchard. You were kind enough to feed me dinner one day, a very long time ago now, fried rabbit I believe it was."

"The architect," she said, "from France?"

"Yes. That's correct. I wonder if there's some place where we could talk in private?"

"Well, I suppose Mrs. Hollis wouldn't mind if we used her office for a bit. It's downstairs, if you'd care to follow."

"That would be fine, Mrs. McReynolds."

At the landing, she turned. "Do call me Alida, if you don't mind."

"Yes," he said, smiling, "and I'm Jerome."

The office was empty, and Alida sat down at the desk. "Have a seat, Jerome, and tell me what's on your mind."

Placing his hat on the floor next to the chair, Jerome sat down, running his fingers through his hair. He'd grown older since she'd last seen him; small lines radiated from the corners of his eyes and mouth.

"The reason I'm here," he said, "is to recruit your help in a problem that has come up."

"Me?"

"Yes. The fact is, Alida, that the McReynolds name carries a lot of weight in this town, perhaps more than you know. We feel that you could be of great help to us."

"Who is *us*, Jerome?"

"A group of businessmen here in Guthrie. You see those buildings out there, Alida? I built them. I built them with my soul and with my sweat. They are *of* me. They are what I leave behind. All of us have invested our lives in this town, our dreams, everything we have, and we are fearful that we might lose it if something isn't done."

"Go on."

"This town has bloomed for one reason: the belief that it is now, and will forever be, the capital of this great state. Without that, we are lost. We are a forgotten city."

Picking up a pencil, Alida doodled on the desk blotter.

"I don't see the problem."

Glancing over his shoulder, he said, "Abaddon Damon is a power to reckon with, as I'm sure you must know. His voice rises from that hill up there like he's Zeus on Mount Olympus. When he speaks, there is no man who doesn't listen, and no man who doesn't fear him. That includes Governor Hodson."

Laying down her pencil, she looked into Jerome's face. "Abaddon's on our side. No one wants to keep the capital more than Abaddon Damon."

Taking out his handkerchief, Jerome dabbed at the sweat that had gathered on his upper lip.

"His editorials against Hodson are ruthless, and relentless, week after week after week. There is no end, it seems, and no purpose but to bring Hodson to his knees. 'Boss Hodson,' he calls him, 'from Blowtown, a man with a little mind and big ideas.' Hodson has told him to stop, to stop the bloodletting, or he will take the capital from Guthrie."

"And what does Abaddon say?"

"That he will see the grass grow in the streets of Guthrie before he gives in to Hodson."

"I see, and what are you proposing to do?"

Leaning forward, he said, "We've organized a group of businessmen and prominent citizens to go talk to Abaddon, to prevail upon him to stop this madness before it's too late. We want you to come."

"And why not ask Creed?"

"There's rumor that soon Hodson might ask for a statewide election to relocate the capital. There's little time to act. Abaddon respects Creed McReynolds and what he's accomplished. We believe your presence could make a difference. Will you come with us?"

Standing, Alida walked to the window. *The Capital City* building rose up from its place on the hill, its dome proclaiming the future of Guthrie station.

"You should know that Creed and I are separated, that I have little influence on him one way or the other."

"Just your presence will help, Alida."

"If you want me to go with the group to see Abaddon, I'll do what I can."

Picking up his hat, Jerome stepped to the door. "You're a noble lady," he said. "I knew it the day you invited me to dinner. We'll be at Abaddon Damon's at noon tomorrow."

As they gathered at the steps of *The Capital City* building, the wind swirled eddies of sleet about their feet, and gray clouds churned in the sky. Jerome took Alida's arm and guided her onto the steps. One man stood near the curb. He wore a derby and a tie, and his vest buttons strained against the pressure of his rotund stomach. Every now and again, he would retrieve a pocket watch from his vest and check it. Another man sat on the stoop, his hands up his sleeves against the cold. A wet cigar protruded from the corner of his mouth, and his eyes were damp with the wind. From the street, a man with stumpy legs adjusted his hat. His pants were cuffed two turns, and he shifted from one foot to the other as if he were in pain.

"This is Alida McReynolds," Jerome said to the men. "She's joining us today to talk to Abaddon." The men tipped their hats and gave knowing glances to one another. "If there's no objection, I'll serve as spokesman. Abaddon's expecting us at one o'clock." The fat man checked his pocket watch once more, nodding his head.

When they entered the building, the clatter of presses emanated from the basement. Bookcases rose to the ceiling. Young men, with sleeves turned to their elbows, rolled ladders back and forth, stacking and retrieving documents from the shelves. The smell of paper and glue was strong, and typewriters chattered from all corners of the room. Filling the corner was a great walk-in vault with a black-enameled door and gold lettering, its steel hinges as thick as buggy axles.

A woman approached them from the back, carrying a tablet and pencil. Her hair was stacked in a great swirl on the top of her head.

"May I help you?" she asked.

"We've an appointment with Mr. Damon. My name is Jerome Bouchard."

"Yes," she said. "Mr. Damon is expecting you. His office is on the second floor. Follow me, please."

Abaddon Damon sat behind his desk studying a document. He wore a black suit, buttoned high over a starched white shirt. There was a gold pin fastened to the lapel of his suit. He was extraordinarily thin, Alida thought, for someone so powerful, and had a dainty mouth, almost feminine. His fingers were long and delicate, and when he looked up, his eyes fell on Alida. She glanced away.

"Jerome," he said, "what brings you and this delegation to my office?"

Jerome removed his hat, looked about for some place to sit. Finding none, he held his hat in front of his lap as he introduced the group.

"And this is Mrs. Alida McReynolds," he said.

"Creed McReynolds's wife?" Abaddon asked.

"Yes," Jerome said. "She's graciously agreed to come at our request."

"I see. Your husband and I know each other very well, Mrs. McReynolds."

"Yes," she said. "It's a pleasure to meet you at last."

Setting his papers aside, Abaddon lay his hands on his desk.

"Now, Jerome, what business do you have with me? As you can see, this is a very busy place."

"Mr. Damon, we represent the businessmen of Guthrie, and, we believe, the best interest of the citizens as well."

"I'm sure you must," Abaddon said.

"You see, we've been discussing the state of affairs, as concerns Governor Hodson and the future of Guthrie. Many of us believe that, well, that he's cornered and dangerous. He's making a lot of noise about taking the capital if the editorials don't stop. And, well, we just thought that it might be prudent to give him some room, you know, just for awhile, to let him cool off."

Standing, Abaddon's face grew dark, and his jaw tightened.

"And what about you Mrs. McReynolds?" he asked. "Do you feel it's time to give him some room?"

Alida swallowed and looked at the others. "Maybe if he weren't pressed so hard to defend himself, he'd be more willing to work with us; after all, we've everything here for the capital now. It only makes sense."

Walking to the front of his desk, he folded his arms across his chest. "I want you good people to look around at the workings of this great paper. We have subscriptions of over twenty thousand citizens, twenty thousand who look to our editorial for the truth, twenty thousand who understand that when it says that our governor is an ignoramus and fool, it's truth in a most rare and unadulterated form. For me to back off from that would be tantamount to betrayal, and that, my friends, I'll never do."

Sitting back down at his desk, he folded his hands.

"The Grand Seal of the Territory of Oklahoma was designed right here in this office, as was the motto for this great state, *Labor Omnia Vincit*, Labor Conquers All Things. These are also words of truth, and the epitaph for any man who dare challenge the capital. I trust this will be the end of it. Now, good day."

Alida sat at her window and watched the evening descend over Guthrie station. Laughter rose from the lobby below. A wind swept down the street, whipping and snapping the store canopies and lifting peoples' hats.

The committee had left Abaddon's office in silence, going their separate ways without so much as a good-bye among them. Even now, she could feel Abaddon's unfaltering stare, buttressed by resolve and steel, and by disdain for anyone beneath him.

Pulling the blind, she tried to read, her mind wandering to the day's events. Jerome had been right, and what she had done by going had been right, of this she was certain. To leave the governor with no escape, no pride, no way out, was to court disaster for Guthrie. Abaddon would not have to retract a single word that he'd written, but simply desist from the scathing editorials that spewed forth from *The Capital City* on a daily basis.

As she dressed to go to bed, there was a knock, soft but business-like. Slipping on her robe, she leaned against the door.

"Yes?" she said.

"Mrs. McReynolds?"

"Yes. Who is it?"

"It's Abaddon Damon. May I speak with you?"

Alida's heart ticked up as she finished buttoning her robe. Opening the door a crack, she said, "It's rather late, Mr. Damon, to come calling."

"And I do apologize," he said, "but the matter is urgent."

When she opened the door, Abaddon removed his hat. He was wearing the same black suit that he'd had on at the meeting earlier that day. An overcoat was hung over his arm, and he smelled of cologne and cigar.

"I'm dressed for bed, Mr. Damon. You'll have to forgive me."

"I'll only be a minute," he said. "May I come in?"

"Well, yes, I suppose."

Closing the door behind him, Abaddon moved to where the light shone through the window. His face was thin and chiseled, and his hair was tousled from the wind.

"May I get you something?" Alida asked.

"I'll be to the point," he said, laying his overcoat on the back of the chair. "I have talked to the members of your delegation tonight, Mrs. McReynolds, one by one, and in private, of course, as it should be. You see, there's not a man among them who has not profited mightily from *The Capital City*, not the least of which would be Mr. Jerome Bouchard. I felt it my duty to remind them from whence they came, and from whence they may fall. A lack of loyalty is a detestable trait, wouldn't you agree?"

Abaddon's eyes cut through the waning light, and his mouth turned up slightly.

"I saw no disloyalty today, Mr. Damon, only men concerned about the future of this town."

Picking up his overcoat, he moved to the door. "Let me put it this way, Mrs. McReynolds. Your husband is a wealthy and powerful man. He is so because of *The Capital City*."

Heat rose in Alida's throat. "He is so because of Creed McReynolds," she said. "Because of who he is."

Opening the door, he hesitated. "I can shut down Creed McReynolds's access to the railroad tomorrow. I can close the spur to Stone Mountain Quarry. In a week it would be a worthless pile of rocks. I can end his land deals and his contracts to the city of Guthrie. I can do all these things," he said, turning, "and let there be no mistake, Mrs. McReynolds. I will."

C reed had not seen the completed *Capital City* building. It sat tall and proud, right atop the goddamn world, just as Jess had said. He studied its tower, its stone base hewn from the flesh of Stone Mountain Quarry. It was a grand building, as Abaddon had promised, dominating the heart of Guthrie station. Turrets and chimneys stood sentry atop its peak like knights on a castle wall, and light poured into the windows that opened onto each floor of Abaddon's kingdom. As Creed climbed the steps, he thought of the day he'd stood guard over his claim, of Samuel and Lena, and of their dream now buried somewhere under Abaddon's building.

Presses and linotypes clattered from the work rooms as he entered. Laughter rose and fell, and the smell of cigar smoke circulated under the ceiling fans. A vault dominated the room, gold lettering rendered across its top. Inside were Creed's land deeds and the secrets of Abaddon's power.

Abaddon Damon sat behind his desk, glasses dropped on the end of his nose as he studied the copy before him. Jimmy sat on a bucket near the door, counting papers. He'd grown since Creed had last seen him. Now that Creed knew who he was, he could see the toughness of Mavis in the boy's eyes, a grit belying both his age and experience.

When Creed knocked on the door, Jimmy ducked under Creed's arm. Abaddon looked up, his blue eyes leveled at Creed.

"Creed McReynolds," he said, motioning for him to sit down.

Pulling up a chair, Creed hooked his hat over his boot and took in the room. Rich paneling covered the walls, and shelves reaching to the ceiling were filled with leather-bound books printed by *The Capital City*.

"You've come a ways since that old tent, Abaddon."

"It's only the beginning, my friend," he said.

"You wanted to talk to me?"

"That cowhand of yours quit on you, I hear," Abaddon said.

"Roop's a good man."

"Good for sitting a horse," Abaddon said. "There's land yet to be bought. Delays will cost you, that's sure."

"I don't plan on any delays," Creed said.

"I met that young bride of yours. Right pretty girl. I hear she's living in the Capitol Hotel."

"Yes, that's right."

"Independence is a fine trait in a woman," he said, "unless it interferes with a man's business."

"She's nothing to do with any of this," Creed said, bristling.

"Just an observation, my friend. No harm meant. Now, bring me up to date."

"I've got Max in charge of the quarry, and I plan to work the land deals myself until I can get someone lined up. We've had a breakdown with the pugmill, but we're keeping up with the orders. I've been thinking that maybe it's time to build the McReynolds Building. What is it that you wanted, Abaddon?"

Walking to the window, Abaddon looked down on the street below.

"We've got a little trouble brewing," he said. "It seems Governor Hodson is unhappy with the editorials of *The Capital City*. Appears he's thin-skinned, as well as incompetent. Fact is, he's making noises about a popular referendum to move the capital to Blowtown, if the paper doesn't cease and desist." Opening the desk drawer, he asked, "Whiskey?"

"Thanks, no."

Putting the bottle back, Abaddon stood at the window again, looking out over Guthrie.

"Governor Hodson claims that Guthrie's a Republican nest, and he's going to clean it out if it's the last thing he does. Says that Guthrie's no more than a tool of the railroad. He's been pressing my bankers to foreclose on *The Capital City*. There was even a pack of Guthrie's finest citizens up here the other day, running scared. We got that straightened out in a hurry." Slipping his long fingers into his coat pockets, he turned. "Thing is, if another town or two jumped in the race for the capital, it could split the vote."

"What are you going to do?"

"The one thing I don't do is run from a fight. No man tells me what to write, and no man's going to take the capital. I figure to run Governor Hodson and his henchmen back over the Kansas border with their tails between their legs."

Sitting down, Abaddon leaned back in his chair and slid his pencil behind his ear.

"Did you take a good look at this town when you rode in? We got ten hotels now, a Carnegie Library, and fifty miles of brick sidewalk. There's the Shakespeare Club, and the Masons, and the Saint Joseph Academy, just finished up this week. There's breweries, churches, and more whores than Kansas City on a Saturday night. We've an orphanage starting up on the edge of town and a marble bathhouse, by god, that Caesar himself would envy. There's cotton coming, too, and vineyards down on the creek bottom, a two-story privy, and a new capitol building up on the hill. Not Governor Hodson, nor any other man, is going to change those facts."

"Any dog will fight in a corner, Abaddon. Maybe you should consider buying a little time, make sure we got the people, the votes."

"Don't you worry about the people. By the time I'm through with Hodson, they'll lynch him off the Cottonwood bridge. Guthrie isn't a town growing but a town grown, born grown, she was, born in a day, with the body of a woman and the mind of a child. With this paper, this thing of flesh and blood, I've taught her everything she knows.

"You and I have made a lot of money. Now, we need to circle the wagons, that's all. There's plenty more for *The Capital City*, and for you, too. Half these homesteaders couldn't farm paradise in a wet year, and now they're crying to get loose with anything they can salvage."

He paused a second. "Jimmy, get those sale bills from the clerk for Mr. McReynolds. He's got to be on his way."

Taking the sale bills from Jimmy, Abaddon handed them to Creed.

"When you get back, you and I are going to have a talk. A man with your education and wealth ought give serious thought to running for governor."

"Governor?"

"And don't you worry about that pretty wife of yours," he said, turning to his work. "I have a feeling, she'll come around just fine."

On the way out of town, Creed stopped at the siding to check on the orders and on the new man installed by Roop. From there, he rode past the Capitol Hotel, pausing at the corner for a look back. At the bottom of the hill, the Red Horse Cafe sat under the yellowed leaves of the catalpa grove, and the aroma of fried rabbit drifted in.

The colored woman at the grill turned, mopping at her forehead, when Creed entered.

"You got the wrong cafe, feller," she said. "Maybe you lookin' for the Ione up the street."

Taking off his hat, Creed waited for her to come around the counter.

"I'm a friend of Buck Reed," he said.

"Buck Reed ain't here no more."

"I just wondered if you'd heard from him?"

Walking to the door, she hooked her hands on her waist as she looked out into the street, as though Buck Reed would appear from around the corner if she looked long enough.

"Buck Reed just got up and left, that's all, and ain't come back. Some say there was nothing left standing between him and evil no more."

"Buck was a good man, a good deputy," Creed said.

"Yes, sir," she said. "Every once in awhile a man comes along big enough to take on the wickedness in this world. When Buck Reed left Guthrie station, all the good, whatever was in this town, left with him, I suspects."

Turning about, she lined up the salt and pepper shakers on the table, sliding the breadcrumbs off onto the floor with the edge of her hand.

"Lordee, but that man could eat," she said, "good lookin', too. You hungry, boy? You look half starved, I swear. I got fried rabbit and greens."

"Thanks, but I've got people to see, land to buy."

Shuffling back to her grill, she turned the frying rabbit with the tips of her fingers, her back to Creed as she bent over the heat.

"It ain't land, boy," she said, "what makes a man smile."

"You see Buck, tell him I came."

"Oh, yes, sir, I will," she said, nodding.

Creed rode from homestead to homestead, observing soddies no bigger than horse stalls, dugouts shoveled from hillsides, rocks stacked into hovels. He took of the farmers' salt pork, of their cornbread and milk, of their biscuits smeared with lard. He ate their beans from tin lids and listened to their stories of no rain, of lost crops, of loneliness and despair.

Taking his money roll from his pocket, he'd peel off the bills. At his knee were children, their bare feet pockmarked from sand burrs, arms sunburned, hair tangled. It was, he told himself, legal and bloodless, the way of the future. He was, after all, their salvation. Without him, without the money that he paid, they would be stranded and hopeless.

The heart of the country was littered with half-starved milk cows, chickens, and jaded workhorses. With the coming of frost, the buffalo grass turned to straw, and the livestock grew thin and weak as they snubbed what they could from out of the rocks. If a man's crop had failed and his field was withered, it was easily spotted by Creed. He knew there was precious little for his family and his animals to eat. With winter ahead, he was inclined to find Creed's offer of cash irresistible. Soon Creed's saddlebags bulged with deeds, and his empire grew, its tentacles spreading into the far reaches of the state.

Often, Creed slept alone on the prairie. He preferred the quiet of the winter night, away from the clamor of kids, or the stink of a barn stall. He thought often of Alida, the turn of her smile, the way she leaned against him in moments of quiet. Sometimes, in the darkest hours, he imagined he could hear the drums of his mother's people out there somewhere on the prairie.

But as the weeks passed, he came to hate the homesteaders' plight, their ignorance and failure, the stink of their huts. Sitting on Roan's back, he would make his bid, holding the bills to flutter in the wind. "It's a good offer," he'd say, "and the last you'll get from me." And then at night, their faces would come to him, keeping sleep at bay.

At the defunct stage depot in Kingfisher, he'd heard that Abaddon's fight with Governor Hodson had escalated, that they'd declared war, and with no prisoners taken. But this much Creed knew about Abaddon Damon: he was never more at his best than when toe to toe with an adversary. Confident that in the end, Abaddon would prevail, he rode north into the flatlands to buy yet more homesteads.

When at last his money was spent, and the smell of spring drifted in, he saddled up Roan and turned south for Guthrie station. In the months he'd been gone, the countryside had emptied. Abandoned dugouts and soddies were everywhere, their doors swinging in the wind. Corn listers, sorghum mills, hay rakes, anything too heavy to take in a wagon, had been left in the fields. Some of the homesteaders had no doubt sold out to buyers like himself. Others, evidently, had simply packed up and ridden away, their hopes and dreams left to decay in the prairie.

Dismounting, Creed led Roan down the trail that wound into the Cimarron valley. As he came out of the trees, he could see the river, its water shimmering as it eased seaward. A man was riding along the bank, a bag in his hand. When he turned to cross the river, Creed could see that it was Jerome Bouchard, and he rode out to meet him.

"Hello, Jerome," he said.

"Creed, what are you doing out here?"

"I've been gone the winter, buying up land," he said, tying Roan's reins to a brush. "Looks like there's been a fair amount of weeding going on. Half the homesteads are abandoned, packed up and left."

Holding his hand against the sun, Jerome studied his face. "You don't know?"

"Know what?"

"Oklahoma City's taken the capital. I tried to tell Abaddon, everyone did, him and his cursed editorials against the governor, but he wouldn't stop, just hammering and hammering, day after day."

Dropping the reins, Creed turned to look at Guthrie, its buildings just visible in the distance.

"Has taken the capital? It's not possible."

"The governor pushed through the vote before anything could be done. There was no time to regroup. We've lost, that's all. We've lost it all."

"But we couldn't have, Jerome. We have the capitol building. We have Abaddon Damon and *The Capital City* paper. We have the Great Seal of Oklahoma, for christ's sake."

Sitting down on his bag, Jerome took off his shoe and poured sand out of it.

"The governor signed a proclamation calling for an election. Shawnee was put on the ballot to divide the vote. The whole thing was kept a secret for five days while they did their deeds. We lost, that's all. We lost everything. The governor moved his office into the Lee Huckins Hotel over in Blowtown. That same night he sent his boys back to steal the seal. Wrapped it in Hodson's dirty clothes and walked right out with it, just like that."

The wind whipped leaves from under the salt sage and into the current of the river. Creed watched them drift away.

"What's happened to Guthrie?" he asked.

"She's dead, emptied out in twenty-four hours. It's like the plague took her, stripped her of life. Property can't be sold, not for any amount. It can't be given away, I tell you." Looking back at Guthrie, he shook his head. "She is a forgotten city. My buildings," he sighed, "my poor lost daughters."

"But it can't be," Creed said.

Putting his shoe back on, Jerome stood. "That old lady asked me to check on her man's grave, if I ever got the chance. I never did."

"Where will you go?"

Mounting up, Jerome shrugged. "Maybe I'll just follow this river and see where she runs. She's the grand architect, they say, and no man's fool."

At the tracks, Creed pulled up to let Roan rest. From there he could see the railroad siding south of Guthrie station, the rows of freight cars still loaded with lumber. Gone were the wagons, the lines, the men at work.

Mounting up, he rode on, past the culvert where he and Roop had swept down the stream, the water now green with spring moss. At the Cottonwood, he eased Roan up the bank, where he'd crossed on that day to make his run through the soldiers' tents.

Now, buildings stood abandoned and forlorn. Windows blared in the sun, empty and unreflecting like dead men's eyes. Somewhere a sign twisted in the wind, its squeak singular and telling. Gone were the children, the yap of dogs, the smell of kerosene. Gone, too, were the saloons, the stink of cigars, the curses of men at their games. Gone were the women, the fragrance of flowers, even the whores with their well-kept secrets.

Here and there wagons rumbled down the road. With their belongings tied in the wagon beds, the people rode away, with no good-byes or waves of the hand, their backs hunched against the calamity behind.

At the Red Horse, Creed tied Roan to the gate. There was no frying rabbit, no greens, no Buck to be seen. When he opened the door, a cat darted out, hissing, its ears laid flat against its head.

At the top of the hill, he stopped at the Capitol Hotel. The door was ajar, boxes strewn about, chairs stacked against the wall. A man was throwing clothes into one of the boxes.

"Excuse me," Creed said.

"There ain't no rooms," he said. "Well, that ain't true, exactly speaking. Right now this town's got more rooms than anywhere in the world, I expect."

"I'm looking for Alida McReynolds," he said. "Do you know where she is?"

"That pretty girl lived up on second? She rode out of here in a rickety old wagon with her brother, the same day ole Abaddon Damon sent us all to hell."

"Did she leave word where she might be going?"

"Naw," he said, picking up his box. "Ain't nobody leaving nothing. They just want the hell out of here. Most of these bastards lit out without paying their bills."

After leaving the hotel, he turned up the road to *The Capital City* building. Jess Clayborn was loading his wagon at the door. Jimmy sat on the wagon seat, kicking his foot, whittling a stick with Creed's old bone-handled knife. The stink of army slop was unmistakable, drawing flies as Jess loaded his loot into the back.

"Hello, Jess," Creed said.

"If it ain't Creed McReynolds," he said, peeking around a chair he clutched in his arms. Tossing it in the back of his wagon, he pushed back his hat.

"Well, you're too late, ain't you, 'cause there ain't nothing left, nothing at all."

"Where's Abaddon, Jess?"

"Gone, ain't he. Gone in the night."

"Just like that, without a word?"

"Left nothing behind, 'cept empty buildings and lost dreams, and this here feral boy."

Holding his hand against the sun, Creed looked up at the dome of *The Capital City* building. From its shadows sparrows darted with bits of straw and twigs in their beaks.

"And the people?"

"Who's to say," he said, looking down the emptiness of the street. "Maybe to Blowtown, the new capital city, 'cause it ain't here no more, or maybe home for sugar tit. Maybe they gone to hell for what I know."

"My deeds were in his vault, everything I own."

Climbing up on the wagon seat, Jess picked up the reins.

"Help yourself," he said. "Abaddon lit out in a hurry, for fear of being lynched, I 'spect, leaving behind what he couldn't carry in his wagon. You best take your papers and move on to better pickin's, 'cause it's all over here. Maybe she *was* a thing of flesh and blood, like Abaddon said, but she ain't no more, just a dead carcass shriveling up on the prairie. She won't be needing no more lumber, nor stone, nor slop-hauling either, for that matter. Anyways, might take a look in that vault. Didn't take time for papers, did he?"

"Thanks, Jess."

"It was such a place for lions and kings, wasn't it," he said, snapping the reins, "sittin' right atop this goddamn hill."

The vault was open, as Jess had said, the smell of mouse and dust already settling into the scattered papers. There was the cling of webs about the door and the quiet of the tomb inside the vault. Rummaging through the shelves, he found his deeds, sweat-soaked and sad, stacks of them, legends of despair.

Looking for something to carry them in, he searched the debris. At first he didn't recognize it, there in the shadows, the leather bag now cracked and stiffened with age. Picking it up, he turned it over, holding it to the light that seeped through the door. Embossed on its bottom was the signature "Joseph McReynolds, M.D., Seventh Cavalry, U.S. Army." It was his father's medical bag, stolen the night he'd ridden into the territory on the lumber car.

Dumping it out, he went through the contents: woolen socks, shirt, gloves still smelling of pine. Abaddon Damon had begun and ended by taking all that was Creed's.

After packing the deeds in the bag, he tied it on the back of his saddle and rode from town. With Roan strong beneath him, he crossed the Cimarron and entered the open plain. Reining up, he looked back on

Guthrie station, the deserted buildings so silent on the horizon, comprising a city born in a day, a city that died as it was born.

Where the blackjacks thickened, he turned down the trail to check on the old man's grave. The soddy had collapsed, its chimney toppled, its walls melting into the prairie. The grasshopper plow was half-buried in sand, thistle growing through its handles. Bramble covered the opening of the well. Kneeling down, he dropped in a stone. The water smelled sour and tarry. It was revenge this land had taken on him to the end, with her water black and stinking of oil.

The old man's grave was sunken but untouched, and Creed stacked rocks to mark its place. As he worked, a wild pig appeared, watching from the scrub, progeny of the old lady's sow, he figured. When he looked again, it was gone, somewhere into the stand of trees. Securing Roan, he followed its tracks into the timbers. Grapevines hung like curtains, their leaves swirling and whispering about his feet.

At the edge of the scrub, he leaned against a hackberry and looked out on the hills. His own mother's grave was lost to eternity. She'd never know all that he'd accomplished, all that he owned. Nothing would ever change that. He thought once to call out her name, but he didn't. From behind, the pig snorted once, peering at him from beneath floppy ears, before tossing its head and darting away.

Mounting Roan, he rode toward the Cimarron valley. With luck, he could hop the northbound to Kansas, ride out the way he'd come in. Alida was gone—Bram and Roop, too. His lumber business was dead, his property and quarry all but worthless. He wanted nothing more than to leave this cursed land forever. He was still a lawyer, a damn good one. What he did once, he could do again somewhere else.

Where the train tracks climbed from the valley, he untied his bag and took off Roan's saddle. With a handful of sage, he brushed her down, tucking her chin in his hand. "Buck told me you were a thinking horse," he said, slipping off her bridle. Slapping her on the rump, he watched her gallop away. "I figure he was right, and you're thinking to get the hell out of here, too."

Black smoke boiled from the northbound as it chugged up the grade, and the throb of its engine settled in Creed's chest as he waited. The stink of sulfur and heat burned his nostrils as the train labored by. Biding his time, he waited for a flatcar, and at the right moment, broke into a run, tossing the bag onto the car, swinging up on the ladder. After catching his breath, he moved forward, taking cover under a threshing machine chained down near the front of the car.

Once out of the valley, the train gathered speed. The click of its wheels, the distant moan of its whistle calmed him. Wearied, he slid the bag under his head and slept.

When he awoke, night had fallen. Uncertain of the time, he turned on his side, the prairie sliding by in the moonlight. By morning, the Territory would be but a memory, gone from his life forever. Sitting up, he took off his hat, and the wind blew through his hair. Why had the hunger consumed him? Why was there never enough?

When he saw the blackness on the horizon, he first thought it a gathering storm, but it was the face of Stone Mountain, its ascent looming into the sky. He clenched his teeth, his heart aching at the sight of the mountain. What had happened there had changed his life forever.

The train slowed, its wheels clacking over the Stone Mountain spur switch, its whistle rising and falling. Soon it gained speed, bearing on to the Salt Fork trestle, on to the Arkansas River, on to civilization. But the train continued alone, without benefit of an illicit passenger.

Dusting off his pants, Creed searched for his bag, finding it not far from the switch where he'd jumped. As he walked toward Stone Mountain, crickets sawed from the low-water bridge that he'd built for the spur road so long ago now. Beyond in the grove, the stables were empty, the crew quarters silent and dark. There was no steam boiling from the jenny, nor thunder of dynamite from the rift. It was all a thousand years ago, a thousand lives past.

As he climbed from the meadow, the air smelled scrubbed and clean, and a soft breeze blew through the trees. At the dugout he stopped, laying his hand on the door, listening to the sounds of the mountain. It was here that he and Alida had been the happiest, had built traps and laughed about hoopers, had made love and planned their future.

From the clearing, he could see the monk's cross high up on the ledge. Taken from its sanctuary, it now leaned against the prevailing winds. Perhaps it had all started that day he'd blown the rift, defied Alida's wishes, set aside his own conscience for a lost town and a sack full of deeds. In the end, what had mattered most, he'd lost, the people he'd loved, those who'd loved him. But no matter what the future held, this much he knew: this land was where he belonged; this land was where he'd stay.

When something moved behind him, he whirled about, "Who goes?" he said, the hair crawling on the back of his neck.

Flea Bag stood at the edge of the clearing, panting, his tongue lolling from the side of his mouth, his tail sweeping from side to side. Alida was behind him, her hands clasped in front of her. Her face was the color of pearl in the moonlight.

"Creed," she said.

"Alida, I've been such a fool. Can you ever forgive me?"

"I forgave you long ago. I've been waiting, you know."

"I've lost everything."

"No," she said. "You have me, this mountain. Down there at the Spring House, there's Bram and Roop, all waiting."

His throat tightened. "They've come back?"

Reaching up, she kissed him. "No one was ever gone, Creed. No one but you."

Afterword

Guthrie was settled in the Land Rush of 1889 in a single momentous day. Located a few miles north of Oklahoma City, it was selected the first territorial capital, May 2, 1890. On August 26 of that year, the first Oklahoma territorial legislature met there.

From the beginning, the permanent location of the state capital was a matter of contention. No one was more fierce in his determination to keep the capital in Guthrie than Frank Greer, editor and owner of the State Capital Publishing Company. His publishing house still stands on the square and is open for public viewing.

On the sixteenth of November, 1907, Oklahoma was designated the forty-sixth state. In 1910, following a bitter political conflict between Greer and Governor Charles N. Haskell, the capital was lost by popular referendum to Oklahoma City. In spite of the vote, it was considered stolen by many Guthrie citizens. Governor Haskell removed the state seal from Guthrie in the dark of night and set up business in the Lee Huckins Hotel in Oklahoma City.

Frozen by circumstances, Guthrie's grand Victorian buildings have survived the passage of time. Only in the last few years have they been recognized for their historic value and beauty. They stand as testament to the glories and to the broken dreams of the past. Joseph Pierre Foucart, architect and Belgian-born immigrant, was responsible for many of the most glorious of these structures. His unmarked grave was only recently discovered in Muskogee, Oklahoma.

From the beginning, blacks played an important role in the settlement of Oklahoma Territory, and of Guthrie in particular. To its credit, Guthrie was, at least for the times, an egalitarian society, with highly successful black politicians, doctors, and law enforcement agents. To the east of Guthrie is Langston University, one of the first all-black universities in the country. Its history is inextricably linked to Guthrie and to the Land Rush of 1889.

Many changes have taken place since the loss of the capital and Guthrie's fall from grace. In the 1970s, the town was placed on the National Register of Historic Places and claimed its right as the largest contiguous urban historic district in the United States. In 1999 it was awarded National Historic Landmark status, and in 2004 was selected by the National Trust for Historic Preservation as one of the top dozen most important historic sites to visit in the United States.

A leader in restoration and preservation, Guthrie attracts visual artists, writers, and performers from all over the country. It hosts numerous festivals and conferences, and more than 250,000 tourists visit annually to enjoy its rich history.

Today, one can stand on Oklahoma Avenue, where thousands of people once clamored for lots, and see a magnificent 400,000-square-foot Scottish Rite Temple sitting right atop Capitol Hill.